Praise for STEPHEN COONTS AND HIS NOVELS

THE TRAITOR

"The prevailing spook mode shifts from cloak to dagger, and suddenly the guys they thought were watching their backs are aiming at them."

—*Kirkus Reviews*

"*The Traitor* contains layer upon layer of deceit and deception . . . plenty of fistfights and explosions . . . Coonts's trademark excitement keep[s] the pages turning to the book's ultimate conclusion."

—Bookreporter.com

LIARS & THIEVES

"This book is vintage Coonts . . . plenty of action and intrigue, with the added benefit of a new lead character."

—*The Dallas Morning News*

"Coonts knows how to write and build suspense . . . this is the mark of a natural storyteller."

—*The New York Times Book Review*

"Former Grafton sidekick Tommy Carmellini, ex-burglar and CIA operative, has been promoted to star in what's sure to be another excellent, long-lived series . . . Tommy is smart, brave, skilled, and possessed of enough self-deprecating, wise-cracking wit to endear him to readers . . . readers of the Jake Grafton series will easily make the leap to Tommy Carmellini, and new readers can be expected to sign up for this hipper hero."

—*Publishers Weekly* (starred review)

"Tommy is a self-deprecating and wise-cracking narrator who brings a welcome energy to the genre. And fans will be pleased to see a now-retired Jake Grafton and his wife, Callie, make an appearance."

—*Library Journal*

MORE . . .

"Readers who have not previously treated themselves to a Coonts thriller should definitely pick up this one."

—Bookreporter.com

"Fast-paced . . . reminiscent of Carl Hiaasen or even the master himself, Elmore Leonard."

—Hintonnews.net

LIBERTY

"Gripping . . . Coonts's naval background and his legal education bring considerable authority to the story, and the narrative is loaded with detailed information about terrorist networks, modern weaponry, and international intrigue . . . the action is slam-bang."

—*Publishers Weekly*

"An action-packed thriller . . . [a] high-octane tale."
—*Midwest Book Review*

"Frighteningly realistic."

—*Maxim* magazine

AMERICA

"This master of the techno-thriller spins a bone-chilling worst-case scenario . . . [Coonts] rivals Clancy for fiction-as-realism and Cussler for spirited action . . . [He] never lets up with heart-racing jet/missile combat, suspenseful submarine maneuvers, and doomsday scenarios that feel only too real."

—*Publishers Weekly* (starred review)

"Coonts's action and the techno-talk are as gripping as ever."
—*Kirkus Reviews*

"Give a hearty 'welcome back' to Admiral Jake Grafton . . . Thrilling roller-coaster action."

—*The Philadelphia Inquirer*

ALSO BY STEPHEN COONTS

NOVELS

Liars & Thieves
Saucer: The Conquest
Liberty
America
Saucer
Hong Kong
Cuba
Fortunes of War
The Intruders
The Red Horseman
Under Siege
The Minotaur
Final Flight
Flight of the Intruder

WITH JIM DeFELICE

Deep Black: Jihad
Deep Black: Payback
Deep Black: Dark Zone
Deep Black: Biowar
Deep Black

NONFICTION

The Cannibal Queen

ANTHOLOGIES

On Glorious Wings
Victory
Combat
War in the Air

THE
TRAITOR

STEPHEN COONTS

St. Martin's Paperbacks

This is a work of fiction. All of the characters, organizations, and events portrayed in this novel are either products of the author's imagination or are used fictitiously.

THE TRAITOR

Library of Congress Catalog Card Number: 2006042505

ISBN: 0-312-99447-8
EAN: 978-0-312-99447-1

Printed in the United States of America

St. Martin's Press hardcover edition / July 2006
St. Martin's Paperbacks edition / March 2007

St. Martin's Paperbacks are published by St. Martin's Press, 175 Fifth Avenue, New York, NY 10010.

10 9 8 7 6 5 4 3 2 1

To Deborah

Tangle within tangle, plot and counter-plot, ruse and treachery, cross and double-cross, true agent, false agent, double agent, gold and steel, the bomb, the dagger and the firing party, were interwoven in many a texture so intricate and yet true. The Chief and High Officers of the Secret Service reveled in these subterranean labyrinths, and pursued their task with cold and silent passion.

—WINSTON S. CHURCHILL

PROLOGUE

She was on the other side of the room when she fastened her eyes on me and made a little kissing motion with her lips. There must have been forty people crammed into the space, which was the living/dining room of a rather opulent Georgetown apartment. The place was hopping with hot jazz and loud, lively conversation. Ooh yeah, Friday night, a party, people drinking and laughing, and this really foxy chick across the room had the hots for me.

Yes, it *was* me she was zeroed in on. I casually glanced left and right just to make sure.

I know what you're thinking: *That Carmellini is bragging again,* but I'm not. I'm telling it exactly the way it went down. Truth is not one of my major virtues, yet I promise I won't lie to you too much.

I was chatting up a Georgetown law student when the hot chick gave me the come hither, so I finished my remarks, got the future counselor's phone number, just in case, then sort of circulated on, which meant I squeezed between people while trying not to spill my drink, a club soda with a twist.

The hot woman was in her mid- to late twenties——it was difficult to say with any certainty——with dark brown hair brushed over, exposing her right ear. She watched me drift toward her, lifting her cocktail glass occasionally to take a sip without taking her eyes off me. High cheekbones, brown eyes set wide apart, all this above a dress with a neckline that plunged almost to her navel.

"Hi," she said when I cruised up.

That wasn't an American accent, or my name isn't Tommy Carmellini. "Hi, yourself," I said as I looked over the situation.

"You look bored," she said, as if that were the most interesting of the seven deadly sins.

"I don't really know anyone except the host."

"Oh, Jacques." Actually his name was Jack, but it sounded like Jacques when she said it.

"Is that a French accent?"

"Yes. I am Marisa Lamoureux."

"Travis Crockett," I told her, holding out my hand to shake. "From Manor, Texas." I pronounced it the Texas way, as if it were spelled Maynor.

"You don't have a Texas accent."

"I have a set of cowboy boots. Will that do?"

She glanced down at my feet and saw that I was lying, and we laughed together. Soon we were getting along fine. And yeah, I lied to her about my name, but it was okay because she lied to me about hers.

Her real name was Marisa Petrou. Lamoureux was her maiden name; she was the daughter of a big mucky-muck in the French embassy, one Georges Lamoureux. She was still legally married to a Jean Petrou, the dirty-rich son of a filthy-rich French financier, but estranged, and was here in Washington for a few weeks visiting her father. Several years ago she spent a couple of semesters at Harvard studying medieval art, then moved on. She didn't tell me any of this, of course; I had gotten it from her file earlier that afternoon.

What else? She liked white wine and champagne, had ended a relationship with a French heart surgeon several months ago and was now having a fling with the director of the French intelligence service, one Henri Rodet, who was twenty-five or thirty years her senior. A note in her file said she liked kinky sex. Where that tidbit came from I have no idea; I seriously doubted that I would get to know her well enough to prove or disprove it.

On the other hand, standing there looking down into those

gorgeous brown eyes, I was acutely aware of the ripe state of her health. And everything else.

We mingled socially. I told her one lie after another about myself—all a part of my Travis Crockett, dude from Manor, Texas, identity—and we replenished our drinks when a waiter bearing a tray hovered into the neighborhood. Marisa was drinking white wine. I stuck to club soda since there was a faint possibility that I might need a wit or two later in the evening.

Out of the corner of my eye I saw our host, Jack Zarb, glance my way. He was a young lawyer who inherited a pile from his grandparents and liked to party. His little black book of hip, trendy women was legendary. I knew him through the friend of a friend. I told him I wanted to come to his party under a nom de guerre and meet a certain woman who might or might not show up. He thought it over, asked no questions and said he understood.

He didn't know I worked for the CIA, or any government agency, for that matter. He must have thought I was a ding-dong or a predator, yet if he ratted me out, no big deal. I doubted if Marisa Petrou was going to think I was as cool as I pretend to be. Still, it was worth a try. With women, one never knows. An evening or two was a small investment, and if it didn't work, I could always try something else.

We ended up on Jack's small balcony looking at the traffic on the street three floors down. Somehow the crowd got so numerous that she was pressed up against me. It was a pleasant sensation. I grinned at her and she grinned back.

We continued to tell each other lies, mixing and mingling, and finally she suggested we leave. A capital idea.

She didn't mention how she arrived at the party. I didn't ask. My old red '64 Mercedes 280SL was parked in the next block, so we took that. I put the top down and she didn't whimper, just climbed right in, which was a plus for her.

Rolling along the streets of Washington with the wind in her hair, she looked pretty good, let me tell you. "You dance?" I asked.

"*Oui.*"

I love it when they talk dirty.

"I know a place," I told her, and aimed the car in that direction.

Since it didn't look like rain, I left the top down when we got to the club in Alexandria and tossed the key at the valet. We danced fast and we danced slow. She knew how to do it. Her body seemed to mold itself to mine. Fate—that was what it was. I began thinking I was living a dream, and it was a chick flick. Actually I was wishing that I was on my own time, not Uncle Sugar's.

Finally she whispered, "Your place or mine?"

I had a little story all prepared about why it couldn't be my pad, and now I didn't need it. "Yours," I said.

"Let's go."

It was that simple. We were past the lying stage.

Now I know what you're thinking: *That Carmellini must be the most conceited bastard alive, going to a party expecting to be picked up by the girl who did indeed pick him up,* but I beg to differ. Men and women do it every day. Besides, it wasn't an expectation, it was merely a hope. Hope is the reason people buy lottery tickets and condoms. Let's make a happy noise for hope.

I drove and she gave me directions—right to her father's house, which was an old mansion in the northwest section of town, a few blocks from the French embassy. She hadn't mentioned what her pop did for a living and I didn't ask. I parked on the street in front of the joint, put the lid on and locked 'er up. There was a guard standing near the door. It looked to me like he was packing heat, but I couldn't be sure.

"Wow," I remarked to Marisa as we walked toward the door. "Quite a pad! Does this belong to a friend of yours?"

"Of course."

I gave the guard my best innocent smile, while he maintained a professional diffidence. He made eye contact with Marisa as he opened the door to let us pass. I wondered if he and Marissa had ever . . . Oh, well. Better luck next time, buddy.

Inside, surveillance cameras were mounted high in every

corner. I suspected the floor had pressure-sensitive pads mounted under it, but I could see no evidence. Then I stepped on a place in the hallway that seemed to give just a fraction of an inch. Yep.

Marisa led me along the hallway to a large door that opened into a spacious library with a ten-foot ceiling. Two men were sitting in the chairs reading, even though it was almost three o'clock on Saturday morning. "My father, Monsieur Lamoureux. Travis Crockett, Father, from Texas. He has the boots."

Georges Lamoureux smiled, stood and shook my hand.

"Alain Frechon," he said, nodding toward the other man. Frechon didn't rise from his chair, merely stuck out his hand for a limp-wrist waggle.

Lamoureux had fashionably gray hair and a trim figure, no doubt because he worked out four times a week. That was in his dossier. When I told you he was a high mucky-muck, I should have been more precise. He was the number two in the embassy, the guy who actually did the paperwork while the ambassador fretted policy issues and went to cocktail parties with Washington's society mavens.

I had never seen any mention of Frechon in the files so knew nothing about him. He was of average height, late fifties perhaps, with a face that looked as if it would crack if he smiled. He didn't bother flashing the chompers at me, just glanced at Marisa and me and went back to looking sour.

If Lamoureux thought it unusual that his married daughter was bringing a man home at three in the A.M., he hid it well. These modern Europeans . . . We chatted as if I were merely taking a tour of a historic home.

Three polite platitudes later, he bussed his daughter on the cheek, and she took me by the hand and led me out of the library. We stopped in the kitchen for a glass of wine. I really needed every last wit I had, yet I accepted a glass and even took a sip. It was delicious.

"Do you know wine?" Marisa asked.

"Red with meat and white with fish." I smiled. "In other words, no."

"Nor I," she confided, leaning closer and lowering her voice. "I drink what I like, and the label . . ." She flipped a hand in dismissal. I was ready to classify her as a dangerous subversive until I reflected that Marisa Petrou probably hadn't been served a glass of poor wine in her life.

As she turned toward me, I gathered her into my arms for a serious kiss. She smelled delicious. She put her glass on the counter and used both hands to hold me. That was when I slipped the little pill into her wineglass. I held the kiss for another fifteen seconds, which was more than enough time for the drug to dissolve.

"Well!" she said, when we finally broke for air. "Texas must be a wonderful place."

"I was thinking the same about France."

She reached for the glass and took a healthy sip as she eyed me.

"You want me, yes?" she whispered huskily.

"Un-huh." That was the only absolutely true thing I had said all evening. My old heart was pounding and I had a sheen of perspiration on my forehead. I took another tiny sip from my glass. It was the high-dollar stuff, all right, smooth as wine can get.

Marisa took a swig from her glass, then seized my hand. "Come," she said. She brought her glass along.

Her bedroom was on the second floor. Tiny night-lights glowed on the staircase and along the hallway. There were the usual surveillance cameras in the hallway, but none in her room. That was a relief. I wondered if the cameras could function properly at those low light levels.

In her bedroom, she skinned out of her clothes and helped me out of mine. Two minutes after she locked the door, we were in bed.

Of course I wondered if she had had enough of the drug to put her under—she had drunk about a third of the glass—and if so, how long we had before she went to sleep. The answer was yes, she had ingested enough, and the time was six minutes. She merely went to sleep in my arms.

How long she was going to remain asleep was another

question. Just to be on the safe side, I removed a small patch from the pocket of my trousers, which were heaped on the floor. I peeled the paper off the sticky side and pressed the patch against the back of one of her hands. The drug would be absorbed through her skin and would keep her under. With a little luck, she wouldn't even know it had been on her.

I looked at my watch. The guards—there were two—made rounds hourly, and unless I stayed in bed with Marisa, they would find me on one of them. I had to find what I was after and get out. I tossed my clothes on, draped my tie around my neck, left my shirt sleeves unbuttoned.

After making sure Marisa was comfortably arranged in the bed, I turned out the lights and opened the door to the hallway.

I stood there listening. The old house was silent. The night-lights were glowing comfortably.

I hoped her father and his guest were still in the library. I went to the head of the stairs and looked. The lights in the library were still on.

His room should be the one at the end of this hallway. Fortunately he slept alone. I tried the knob. Locked. I put a small stethoscope up to the door and listened. Nothing.

Lamoureux might come upstairs at any time, and I wanted into that room. I picked the lock. That took a long four minutes. I could have done it faster if I hadn't been trying to keep quiet and wondering if the surveillance cameras were getting all this. As dark as the hallway was, I doubted it. I would certainly find out soon if they were.

When the lock opened, I stepped into the room and locked the door behind me. It would be nice if I could find another exit. Two night-lights illuminated the room. A thick carpet covered the floor, and thick drapes obscured the windows. Cool air came from vents high in the walls. I pulled the drapes aside and inspected the windows. The paint on the sills and sashes revealed that they hadn't been opened since the building was erected.

The closet was a walk-in. Yes. It went through to a spare bedroom, which was set up as an office. This was my escape hatch if I needed it.

I flipped on my flashlight and began searching—and quickly found what I was looking for: books. Lamoureux had perhaps two dozen in his bedroom, all in French. One of them, one here or one in the library or perhaps one in his desk or locked up in a safe, he used as a key for a cipher. Since it was based on a random word that appeared somewhere in the text of the book, and that word probably changed with every message, the cipher was essentially unbreakable. Oh, sure, with a big enough computer and years to watch it work, eventually a cryptographer would find which of the billions of possible letter combinations would unlock a message. Then the code breakers could do the drill all over again on another message, and so on.

That method of cracking the cipher being unfeasible, the wizards had asked for help. I was the help. I was supposed to photograph the title of every book Lamoureux had routine access to and, if possible, figure out which one was *the* one.

Since I wasn't anywhere near as smart as Sherlock Holmes, I decided to photograph all the books. I turned on the room lights, all of them, and began clicking away with my camera. Back in the good old days spies snapped away with Minox cameras, but we were digital now. I used a Sony Cyber-shot. When I had photographed all the books, I opened and closed drawers. No books in the drawers.

He had a desk in the room, and I attacked it. In seconds I knew the drawers were empty. I turned off the lights, then went through the closet to the office. More books. I snapped on the lights and got busy with the camera. On a bottom shelf, lying on its back as if it had just been tossed there, was a well-thumbed paperback, *The Sum of All Fears* by Tom Clancy, the only book in English I had seen.

I picked it up. The light wasn't good enough. I turned on the desk lamp, held the pages under it and flipped quickly through them. I was looking for pencil or ink marks. Didn't see anything.

I put the book back on the shelf and looked at it again. The spine was crazed, completely broken down. The pages refused to close neatly. This book had been read and reread.

Of course the wizards hadn't bothered to tell me how Lamoureux sent his messages, or to whom, or how frequently. I didn't know if he sent letters, postcards, or e-mail, or whether his missives went out in the diplomatic pouch or via snail mail. All I knew was that I was looking for a book that was used as the key to a code.

Maybe Lamoureux was a Clancy fan. And maybe—

I heard a noise.

I had the lights off in a twinkling and strode for the closet. I heard the door opening in the bedroom. That told me which way to jump.

I went over to the office door and carefully turned the knob. It was locked, naturally, with a Yale that took a key on both sides.

I immediately looked for a place to hide, just in case the old monsieur decided that right this very minute was a good time to send a coded letter to his mistress in gay Paree.

There was just enough room behind a large padded leather chair. I hunkered down behind it and tried to control my breathing and heart rate.

He knocked around in the closet, then went to the bathroom beside the closet—I had forgotten to look in there for books. When the door closed and the water started running, I hopped out from behind the chair and scooted through the closet, past the bathroom door and across the bedroom. The door was locked, but there was a knob to unlock it. I twisted the knob, slipped out into the empty hallway, and eased the door closed behind me.

Marisa was still sound asleep. I stayed just long enough to remove the patch from the back of her hand. The drug should wear off in about an hour, and with luck she should sleep soundly for the rest of the night. "Au revoir, baby," I whispered, and gave her a kiss.

I sidled along the dark hallway, pausing at the head of the stairs. No one in sight. Down the stairs I went, trying desperately to be quiet.

The lights in the library were off. Three small night-lights were the only illumination, and they certainly didn't give enough light for photographs. I looked at the entrance from the hallway. There were two large oak doors, but closing them would probably wake the dead. No curtains on the windows. I looked out. The lawn was there, quite spacious for Washington, with a few trees and shrubs, bounded by a high masonry fence topped with barbed wire. Beyond the fence was another building. I could see windows.

If Lamoureux encoded his messages in here, anyone in the yard could look in the window and watch him do it. If he did it in the chair he was sitting in when Marisa introduced me, anyone in the window of that building across the way could see him with binoculars.

No, he didn't encrypt messages in here. He did it at the embassy or upstairs in his bedroom or office.

I glanced at my watch. I had been in the building for sixty-seven minutes—far too long—and I was going to have to turn on every light in this library if I were going to photograph all the book spines. I scanned the shelves. A good many American and British authors, even a few German, but the works were in French.

The Sum of All Fears. That might be it.

As I walked out of the library I almost bumped into a guard. My heart nearly leaped from my chest. At least, I assumed he was a guard; he was a fit man wearing a suit and he looked quite capable.

"Ah, I wonder if you could show me the way out," I said thickly, as if I had had a bit too much to drink. "I seem to be a little lost."

"Of course, sir," the guard said in good English. "Right this way."

Four minutes later I unlocked the Mercedes and climbed in. The sky was getting light to the east.

On Monday at headquarters I gave the digital camera to the wizards and told them about the Clancy paperback. They thanked me and that was that.

The person who said "Silence is golden" must have worked in the intelligence business. If you pull off a difficult assignment you never hear another word about it. I must have done okay on this one because no one ragged me about what I should have done. They wouldn't even tell me if one of the books I photographed was the key they were searching for to Lamoureux's codes.

So Marisa Petrou faded into my past. A few weeks later, just as the baseball season got interesting, the trolls in the inner sanctum sent me to Iraq, which is one of the world's hell-holes, let me tell you. It was truly a long hot summer; I couldn't wait to get back to the land of the beer and home of the hot dogs.

CHAPTER ONE

Maurice Marton died of a heart attack thirty-seven thousand feet above the Mediterranean. He did it quietly, the same way he had lived his life. He felt a sudden, severe chest pain, couldn't breathe, and reached for the call light above his seat. As he looked up, gasping, groping for the button, his heart quit beating altogether. Maurice Marton slumped in his first-class airline seat. By chance, he was in a window seat and his head sagged toward the window. Also by chance, the aisle seat beside him was empty.

It was several minutes before the flight attendant noticed Marton. The man was slumped down, facing the window, and although his eyes were open, the attendant couldn't see them and thought he was asleep. As is customary in first class, he let him sleep.

A half hour later as the aircraft began its descent into Amman, the seat-belt light came on. It was then that the flight attendant tried to wake his sleeping passenger. As soon as he saw the open, unfocused, frozen eyes, he knew the man was dead.

An old hand at the business, the attendant felt for Marton's pulse. Finding none, he covered the man with a blanket and turned his head back toward the window.

The plane made a normal landing in Amman, and after the other passengers were off the plane, a doctor and two policemen came aboard. As the senior cabin attendant watched, they loaded the corpse onto a stretcher and carried it off.

With the airplane empty of people, the senior attendant removed Marton's attaché case from the storage compartment over his head and opened it. The case was crammed full, mostly letters and spreadsheets and a few printed statements. Roughly half were in French and half in Arabic. The attendant sat down and began rapidly scanning the documents.

Three weeks after the death of Maurice Marton, a man from the American embassy entered a nondescript building in Tel Aviv and was ushered to a basement room. The walls, floor and ceiling were poured concrete. A naked bulb on a wire hung from the ceiling over the only desk, a small, scarred steel one that at some time in the historic past had been painted a robin's egg blue. Behind the desk was a tanned man with close-cropped brown hair wearing a white short-sleeved shirt. He had a comfortable tummy, and a firm grip when he shook hands.

"Good to see you, Harris. How was Washington?"

"A steam bath," the American said. "With a whole continent to play with, they managed to put the capital in a place that's cold, damp and miserable in the winter, and hot, humid and miserable in the summer."

"I've never been there. Should I make the trip someday?"

"Only if the airfare is free."

The men were seated now. The host said, "I have a story that I thought would interest your colleagues."

"Anything that interests the Mossad will interest my crowd," Harris replied candidly.

"On the twenty-seventh of last month, a French intelligence agent named Maurice Marton died on an Air France flight between Paris and Amman. Had a heart attack, apparently, and quietly expired. In his attaché case were some interesting documents that I would like to share with you." The host picked up a small stack of paper and handed it to his guest.

The American examined the sheets carefully. They were obviously copies. After a few minutes, he remarked, "I understand most of the French, I think—it's been a few years since college—but my Arabic is a little rusty. It appears someone named Henri Rodet is buying stock in the Bank of Palestine, two million euros' worth."

"I think so, yes," murmured the Israeli. "Do you recognize the name?"

"No."

"Henri Rodet is the head of the DGSE." The *Direction Générale de la Sécurité Extérieure* was the French intelligence agency.

Harris lowered the sheets and stared at his host. He blinked several times. "Really!"

"Indeed."

Harris spent another minute scanning the documents, then raised his head and said, "They'll want to know how you got these."

"As I said, Marton, a career clerk in DGSE headquarters, was on his way to Amman, presumably to do this deal for his boss, Rodet. He died en route. One of our men got his hands on Marton's attaché case, saw that these documents were of interest, and managed to run the originals through a copier and return them to the case."

"Luck," muttered Harris.

"On rare occasions that sprite does indeed smile," the Israeli said casually. He said that to be polite; the only kind of luck he believed in was the kind you made for yourself. The men and women of the Mossad used every morsel of wit and guile they could muster, and every penny of their budget, to keep agents in place in key positions in Cairo, Amman, Damascus, Beirut, Riyadh and two dozen other places around the globe. Because agents were there, in place, good things could happen. Good things had to happen for Israel. Without timely, accurate, reliable intelligence for its decision makers, the nation would cease to exist.

The American settled himself to study the documents in detail. When he finished he put the sheets back on the desk.

"You may have those," the Israeli said.

Harris folded the sheets carefully. "You are convinced these are genuine?"

"Marton was very dead, right there in a first-class seat. From all appearances, it was a natural death."

"Why first class? Why not coach?"

"The French government bought the ticket. Air France upgraded it because there was room in the front of the plane."

After Harris placed the copies in his trouser pocket, he asked, "Did your man raise any suspicions?"

"He thought not. The attaché case and the dead man's luggage were held by the airline. After his family was notified, a man arrived on the next day's flight and claimed them."

"His name?"

"Claude Bruguiere. We believe he, too, is DGSE."

"And what did he do with the attaché case?"

"This happened in Amman," the Mossad officer explained. He spread his hands. "We have limited assets, as you know."

"So you're not going to share that." It was a statement, not a question.

The Mossad officer smiled.

The American intelligence officer scratched his head, then smoothed his hair. He didn't have much; the motion was an old habit. Finally he stood and stuck out his hand. "Thanks for the information," he said.

"You're welcome," the Israeli replied as he pumped Harris' hand.

"You've opened a whole can of worms, you know."

"The worms were already there, my friend."

"I suppose so," Harris said.

By pure coincidence, the day the American named Harris had his interview with a senior Mossad official, a well-dressed man in his late forties or early fifties joined a group of tourists waiting for a guided tour of the Château de Versailles, the Sun King's palace that is today in the southwestern suburbs of metropolitan Paris.

The man had a dark complexion, as if he spent much of his life in the sun. Of medium height, he was perfectly shaved and barbered, with a lean, spare frame that showcased the dark gray tailored Italian suit he wore. He wore hand-made leather shoes; on his wrist was an expensive Swiss watch. His deep blue tie was muted and understated, the perfect accent for a wealthy man in the upper echelons of international society, which was, of course, precisely what the man was.

An American college professor on sabbatical spoke to the man in heavily accented French, asking if he had ever before toured the palace. He replied with a hint of a smile, in perfect French, that indeed he had, although many years had passed since his last visit. The professor, a single woman who had always been enthralled by France and all things French, gave the man her absolute best smile.

He answered it by discussing the history of the palace as they waited for the professional guide. He knew so much about the palace that the American asked, "Are you a scholar?"

"A businessman, madame," he said with another hint of a smile. The lady thought him charming. She would have asked more questions, but the guide showed up and launched into a canned speech, and a minute later the group straggled off after her.

The American woman stayed close to the well-dressed man in the dark gray suit. Occasionally, when the guide glossed over some fact that the woman thought might be intriguing, she asked the man, who knew the answers.

The group—there were several dozen tourists, mostly couples—made their way through the palace. They worked their way through the north wing, looking in on l'Opéra, the site of the marriage of the future Louis XVI and Marie Antoinette, the Chapelle Royale and the picture galleries, then made their way into the center section of the palace. The guide led the group through the library, the Cabinet du Conseil, and the king's bedroom. From there they went to the queen's bedroom, where the queens of France gave birth to their children as members of the court watched with bated breath.

"That way there could be no question as to who was the

lawful heir to the throne," the man whispered to the American, who was slightly appalled at the public nature of what she considered a very private event.

From there, finally, they entered the Hall of Mirrors, the great room of state for eighteenth-century France. "In fact," the guide intoned in heavily accented English, "this room is still used for great state occasions. For example, in 1919 the Treaty of Versailles that ended World War I was ratified in this room."

It was a huge room, about eighty yards long, with a high, vaulted ceiling covered in gold leaf. The long wall on the exterior side of the building was perforated with tall arched windows, from which one could gaze in awe at the magnificent gardens behind the palace. The opposite wall was lined with mirrors, and the entire room was lit with dozens of dazzling chandeliers.

"*Very* impressive," the American lady whispered to her fellow tourist.

He nodded in agreement, and stood rooted as the group moved on.

This is the place, the man thought.

They will be here before the cameras, surrounded by television crews, reporters and security guards. The world will be watching.

We will kill them here.

CHAPTER TWO

"How would you like to do a month in France?" my boss, Blinky Wooten, asked. We were seated in his office at the Special Collection Service, or SCS, on Springfield Road in Beltsville, Maryland. The SCS was the bureaucratic successor to the National Security Service's Division D and was a joint CIA/NSA effort. Our job was to find the easiest and cheapest way to collect the intelligence necessary for national survival in the modern world. Since I wasn't a scientist, by default I ended up a grunt in the electronic wars.

It was October, and the weather on the East Coast was glorious, the leaves were changing, and football season was in full swing. After four months in Iraq, the place looked like God's garden. I was in no hurry to leave. On the other hand, I do have to work for a living.

France. I shrugged. "At the embassy? Sure."

"Huh-uh. As an illegal. The embassy is full as a tick right now. France is going to host the summit meeting of the G-8 leaders at the end of the month. Our people are working with the Secret Service and FBI on a temporary basis to ensure it goes off without any incidents." Terrorist incidents, he meant.

"If I'm going to stand around wearing a lapel mike and looking tough, why the cloak-and-dagger? I could just pretend to be Tommy Carmellini, loyal federal wage slave."

"I don't think they need any more door decorations. They have something else in mind for you."

Hoo boy! Like every other nation on earth, France has

laws against espionage, conspiracy, theft, and breaking and entering, which is, by definition, what spies are employed to do. When sent overseas, most CIA officers in ops and tech services were assigned to an embassy or consulate staff, and consequently enjoyed diplomatic immunity if they were caught violating the laws of the host nation. As an illegal, I wouldn't have diplomatic immunity as a safety net.

But I was used to dancing on the high wire without a net. The SCS staff flitted here and there all over the world, installing antennas, breaking into computer facilities, bugging embassies and consulates, bribing systems administrators, that kind of thing. In and out fast, like an Italian government, was usually the best way. "I've heard that France is a friendly country, more or less," I remarked.

"Well, if they catch you red-handed, they probably won't give you a firing party, with a blindfold and last cigarette," Blinky said judiciously, "but they might rough you up a bit." He looked at me over his glasses while he batted his eyelids another twenty or thirty times. He was sensitive about his nervous habit, or tic, so no one called him Blinky to his face. I averted my eyes so he wouldn't think I was staring.

I focused on a golf ball he had glued to a tee on his desk—a sacred, hole-in-one ball—as I pondered my options. If a fellow is going to make his living as a spy, France is probably as good as it gets. *La belle France*—great food, nice climate, fine wine, and the world's most beautiful women. On the other hand, France *is* the home of the French . . .

A woman I knew had tickets to all the Redskins home games. She enjoyed my company. She had bought the tickets, so I bought the beer and hot dogs. She was also really cute. "I just got back from Iraq two weeks ago," I pointed out, quite unnecessarily. Blinky knew damn well where I'd been and when I'd returned.

"You volunteered for France." He rooted in a file on his desk and came up with a sheet of paper. "See, here it is." He fluttered it where I could see it.

"That was a dream sheet I filled out years ago," I remarked, and waved a hand in dismissal. All this drama was for show, of course. The heavies cared not a whit whether I was happy in my work; Blinky could send me to any spot on the planet with a stroke of his pen.

"So?"

"As I recall, when I volunteered I wanted a chance to make a personal contribution that would improve our relations with our French allies. I was thinking along the lines of assistant passport officer at the embassy, black-tie diplomatic parties, meeting a few nice French girls, invitations to the country for the weekend—"

"You've been watching too many movies," Blinky said crisply. "The new head of European Ops asked for you by name."

"He did?"

"Indeed."

I was dubious. My stock at the agency hadn't been very high since that disaster with the retired KGB archivist who defected the summer before last. "What's his name?" I asked, trying to keep my skepticism from showing.

"Jake Grafton."

Uh-oh! I ran across Jake Grafton a few years ago in Cuba, and he and I had crossed paths a few times since. He had my vote as the toughest son of a bitch wearing shoe leather. He was the man the folks in the E-ring of the Pentagon and over at the White House handed the ball to when things got really rough. "I thought he retired?"

"From the Navy. He's working for the company now. But what the hey, if you don't want to go to France, we can ship you back to Iraq—they're asking for you, too."

I was underwhelmed. "I work too cheap," I remarked.

Blinky ignored that crack. "So which will it be?"

It wasn't as if I were being asked to hang it out on a secret mission behind the Iron or Bamboo Curtain. Blinky was talking *France,* for God's sake, the good-living capital of the world, where snootiness was de rigueur and fleecing tourists a way of life. Still, the folks in the DGSE played hardball. That agency was the successor to the *Service de Documentation Extérieur et de Contre-Espionage,* the SDECE, the spy agency de Gaulle founded after World War II. The name was changed after the SDECE's reputation for murder, kidnapping and torture became a political liability. The same kind, gentle, in-tight-with-Jesus Samaritans were still there, however.

"Eenie, meenie, minie, moe . . . France."

"How's your French, anyway?"

"Voulez-vous couchez avec moi?"

"Fluent," he muttered, and launched into an explanation of my assignment. London first for a briefing, then France.

A few minutes later Blinky stood and held out his hand. That was my signal to leave. "Try not to get caught," he said as he pumped my hand perfunctorily.

"Yes, sir."

He followed me to the door and muttered, "I once spent a summer in France." He blinked a dozen or two times, seemingly lost in thought. "I've always wondered—," he began, then fell silent and blinked some more. His Adam's apple bobbed up and down.

He shoved me gently through the doorway. The door closed behind me with a *thunk*.

So I cleaned my apartment, put the car back in storage, and took a cab to the airport on Sunday afternoon. I was in a fine mood as I strolled down the concourse at Dulles International.

Boarding was ten minutes away as I approached the gate area. I automatically scanned the crowd . . . and there she was, sitting with her back to the window reading a magazine. My old girlfriend, Sarah Houston. Oh, no!

Of course, she glanced up and saw me at about the same instant. Our eyes met for a second or so; then she turned the page of her magazine and concentrated upon it.

Oh, *man!*

After the mess with the KGB archivist, Sarah decided I was boyfriend material. Everything went fine for a couple of months, then, you know . . .

She was tall, brainy and gorgeous and worked for the NSA—National Security Agency—as a network and data mining specialist. She had a seriously twisted past and was a little cross-wired upstairs, but I was big enough to overlook those smirches. If you hold out for a saint, you're going to die a virgin.

The lounge was filling up and there weren't many seats left. That was fine—I was going to be sitting for hours.

I sneaked a sideways look. She was examining me over the top of her magazine. She instantly averted her eyes.

Of course it all came flooding back. She had gotten so serious . . . Did she have another guy now? I wondered if she was wearing a ring—and sneaked a look. Couldn't see her left hand from this angle.

I know it sounds stupid, but suddenly I wanted to know. I walked to the window on her left side and stood looking at our jet, which was nosed up to the jetway. Finally I shot another glance at Sarah. Well, hell, I couldn't tell.

They began boarding the flight, and since I was sitting in the back of the plane, they called my row immediately. I got in line and went aboard. Sarah was still sitting by the window when I last saw her.

I had drawn an aisle seat three rows forward of the aft galley and had a lady beside me who was fifty-fifty—about fifty years old and fifty pounds overweight. She sort of spread out and I tried to give her room.

The herd was pretty well settled when I saw Sarah coming along the aisle with her shoulder bag and wheeled valise. She had her boarding pass in her left hand. I ooched down in the seat to hide the bottom half of my face and took another squint at her left hand. No rings.

Then she spied me. She took a step or two closer, checked the seat numbers, turned and called loudly for a flight attendant. One appeared almost immediately, as if she had been waiting offstage for a summons.

"I want another seat," Sarah declared in her I-am-not-putting-up-with-any-more-of-this-crap voice.

"We're pretty full—"

"I'm not sitting near *him*!" This announcement carried all over the ass end of that cattle car, and to ensure everyone knew which cretin she was referring to, she pointed right at me. "I just *couldn't*!"

The flight attendant zeroed in on me, even took a step closer and gave me a hard look to see if I was drooling.

"I'll see what I can do," the uniformed witch said. She whirled and marched forward. Sarah followed her up the aisle, her head erect, her back stiff.

As I watched them go I realized that everyone within twenty feet was sizing me up. "Jerk," the woman beside me announced, then studiously ignored me.

We were somewhere over Long Island when I finally got around to wondering why Sarah Houston was aboard this flight.

The next time I saw Houston was at the baggage carousel at Heathrow. She stayed on the far side of the thing and refused to look at me. I was getting a little browned off at the public humiliation and tried my best to ignore her.

It wasn't as if I left her stranded at the altar or branded with a scarlet *A*. For heaven's sake, we were both adults, nearly a decade over the age of twenty-one, perfectly capable of saying, "No, thank you."

I dragged my stuff through customs and joined the taxi queue. It was early on Monday morning in London, and I didn't get a wink of sleep on the plane; I was tired, grubby and stinky. On top of that, just when I was in the mood to kill something, everyone was so goddamn polite, nauseatingly so. I snarled at the lady in front of me when she dragged a wheel of her suitcase across my foot and she looked deeply offended.

The CIA had an office in Kensington on one of the side streets, a huge old mansion that sat in a row of similar houses, all of which had been converted to offices. The sign outside said the building housed an import-export company. As my taxi pulled up in front, I saw Sarah Houston get out of the cab ahead. I knew it! My luck had turned bad; it had gone sour and rotten and was beginning to stink. People were going to avoid me, give me odd looks, leave rooms when I entered. I've been through stretches like this before—and some woman usually triggered it.

Houston went up the steps and was admitted to the building while I rescued my trash from the trunk of my hack and paid off the cabbie.

The receptionist was a guy named Gator Zantz. I met him a couple of years back when I was bugging an embassy in London. He was a big, ugly guy with a flattop haircut; I figured he probably had the only flattop east of the Atlantic, but who knows—maybe there was a U.S. Army private somewhere in Germany more clueless than Gator.

"Hey," Gator said when he took my passport. Mr. Personality.

Sarah and I wound up in chairs on the opposite side of the reception room. We ignored each other. Sarah pretended to read a newspaper.

When Gator returned our passports, he leered at Houston a while—she ignored him—and then, when he realized that relationship was not going to get off the ground, turned to me. "So how's it going?"

"Okey dokey," I said.

"The Patriots are going to win again tonight," he informed me. "I think like ten pounds' worth."

"Who they playing?"

"Pittsburgh."

"You're on." Actually, this was a pretty safe bet for me. Gator's affection for a team was the kiss of death. Two years ago I won fifty pounds off this clown during football season. God help the Patriots.

Gator went away and came back five minutes later. He crooked his finger at us, and we dutifully followed him.

He led us along a hallway to a flight of stairs, then down to the basement, which was a "skiff"—a Sensitive Compartmented Information Facility, or SCIF. This area had elaborate safeguards installed to prevent electronic eavesdropping. As a member of the tech support staff, I had helped do the work the fall that Gator kept me in beer. We had even driven long steel rods into the earth under the house and wired them to a seismograph so we could detect any tunneling activity.

Since the new cell phones had the capability of taking photos and recording conversations without transmitting, all cell phones were banned in the SCIF. Sarah and I each dumped ours in the plastic box outside the door before we went in.

We walked along a short hallway and stopped in front of a door, which Gator rapped on. A muffled voice was the reply. Gator opened the door, waited until I was in, then closed it behind me.

It was a small office, perhaps ten by ten; most women have larger closets. Two folding chairs were arranged in front of one desk. Jake Grafton was seated behind the desk in a swivel chair.

He smiled at us now, a solid, honest smile that made you feel comfortable, and stood to shake hands. "Tommy, Sarah, good to see you again."

Grafton was about six feet tall, maybe an inch or so more, ropy and trim, with graying, thinning hair that he kept short and combed straight back. He had a square jaw and a nose that was a bit too large. On one temple he had an old faded scar, which someone once told me he got from a bullet years and years ago—you had to look hard to see it.

"I thought you were retired, Admiral," Sarah said. Her path had crossed Grafton's in the past and he had taught her some hard lessons. She didn't carry a grudge, though. At least, I didn't think she did.

Grafton sighed. "They caught up to me, offered me this job. I said no, and Callie said I ought to take it, and . . ." He grinned. "She's hard to say no to and make it stick. She convinced me that I had loafed long enough and desperately needed a challenge."

We chuckled politely. I knew Grafton well enough to think that statement was probably true. I liked him, and I really admired his wife. Callie was first class all the way.

"The good news is she's coming over to Paris. We're getting an apartment."

"Sounds like an adventure."

"Yeah." The smile faded. "As you know, in the age of terror, we need all the help we can get from the European intelligence agencies. Washington sent me to see if I can get a little more cooperation. No one in Europe knows me, so I'll have a little grace period."

I tried to smile. That was a Grafton funny. He didn't do many, so you had to enjoy the occasional *mot,* even if it wasn't so *bon.*

Now he turned serious. "You've probably been reading about the G-8 summit coming up in Paris in two weeks. The folks in Washington are nervous, and rightfully so. The heads of government of the eight largest industrial powers all in one place, at one time—it's a tempting terror target. After the Veghel conspiracy was busted, it finally occurred to them that Al Queda or a similar group is fully capable of mounting such an operation in Europe."

Named after a town in the Netherlands where a group of Islamic fundamentalists lived and did their plotting, the Veghel conspiracy was the latest suicide plot against the United States to be broken up and the conspirators arrested. The arrests happened about six months ago; the accused conspirators had yet to go on trial. According to the newspapers, they planned to blow up the New York Stock Exchange with a tractor-trailer full of explosives, à la Oklahoma City.

"One would think they learned that years ago when the Israeli athletes were attacked and murdered at the Olympics," I remarked.

"They're slow learners," Grafton said. "Veghel was the catalyst."

"Weren't the U.S. authorities tipped about the conspiracy?"

"They were," Grafton said, nodding. He didn't say anything else, so Sarah asked one more question.

"Who tipped them?"

"Henri Rodet, the director of the DGSE."

"How did the DGSE learn about Veghel?" Sarah asked. She wasn't the shrinking-violet type.

Now Grafton grinned. Sarah had asked the right question. "I don't know, and Monsieur Rodet refused to tell our people. So we are going to find out."

Uh-oh. There was going to be more to this than sitting around French waiting rooms and chatting with bureaucrats.

Grafton continued. "Rodet's an office politician who rose through the ranks of the new DGSE to replace the hard-line, right-wing leaders who were systematically retired or fired during the 1980s under François Mitterand. Twenty-five years ago he went to the Middle East. He's been working hard ever since to ensure that France got its share of the Arab pie. Ten years ago he was picked to run the agency. When Jacques Chirac sent a letter to Saddam Hussein pledging that France would veto any Security Council resolution authorizing a U.S.-led invasion, Henri Rodet hand-carried the letter to Baghdad and personally placed it in the dictator's hands."

"I thought France was an old American ally," I said as Grafton paused for air.

"France has never helped anyone unless it was in France's best interest," Grafton said flatly. "These days they are busy taking care of number one. Baldly, the French intend to eventually rule a united Europe on the principle that what's good for France is good for Europe, and vice versa."

"I seem to recall someone saying that about GM and America," I remarked.

Sarah Houston studiously ignored me, pretending she didn't even hear my voice.

Grafton's eyes flicked from me to her and back to me. He took a deep breath and went on with the story. "Rodet's number two is Jean-Paul Arnaud, the head of counterespionage. Arnaud's specialty is commercial espionage, which is a nice way of saying that he runs a string of agents who have bought stolen trade secrets from foreign companies and passed those secrets on to French companies. There was a scandal a few years back—Arnaud's boss at the time got canned and the DGSE was reformed under political pressure. That was window dressing, of course. They stayed in the commercial espionage business and Arnaud got promoted."

"So counterespionage is basically the French government spying on foreign companies with offices in France?"

"Well, they don't limit their activities to France. The primary targets are American companies, and they go after trade secrets anywhere they can find them. They are also very interested in muscling in on international deals, winning contracts with bribery or whatever."

"They still doing it?"

"The world is still turning," Grafton said. He made a sweeping motion with his right hand. "That is a problem for another day. We're going to have a chat with Rodet. Tell him, Sarah."

She didn't look at me but at the admiral. "Rodet apparently came into a couple of million euros by way of the U.N.'s Oil-for-Food program, which essentially went away with the American invasion of Iraq in 2003. The money came from a series of transactions between five small companies that were providing goods and services to Saddam Hussein. Rodet invested the money in the Bank of Palestine, which is a honey pot or piggy bank for Islamic radicals out to overthrow Israel—and America and Western civilization and so on."

I had heard of the Bank of Palestine. Somehow bank money wound up being used to pay survivor's benefits to the families of terrorist suicide commandos who had gone on to their reward, whatever that might be. "He owns stock in *that* bank?" I asked.

"He does, and he tipped us on the Veghel conspiracy. It doesn't compute. We're going to try to figure him out and find a way to exploit his relationships with the Bank of Palestine and the various extremist groups in the Middle East." I knew what "exploit" meant. I figured Sarah did, too. "Sarah, you are going to be our computer wizard. Tommy, you're going to be my tech guy and point man."

"Tell me some more about Rodet," I said.

"He's married to an heiress almost ten years older than he is. They're estranged. No children. He has a live-in girlfriend, a château upriver from Paris and a luxurious flat in town. I hear it's quite a place."

"I think I met Rodet's girlfriend this past spring. Gal name of Marisa Petrou. She still his main squeeze?"

"That's her," Grafton agreed, nodding.

Suddenly I realized that Sarah Houston was giving me the

once-over. One of her eyebrows was higher than the other. Now she turned back to Grafton.

"I seem to recall seeing a television interview with Chirac just the other day," I said, "where he was bragging about co-operating to fight terrorism."

"The French are cooperating, but we think they know more than they're passing on, a lot more, and we aren't getting it. Henri Rodet is the key. He's in the crosshairs, partly for the Veghel conspiracy, and partly because the French government has him running the security team for the G-8 summit.

"The question is, How did Rodet learn of the Veghel conspiracy? After careful analysis, we don't think he got it from a DGSE operation, or from one of their agents. It's possible, but . . . We think it's more likely that Rodet has an agent in Al Queda, and that agent was the source of the information on the conspiracy."

"Whoa," I said. "That's a big leap."

"No, it isn't. *Someone* told him."

I threw up my hands. "What does Rodet say?"

"He isn't saying anything. He refused to discuss the matter with the Paris station chief."

"Oh, boy."

Grafton motored right along. "So that's our assumption—Rodet has a spy in Al Queda. We know a few things about this guy." He began ticking them off on his fingers. "One, the agent hasn't yet been caught, which means that he has never been suspected. Two, he's high up in the organization, or he would not have known about the conspiracy. Three, he's been inside a long time. Al Queda is a criminal conspiracy, which means it is composed of extremely paranoid people who don't trust any outsider. Ergo, he's not an outsider. Four, there hasn't been a leak from inside the DGSE, which means that the agent isn't being handled routinely, by the usual professional staff. He's being handled from the very top, perhaps even by Rodet himself."

"If all that's true," Sarah mused, "how do the agent and handler communicate?"

"That is precisely what I want to know," Jake Grafton shot back. "I want you to help me find out."

Grafton talked for another minute or two about logistics. Finally he said good-bye to Sarah, and she got up and left. Didn't even glance at me. When the door closed, I was alone with Grafton.

"I take it you and Sarah aren't getting along very well these days," he said.

"You noticed, eh?"

"Uh-huh."

"Well, you know the course of true love. There are bumps and potholes in the road."

"She going to shoot you or start amputating parts?"

I tried to smile. "I hope not."

"I'm going to need some serious help on this job," he said, looking me straight in the eyes.

"I'm on the shit list after that adventure last year," I replied. "I've been told to stay out of trouble or else."

Grafton's eyebrows knitted. "How come you're still working for this outfit, anyway? A year ago you were talking about taking a banana boat south."

"You know my tale of woe. They have me by the balls. The statute of limitations still has a couple of years to run." Grafton knew I was referring to the felony theft charge that was shelved when I joined the agency. The fuzz didn't catch me, you understand; my partner ratted on me. Same difference, I suppose, but a guy has to keep the record straight.

"In the Navy we didn't have people quite so firmly in our grasp," he said with a straight face.

I snorted. "Don't give me that bullshit. Sounds as if you intend to jam Rodet's nuts into a vise and crank until he screams. That's his problem, not mine. Just what, precisely, do you want from me?"

Grafton picked up a pencil and twirled it between his fingers. "For starters, I want you to bug his flat in town and his house in the country. We'll set up listening posts."

I admitted those chores were in my area of expertise.

"Then I want you to turn traitor. I want you to walk into DGSE headquarters and offer to sell them the Intelink."

Okay, I am an idiot—I admit it. I accepted another assignment working for Jake Grafton! I could be on my way to fun in the sun in Iraq this very minute. God damn!

Grafton kept talking. "You and your girlfriend, Sarah Houston, are looking to make a fresh start, which would go a lot better if you had a couple million tax-free euros in your jeans. You'll give them Intelink-S first, as proof of your bona fides. When the money is in your bank account, you'll give them Intelink-C." Intelink-S was a network, a government Internet, if you will, which contained information classified secret. Intelink-C was the top secret network whereby the United States and its closest allies, Britain, Australia, and Canada, shared intelligence.

"You have got to be kidding!"

"I'm not."

"In the first place, I don't have an access code to any level of Intelink. I have never had an access code."

"I do."

"They change it every week. Rodet isn't going to buy a week's subscription."

"He is going to buy the fact that Sarah helped design these networks, that she's foolishly fallen for a swine like you, that at your insistence she installed a trapdoor, and that you will sell him the key."

I thought about it. "NSA would never let Rodet peek. Ever."

"That's true, of course. We don't even want Monsieur Rodet to know the type of information that is really on Intelink-S, so we've created a parallel, fake Intelink-S. It will look good enough to fool the French, we think. That's what we're going to give Rodet access to. He'll never see the real Intelink-S, and we'll have hooked and boated him long before it's time to reveal Intelink-C."

"He'll never buy it."

Grafton waved that away. "Corrupt people think everyone's corrupt."

I felt nauseous. My forehead was covered in perspiration. I swabbed at the sweat and wiped my hand on my trousers. "They're going to smell a rat. This could be the biggest intelligence debacle ever. What I'm trying to say, Admiral, is that if we live through this, we could go to prison. Like, forever."

Now he smiled at me.

I tried to reason with him. "The frogs will be all over me like stink on a skunk. And through some tiny bureaucratic oversight, I don't have diplomatic immunity." I waved a hand at the door. "They gave all the embassy spots to those security people combing the crowds for terrorists going to the G-8 meeting." I couldn't believe I had the bad luck to fall into a mess like this. The head of the DGSE! God almighty! "If Rodet doesn't buy what we have to sell, what then?"

The admiral turned his hand over. "The Veghel conspirators were going to blow up the New York Stock Exchange. A half dozen Middle Eastern fanatics living on welfare in the Netherlands don't go charging off to America with passports and credit cards and traveler's checks to rent trucks and make bombs without some serious help. Henri Rodet has some questions to answer. Our job is to convince him to do the right thing."

"You, me and Sarah."

Grafton grinned. "Have faith, Tommy."

"It's going to take more than faith, dude. No one in France is going to want us digging up smelly little secrets. Not a single solitary soul."

"I have faith in you," Jake Grafton said firmly.

"It'll take a couple of weeks to scope out those two places and bug them. I'll need a couple of vans, all the good people we can get—and I mean real damn good—and a whole lot of luck."

"We got the vans in Italy. They are in Paris now. I've raided the warehouse in Langley, and they used the diplomatic pouch to send us everything I thought you might need. And we don't have a couple of weeks."

It took a moment for the implications of that remark to sink in. Grafton didn't come up with this caper last night.

When the guys at the very top start scheming, it's time to run for cover. "Oh, man!"

"I want you to go to France tomorrow, rent this apartment"—he passed me a slip of paper with an address on it—"and wait for a telephone call. The caller will give you a place and time. Subtract four hours from the time. Two guys you know will pick you up in a Citroën precisely at that time. If you're followed, don't go there. They won't make the meet if they are under surveillance." He removed a cell phone from a desk drawer and slid it across the desk.

I didn't touch it. "It's sort of funny," I said, "how people talk. For instance, you don't say, '*we* want,' you keep saying, '*I* want.'"

"I'm the man they gave the job to," Grafton said curtly. "I'm responsible for results. You could assume that I've discussed with my superiors how I intend to get the results they want. On the other hand, if your view of my character is a little darker, you might assume that I'm some sort of idiot rogue, that if my actions wreck the Franco-American alliance, it won't bother me. Make any assumption you like—doesn't matter an iota. Your job is to do what I tell you to do. You can bet your ass on that. Got it?"

"I am betting my ass. That's the problem."

His features softened. "That's the job, Tommy."

"You made any arrangements to get us some luck?"

"You're going to supply the luck. Be careful, professional. Think every move through, keep your brain engaged and don't get sidetracked. We'll peel the onion one layer at a time. I want to know what you're doing and when you're doing it and what the results are. Keep me advised, keep your eyes open and you'll be lucky."

The last twenty-four hours of my life had been rocky. Now, faced with the prospect of another Jake Grafton adventure, the gloom was setting in, which was why I said, "When they told me you were getting in this game, I should have bailed. I've had it up to fucking here with this spy shit."

Not a muscle in Grafton's face twitched. He should have

been playing poker in Vegas instead of wasting his talent in the CIA.

"Maybe I need to do some research on the federal statute of limitations," I muttered. "The diamonds the rat and I lifted were from a museum in the District of Columbia. That info should be online."

"Tell you what," Grafton replied, locking me up with those gray eyes, serious as a hangman an hour before dawn. "You help me out on this, and I promise you there'll be no prosecution, even if you leave the agency."

"Maybe a pardon, huh?"

"No prosecution. That's the deal."

I took a deep breath. "I want someone to watch my back."

"The people I have lined up are career professionals." He gave me their names.

I waved the names away. "Three guys. This is a joke. We couldn't follow Martha Stewart's limo through Manhattan with three guys."

"Three plus you."

"Like I said, I want someone to watch my back."

"Is there a reason you don't trust these people?"

"The agency has had its troubles in Europe—hell, that's why *you're* here!" I spread my hands. He knew as well as I that any of these pros could be a mole or double agent. True, the odds were remote, but it *had* happened. "You don't want this op blown and I don't want to stop a bullet."

"Who do you have in mind?"

"Willie Varner, my lock-shop partner."

"He isn't with the agency."

"That's one reason I trust him."

"He's a convicted felon."

"Indeed he is. Willie got caught and went to the joint. Twice. I hate working with people who think they're too smart to get caught. Willie's careful, competent and paranoid—just my kind of guy. And he's one more guy. Believe me, we'll need him."

"If he'll come, we'll make the arrangements."

"I'll offer him a free trip to a French penitentiary—he'll be on the next plane."

"We'll pay him contract wages."

Willie wouldn't sign up for this gig if I told him what the job really was. Still, he had never been to France and was probably foolish enough to want to see it, so I wouldn't level with him until he was here. Like Jake Grafton, I'm sort of short on scruples.

"He's going to need a passport," I told Grafton. "One in his own name would probably be best. He's a good liar but there's not much time and I need him now."

I sat there thinking about Henri Rodet and the DGSE. Some years back the French spooks used murder and kidnappings to squash their enemies. In Algeria they used teams of assassins to take out people they didn't like; when the assassins had done their job, the spooks blew up the hotel the assassins used as headquarters—with the assassins in it, of course. This being *la belle France,* after the explosion leveled the hotel someone whispered the names of the bombers to the newspapers.

If I got put through a grinder and turned into lean meat, bone meal and gristle, there was a shadow of a possibility that someday someone in the DGSE would leak the amazing facts to the press. If they did, that was probably all the epitaph I would ever get.

"I hope I don't regret this," I muttered.

"I just hope you live through it," Grafton said, and smiled again.

A cold chill ran up my spine.

CHAPTER THREE

I called Willie Varner from a phone in the SCIF. Due to the time differential, I got him at home before he went to work. Way before.

"Jesus Christ, Carmellini! You know what time it is?"

"Early."

"It's five thirty in the fuckin' mornin', man. You in jail or dead or what?"

"I need some help, Willie."

"You need a new watch, that's for sure."

"I want you to come over to Paris and help me for a few weeks."

"You mean, like, in *France?*"

"Yeah."

A long silence. "*France,*" he said. I could tell he was warming to the idea.

"We'll pay you for your time, of course," I said casually. "All expenses covered. Nice hotel, some time off. Sort of a working vacation."

"Doin' what?"

"Helping me. I need some backup."

"Backup for what?"

"I really can't get into it on the phone. Nothing dangerous."

"No shooters, man. Nothin' that goes bang. No knives, neither."

"Oh, no. Nothing like that."

"I done my time and I done my bleedin'. Don't want to do no more of neither one."

"I know where you're at. This will be cool."

"Well . . ." He was seriously tempted, I could tell. "Hell, I ain't got a passport."

"We'll get you one. Be a fellow around to the shop later today to take your picture and get your information. In a couple of days someone will bring you a passport and give you some tickets."

"*Goddamn! France!* Okay, I'll come. I can always boogie if things get too iffy. I'm no spring chicken, you know."

"Sure."

"More like a jackrabbit. I like to screw and I can really run."

"The airport's open seven days a week."

"The Folies . . . I heard about *that!* That's what I want to see."

"Works for me. Man will be in to see you later today." I hung up.

Grafton was looking at me with raised eyebrows.

"He's never been out of the country before," I explained, "so he's hot to trot. He'll cool off when he gets to thinking about it, but he'll come. I'll keep him busy and out of trouble while he's here."

When he was seated at his desk in DGSE headquarters in the Conciergerie, Jean-Paul Arnaud could see the Eiffel Tower. From his large, padded swivel chair he could also see the stately walls of the Louvre and bridges all the way downriver to the Pont de la Concorde. If he were so inclined, he could watch the tourist barges, the bateaux, cruising up and down the river with their loads of sightseers, or cloud formations soaring across the skyline of Paris, clouds that had enchanted armies of artists. Jean-Paul Arnaud never looked.

He sat at his desk day in and day out as the seasons changed and the sun and rain came and went, chain-smoking cigarettes as he worked. Occasionally he wrote orders, case summaries and the like; once a quarter he devoted a day to the budget battles; one afternoon a week he turned his attention to personnel matters; on Monday and Wednesday mornings he sat down with the agency head, Henri Rodet, to discuss business; and when asked, he accompanied his boss to meetings with the minister. Otherwise, Jean-Paul Arnaud sat at his desk smoking and reading reports.

So it was at his desk, while sunlight and shadow played on the great city beyond his window, that Jean-Paul Arnaud learned that Jake Grafton, now believed to be associated with the U.S. Central Intelligence Agency, was temporarily attached to the American embassy as a State Department employee and would soon be arriving in Paris.

And it was here, this morning, that he learned that Tommy Carmellini, CIA officer assigned to the SCS, was coming to Paris under a false passport that gave his name as Terry G. Shannon. The report noted that he would arrive in France tomorrow and rent an apartment on Rue Paradis, then speculated a bit on why he might be in Europe.

Using his pen that wrote in green ink, Arnaud made a note on the margin of the report. *Keep me informed.*

He tossed the form into the out basket and picked up the next one from the in basket.

After my interview with Jake Grafton, Gator Zantz gave me a ride to a hotel, the Royal Garden. I was his only passenger. "Where's Houston?" I asked.

"She'll be along."

I grunted. I didn't want to be in the same country with Sarah Houston, let alone the same hotel, not after that stunt she pulled on the airplane. Oh, well.

My hotel room was on the eighth floor. I pulled the curtains, got undressed and climbed into bed—had a devil of a time getting to sleep but eventually drifted off. Not long after that the maid began pounding on the door. I ran her off, watched television for a while, then finally went back to sleep.

A nightmare woke me up at 9:00 P.M. local time, and I lay in bed tossing and turning, unable to get comfortable. I had been trying to catch a plane, and the security people kept finding something else to check as the minutes ticked away. Then I left my watch at the checkpoint and had to run back for it . . . An anxiety dream. What do they mean?

Jet lag is always worse traveling east. On top of that, I was hungry.

When I realized that I was wide-awake, I showered, shaved and got dressed. Went downstairs and looked in the bar. Naw. Went outside and saw a pub just down the street. Perfect.

I don't know about you, but I like London. It's a great town, and the Brits are terrific. They even speak an obsolete form of English that some folks find amusing. Sitting in the pub, I ordered fish and chips and my favorite cider and submerged myself in the delightful atmosphere, surrounded by conversation and laughter as a tennis match played on the telly over the bar.

In a few minutes the world began to look better. Yeah, I had another Jake Grafton adventure ahead of me, but it was the last one. Yeah, I had woman troubles, but who doesn't? I was munching chips and sipping cider and meditating about what I was going to do after I got out of the Christians In Action when Guess Who came into the joint.

She looked around, saw me, thought she would leave, then changed her mind and came over. I stood as she approached the table.

"May I join you?" she asked coolly, formal as hell.

"Please do."

I enjoy the company of women—being around them, watching how they move, how they carry themselves, their gestures, listening to what they have to say, all of it—and I had really enjoyed being around this one. I wasn't so sure I was going to like it this time.

Sarah Houston was seriously brilliant, with a quick, darting mind and a feminine presence that seemed to radiate heat. In addition, she had an erect, athletic carriage and was pretty darn good-looking. Tonight, as usual, people at other tables and at the bar had turned to watch as she walked across the room. They kept their eyes on her as she seated herself, and only reluctantly turned away.

"Couldn't sleep?" I asked.

"No."

"Umm."

The waitress came over and Sarah ordered white wine. "I'm not hungry," she told the young woman in jeans when she asked if Sarah wanted something to eat. The other patrons accepted us as members of the pub community and ceased to pay attention. Sarah helped herself to a small piece of fish off my plate and nibbled on it.

"Ever been to London before?" I asked, just to make conversation.

"Back in my dark days." She meant back when she was known as Zelda Hudson and was on a holy quest to get filthy rich. I had known that and forgotten. Since we weren't supposed to talk about Zelda, her former identity, I changed the subject.

"How about Paris?"

"No."

"Great town."

She didn't respond to that inanity.

"After this assignment, are you going to stay with the company you work for?" I meant the National Security Agency.

"I'm still in the process of rehabilitation, I guess." She grimaced. "Not that I have a choice. You sprung me from prison, remember?"

For some reason the subject wasn't changing. I thought about telling Sarah about my own checkered past, and Grafton's promise, but refrained. Sharing personal secrets with ex-girlfriends is always a bad idea.

"I'm sorry about the scene on the plane," she said, when the silence had gone on too long.

I muttered something.

She took her time on my fish, thoroughly chewing each tiny bite. She didn't look at me.

When she had finished the last morsel, she cleared her

throat. "It was the first time for me." Then she decided that comment could be taken several ways. "The first I fell in love," she said as an addendum.

I knew I was also the first man she had welcomed into her bed, but she didn't want to discuss that. Nor did I. The silence got wider and deeper.

"A man once loved me," Sarah said softly. "But I didn't love him." She sat immobile, her eyes focused on infinity.

"These things happen," I said as gently as I could.

When the silence was threatening to strangle us both, she said, "Now I know how it feels."

She got up and walked out. The waitress bringing the wine stopped and watched her go.

The wind off the Atlantic carried in low clouds that evening, and rain fell across most of northern France. About ten o'clock a man came walking slowly and unsteadily along a street in a working-class district of suburban Paris, a street lined with cars and small trucks, with scooters and motorcycles parked sideways between them. The man wore an ankle-length coat and a hat that shed the rain. Under the coat, he had a muffler wrapped around his neck. Sticking from the pocket of his coat was the neck of a bottle.

He took shelter in the doorway of a closed business. There he extracted the bottle from his pocket, sipped on it and lit a cigarette. Working carefully, keeping one hand on the locked door of the building and the other firmly around the neck of the bottle, he lowered himself to the concrete. Once in position, he took the cigarette from his mouth and exhaled slowly, savoring the smoke. Then he took another nip from the bottle.

Pedestrians, and there weren't many, ignored the man. The people were going into and out of a bar across the street. Even those men and women who glanced his way couldn't see him very well, with the hat obscuring his eyes and his coat collar turned up against the invigorating night breeze, which occasionally whipped a small shower of raindrops into the doorway.

An hour passed as the rain made puddles in the street and

on the cracked, broken sidewalk. Half of another hour had slipped by when a dark blue motorcycle came down the street at a good rate of speed and stopped in front of the motorcycle parking area near the bar. In the rain the motorcycle looked black, except when a streetlight shone directly on it.

Unfortunately the motorcycle parking area was full. The rider eased his steel horse into motion, rode to the end of the block, then turned around. Coming back toward the bar, he saw a place on the sidewalk near a pole that he could squeeze the motorcycle into. No sooner thought than attempted.

The man in the doorway was standing now. The motorcyclist ignored him and set about securing the vehicle with a chain lock, which he threaded around the drive shaft and through the spokes in the rear tire.

The light was bad, and the lock on the chain quickly became wet and slippery. The motorcyclist put his helmet on the seat of the bike and bent down, trying to see where he needed to put the chain.

He realized that the man in the doorway had left it and was behind him, and glanced around. As he did so, the man in the coat fired a pistol into the motorcyclist's head. The bullet entered it above his left ear. The shot was muffled, a wet pop that was lost in the sound of an oncoming truck. The victim slumped to the pavement, his legs splaying out.

The man in the coat quickly bent down and fired another bullet into the motorcyclist's head, then put his pistol back into his coat pocket.

The shooter walked away along the sidewalk with his hands in his pockets as the truck passed. In the dim light and rain, the driver of the truck didn't notice the man lying on the sidewalk.

The falling rain diluted the blood that had leaked from the holes in the victim's head and washed his open, unseeing eyes.

CHAPTER FOUR

Jean-Paul Arnaud saw the flashing lights in the wet street and pulled his BMW as close to the curb as he could, then parked and locked the car.

He walked toward the nearest policeman and flashed his credentials. The policeman pointed. "Inspector Papin."

The inspector was a man wearing an English raincoat with the collar turned up and a brimmed hat, standing under a bit of awning watching the photographers work. The body still lay in the gutter by the motorcycle, just as it was when it had been discovered an hour ago. The rain was almost a mist now, given weight and substance by a cool breeze that swirled through the streets.

"I'm Arnaud, DGSE." He offered his credentials for inspection.

The police officer gave them a cursory glance, without touching them, and produced a set of DGSE credentials from his pocket. "He had these on him. One of your men, apparently."

Arnaud accepted the building pass, looked at the photo, and studied the name. "Claude Bruguiere," he said softly, and handed the credentials back to the inspector. "What can you tell me about it?"

"We're just getting started. The body was found about an hour ago, in the position in which it lies now. The doctor who examined it said the man has been dead no more than two hours. He was apparently killed by two bullets to the head.

They appear to still be in the skull and will be recovered during the autopsy. I have officers canvassing the neighborhood trying to find someone who saw or heard the shooting, but I expect they will find no one—no one telephoned the police when it happened. Still, we shall see."

The inspector took the time to light a cigarette and return his lighter to his pocket. "Bruguiere came to this bar," he nodded toward it, "several times a week to see a woman who works there. She is married to another man. She was in there all evening—no one saw her leave the premises—and was there when the body was discovered. Only when someone said there was a body on the street outside did she come out to see if she recognized who it was. She's inside now, crying. We have an officer getting her statement."

"Her husband?"

"He works nights. An officer is interviewing him now."

"Was Bruguiere robbed?"

"I doubt it. He had his wallet on him, his credentials, a wad of keys on a ring . . ."

"His family?" Arnaud asked. He was almost embarrassed to ask—he couldn't remember if Bruguiere was married or not, nor had he asked the duty man at the office to find out when he called to notify him of Bruguiere's murder. It hadn't occurred to him.

"Your office says he isn't married. We got his address from his driver's license. We have a man on the way over there."

The photographers finished their work and began packing their gear. Inspector Papin motioned to the crew of the ambulance, who had been standing out of the way. They began preparations to move the body to the morgue.

The inspector conferred with his officers, listening to their reports and sending them off on other errands, but he had nothing more for Arnaud. The DGSE official lingered until the body was in the ambulance, then walked back through the rain to his car.

• • •

My mood wasn't great that morning. Before I went to the train station, I went over to the company for an interview with one of the paper pushers, a man named Rick Odell. While I was waiting Gator walked past pretending he didn't see me, so I knew the Patriots had lost.

"Hey, Gator, sports dude. What's the news from the U.S. of A.?"

He looked blank.

"Ten pounds, buddy."

The blank look disappeared. "You look like a sport, Carmellini. How about double or nothing?"

"How about paying up, Gator-bait? The Patriots ought to pay you to bet on somebody else."

He counted out pound coins with little grace. He acted as if it were my fault that the Patriots couldn't cut the mustard. "I'm really sorry your life sucks," I said.

"Fuck you, Carmellini."

"I'm sure you'd like to," I replied, "but you look like the kind of guy that would kiss and tell."

I knew Rick Odell from previous trips to Europe. He was perhaps forty, prematurely bald, and never smiled. He ran through contact procedures, telephone numbers, whom I should call if I got burned, the address of a safe house, all of the procedures and info that an agent in a foreign country needed to do his job and stay alive. Everything had to be committed to memory, so after we had run through everything twice, he quizzed me.

Finally Odell shuffled the papers together and replaced them in my op file. "This isn't a vacation, Carmellini. You'll be onstage every minute. The DGSE is competent."

I had tried to make that point with Grafton the day before. I reminded myself that Odell was just the hired help. "Okay." I said.

"And stay away from the women."

I wondered what generated that remark. Did he know about Sarah and me? "I'll try," I said earnestly, "but I get these urges. Isn't there a pill for those, some kind of anti-Viagra?"

Odell wasn't amused. If it weren't for the scene in the pub last night, I would have probably kept my mouth shut; that's usually a wise choice in the spook business.

"I've read your file. You have a bad habit of going off half-cocked. You're on thin ice. For a change, use good judgment."

I figured he was referring to the KGB defector mess that Grafton helped me with last year, but I'd had enough. "What's that supposed to mean?"

"You know the regs. Report all contacts with possible foreign agents."

"That's everybody in France. The damn place is full of foreigners."

Odell continued as if I hadn't spoken. "Don't get yourself in a compromising situation—no sleeping with the enemy." He sighed. "There's always the possibility that you might get the clap."

Donning a new identity always feels strange. It's as if you are borrowing someone else's life. When I set out for Waterloo Station in a taxi, I was Terry G. (for George) Shannon, from Los Angeles, California. I had a passport to prove it, too, a genuine U.S. government forgery. The document bore a smattering of entry and exit stamps that would tell anyone who looked that ol' Terry G. had logged his share of frequent flier miles.

To back up the passport, Terry had a driver's license with my mug on it, a library card, a telephone company calling card, three credit cards—all real—and a AAA card, in case his car crapped out on the freeway. According to Terry's legend, he worked as a freelance travel researcher, checking on hotels, restaurants, and travel facilities for various tourist publications.

A legend is a history of a person who never existed. It has to be built up layer by layer, a task that occupies a building-full of folks at the agency. In fact, they maintain over fifteen thousand legends, which they dole out when the need arises, complete with all the paper to prove the fake person really exists. No legend is perfect; anyone who backtracks far enough will find that the tracks of the fictional person completely disappear. Yet extensive backtracking costs money and ties up manpower, so there is a very real practical limit. I was confident my Terry Shannon identity would withstand a quick check. It was going to get a lot more than that, however. I had my fingers crossed that it wouldn't happen until the proper moment.

Anonymity is a spy's best friend. As usual that morning, I wore a cheap watch on my left wrist and no other jewelry of any kind. My hair was medium length, my sunglasses were from a drugstore, and my clothes looked as if they came from Wal-Mart. They hadn't: I had had them specially tailored so that when I wanted to pass unnoticed, my clothes would mask my narrow waist and wide shoulders; these features were so out of the ordinary that people might remember me because of them.

At Waterloo Station I bought a ticket to Paris on the Eurostar, checked my bag, and went through immigration to the departure lounge. I bought a few newspapers and a paperback novel; then sat reading in the most inconspicuous corner of the lounge. Now I was taking precautions against meeting that old pal from high school. I need not have worried; he didn't show.

I was, however, now onstage. Someone from French intelligence would be scrutinizing all visitors to France, looking for known agents and suspicious persons. This was the reality that every intelligence officer lived with when off his home turf. I have heard it referred to as occupational paranoia, which is a good description, I suppose. One won't last long in the business without it. Actually, I sort of enjoyed it. Some people do.

Soon I was seated on the train, which glided out of the station and eventually dove into the Chunnel. When there was again something to see out the window, we were in France. I rode along looking at the manicured fields and small farmhouses, thinking about Sarah Houston. *Got to stop that,* I told myself.

I picked up a newspaper and tried to get interested.

Those were tough days for spooks. Some folks said the days of the conventional spy were over, that human intelligence, or HUMINT, cost too much, was unreliable and too vulnerable to foreign penetration of our intelligence services. It had certainly been hard to get during the cold war, so NSA, the code breakers from World War II, grew and grew and grew. NSA gathered electronic intelligence, ELINT, which was made up of communications, imagery, and measurement and signals, all with their own acronyms, such as COMINT, communications intelligence. NSA had satellites, airplanes and listening posts all over the world. They listened to radio transmissions, radars, taxicabs, airplanes, infantry squads, cell phones—almost anything that radiated. After they collected this huge, raging river of information, they ran it through the largest computer systems on the planet and distilled it into intelligence. Intelligence about everyone. Some of this product, if you will, was shared with American allies.

America went electronic for several reasons, one of the most important of which was traitors—such as Aldrich Ames, for example—who sold the Soviets the names of America's handful of in-place agents in the Soviet Union. The Soviets executed the agents and reduced the flow of human intelligence from the Soviet Union to a trickle, forcing the United States to go in another direction.

Now the world was changing again—and damn fast. More and more communications were going over fiber-optic cables, not broadcast, and more and more of the things the English-speaking world wanted to know about everyone else were on computer databases. The information wasn't inaccessible—it was just sometimes more difficult to get to. Our job was to get to it.

The goal was to know everything that was going on, everywhere on the planet. Impossible? With COMINT, perhaps. It couldn't tell you what your adversary was thinking or what he might do next. It could not predict the future. It was also grotesquely inefficient in gathering intelligence about terrorists, who were stateless, rootless fanatics at war with civilization. To fill in the COMINT gaps, one needed human intelligence, spies.

Henri Rodet obviously had a spy, or spies, who were turning up more real information on Al Queda than our guys, and Jake Grafton wanted access to that info. But how would selling Rodet a bogus information network help us get it? The answer, I concluded, was that Grafton was going to sell Rodet a pig in a poke, and the price was access. On the other hand, conning someone didn't sound to me like the way to start a long-term relationship. In any event, it had never worked with me and women.

Perhaps I should have asked—but perhaps not. I reminded myself that my job was to obey orders, not figure them out.

Before he left for France, Jake Grafton took the time to visit the SCIF in the basement of the Kensington safe house to check the Intelink for the latest update on Europe.

It was there he learned about the murder of DGSE officer Claude Bruguiere the previous evening. Intercepted police radio voice traffic had been the first reports; then, finally, the policeman examining the crime scene radioed in the information from Bruguiere's driver's license. The NSA computer matched the victim to a list of DGSE officers.

Bruguiere, Grafton knew, had been the man who completed Roget's stock transaction in Amman, Jordan.

He was in a somber mood when he turned off the computer.

Although it's an ancient European city, Paris has a different feel than most European cities; it has wide boulevards and large squares and scenic vistas. The difference is urban renewal. While the Germans had extensive help with theirs in the early 1940s, the French rebuilt Paris in the 1860s. They turned the job over to an urban engineer, one Baron Haussmann, who gave the world a beautiful city; indeed, some say the loveliest on earth.

It is also just about the world's biggest, most expensive tourist destination. The only thing that saves the place, in my opinion, is the French. They are wonderful, impractical people with incomprehensible politics who love art, music, clothes, their city and each other. Boy, do they like each other. Lovers are everywhere, or at least they were that day I arrived at the Gare du Nord, stuffed my bag in a taxi, and went riding off through the streets as if I were a dentist from Scranton armed with four guidebooks. Holding hands and clinging tightly are part of the French social order. All things considered, it's a wonder there aren't more French.

However, I had had it up to here with love. Maybe the Parisian taxi driver had, too; he was a surly rascal who seemed to take personal offense that I was riding in back while he had to sit up front and drive.

The address Jake Grafton had given me was a building on a small side street just off the Rue Paradis, which by some miracle wasn't too far from the train station. The building was about six stories high, stuck in the middle of a block, one of a string of them. The street was narrow. Apparently the baron didn't do this one.

I got my stuff out of the trunk, paid off the hackie, and spent fifteen seconds looking around. As usual, I kept my eyes moving. I didn't see anyone paying any attention to me, which I hoped was indeed the case. If the French already had a tail on me, I might as well head back to the States right now.

Inside the building I dusted off my French and tried it out on the concierge. Terry G. Shannon. My company arranged for an apartment? After listening to my French, she wanted to see my passport. She made a note of the number and returned it.

The building had no elevator. Yep, I had the top apartment. I took a look at the steep, narrow staircase and left my suitcase for the second load. The concierge didn't offer to climb up and show me the place—she simply gave me a key. Two keys, actually. One was to a mailbox in a bank of similar ones in the small lobby.

The flat was right under the roof. The space had probably been the attic; at some time in the geologic past it had been finished out and rented. About six feet in from the door, the ceiling began slanting toward the street, except for the dormer for the one window. The place was large enough for a double bed, a chair, dresser and desk, a closet and a bathroom. No shower in the bathroom, just an ancient tub with four feet. I'm a shower man myself, but in Iraq I bathed from a bucket. I told myself that the tub was very French.

And the window opened. I pulled back the sashes, leaned forward and looked out. The sounds of Paris assaulted me. I took a deep breath. I fancied I could smell the butter.

Well, heck. This wasn't bad.

I took my time unpacking. When I had my duds stored in the ramshackle dresser and closet, I sat in the chair and played with my cell phone. I turned it on and it seemed to find a cell tower. Back in the bad old days spies had to sneak around looking for chalk marks on walls and upside-down flowerpots; now they just call you. Progress is wonderful.

I stowed the phone in my pocket, yawned—I had had another two hours' sleep after my pub visit—and decided to go for a run. Maybe before dinner I could get a nap.

Paris. Any way you cut it, the place beat the hell out of Baghdad.

Jake Grafton and Sarah Houston checked into a hotel on a side street just off the Champs-Elysées. Grafton telephoned the embassy from his room, and thirty minutes later a car picked him up in front of the hotel.

The embassy was situated immediately beside the grandiose Hotel de Crillon, the royal palace of Louis XV, which faced the Place de la Concorde. Jake Grafton remembered some of his college history, so he looked with interest at the Egyptian obelisk in the center of the huge square. Napoleon stole it from Egypt before his North African adventures were terminated by the Royal Navy. The stone pillar had replaced the guillotine that Louis XVI lost his head upon. Twenty thousand people were executed during the most intense period of the Revolution, the Reign of Terror.

As one commentator noted, the French married mechanization to political death to create industrial decapitation.

Oh, people had been murdered in droves before, that was nothing new—whole cities-full of inhabitants hacked and stabbed and slashed, and heretics tortured and burned—but it was piecework, each killing a personal, unique work of mayhem. For the first time in European history whole classes of people were condemned and mechanically slaughtered, not because of their deeds but because of their status. Eventually Stalin and Hitler, the heirs of Robespierre, took the process a step further and bureaucratized industrial murder, thereby raising it to a whole new level. Instead of tens of thousands, millions of people were declared enemies of the state by the dictators and institutionally terminated. And it all started right here in the heart of Paris, in what is now the Place de la Concorde.

The admiral cooled his heels in a reception room for twenty minutes before he was ushered in to see the U.S. ambassador, who had a huge office with a view of the plaza and the Paris skyline. The person who did the ushering was a woman, a career diplomat. "Mizz Agatha Hempstead," she said, emphasizing the "Ms." in case Grafton had forgotten.

He hadn't. "A few years back, in Russia, wasn't it?"

Her lips compressed into a thin line as she nodded her head half an inch.

The ambassador, Owen Lancaster, wasn't a career diplomat. He might as well have been, though. He was one of those establishment pillars who are routinely appointed to key ambassadorships by presidents of both parties. If he had a political affiliation, he never let it show. Owen Lancaster seemed the incarnation of capitalist success, but Jake doubted that he had ever dirtied his hands earning money. He had come by it the tried-and-true traditional way: He inherited it. He was tall and lean and had a head of immaculately barbered gray hair. Today he was impeccably togged out in a tailor-made wool suit and hand-painted silk tie. A red one. On his lapel was a small red flower. Jake thought the suit looked Italian, but how would one know?

Grafton unconsciously adjusted his new suit and straightened his tie. Last week he and Callie had picked out four new suits at a department store in a Washington mall. To the relief of both, the suits had been on sale for 30 percent off.

"*Admiral* Grafton," Lancaster said with a frown. "The last time our paths crossed was in Russia." So much for the social pleasantries.

"I remember, sir."

"I was not happy to see your name again," Lancaster said baldly. "You made a hell of a mess in Russia."

"Just doing my job," Jake said mildly. He checked the shine on his new shoes. They hadn't been on sale.

"I confess, I was surprised when CIA brought you in as their European Operations chief. You're a retired naval officer. Do you have any experience in intelligence?"

"A little," Jake replied curtly. He had no intention of discussing his qualifications for his job, or lack thereof, with someone outside the agency. The ambassador should know better, he thought.

When it became obvious that Grafton was not going to say more, the ambassador said sharply, "I know your reputation, sir. Russia, Hong Kong, Cuba, New York—oh, yes, I know who you are. You've been in the middle of some of the biggest crises of the last ten years. And if I know, don't you think the French will?"

"I'd be surprised if they didn't do their homework," Jake responded.

"This G-8 summit in two weeks—the president has made normalization of our relationship with France his number one foreign policy objective. He's coming to Paris to see to it personally. France is the key to Europe, and we need Europe on our side."

"They said much the same to me in Washington," Jake said mildly. "We'll try to keep the terrorists and spies out of your way."

"This summit had better not be torpedoed by anyone. You understand about torpedoes, don't you, Admiral?" Lancaster was of an age and station in life that meant he didn't have to be polite. These days he rarely bothered.

"I do."

"I want a promise, sir. In Russia you charged off to tilt at windmills without informing me of your activities. Fortunately it worked out, but that was just shit-house luck."

Jake was shocked—he didn't know that Lancaster had that kind of language in him. Ms. Hempstead didn't turn a hair. Lancaster steamed on. "I don't want to be blindsided by any shenanigans this time. I'm not a babe in the woods—I've been in the middle of more international crises than you've ever read about. Talk to me before you kick over anyone's applecart."

"I'll do my best, sir."

"I need more assurance than that," Lancaster snapped.

Jake Grafton had had enough. "That's the best I can do. Take it up with Washington."

On that note the interview ended. Clad in his new shoes, department-store suit and made-in-China tie, the admiral was ushered out of the ambassador's office.

When Agatha Hempstead returned from escort duty, Lancaster was standing at the window with his arms folded across his chest, looking out.

"You knew CIA was going to replace their European chief," she said. "What is so remarkable about Admiral Grafton?"

"He isn't a career man—he's a shooter. With the G-8 summit just around the corner . . ." Lancaster sighed. "Washington is obviously worried." He held his hands out and looked at them. "I feel as if the world I know and love is dying." He balled up his hands into fists. "Civilization is mortally wounded, and something truly evil is being born to take its place."

George Goldberg, the CIA's Paris station chief, was a large, balding man with a serious paunch who moved slowly and deliberately. He had a square jaw and heavy brows on a face that was usually expressionless. He never smiled or frowned, looked excited or disappointed. On first meeting him most people thought he was stupid. They couldn't have been more wrong. He had attended college on a football scholarship, playing tackle, and been drafted by a pro team but refused to sign. Instead, he stayed in school to complete his PhD in economics.

He and Jake Grafton sat in the SCIF in the basement of the American embassy chatting about their careers as they got acquainted. "Perhaps I should have gone to the NFL, just for the heck of it," Goldberg told the admiral, "and after a couple of years returned to school. There were days in Moscow when I wished I had done it that way."

"Ah, the road not traveled . . ."

"At the time the London School of Economics looked more interesting than the Cleveland Browns. I'd been to Cleveland, the Mistake on the Lake." Watching the way Goldberg said that, with his deadpan face, Jake Grafton was reminded of Buster Keaton.

"How well do you know the folks at the DGSE?"

"Very well. We have a liaison officer, of course, but when he goes to the Conciergerie, he talks to some guy in a tiny office. To get any cooperation I have to go over there. I get to see Arnaud any time I want. Occasionally Rodet."

"Tell me about Henri Rodet."

"He's a smart, ambitious survivor," Goldberg replied thoughtfully. "He's built his career in the Middle East. I would bet he knows the Arabs better than anyone else in Europe—well, better than any other intel pro. Nobody knows more Middle Eastern scumbags than he does. He speaks fluent Arabic and Farsi, and he's got a GI system that's as impervious to germs as a sewer pipe."

"So he can talk the talk and grab the goat."

"You got it. He spent twenty-five years listening and connecting the dots."

"Arnaud, Rodet's number two?"

"Shrewd, smart and unscrupulous. There's another guy looking out for number one."

"So what was your reaction when you heard Rodet was buying stock in the Bank of Palestine?"

Goldberg shifted his weight as he considered his answer. "My first reaction was that he had figured out another way to make money from other people's troubles. You see, Rodet's the son of a couple of schoolteachers. He wound up in the intelligence service and spent a lot of time in the Middle East. Then he married the daughter of a rich French merchant who sold hardware all over the Arab world. She was ten years older than he was. Maybe it was love, maybe it was money, but . . . when the passion cooled the father-in-law gave him a ton of money and the wife moved out. Then there's all this smoke rising from the Oil-for-Food debacle. Some folks say some of that money wound up in Rodet's pocket. I don't know if it did or not. In any event, when I heard about the bank stock, I thought that story might be true."

"And now?"

"Well, now I'm not so sure. It could be a slick smear."

"Tell me about the Veghel conspiracy."

"It was just another day, like any other. I was at the Conciergerie talking to Arnaud when a messenger or someone stuck his head into the room and said the director would like to see me. So I got up and trooped off behind the guy, leaving Arnaud sitting there."

"Did he know why Rodet wanted to see you?"

"Didn't act like he did, but these guys are pros. Who could say?"

"So what happened?"

"I went in to see Rodet and he shook hands, put me in a chair. Told me about the Veghel conspiracy, who they were, what they intended to do, when, and so on. What he didn't tell me was how he learned about all this. So that was the question I asked. Do I call the president right now, wake him up with this hot tip, do I send it to Washington flash immediate, or do I put it on the computer and let the bureaucracy grind it up for the in baskets?

"And Rodet looked at me innocent as a lamb and said, 'I cannot tell you that.' Didn't feed me a line about secret sources or broken codes or any of that other bullshit. Just, 'I cannot tell you that.' Of course I decided it was gospel, and by God, that's the way it is turning out. Those raghead bastards *were* going to blow up Wall Street and everyone in it, including themselves."

"Got any theories on how the DGSE found out about this group?"

"I asked Arnaud that question again the next time I saw him, and he just stared at me. Didn't say a word." Goldberg shrugged.

"I read your report. What I want to know is what you think. You've been talking to these people for years."

"Four years." George Goldberg scratched his nose and eyed Jake Grafton thoughtfully. "I don't think the DGSE came by this info. Arnaud always tells me what the organization wants me to know. Rodet is the political guy. On the other hand, this was big. Really big. Maybe Rodet thought he should do this himself for political and PR reasons."

"If the DGSE didn't come up with this information, how did Rodet get it?"

Goldberg raised his hands. "Rodet has always been well informed about Middle Eastern terrorists—the radical imams, the financiers, bankers, sympathizers, possible targets, methods . . . We always thought he had people here and there who heard things and passed them along, the classic way to gather intelligence. French businesspeople roam the Arab world at will and they talk to the DGSE. On the other hand, the Veghel thing wasn't something someone overheard down at the mosque. One suspects someone inside the conspiracy or inside Al Queda passed the information to Rodet. In any event, he isn't saying anything to anyone about his sources."

"You're saying that Henri Rodet may have a secret source inside Al Queda, one known only to him?"

"That's a possibility. The most probable possibility, in my opinion. The Veghel stuff was hot—really hot." Goldberg shrugged. "You know as much as I do."

"If you could construct that hypothesis, other people can, too."

"They could," Goldberg agreed.

"Washington has a name. They say the spy is a guy named Abu Qasim."

Goldberg looked skeptical. "Where did they get that tidbit?"

The admiral shrugged. "I wasn't told the source."

"If my memory serves me correctly, Qasim is one of the aliases of a top Al Queda guy, who also goes by the name of Abdullah al-Falih." Goldberg made a face. "Getting a name from some illiterate holy warrior doesn't make it so."

"You think that's where they got it?"

"Probably. The Egyptians, the Pakistanis and even the Saudis torture those guys, who will say anything to stop the pain. That kind of information is worse than worthless, and the fools in Washington take it for gospel. 'Let's raise the security level to yellow this weekend—a guy in a Cairo prison said his pals are going to blow up Washington.' "

Grafton sat lost in thought. Finally he sighed and spoke, on a different subject. "This DGSE agent who was killed last night, Claude Bruguiere—any whispers on who might have killed him?"

"I haven't heard any."

"The G-8 conference? What are the French authorities doing about security?"

"Everything they can, and I mean everything. Rodet is chairman of the security committee. They are making life uncomfortable for the French Muslim communities. The trick is to keep track of the suicidal fanatics without triggering more rioting. They are tightening border security and shifting police and army units here from all over the country. By the day the G-8 leaders arrive at Charles de Gaulle, the Ile de France—that's the heart of France, Paris and the surrounding area—will be an armed camp. The French have absolutely no intention of giving terrorists any cracks at all to exploit. While the foreign leaders are on French soil, Paris and the surrounding area will be the most heavily policed area on earth."

They talked over the G-8 security arrangements for several minutes before Grafton moved on to another subject. "I'd like to go over the past year's DGSE intercepts and summaries with you, if that's possible."

"Certainly," George Goldberg said. "We'll use the Intelink." He swiveled to the computer beside him and began to type.

Two minutes later he said, "Here's your name."

"What?" Jake looked at the screen. His name wasn't on the Intelink this morning. The folks at NSA must have just posted it. As he read the entry he saw another name he recognized: Tommy Carmellini. Let's see . . . this was an interception of an encrypted landline data transmission . . .

So the French knew that Jake Grafton and Tommy Carmellini were in Paris and both were CIA.

"There's a leak somewhere," Goldberg muttered.

"Yes, but where?" Jake Grafton shot back.

CHAPTER FIVE

Jean-Paul Arnaud cooled his heels in the director's outer office while he enjoyed the presence of the secretary, a tall, stately woman who owed her position more to the boss's appreciation of beautiful women than to her professional accomplishments. She smiled wanly, as if apologizing for Rodet's uncharacteristic tardiness. Arnaud tried to swallow his churlish mood. He didn't appreciate being kept waiting.

Twenty minutes after the hour, he was ready to stomp off with orders to call him if and when Rodet arrived. He managed to stifle himself—a good decision, he concluded when Rodet came marching in five minutes later. The director ignored the secretary, who stood for The Arrival, and motioned to Arnaud with a jerk of his head.

Inside the director's office with the door closed, Rodet said, "Sorry I'm late. Traffic becomes more and more impossible." The director was of medium height, a fit, trim, vain man who spent an hour a day on a tennis court and a half hour a week in a tanning bed. He was smart, a shrewd judge of character and an even shrewder politician, psychotically ambitious and absolutely ruthless. Arnaud suspected that in his heart of hearts Henri Rodet wanted to become the first president of the European Union. Of course, if this were true, Rodet was wise enough to have never mentioned it to a living soul.

Arnaud made a sympathetic noise. "How was Bonn?" he asked.

"They are not sure the politicians will go along with secret data mining of bank records," Rodet said as he plopped himself into his chair behind his huge custom desk. He held out his hand for the weekly report, which Arnaud passed to him. Rodet had been talking to his counterpart at the BND, the Bundesnachrichtendienst, or German Federal Intelligence Service. "They are worried about scandals. They got burned years ago when they went after the Red Brigades."

"Scandals are the nature of the business," Arnaud said reasonably. "It's the world we live in."

"Indeed," Rodet said, and took a deep breath. He exhaled with a sigh as he surveyed his corner office. It was tastefully decorated in understated elegance, with a few simple pieces of art. The people who visited Rodet's office who weren't with his agency were exclusively government officials. Only the initiated realized that the art was horribly expensive, and those few were precisely those whom Rodet wished to impress.

Rodet opened the classified morning briefing sheet and scanned it. He read for a few seconds. "This American— Admiral Grafton. Who is he?"

"The CIA is reshuffling again. Grafton is their new head of European Ops. He's an amateur, a dilettante."

"And this illegal Yankee Doodle? Carmellini?"

"A professional. Strictly technical. He was in Iraq this past summer. We are not sure—you know how hard it is to build dossiers on foreign agents—but we believe he and Grafton worked together on several occasions when Grafton was still on active duty in the American navy. Cuba and Hong Kong."

"Now I remember. This is that Grafton?"

"Yes, sir."

"There are no aircraft carriers in Paris, no jet airplanes, no revolutionaries," Rodet said, not bothering to hide his sarcasm. "Ah, these Americans! What are we doing to keep track of these two?"

"We monitor reports from agents. I have the reports sent directly to me."

"No surveillance?"

"No, sir. I didn't think that wise at this point." This was a lie, and Arnaud told it readily. He had learned long ago that the key to survival in the DGSE was to know more than the boss. What the boss didn't know wouldn't hurt Arnaud; what Arnaud knew was capital in the bank. Professional survival was high on his priority list.

Rodet paused, thinking of his conversations with the Germans. Unfortunately they, like all other Western intelligence services, talked with their counterparts in foreign services, including the Americans. Especially the Americans, who were sharing information on suspected terrorists and their activities and demanding reciprocity. In today's world it was politically impossible not to cooperate. Correction: impossible to appear to be not cooperating.

The hard reality was that America was an attractive lightning rod for Islamic extremism. America's arrogance, pride and worldwide commercial interests made Americans easy to dislike; they made wonderful villains. As any student of realpolitik intuitively understood, every holy warrior crusading against an American target was one less aimed somewhere else. Also, although it could never be said aloud, the difficulties American companies experienced doing business in the Middle East created opportunities for European concerns. After all, in the final analysis, the misfortunes of others were profit opportunities.

The director of the DGSE toyed with the report in his hands, neatly folding and unfolding a corner. "I concur," he said. "Now is not the time to beard the Americans, not a few days before the G-8 summit, at any rate. Let this sailor, Grafton, have his honeymoon."

Rodet went on to the next item on the weekly report, the murder of DGSE officer Claude Bruguiere.

"The police are investigating it as a routine murder," Arnaud said. He had, of course, already talked several times with the police officer in charge of the investigation, the last time just this morning. That fact was in the report in front of Rodet.

"Bruguiere was shot in front of a bar he regularly frequents," Arnaud continued as Rodet scanned the report. "A married woman friend worked there. Two bullets in the brain. No one heard the shots. The weapon was nine-millimeter, yet the cases probably had a reduced powder charge, one barely sufficient to activate the mechanism." Arnaud and Rodet both knew that such weapons were the choice of professionals using a pistol with a silencer, so Arnaud didn't bother to point out this fact. "He was not robbed."

"The woman's husband?"

"At work. The police believe he knew nothing of his wife's affair. The news was quite a shock."

"Indeed," Rodet said dryly. "What was Bruguiere working on?"

Arnaud passed the files across.

Rodet flipped through them. "Nothing leaps out. Perhaps something from the past."

"Perhaps."

"Look into it, please, and keep me briefed."

"Yes, sir."

Rodet went on to the next item on the list, a prominent minister's secret affair with a woman believed to be a BND agent. "The Germans never mentioned this."

"Perhaps she isn't really a BND agent."

"Without sex to complicate human affairs, newspapers would be much thinner and you and I wouldn't be nearly as busy," Rodet said as he studied Arnaud's notes.

"One wishes politicians would get too old for this sort of thing," was the good-natured riposte, "but age seems to make them more susceptible."

"So it seems," Rodet murmured, and wished he had kept his comment to himself.

They spent the next twenty minutes discussing security for the summit, with a heavy emphasis on surveillance of Islamic militants residing in France.

After Arnaud left the office, Rodet made a call to his minister. They chatted briefly about Rodet's trip and talked extensively about security for the upcoming G-8 summit. "The president insists on ironclad security," the minister said. "We are relying on you. The security apparatus of the nation is yours to command."

"I understand," Rodet said politely. Indeed he did; if there were a terrorist incident in Paris while the summit was occurring, he would be the scapegoat. The politicians would publicly blame him and, of course, sack him. That outcome was inevitable, perhaps, but the minister wanted to be able to say that he told Rodet he was responsible and accountable. Actually the minister had said it four or five times—Rodet had lost count.

The two men agreed to talk again later that afternoon and terminated their conversation.

Alone at last, Rodet stood at the window looking at his view of Paris. Beyond the double-pane, electronically protected windows the autumn wind swirled fallen leaves in clouds through the streets, but he was thinking about the desert.

He had been young then, only twenty-four.

The heat and cold, the wind, the hard-packed, scoured dirt that stretched away to the horizon in all directions, and the occasional small stone outcrops . . . that was the desert. There wasn't a grain of sand for a hundred miles, just endless vistas of naked dirt under a cloudless sky—and the oil pipeline, which ran from horizon to horizon. The company that built it hadn't bothered to bury it, of course. They had laid the pipe on top of the dirt and rock, here and there putting it up on posts to keep it level where it crossed a wash or low place, and burying it only when necessary to provide a crossing place for vehicles—or the occasional Bedouin. The pipeline ran from the wells in the south across the desert, across the mountains, to the sea.

Algeria! Not the Algeria of the coastal plain, but the Algeria of the desert, the Sahara.

In the summer there was the pitiless dry heat that sucked the moisture from living bodies, literally beginning the mummification process while one was alive. In winter, the desiccating wind was bone-chilling cold. Was hell hot or cold?

Summer and winter there was the wind-borne dirt, getting into everything, clothes, food, water, every nook and cranny, accumulating in ears, eyes, hair, every fold of skin, sandblasting metal, windshields, exposed skin, ruining engines, contaminating oil, turning grease into an abrasive . . .

He had hated the desert. Hated the circumstances that brought him to it. Hated the people who lived in it, the dirty, smelly Arabs in their filthy robes, with their goats and camels. Most Westerners, Rodet included, discovered that the Arabs did not understand the concept of truth, used an incomprehensible logic, and were reliably unreliable. The world's worst thieves, they would steal anything they could carry, actually anything they could disassemble to pieces small enough to carry, even if the object was useless, even if they didn't know what it was. They were illiterate and ignorant, knowing nothing of the outside world, nothing of germs or bacteria or sanitation, nothing about anything except the desert and the animals—and, of course, the Koran, which they committed to memory in the ancient tradition of oral literature. They were religious in the way that illiterate nomads have always been religious, in tune with nature, convinced that the eternal, immortal spirit surrounded them in this grand desolation in which they lived.

Rodet's job, back when he was young, had been to prevent theft and keep the pipeline intact and operating. So he drove the road beside the pipe and checked on the toolsheds and supply depots located at convenient intervals. The job was mind-numbing.

Standing in Paris all these years later, he could still remember that hot summer day, the brassy sky, the choking dirt raised by the truck that blew in through the windows, coating the dashboard and windshield and seat and every square inch of every single thing, clogging his nostrils, burning his eyes. Oh, yes, he could still see it in his mind's eye: see the figure in the great distance running from the toolshed, leaping up on a camel, and trotting directly away from the pipeline.

He gave chase, of course. Caught up with the trotting

camel and the barefoot man aboard it. Motioned for the rider to stop his mount.

He didn't. Kept whacking at the camel with his bare heels.

Rodet waved the revolver. The rider urged the animal to greater speed.

Rodet lost it then—shot the camel from a distance of a dozen feet and watched the thing trot on for a few more strides, then slow, stumble, and go down. The rider went flying and landed all in a heap.

Rodet boiled out of the truck with the pistol in his hand.

The rider was a boy with only scraggly facial hair. He was dressed in rags.

They were a hundred miles south of the nearest collection of mud huts, in the midst of a great plain of mud and rock, broken only by an occasional thorn bush. To the east lay the low hills that the boy had been running toward. Once in the hills, he could have found a place to get out of sight until the infidel in the truck tired of waiting and drove on. Now, of course, Rodet had him.

As he stood with the pistol covering the boy, who was sitting, not trying to stand, he looked back at the pipeline and the tool depot. The door of the storage shed was standing open; no doubt the boy had broken the lock and entered to see what he could steal.

The camel flopped around a few times, groaning, then lay still.

Staring at the young man, Rodet realized that he could kill him and no one would know. Or care. For the first time in his life he felt the power of life and death, felt the power of the blued steel he held in his right hand.

The Arab stared at him, watching every move, expressionless. He made no attempt to stand, or even move. Not that anything he could have done would have done him any good. Only fifteen feet separated them, and Rodet held the revolver, which still had five cartridges in it. Five was probably four more than enough.

Damned dirty Arab thief!

He stood there, tempted, acutely conscious of the heft of the revolver.

Not a trace of emotion crossed the brown face before him. It was only when Rodet glanced away from the dark eyes that he realized the young man was holding one arm with the other. The arm being cradled had a sliver of white bone protruding through it.

The kid was extraordinarily tough. Rodet had never seen anyone with this kind of physical courage.

He stuck the pistol in his hip pocket and went back to the truck for the first aid kit. When he returned the youth hadn't moved. As he inspected the broken arm, he realized that if he didn't set it, it would never be set. This boy was from one of these ubiquitous collections of mud huts that surrounded the "towns"; the arm would either heal or fester, and if the latter, be taken off by some self-taught surgeon to prevent the infection from killing the patient. People with missing limbs were a common sight in the third world.

He touched the limb, explained in French what had to be done. The boy's expression never wavered. "Do you understand?" Rodet asked.

"*Oui.*"

So he seized the arm and braced his foot against the elbow and pulled until the bone came back inside the skin. The boy groaned once, a moan that escaped from deep inside. Rodet felt the arm to make sure the bone was where it should be, more or less, and then splinted the limb. He left an opening in the splint for the wound, which he sprinkled with a disinfectant powder and dressed.

When he was finished, he half-carried the boy to the truck.

His name was Abu Qasim. His arm healed, and as it did, he taught Henri Rodet to speak Arabic. Not shooting Abu Qasim was the turning point in Rodet's life, the most important thing that ever happened to him.

Abu Qasim . . .

Henri Rodet turned away from his palatial window and tackled the paperwork piled in his in basket.

◆ ◆ ◆

I spent the evening riding the subways and walking into and out of department stores. Those exercises, I have learned through the years, give me an excellent opportunity to see if I am under surveillance. I was well aware of the fact that if the DGSE wished, they could devote so many agents, cars, and helicopters to the task that the subject would be under continual surveillance and, unless he was very astute, be unaware of it. During the cold war the Soviets took this kind of roving surveillance to a whole new level in Moscow. Fortunately this was France. A government bureaucracy, the DGSE had no more extra people than any other agency of a democratic government; God willing, they had no reason yet to pull out all the stops to learn what that American wart Terry G. Shannon was up to. All I was doing was checking to see if, for any reason, I had aroused enough suspicion somewhere to warrant a little checking up on by one or two officers. I didn't see anyone paying any attention to me, and after two hours of strolling, I was certain I was clean.

I needed to be, because I was going to a meet with two agency types. This meet was set up by the call Grafton told me to expect. These men had diplomatic cover, which was a mixed blessing; as personnel assigned to the embassy, the counterintelligence section of the DGSE would automatically be interested in them and would routinely, from time to time, devote people and assets to checking on their movements and activities. They had to be loose when they met me or I would come under suspicion and my future activities would become more difficult. I hoped those two were pros and knew what the heck they were doing.

When trying to spot surveillance, the secret is not to appear to be looking for it. A surveillance subject who stops to look for reflections in windows, pauses to tie his shoes, darts across traffic or jumps on or off a subway at the last moment red-flags himself, telling the watcher that, indeed, he is worth watching.

I checked my watch and, exactly at twenty-one minutes past eight in the evening, stepped out of a Left Bank bar onto the sidewalk. I turned right and was walking along when a blue Citroën pulled over to the curb. A man was in the right seat with his window rolled down, and he was smoking a cigarette. I recognized him; his name was Rich Thurlow, and he was originally from Brooklyn. "Need a ride?" he said, just loud enough for me to hear.

"Yeah," I said. I opened the rear passenger door and climbed in. The car was in motion again as I slammed the door. I lay down in the rear seat.

Rich turned around and looked at me. He nodded toward the driver. "You know Al."

"Hey there," I said, and tried to make myself comfortable. The back seats of Citroëns are not designed for guys over six feet to lie down in.

"Hey," the driver said, and concentrated on driving.

"Long time no see," Rich said. He tossed his weed out the window and fished another from a pack in his shirt pocket.

"So how's everything?" I asked.

"The frogs had two cars on us tonight. We led them around for about an hour before we put some moves on them." They laughed.

Well, if you couldn't brag a little about your exploits, why be a spy?

"Think you're clean?"

"Yeah, but hell, you never know. Fucking frogs . . ."

I sat up, putting my head into one corner so I would be difficult to see from a trailing car. "Won't getting ditched make them suspicious?"

"Would if this was the first time we did it," Al Salazar said with a laugh. "We do it every time we go anyplace. They expect us to. They play the game awhile and let us go."

Or follow unobtrusively. Well, this was Thurlow and Salazar's station—all I could do was hope they knew what they were doing.

I knew them both, so I had reason to believe they did. Rich Thurlow and I had broken into a bank in Zurich, among other things. I had known him for about three years. He had a wife who cheated on him if left alone too long and a teenaged son who experimented with marijuana. He lived to fish and carried a telescoping rod with him everywhere. He even fished in the Seine during his lunch hour.

Alberto Salazar and I had worked together during my four months in Iraq. We ran on-the-job experiments with new technology to detect explosives through walls and in vehicles. He was about five and a half feet tall, very athletic, and single. Al was from Texas and spoke machine-gun-quick Spanish. His English was lightly accented, his Arabic pretty good, and his French tolerable; he could cuss a blue streak in any of those languages. He had an innate grasp of how a thing should work, so he was easy on the equipment and got results.

In short, Thurlow and Salazar were competent career professionals. When I told Grafton that I didn't trust my colleagues, that statement might have conveyed a false impression. I had no specific complaints against anyone. And yet . . . sometimes it seemed that the harder we worked, the fewer results we had to show for it. Now and then a subject found out we were doing surveillance, or the other side transferred the guy we wanted somewhere else, making him unavailable, or people stopped talking in rooms we had bugged. Things are going to go wrong occasionally—that's life—yet it seemed to me that in Europe, especially in Europe, things went wrong a little too much. Occasionally. Nothing I could put my finger on. Or maybe I've been in this game too long.

Hell, maybe we all had.

"So Goldberg says you want a brief."

"That's right. Need to know everything you know about Henri Rodet."

Both men turned to look at me. Salazar got his eyes back on the road two seconds later as Rich whistled. "Rodet, huh? Gonna start right at the top and work down."

"Yeah. I want to see DGSE headquarters and Rodet's residences. I hear he has a flat in Paris and a château somewhere outside the city."

"Well, yeah, we can do that," Salazar said, glancing at me again in the rearview mirror.

"Gonna get to know him better, are you?" Rich muttered.

"I know him on sight, but that's it. Never met the man and don't want to. Real asshole, from what I hear—one hard, ruthless, tough son of a bitch. Made a lot of money somehow or other and runs a tight ship. Used to be the DGSE was a bunch of Inspector Clouseaus with attitudes, strictly amateur hour. Every naughty little thing they did got leaked to the press. You opened the morning paper to see what the spooks had been up to last night. Murders, kidnappings, smears of political enemies—they did it all. Rodet stopped the leaks. Hasn't been a leak in years. They may be doing the same stuff, but you won't read about it in *Le Monde*."

Salazar was wending his way through the streets as Rich talked. I could see his right eye in the rearview mirror. His eyes never stopped moving—checking the mirrors, looking at traffic to the right and left, oncoming, checking pedestrians . . .

Rich finally tired of talking about the French spooks and got started on Paris station gossip. He and Salazar gave me the latest on the boss, George Goldberg, who was trying to eat his way through every restaurant in Paris during his tour. He had eaten in 237, by his count, according to Salazar. They discussed the possibility that George might be lying about that number. They condemned George's practice of eating dinner in one establishment and dessert in another and adding both to his list.

Rolling through the streets and listening to my colleagues gab, I thought about how nice it was to once again be in a place that had toilet paper in the restrooms. I have a theory about toilet paper: Social organization is required to get it into the restrooms, public education tells the average Joe what it is and how to use it, and public order prevents the first guy who sees the stuff from stealing it. Paris had all three; Baghdad none of them.

Salazar rolled into a square and found a spot at the curb where we could sit for a moment. He pointed. "Over there, the second building from the left, second floor above the arcade. That's Henri Rodet's apartment."

I thought I knew the square. "Isn't this the Place des Vosges?"

"Yeah. These houses date from the Renaissance. They're about four hundred years old."

"So which apartment does Rodet have?"

"Man, he's got a whole floor. Not that the flats are all that big, but they're cool, y'know?"

"Who does he keep here? Wife or mistress?"

"Top secret stuff like that is way above my pay grade," Salazar said solemnly.

"You see him, you ask him," Rich chimed in. "Then tell us."

"Okay," I said. "Let me out. Come back and get me in thirty minutes."

"Sure."

I got out of the car, and Salazar got it under way.

Nine symmetrical houses lined the east, west and south sides of the square, with seven on the north. Whoever designed it four hundred years ago was probably very uptight. If you really like symmetry, this is the sort of thing you will like. A people place, complete with sidewalks, trees and wrought-iron benches, formed the interior of the square. The ground floors of all the houses formed an arcade that stuck out over the sidewalk. When the houses were built back in the good old days, pedestrians were probably grateful for the arcade since the folks in the top floors of the houses emptied their chamber pots out the windows into the streets, symmetry or no symmetry. France had its pre-toilet-paper era, too. The wonder is that the people lived long enough to reproduce.

I walked across the park toward Rodet's building as I looked it over. Streetlights lit the fronts of the buildings, so every feature was visible. Some of the windows had drapes, others did not. Some buildings, especially those on the west side of the square, looked as if they were being renovated. That meant contractors and craftsmen and their vehicles.

I could see lights in Rodet's windows. He had four windows, two with drapes and two without. The main entrance to the building was off the arcade. I looked for security cameras and didn't see any. Still, the head of the DGSE probably rated a bodyguard or two, and no doubt they were upstairs or somewhere out here on the square, keeping watch.

There was a walkway under the center building in the block, so I passed through. Sure enough, a narrow alley led behind all the buildings. Metal fire escapes were arranged on the exterior walls. There should be a rear staircase, too, I reasoned, because even before fire escapes, people in buildings didn't want to be trapped.

I walked along the alley and found doors into each building, although whether the doors were original or later alterations was impossible to say. The locks were old large-key door locks, the kind that were popular in Europe between the world wars. They probably dated from a renovation during that period, which I thought must have been the last major one. I glanced at Rodet's back door. It was not alarmed, at least on the exterior, but high above, pointed down at a fairly steep angle, I saw a security camera. The thing seemed to be aimed straight at the doorway. If the video feed was not monitored inside the building, then it must be monitored off-site, which meant there was a dedicated telephone line or an Internet connection. I continued strolling along the alley, craning my neck left and right like your average tourist.

If you think it would be easy to go in through Rodet's back door, think again. I would have bet serious money that the old door was there because local ordinances prevented exterior modifications on historical buildings. Immediately inside, I suspected, was another door, a steel one with terrific locks, festooned with alarms. Yet the exterior walls, with old metal drainpipes coming down off the roofs, could be climbed.

When I got back in the square I looked again at the roofs. Above Rodet's apartment was an attic with dormer windows. I wondered if that attic was part of his apartment. A careful man could go over the roof and enter through one of those windows. It was something to think about.

I was also thinking about Marisa Petrou, Rodet's mistress. Could I use the fact that I knew her to gain entrance to this apartment?

I spent the rest of my half hour just looking, trying to make the scene and details stick in the gray matter. Alberto Salazar and Rich Thurlow arrived right on time to pick me up.

"I thought we'd look at DGSE headquarters tonight and save the château for tomorrow," Rich said after I was in and the car was rolling again.

"Sure. Drive on."

We hadn't gone two blocks before Salazar said, "Sure is different from Iraq, isn't it?" He directed that comment at me. "There's a place I don't miss, let me tell you. Squalor, dirt, heat, fanatics, car bombs, blood on the street, body parts strewn around . . . It's the contrast, y'know? I have nightmares about the place. How about you, Tommy?"

"Hard to forget a resort spa like that," I agreed.

"Remember that time we located those explosives inside that house, and when the soldiers surrounded the place, that woman walked out? She was wearing one of those chadors, those black robes that cover her head to toe, and she had a baby in her arms, a kid maybe a year old. She walked right toward the lieutenant."

I knew how this story ended, and I wasn't in the mood for it. "Let's talk about something else, Al," I suggested.

He ignored me. He glanced at Rich to ensure he was listening and continued. "She was walking toward the lieutenant and interpreter, who were standing behind an APC, when she blew up. Had explosives around her waist in some kind of belt. Goddamnedest thing I ever saw. One instant she and the kid were there, then they weren't. Gone in the blink of an eye. When the smoke and shit cleared so we could see, there were little pieces of skin and bone and bloody tissue splattered for blocks. Everybody was watching when the bomb went off, so everybody got hit with this stuff, and six or eight guys got scratched up with shrapnel or something."

"That's enough, Al," I said.

"If they try to send me back, I'm quitting."

"Okay," Thurlow said, "but enough's enough. I don't want to hear any more, either."

"Fuck you," Al shot back. "You too, Carmellini! Fuck both you dickheads."

Of course, he would be the guy behind the wheel. He was hunched over, gripping the wheel so tightly his knuckles were turning white, staring straight ahead as the car rolled along.

"Hey, man, it's over," I said, trying to calm him. "You're out of the sewer. Lay it down and let it go."

"If I can't talk to you guys about it, who the hell *can* I talk to?"

That, I thought, was the most insightful question I had heard in years. Be that as it may, I still didn't want to chin about Iraq with Al Salazar or anybody on planet Earth.

If I never again set foot in Iraq, that would be fine by me. Remembering Grafton's promise, I silently vowed to make this assignment my very last for the agency. After this, you can color me gone. Au revoir, baby.

The French spooks, the DGSE, had their offices in an unlikely building, the Conciergerie. This was an old, old building on the Ile de la Cité that had been used for a lot of things down through the centuries, including a prison. Here the revolutionaries imprisoned Marie Antoinette and Charlotte Corday, the assassin of Marat, as well as Danton and Robespierre before they each made their one-way trip to the guillotine. The history came from Rich Thurlow, who had apparently spent a few evenings with a guidebook. He said that during the Revolution over four thousand prisoners were held here. We found a place to park and did some walking.

Standing on the right, or north, bank and staring at the building, I thought it looked ominous. It was made of cut stone and stood about six or seven stories high—it was hard to say because I didn't know how high the ceilings inside were. There were towers where the walls cornered, and the whole thing had one of those Paris roofs broken with dormers. The place had obviously been built as a medieval palace. In those happy days a palace was a fortress, a stronghold, where the king's men could hold off starving mobs or armies led by unhappy lords and barons. The river had been the moat. No crocodiles, but since the Seine was the city sewer, who needed them?

"When was that thing built?" I asked Thurlow, our walking Baedeker.

"Thirteenth or fourteenth century. It's roughly contemporary with Sainte-Chapelle, which is immediately on the other side of it."

I knew about Sainte-Chapelle, a magnificent medieval church that King Louis IX built in the thirteenth century to house Christ's crown of thorns and fragments of the true cross. He purchased these relics, properly authenticated, of course, from the emperor of Constantinople for an outrageous fortune. No doubt the emperor laughed all the way to the bank. This transaction set the record for the largest swindle ever successfully completed, a record that stood for centuries. If you take inflation into account, it may still be the con to beat. The pope was so impressed that he made Louis a saint; the good folks in Missouri even named a city after him.

Staring at the walls of the Conciergerie, I wasn't in a laughing mood. I saw my share of old black-and-white movies when I was growing up, so I knew damn well what they had in the dungeons of that rockpile: lots of cells and a torture chamber. Probably had a rack and screw and a wall where they hung people in chains, the way the King of Id tortures the Spook. Just looking at those massive sandstone walls gave me the willies. I turned and looked the other way. Well, heck, half of Paris was to the north, and half to the south.

"You going in there?" Rich said, jerking his head at the building.

"I sure as hell hope not. But I do what Grafton tells me. He says go, I'm off like a racehorse."

"More like a mouse."

"That's probably a better analogy, I suppose."

"Better you than me."

We discussed equipment, what they had on hand and what they could get in a reasonable amount of time. "Bugs," I said. "Audio and video. How many?"

"We got about twenty of each on hand. Most of them are the new ones, so tiny you could swallow them and listen to your lunch digest."

I grunted. One of my instructors had done just that to

demonstrate the capability of the new units. It had been funny . . . then!

"Take me to a subway station and drop me off," I said. "Tomorrow, when you're clean, you come along this street right here, and I'll be standing over there by that bus stop. About ten in the morning. Will that be enough time?"

"It's after rush hour. We should be clean by then."

"Have the guy driving the van meet us somewhere. I want to see him and the stuff in the van."

"Okay," Rich said, and flipped a cigarette away.

Al stood looking at the Conciergerie with his hands jammed in his trouser pockets. Finally he pulled one out, turned his jacket collar up to ward off the late-evening chill, then jammed that hand back where it belonged and started walking toward the car, which was two blocks away.

"Assholes," he muttered.

I wasn't sure whether he was referring to the French spooks or his present companions. He was going to be fun to be around for the next few weeks.

Jake Grafton had an interview with Sarah Houston at the American embassy.

"So how are you and Carmellini getting along?"

"Fine," she snapped. She had no intention of discussing her relationship with Tommy Carmellini with anybody alive.

"Do you have any objection to working with him?"

"I have absolutely no desire to go back to Alderson." She had served some time in the federal women's prison in Alderson, West Virginia. "To stay out of the can I'll work with the devil."

"I don't think we have to dig that deep for recruits just yet," Grafton said with a straight face. "I merely wished to confirm that you had no objection to working with Mr. Carmellini."

She shook her head. Although her lips were compressed in a thin line, Grafton noticed, she seemed relaxed.

"Or me," he added.

"I don't like where this conversation is going. Just what do you have in mind?"

"Fair question," Grafton admitted. "I was thinking of having you turn traitor."

Sarah Houston's mouth fell open and she gawked.

"I was thinking you and Tommy might sell access to Intelink to our French friends."

She closed her mouth and kept her eyes glued on his.

Grafton kept talking. "Terry Shannon is a CIA traitor who wants to make a big score and live happily ever after. You are his girlfriend, the NSA analyst with the access to Intelink. You were on the software team and Shannon has convinced you to install a trapdoor. You hate your job, your bosses don't appreciate you, and you're madly in love with Shannon."

"They'll never believe *that!*"

"We'll have to make them believe it."

"Do you really intend to give them Intelink?"

"I'll give them a peek at a fake Intelink. That'll be enough."

She snorted. "You have got to be kidding!"

"I'm not."

She pursed her lips and gave a low whistle. Then she rubbed her forehead. "The French will never buy it."

Grafton waved that away. "Will you give it a try?"

"No. Hell no! I'm supposed to be rotting in a federal prison right this very minute. You ought to know—you put me there. They're going to check me every way from Sunday and find out I'm hot. And by hot I don't mean sexy."

"The last thing in the world they will want is for any information about you or Intelink to get out," Grafton pointed out.

"Rodet won't be the only one at the DGSE who knows. One photo in the papers and I'm toast. One nosy reporter bastard and I'll be in a cell until the day I die. I'm not complaining—I deserve it for what I did—but I am not going to do anything that increases the odds that I'll go back to that shithole. Nothing. I will do *nothing!*" Her voice rose until it cracked. Whispering, she added, "Goddamn hell no, Admiral. Get another sucker."

"Unfortunately, you're the only one I have," Jake Grafton said, and sighed.

CHAPTER SIX

Henri Rodet's château on the bank of the Marne, twenty-some miles upriver from Paris, was the kind of place I am going to buy if Warren Buffett ever adopts me. Salazar parked the car beside an inn across the river from Rodet's little piece of paradise. Through the trees I could see the main building—which looked as if it contained twenty or more rooms.

"A real shack," Rich Thurlow said. "The Department of Defense sent us some satellite photos of the place." He opened a briefcase and handed me the file.

There were seven photos, all marked SECRET NOFORN in caps, and the detail was amazing. One of the things looked as if it had been taken in infrared. I studied the hot spots.

There were actually eight buildings on the grounds. The main house and two smaller ones looked as if they were occupied; perhaps one of the smaller buildings was for servants, guards or in-laws. One structure appeared to be a barn, one a garage, and the others might have been used for storage of some type. There was a pool and a tennis court. And a dog pen.

I couldn't help myself—I whistled in amazement. "This guy is worth serious bucks," I said.

"The end result of prayer and clean living, I suspect," Salazar muttered.

I handed the photos back to Thurlow and got out of the car. Below us was a dock with some rowboats tied to it. Upriver two men were fishing from a boat that looked as if it had come from the collection below. They were fly-fishing as they drifted.

Across the river, on Rodet's side, there was no fence. I suspected he didn't need one. Salazar saw where I was looking and handed me a set of binoculars. The view was fair even though most of the trees still had some of their leaves. Sure enough, I could see several—at least three—surveillance cameras mounted in the trees. No doubt there were also infrared sensors and motion detectors. I suspected that an uninvited guest wouldn't be there long before he became personally acquainted with the dogs.

"Well, heck," I said. "We're here, so let's do the tourist thing, go in and sample the local chow."

"Cuisine," Thurlow said, correcting me. "This is France, remember."

"You say that like Bob Roll does. It's *France,* my man, through your nose. *France.*"

"I'll work on that. You and Al get something to eat. I'm not hungry." Thurlow popped open the trunk of the car and reached for his rod case. "I'm going to dip a hook and see if anything wants to bite it."

The inn looked old, although I didn't think it was. It was decorator old, and the toilets really flushed. After I visited the facilities, Al and I were led to a table overlooking the river. This being a weekday, the place wasn't crowded. In the summer and on weekends, a fisherman should probably pack a sandwich.

Al had little to say. Nor was he interested in the view of Rodet's estate. Everyone around me these days seemed to be adrift.

As I looked over the menu, I thought about Sarah Houston. Aaugh!

Marisa Petrou glanced right and left along the sidewalk before she entered the restaurant. It was a small place, very discreet, in which each party had its own private nook, free from the observation of other diners. The exquisite food and unique physical layout made the establishment a favorite rendezvous for married men and their mistresses, and for married women and their lovers. Part of the charm of the place was the fact that the diners never knew who was in the other nooks, be they politicians, celebrities, neighbors, or, perhaps, spouses.

Marisa was quickly escorted to a nook in the back of the restaurant. The man waiting there stood and embraced her. Behind her, the maître d' closed the drapes.

"It is good to see you again," the man said.

He helped her with her chair and, when he was again seated, poured her a glass of wine. He raised his glass to her. After they each had a sip, he said, "So what message have you today?"

"All preparations are complete. The security teams from the various nations are arriving within the next few days. The city will be covered with heavily armed security personnel."

"As we planned."

"Yes." Marisa had another sip of wine. "Oh, the American CIA has sent a new director of European Operations, a retired American admiral named Grafton. One of the men with him is a man named Tommy Carmellini, who is using the name Terry Shannon. Carmellini knows me, by the way. We met in Washington last spring."

"How did you meet?"

"A party." She brushed it away. "Grafton arrived now, Henri believes, to assist the American Secret Service with security. The Secret Service team will arrive next week. No doubt he will make an appointment to see Henri in the near future."

The man beside her merely nodded.

After a moment he said, "Nothing else?"

"No."

"These meetings are dangerous . . . ," he said, and left the rest of the thought unspoken.

There was a knock; then the drapes opened. The waiter entered, discussed the menu, took their luncheon orders and departed, closing the drapes behind him.

"I wanted to see you," Marisa said, when the silence had gone on too long, "to ask you to reconsider."

"My enemies are closing in," the man said slowly. "This is my time, my mission."

"And when you are gone?"

"Others will pick up the sword. They also have their duty to God."

Marisa sipped wine. "I have never shared your vision of God and duty."

"But you have helped anyway."

"A DGSE man was murdered the other evening. Did he have to die?"

"Henri must be protected."

"You didn't answer my question."

"Yes, I did. In any war there are casualties."

"So this is the last time I will see you?"

"Unless Henri has a message. He understands the risk involved in face-to-face meetings."

"And I don't? Me, a mere woman?"

The man said nothing.

"I wish, for my sake, that I shared your vision of God and duty and obedience to the word of the Prophet. But I don't. I think you are making a great mistake, and when you stand before the throne of God, He will judge you harshly."

"You blaspheme."

"Perhaps. I will stand there, too, one day, and He will judge me then. I am afraid I shall have many sins to answer for."

With that she seized her purse and rose from her chair. He put out his hand to stop her, but she drew away.

"Good-bye," she said, and, defying the rules of the house, she parted the drapes and departed without an escort.

On my third day in Paris, we put magnetic signs that advertised a plumbing concern on the side of the surveillance van and parked it on the Place des Vosges in front of the old houses undergoing restoration. We lucked out—I could see four of Rodet's windows from the passenger seat. I scrambled into the back of the van and turned everything on.

The tech support guys had done some serious work on this van in Rome. It had a white dome on the roof, which didn't look like anything much. It was merely aluminum bent and pounded into shape, then painted white. The interior of the dome, however, was painted black. Under it was a laser and a sophisticated telescope, also painted black. The dome could be manually raised two inches and latched there, then the laser radiated through the gap. It was simple and effective; anyone standing on the sidewalk would never notice the gap between the dome and the van roof.

The laser was aimed at a windowpane, which vibrated from a variety of causes, including sound and wind. Aimed at the vibrating spot of laser light, the telescope focused the image upon a sensor that converted the microscopic movement of the spot into digital signals; a computer processed those signals into sound. The system did not use the reflection of the laser beam, so the angle of incidence was not critical. Amazingly, in perfect atmospheric conditions, the system had a theoretical maximum range of three miles. All one needed was a window—and a wizard, someone who understood the system and could wring human speech from all the other sounds that vibrated the glass, such as traffic in the square, a television inside the building, a washing machine in the basement, planes going by overhead, and so on.

Our wizard was Cliff Icahn. I had worked with him last year for a few weeks in Berlin, and he knew his stuff. He looked sour this morning. "We're not going to hear anything," he grumped. "There's too damn much noise. I'm no miracle worker."

I spend my life in the company of optimists. "Well, let's try it awhile," I told him from my perch on a toolbox near the back doors of the vehicle. We had tools, pipe elbows, brazing equipment and the like stacked there to display to a policeman, should one demand to look inside the vehicle. Between it and the laser was a solid wall of shelving, most of it made of balsa wood to save weight. "If we don't, we can't keep you here. You'll have to go on home."

That comment dried up his objections. Cliff and his wife

didn't get along, which was the reason he volunteered for every overseas job that came along. He spent more time out of the United States than he did in it. I didn't know why they stayed married, and I had no intention of asking.

He diddled with the telescope for a moment, ensured the solid-state accelerometers were working and allowing the computer to compensate for the movement of the van, then turned his attention to the computer. When he eliminated all the extraneous noise, we hoped we would be left with voices. It was a Saturday morning, so who could say? From where I sat I could see tourists wandering along, looking at the buildings. I looked for young or middle-aged men who were interested in people, not buildings. Saw one, finally, who did nothing but sit on a bench and watch people.

Finally Cliff said, "I've still got a buzz that comes and goes."

"Vacuum cleaner?"

"Maybe. I'm going to take it out . . . if I can."

Sixty seconds later he stated, "Now I can't hear a damn thing."

One explanation for this phenomenon, if the equipment was functioning correctly and Cliff had tweaked it properly, was that there was nothing to hear. I refrained from stating the obvious. Outside, halfway across the square, the watcher I had spotted a few minutes ago lit a cigarette. So far he hadn't even glanced at the van.

I got out of the van on the side away from the watcher, crossed the street, and started hiking.

I walked the sidewalks around the square, which were protected from the weather by the overhang of the floors above. There were shops, artists selling paintings, people in casual clothes and people dressed fit to kill. Women pushed strollers along. A derelict wearing a long coat and a brimmed hat sat on one bench.

I was a half block from the door of Rodet's building when a limo stopped in front of it. The chauffeur got out and opened the rear door on the sidewalk side. The woman who emerged was in high heels, hose, an obviously high-fashion dress, and a fur jacket. Brown hair combed so one ear was exposed. I got a glimpse of her face, but she didn't see me. Marisa Petrou!

She used a key on the door to the building, then disappeared into it. The chauffeur got back behind the wheel of the limo and rolled.

When I got back in the van, I asked Cliff, "What have you heard?"

"The maid likes American pop tunes."

"There's hope for the world after all."

"Someone came in a while ago. A woman. The maids turned off their boom box. The woman inspected the place, told the maids to do the toilets again. No names."

Our watcher was still in his seat. I pointed him out to Cliff. "That guy. Scan his face. Put him in our database and send the image to Langley via satellite. I want to know who he is."

The face scanner was another digital toy. The computer placed points on the captured image of a face, then measured the distance between those points, thereby converting the scanned face to a series of digits. Amazingly, faces are like fingerprints, each unique.

It took only a few seconds for Cliff to aim the scanner, focus it and capture the image. The computer did the rest, including sending the encrypted digital signal to Langley via satellite for comparison with the agency's database.

We had our answer in six minutes: the man's name and the fact that he was a DGSE agent.

The derelict huddled in his coat on the park bench watched Tommy Carmellini circle the square. The brim of his hat was turned down all around his head, and it obscured much of his face.

He hadn't been paying any attention to the plumber's van until the athletic young man got out of it. Now he scrutinized it carefully. He could see the white hump on the roof, yet due to the angle from which he observed, he did not notice the space between it and the roof of the van. Still, the athletic man with the wide shoulders and narrow waist was obviously not a plumber, so that made the van suspicious.

The derelict shifted his weight . . . and eased the hard mass of the pistol in his coat pocket so it didn't press against him.

My little garret on the Rue Paradis looked pretty good, let me tell you. I even liked the neighborhood. There were women standing around on the sidewalk at all hours, and they always smiled at me. I smiled right back. Those ladies were the friendliest people in France, by golly. The men I saw weren't so friendly; they tried hard to avoid eye contact, apparently on the theory that if they didn't acknowledge your presence, you wouldn't notice theirs. I always looked carefully at their faces, trying to decide if I had seen them before. Of course, any agency watching me would probably be smart enough to pay a few of these women, but bureaucrats being bureaucrats, who knew?

It rained the night after I saw Marisa, a gentle, steady soaker. I lay in bed listening to the rain patter on the windowpane and gurgle in the downspout right outside the window. The gurgling was nice and loud because I had the window open a couple of inches. The ventilation cooled the room and made it very pleasant for sleeping.

Paris and Baghdad were so different that I wondered if I were still on the same planet. *Man,* I thought just before I drifted off to sleep, *I could get used to this.*

On Thursday I walked around Paris for a while, just checking my tail, and finally boarded the Metro and rode out to the airport. I bought a couple of Snickers bars at an airport candy shop, then rented a car, a little four-seater. The sky was cloudy and there was a cool breeze from the west. The trees were in full color. An hour after I left the airport I pulled into the inn on the Marne, across the river from Rodet's humble shack, got out and looked across the river, then went inside and got something to eat.

After my meal I drove to the bridge and crossed to Rodet's side. I explored the neighborhood and drove along the road that ran the length of his estate on the landward side. I found the power line that went across the fence, a chain-link with barbed wire on top, and slowed down for a look at the main gate. It was a two-piece affair that looked as if it were triggered by a wireless transmitter, such as a garage-door opener.

On the side of the road away from the river was a forest, with occasional driveways that led to small cabins. The ones I could see looked empty. Weekend getaways, I thought.

I was going to go in with nowhere near enough information. I had told Grafton that, to be safe, I needed two weeks of observation to ensure I knew the size and composition of the household and had a good idea of their routine. "We can't wait," he said. "The sooner the better."

Willie Varner was arriving on Saturday, so we settled on Sunday night. I would just have to play it by ear, do the best I could.

I drove around the neighborhood for almost an hour, checking on where each road went. If I had to boogie, I wanted to know where I was boogying off to.

Finally I pointed the car back for Paris. I found a place to park the thing, in a garage only a few blocks from my apartment, and rode the Metro to the Place des Vosges.

The van was parked in a slightly different place, surrounded by traffic cones. I knocked on the driver's door. Alberto Salazar opened it and whispered, "We don't want any. Beat it, bub."

I joined Cliff and Al inside. "Good thing we're all friends," Cliff muttered, squeezing himself over to make room.

"Whaddaya hear?"

"Both maids have dates for the weekend," Al told me. "One of them is meeting an old boyfriend for dinner tonight, then going out with him tomorrow night. She hopes her current fellow doesn't find out."

"Hot stuff, eh?"

"Sizzling."

"What about Rodet?"

"The woman who came in had a telephone conversation

with someone. We only heard her side of it. It might have been Rodet. She said something about dinner. It's hard to say, but I sorta convinced myself that she's his girlfriend or something, and he's coming there after work this evening."

"So he's in town?"

"Maybe. Maybe not. Someone is coming for dinner. I didn't hear her say a name. Do you know who she is?"

"Yes. Her name is Marisa Petrou."

"Want to tell us how you learned that?" Cliff asked.

"No."

"It's a mushroom deal," Rich Thurlow told Cliff.

"Just do your job," I shot back. "I want everything you can get between Petrou and Rodet. At least one of you must stay on duty all the time he is there."

"We can't hear any conversation except those that occur in rooms facing the square."

I knew that, of course. Not wanting to waste the afternoon listening to them bitch, I climbed out of the van, made sure the door locked behind me, and headed for the Metro.

I had to figure out how to get into that flat.

Al Salazar was the only guy in the van at the Place des Vosges when I stopped by that evening. "Catching anything?" I asked.

"Not even a cold. The man went in, and they talked in the kitchen and maybe the bedroom. I got kitchen noises and occasional words. I have no idea what they talked about."

"You make a disk?"

"Sure."

Well, maybe the wizards in Washington could figure out what was said, if they cared. I used a set of binoculars to scan for a watcher. Didn't see anyone.

Al got up and stretched. "Remember in Baghdad, when those two guys with rifles got out of that car?"

"Let's talk about something else."

"What I still can't figure out is how you knew they were bad guys."

"I just knew."

"God, Tommy, it was like a movie or something. Not something real. You pulled out that pistol and gunned those two, bang bang. What if you'd missed?"

"But I didn't. Hey, man, you're going to go fucking nuts sitting here thinking about that crap. You've got to think about something else."

He sat heavily and stared out our window at the symmetrical square and the identical buildings and the French mothers with prams and lovers holding hands. "Like what?"

"Hell, I don't know. Women . . . your wife. Your kid. Fishing. Sports. The stock market. You can't sit here all day listening to those French maids jabber and think about nothing but bombs and blood and bad shit. You can't, Al."

"What if they had been good guys, Tommy? Ever ask yourself that? What if you had shot the wrong guys?"

"I didn't."

"Luck."

"No, goddamnit. It was instinct. I could see them, see how they were acting. I looked and I saw and I knew."

"You were lucky."

I headed home. Unless we got some results with the windowpane gadget, Grafton was going to want me to bug Rodet's flat. I had that to look forward to. Oh joy. I forced myself to think about that instead of bodies lying in the street oozing blood. The hell with Al Salazar and his bad memories! Yeah, I had 'em, too, but damn if I was going to let that stuff ruin another hour of my life.

A half hour later I walked down the Rue Paradis and the few paces up my cul-de-sac to my home away from home. It was the coolest address in Paris, and by God, it was mine.

In the lobby the concierge was showing a new tenant the key to her mailbox. She was about my age, fit and trim, and she spoke French with an American accent. She had two large suitcases.

We ended up climbing the stairs together. I carried the larger suitcase.

"You're just moving in, apparently."

"Yes. My name is Elizabeth Conner. I have the fifth-floor apartment."

"Terry Shannon." I almost said Tommy Carmellini, but caught myself just in time. "From California."

"I'm from Boston."

"I'm your neighbor on the top floor, the one above you."

"And what do you do?"

"I'm a travel writer. Update guidebooks."

"Sounds interesting."

"I eat too much rich food, that's for sure. And you?"

"Art student."

"Welcome to Paris."

"Thank you."

She stopped in front of her door and used the key. She opened the apartment and I put her suitcase inside the door. "Thanks for your help," she said, and smiled. She had a nice smile.

I wished her good night and hiked up to my little corner of the world. I took a bath and fell into bed.

CHAPTER SEVEN

Jake and Callie Grafton found a small apartment to rent by the month four Metro stops from the embassy. The other tenants in the building seemed to be middle managers—at least they left for work every morning wearing nice clothes. The neighborhood had its share of children, who gathered every afternoon on a playground that the Graftons could see from their windows.

"So what do you think of Paris this time?" Jake asked his wife as she unpacked the last suitcase. She had been here on two occasions before she finished college and once with their daughter, Amy.

"The first time I came was with my parents," she told her husband. "I was still in high school. Dad hated de Gaulle and on that trip denounced him at every opportunity, which created some tense moments. He was so thrilled when the socialists took over."

Jake merely smiled. His father-in-law had been a political science professor at the University of Chicago; his politics bumped the far left edge of the spectrum. He had been profoundly disappointed when his only daughter married a career naval officer, although he had tried to be civil to Jake—Callie's mother made sure of that. The professor had been dead for twenty years. Still, when Callie mentioned him, once again Jake heard that sonorous baritone preaching against the evils of capitalism, nationalism, democracy, and all the rest. The professor had been, Jake thought, the most predictable, obstinate, narrow-minded bore he ever had the misfortune to meet, but he had never stated that opinion aloud, nor did he ever intend to.

Callie continued as she folded clothes. "I had read Hemingway and Fitzgerald and loved the Impressionists and the cinema. The summer I was sixteen, walking the streets of Paris, I decided I wanted to learn languages. Paris was so wonderful, exotic and full of life . . . so marvelous . . ." She ran out of words, turned to face her husband, and smiled. "Don't you think?"

"Oh, absolutely."

"You're going to enjoy Paris," his wife told him definitely. "Isn't this better than flying around the United States in that little airplane?"

"Well . . ."

"You were getting bored. I could tell. God knows I was."

He couldn't help smiling. "I suppose."

"Thanks for taking this job." She turned to the window and opened her arms. "Believe me, we are going to *love* this city."

The Secret Service's man in Paris was Pinckney Maillard. He was tall and willowy with jug ears. He came straight from the airport to the embassy. He hadn't been in the embassy ten minutes when he huddled with Jake Grafton in the SCIF. He skipped the social pleasantries and got right to it. "Where are you on this Al Queda spy?"

"Just getting started."

"Okay. This Rodet, the DGSE man. Is he going to cooperate?"

"I haven't talked to him yet. I have no reason to think he'll tell me anything he hasn't already told George Goldberg or his minister in the French government. 'There is no spy.' "

"The Veghel tip—"

Jake held up his hand to stop Maillard. "I know all that. The official French position is that there is no spy. Consequently Rodet has nothing to share."

Maillard took a deep breath and looked Jake Grafton in

the eyes. "Admiral, I know the agency insisted on dragging you out of retirement to take this post. I know you don't give a rat's ass if you get promoted or fired or forced to quit. Here's the deal: In twelve days the president of the United States, the president of France, the prime minister of Great Britain, the prime minister of Japan, the chancellor of Germany—you know the list—are going to be at Versailles with the cameras rolling, talking serious, important political shit, shaking hands, making promises, all of that. You get the picture?"

Grafton nodded.

"They told me in Washington you were the toughest, slickest, meanest, trickiest bastard still wearing shoe leather. They said—"

"They lied," Jake said flatly.

Maillard lowered his eyes for a moment, then again met Grafton's gaze. "Democracy won't work if elected officials can be assassinated by crackpots, half-wits, anarchists, people who want to be famous or suicidal holy warriors on a mission for God. I need all the help you can give me, Admiral."

"You'll get it. And call me Jake."

"I'm Pink." Maillard held out his hand to shake.

"Has there been a specific threat against the G-8 leaders?" Jake asked.

"There's all the usual bar talk, cell phone chatter, that kind of stuff. If anyone in Washington heard about a credible threat, they'd tell me. The question is, If Rodet does indeed have a spy in Al Queda and he hears about a murder plot, will he pass it on to us?"

"There's no reason to believe he won't," Grafton said. "Except for the fact he says there is no spy."

Jake met Sarah Houston in a tiny room of the SCIF twenty minutes later. She was reading the special Intelink net. "So how does it look?" he asked.

"They've done a nice job," she admitted.

"Can you sell it?"

"It looks good at first blush. There's some Al Queda intel,

some juicy inside stuff on the Saudis, a French op against an American software company, some pretty good Russian intel . . . Yet if an intelligence specialist studies the information, I am afraid that they will eventually conclude that there is little here of great import. In other words, they'll smell a rat."

"That's the best seed material we could get permission to post," the admiral explained, and drew up a chair. The first law of disinformation is that most of the stuff must be real and verifiable. The lies must be fashioned so well that they, too, look real, so real that a knowledgeable reader cannot distinguish verifiable truth from fiction.

She scrolled along for a while longer, then logged off.

"Can you sell it?"

"For how long?"

"A couple of days."

"Before or after you insert your essay?"

"Before."

"I can try."

"You won't go onstage for a few more days. How are you coming on hacking into Rodet's computers?"

"I've been into the three computers members of his household have used since I've arrived in Paris. The e-mail files appear to be clean. There are, however, areas in the hard drives that I can't access."

"Tommy is going to try to put a key logger on one of Rodet's computers."

"That would open the can," Sarah agreed.

Jake left her there and went to find George Goldberg. He found him in the offices upstairs. "Let's go to the SCIF," Jake suggested.

As they walked the hallways, Goldberg asked about Callie. "She like the apartment?"

"Oh, yes."

"The embassy staff rented it. It may be bugged. In fact, I would be amazed if it wasn't."

"I thought it might be."

"You want us to send a team to check?"

"No. Let 'em listen."

"Would you and your wife like to go to dinner tonight?"

They made plans.

When they were in the SCIF, Jake said, "I'm concerned that the French know about Carmellini. How did they find out?"

"Two possibilities. They are deciphering one of our codes, or someone told them. I suspect someone told them."

"How many other leaks have you had?"

"One for sure, and eight or ten possibles. Would you like to go over the files?"

"Yes."

They settled in for the afternoon.

On the way back to the Rue Paradis Friday evening, I walked past a shop selling Vespa motor scooters. As I stood in the small showroom looking at the shiny paint, a passing rain shower spattered the window glass. I was getting tired of walking, and parking for the rental car was a serious problem. The Metro was inconvenient, taxis were iffy. What the heck, I was spending taxpayers' dollars. They had a used scooter there, a nifty red one, so I bought it—with a Terry Shannon credit card. The bill would go to the agency, of course, a fact that made me smile. The purchase required fifteen minutes, and insuring the thing took an hour.

I buzzed off into the rain. I was wet and shivering when I climbed the stairs of my building on the Rue Paradis. Didn't see the hot woman from Boston.

I unlocked the door to my flat, walked in, and paused.

Something didn't feel right. I closed the door and stood looking.

Through the years I've broken into my share of houses and apartments. One of the skills I acquired for my job of searching for or planting listening devices is the ability to look at a room and memorize the position of everything in it. You do it by sections, the table, the chair, the kitchen counter, and so on.

I scanned the room, looking . . . ah! The cushions of the couch had been rearranged.

There was nothing incriminating in the apartment for anyone to find. I only had one passport, my Terry Shannon job; everything else I needed for my life as a spy was in my head. True, my cell phone had a couple of numbers on it that I wouldn't want the DGSE praying over, but it was in my pocket.

I scrutinized the lock on my door. It was an old model, the kind commonly found throughout Europe in older buildings. It had not been forced. Picked or opened with a key was my verdict.

After a long, hot bath, I dressed warmly and pulled on a waterproof jacket. I trooped downstairs, unlocked my ride, and motored off. Yeah, Paris in the rain.

I wound up parking in an area marked off for scooters and cycles on one of the sidestreets just off the Champs-Elysées. I picked one of those restaurants on the avenue that had a glass front; the maître d' plunked me at a table right by the window so I could watch the people flow past on the sidewalk outside—and they could watch me.

I ignored the crowd and tried to read a newspaper as I waited for my meal. Didn't make much progress. I kept thinking about Elizabeth Conner, wondering if she was a DGSE agent. Hmm . . . How did a well-spoken American woman, if indeed she was an American, get hooked up with French intelligence? Or did she just get smitten by my handsome mug in passing and decide to check me out before she wasted any more time on me? Perhaps that was it.

The next morning I rode the subway out to the airport to meet Willie the Wire. He and I became partners in a lock shop in Washington after he got out of prison the last time. He was a slim, dapper black man twenty years my senior. From the age of fifteen, he worked as a bellboy in Washington hotels. He would probably still be doing it if he hadn't decided to carry out the guests' luggage and fence it before the guests checked out. He got remarkably good at picking locks—hence his nickname—although it was inevitable that sooner or later he would get caught.

He had gone straight since his last stretch in the pen and

worked middling hard at running the lock shop, taking care of everything while I wasn't there and entertaining me when I was. We got along reasonably well, I thought, considering our age and background differential.

He spotted me instantly when he came out the customs door pulling his suitcase.

"Hey, Tommy."

"It's Terry."

"Huh?"

"I'm Terry while I'm here."

"Hell, I'll never remember that."

"How was your flight?"

"It felt like I was packed in a slave ship. Let's go see the Folies."

"Don't you want to get some sleep?"

"Hell, no. I want to see something."

"They do the Folies at night—this is morning."

We got on the subway and rode it downtown, getting off at the Eiffel Tower stop. When we got to the thing, Willie stood there looking up. Since it soared from a wide base to a point, from the ground it looked as if it reached halfway to Mars. Willie craned his neck, watching the puffy clouds driven by the wind off the Atlantic and the intermittent patches of blue. Finally he tired of it and began ogling female tourists, examining the statues on the Seine bridges, watching the barges go up and down, looking over the whole scene.

Since I was on tour guide duty, I said, "I'll stay with your bag if you want to go up there."

"Naw. Been here and seen it—that's enough. Now tell me about this gig you got goin'."

"I need someone I trust to watch my back."

"Oh. Pray tell, who we gonna get to watch mine?"

"I will."

"Sure! I notice that you haven't told me what you got goin' down."

"Later."

Swine that I am, I didn't pass Grafton's tidbit about the murdered DGSE man on to Willie. Nor did I tell him the happy news that the French spooks knew I was Tommy Carmellini, CIA dude. He would have boogied immediately, leaving me to do Grafton's chores with the help of the three stooges. Okay, okay—they weren't stooges. Still, I wanted Willie the Wire behind me. He was high maintenance and whined a lot, but I trusted him; he knew that I'd kill him if he screwed me over. These other guys weren't true believers like Willie.

Willie eyed me suspiciously. "Ain't doin' no shootin' and ain't stoppin' no bullets. Not for a goddamn soul, includin' you."

I had had enough. "Want to go home now? You've been here and done it and there's a plane this evening."

Willie glanced up at the Eiffel Tower one more time, then waved that away. "I'll stick for a little while, but don't fool yourself, Tommy. The scene gets heavy, you can mail me a postcard in Washington—I'll be there when it arrives."

Right. I had been trying to convince myself that this gig was going to be a piece of cake. Maybe it would be. Besides, the change of scenery would be good for Willie, would broaden his horizons. God knows they could use a little broadening.

The next morning Willie Varner and I drove out to see Rodet's château. We went in the car.

"Since I didn't get a call from an emergency room or the morgue," I said, "I assume things went okay last night."

"After the Folies, I found a cozy little whorehouse. We mixed chocolate and vanilla. Made a lotta shakes."

"International relations."

"It was '*oui, oui, bay-bee*' all night long." Willie the Wire sighed contentedly, then yawned.

"So how do you like France?"

"Pussy's as pricey over here in frog-land as everything else."

"Socialism, I guess."

"One of the women told me it was taxes. They tax ever' damn thing over here, she said."

"Do you have any money left?"

"Still got a few euros burning a hole in my pocket. Just gonna lay around today restin' up—rechargin' my battery, so to speak—and goin' back tonight."

"Not tonight. I'm going to need your help."

We found the place where the power lines went into the property and backtracked to the first transformer.

With Willie at the wheel, I used binoculars where I could. We looked for security patrols, marked and unmarked, and surveillance devices. I could see cameras mounted in the trees inside the fence, but apparently none outside. After we had leisurely circled the entire estate, a circuit close to ten miles long due to the location of the bridges, we headed back for town.

"What do you think?" Willie asked.

"It can be done."

After I dropped him at his hotel so he could get some sleep, I headed back to my pad on the Rue Paradis.

I climbed the stairs making the usual racket, passed Elizabeth Conner's door and unlocked my garret on the floor above. After drawing the blinds on the window, I opened the backpack Al had given me and dumped the contents on the bed.

Someone had packed a wealth of goodies for me to play with. The first item I picked up was the scanner, which was battery operated. I turned it on and went around the apartment looking for bugs, the electronic kind. I didn't find any.

That didn't mean there weren't any; it meant that I didn't find them, if indeed they were there.

I began an inch-by-inch search of the walls, floor and ceiling of the apartment. The job took several hours. I was looking for a hidden camera, or for a bug that could be turned on and off remotely. I moved furniture, disassembled the lamps, removed and reinstalled all the protector plates on the electric sockets and light switches, took off and inspected the air vents, went over the floor and walls with a magnifying glass and pulled the innards out of the television. It was tiring, tedious work. Fortunately there was no telephone or I would have had to take it apart to check the circuitry. When I finally got everything back together and back in place, I was ready to certify the apartment as bug-free. Not that I cared if anyone overheard me humming in the tub or brushing my teeth—I just wanted to know if anyone was curious enough about me to bug the place. Apparently not, and that was good.

I was still bothered by the fact that Conner was in the apartment directly below mine. One of the things she could have done was merely put a listening device on her ceiling, which was my floor. With a simple computer, such a device could be made to work as well as a microphone in my bedroom lamp. That would be a cheap, easy way to keep me under surveillance.

I felt like a racehorse waiting for the gate to open. Tonight was going to be busy. With nothing better to do, I went for a run.

That evening Sarah Houston ate dinner with one of the FBI forensic accountants in Paris going through Oil-for-Food bank records. They ate at a small restaurant he selected from a guidebook. He had asked her to dinner, and she thought, *What the heck,* so here she was. It wasn't as if he were a toad; he was clean-cut and good-looking, with a square jaw and good teeth, and he didn't have any visible tattoos or piercings. She kept a smile on her face and listened to what he had to say. Someone once told her that this was the way to do it: Men need women to pay attention.

"The thing that attracted me to accounting was the beauty of the logic," Wally Slayton told her as they worked on an appetizer of *pâté de campagne*. "Who knew that this career choice would put me in the thick of the action? Enron, HealthSouth, WorldCom, Tyco—I've worked 'em all. Very exciting, let me tell you."

"Lots of travel," Sarah Houston managed.

"Oh, yes. I've got enough frequent flyer miles for a round trip for two to Tahiti."

"Next vacation."

"Oh, yeah."

The waiter served the coq au vin and refilled their wineglasses. "This Grafton," Slayton remarked after he had told her about some of his more memorable vacations. "Do you really think he knows what he's doing?"

She deflected the question. "I haven't thought about it."

"He doesn't think like an accountant, I can tell you that."

Sarah Houston picked at the entree and helped herself to more wine. "I suppose not."

"Accounting requires a logical mind and the ability to pay attention to details. Grafton . . ." He raised an eyebrow, then abandoned the admiral to his fate. "I've worked with some of the best prosecutors in the world. It's amazing to watch them in action. Dynamic personalities, brilliant strategists. You can feel the electricity when they're around . . ." He went on, naming names, regaling her with his experiences in the midst of legal combat. Had he but known about Sarah Houston's past legal adventures, he would have probably been tactful enough to pick another subject. Maybe.

Sarah finished the wine in her glass and stifled a burp. She had a headache.

A few raindrops hit the windowpane beside the table and ran down to puddle on the outside sill. She stared at the puddles and thought about Tommy Carmellini.

I ate a light dinner at a little restaurant I had been walking past. They decided I was a barbarian when I refused wine and insisted on Coke—with ice.

After I returned to the apartment, I mounted a bug on the floor. It had a dish receiver on it, one that acted as a collector of vibrations. I plugged the lead into the amplifier, which weighed about half a pound, plugged the unit into a wall socket, turned it on and put on my earphones. After I adjusted the controls, I found myself listening to a television program in French and the sound of footsteps and doors closing in this building and the hotel next door. The headphone cord was about ten feet long. Still wearing the phones, I got out the infrared goggles, made sure the batteries were charged, put them on and fired them up.

The goggles were the latest and greatest. I'd worn them

for months in Iraq. When properly adjusted, the wearer could look through a normal visual obstruction, such as vegetation or a wall, and see if there was a heat source beyond it, such as a person or animal. I walked to the window and stood looking at the buildings across the street.

The exterior wall still radiated some heat, but it was fading. Fortunately autumn had arrived in Paris. Poorly insulated hot-water pipes stood out in bold relief. I could also see a stove cooking, several hot plates and people. I stood looking at the human figures as I played with the gain on the unit.

I could see them easily. They appeared not as mere blobs of color but as humans, with every limb in clear view. Consequently I could get a pretty good idea what they were doing by their posture and estimated position in the rooms.

I couldn't see anyone across the street who might be using binoculars or whatever to look at me. When I was pretty sure that I wasn't being watched, I bent over enough to see into the apartment below. I could see Conner clearly, watching television, and through the bugs, I could hear the TV.

Okay, I was a high-tech pervert.

In a few minutes Conner turned the television off. A bit later she went to the bathroom and—well, you know. Gentleman that I am, I took off the goggles. Pretty soon she began making noises like she was brushing her teeth. I watched her finish washing teeth and face, get undressed and take a bath. The hot water in the tub obscured her figure.

After a while I saw her climb into her bed and heard it creak. There were no more noises. I turned off the goggles and laid them on my desk.

Who was Elizabeth Conner?

Finally I stowed the toys in the backpack and got dressed for the evening.

CHAPTER EIGHT

The night was cold, almost freezing. I was sitting in a car with Willie the Wire examining Rodet's château through the night vision goggles. I couldn't see any people on either the ambient light or infrared setting.

"It's three o'clock," Willie said. "How long you gonna wait?"

"I don't know. I wish I had a few more nights to scope out this place."

The night vision goggles were amazing. Even though evergreens and branches obscured much of the lawn, I could see a dog wandering along, stopping, moving at random, then lifting a leg on something. Actually I could see his thermal image, which is almost the same thing.

As we sat there Willie had been regaling me with his romantic adventures. "Fella I know gave me some of those four-hour peter pills," he informed me now. "I took one last night."

"Four hours?"

"You know, the ones they advertise on TV. You get a hard-on that lasts more than four hours, you gotta go see a doctor."

"Talk about a great advertising campaign!"

"I don't know how the doc gets it down. Don't want to find out, neither."

"Gives you a different perspective on technical progress, doesn't it?"

"We're marchin' on to the happy ever after."

The dog was probably going to spend the night outside. No sense waiting. I just hoped he was alone. "Okay, give me the backpack."

Willie dug it out from behind the passenger seat. I took off the goggles and looked it over. I had packed it, but I wanted to check where everything was one more time. I was going to have to locate most of this stuff by feel.

Inside the pack were two small two-way radios, each built into a headset that contained an earpiece for the wearer's right ear and a small boom mike that stuck out a couple of inches. I turned them both on, then handed one to Willie. As we put them on, I heard him say, "You get caught in there, I'll send you a card every year on your birthday."

"You don't even know when my birthday is," I replied, and heard my own voice in my ear.

"The Fourth of July, then."

"You have the grenade?"

"The gonad cooker? Yeah, but I'm thinking about throwing it."

"Put it in position, right at the base of the pole, then drive off. There's a sixty-second delay—that'll be plenty."

"Why me?" Willie whined. "How come I got elected for this?"

"I knew you could do it. But with fried gonads and a petrified dick, you're going to be in a hell of a shape when you get home."

I had put tape over the switch that activated the car's interior dome light when the passenger door was opened, so the light stayed off when I opened it.

I checked my watch. Eight minutes after three. "One hour from now. Right here."

"I'll be here."

I closed the door and walked away. Willie got the car under way. It was about a mile to the pole with the transformer on it.

The lane along the fence was deserted. There hadn't been a car in two hours. The temperature was in the midthirties, and there was a breeze blowing. My black jacket, pullover wool cap, and gloves felt good. As I walked I got a Snickers bar out of my jacket pocket and stripped off the wrapper. The wrapper I put back in my pocket. I swung my arms to get the blood circulating.

The dog had scented or heard me. He was behind the brush, but with the goggles, I could see his thermal image, which appeared as a shape, with the hotter spots more intense. His tail was almost a shadow, yet his tongue was quite prominent. He was silent, paralleling the fence.

I came to the spot I wanted, where a tree limb had come down on the barbed wire that topped the chain-link fence. This was where I would cross.

The dog was over there, pointed right at me, waiting, not even growling. He was big, at least fifty pounds. And oh, yes, this one was well trained, waiting silently there in the darkness in the hope I would cross that fence and he could have the pleasure of tearing my throat out.

I toggled the goggles from the thermal to the night vision setting. It took a few seconds for an image to appear. Now the yard and trees and shrubs glowed with a greenish light. I could see everything except the dog, which was behind a clump of bushes. I moved along another ten feet or so to a gap in the dark limbs. The lights of the house glowed like headlights in the goggles. I found myself squinting. I tossed the candy bar over the fence. I saw and heard it hit a tree branch, then drop in the fallen leaves that coated the ground.

Here came the dog. Now he was in view. I watched him sniffing that candy bar. I was pretty sure he would eat it. No doubt he was trained to avoid raw meat, the logical bait. Never saw a dog yet that didn't like Snickers bars.

He looked like he was eating. His head was down.

I was waiting for him to lie down when I heard a distant pop, like a backfire, and all the lights in the château went out. The place became instantly dark, lit only by outside ambient light. Willie had popped the electromagnetic grenade, which emitted one short, intense pulse of energy. That pulse tripped the circuit breaker in the transformer.

The dog moved a little, walking slowly, then stumbled, tried to rise, and lay still.

The drug should keep him down for an hour or so, if he ate the whole bar. I could only hope he did.

I switched the goggles to infrared, scanned carefully, then went up the fence with my hands, grabbed the limb and scrambled across. I checked the dog, which hadn't moved. Then I dropped to the ground.

Silence.

After one last scan on infrared, I switched the goggles back to night vision. The dog lay under a tree. I pulled him over under a bush, just in case someone came looking. Then I jogged across the lawn for the house.

Approaching the house, I found a tree and got behind it. Now I shifted the goggles back to infrared. The walls of the house were cool. I played with the control knobs, adjusting the setting. I wanted to see people inside, if there were any to see. The insulation of a building's exterior walls would interfere with infrared transmissions, a fact the user had to understand and work with.

Still, the goggles were magic. The insulated interior hot-water pipes became visible as fixed lines. I saw the glow of the kitchen: The stove still retained a detectable amount of heat even though it had probably been off for hours.

Someone was moving around inside on the first floor. I could see the human figure walking . . . going down a set of stairs—to the basement, probably, to check the circuit breakers or fuses.

There was another figure, faint, apparently in a room on the far side of the house. It was sitting. I stared and reached for the goggle controls. Oh, he or she was putting on shoes. Or boots. There was no time to waste.

The porch had a roof. I trotted over, found the balcony, leaped to the rail and pulled myself to the roof. Almost lost the goggles. I paused to readjust them and tighten the straps.

Once I reached the side of the house above the porch I re-alized that the house was built of cut stone. There was probably little or no insulation in the walls. This shack was a couple of hundred years old, at least.

There was a window overlooking the roof, and a peek through it revealed no heat sources in the room. Which was good. I didn't want someone wrapped in a comforter to start screaming when I made my entrance.

I flipped the goggles back to ambient light and waited for the picture to blossom. The window, two panels of panes, was locked, of course. I forced a shim into the gap between the panels and started prying.

Just as I felt the latch give, I heard a whistle. High-pitched. Then a human whistling. Now a male voice called for the dog. I couldn't make out the critter's name, but the tone of voice was the same in any language.

I eased the window open and stepped through.

Once I was inside with the window closed and latched, I looked down onto the lawn. The man had a flashlight and was casting the beam around, calling the dog.

If he found him, this gig was going sour fast.

I put the goggles back on the infrared setting and began looking around for heat sources. The interior walls were wooden, and much thinner than the cut-stone exterior walls, so I had to diddle with the adjustment knob.

There was a person in the next room, obviously lying down. No, two people, apparently in bed together—and not moving. Asleep, I hoped.

No one in the hallway beyond the door, which wasn't locked. I opened it and scanned the dark hallway.

There were at least six bedrooms leading off the hallway. Only the one beside me contained a person.

Out in the hallway I looked downward, trying to see if there were people on the floor below.

No.

The hallway and stairs were carpeted. Still, I eased down the stairs, staying to one side in case there was a creaky board. A building this old, I bet there wasn't a nail in it—just pegs.

Taking my time, exploring, I worked through the lower

floor. There was a kitchen, a formal dining room, a couple of sitting rooms, a library with a television, a couple of small bathrooms that looked like they might have been closets way back when, an office and a master bedroom suite. The master suite contained people, two, apparently asleep. Mounted in corners in every room were surveillance cameras, and here and there a motion detector. Without power they were useless, but if the power came back on . . .

There was a safe in the office, a floor-mounted job about three feet high. I noted the brand and model number, just in case Jake Grafton got another big idea.

Then I attacked the office. Working as quickly as I could, I installed a key logger on the computer keyboard cord, under the desk and out of sight, then installed audio bugs on the curtains, up as high as I could reach, and put one mounted on a pin on the back of an upholstered chair. It would be good to know who was using the computer, so I installed three video bugs facing the desk. They would essentially cover the room.

"There's a car coming." That was Willie's voice in my right ear.

I headed for the library, then the sitting rooms and dining room, and installed audio bugs in each one. These were top of the line, so small that they fit nicely on the head of a pin. I worked a couple into the edges of the carpets.

"He's slowin' down and lookin' me over, Tommy."

The bedroom was the place I wanted into, though, and there were people in there. I tried the doorknob. It was locked. As I bent down to examine it with the goggles on the ambient light setting, I heard a noise: a door closing somewhere in the building.

Back to infrared. As I waited for the picture to change I groped for the stairs.

I had just reached them when I saw him, coming around the corner from the kitchen. He had a flashlight, which looked like a tiny glowworm in infrared. He opened a doorway and began descending the stairs.

"Okay, he's goin' on. Might call the police, though.

Maybe you'd better hurry up and get your sneaky ass out of there."

Call it intuition, but I just knew the man in the house was going to the basement to fire up an emergency generator.

Flipping the goggles to ambient light, I came back down the stairs and made for the kitchen and the door that led out the back, the one the man had just entered. It was unlocked, of course. I pulled it shut behind me.

Turning, I saw a dog coming at a dead run, a speeding green shape against the light green background, and, quicker than thought, he was *there!* I just had time to set my feet. He growled as he leaped for my throat.

I balled my right hand into a fist, pivoted on my left foot and hit him in the side of the neck with everything I had. By sheer dumb luck my timing was perfect—I couldn't do that again if my life depended on it. The impact of the blow deflected him to the left, and his tail slapped me on the side of the face as he went flying by.

The dog splattered against the ground—didn't try to break his fall. Lay there motionless. Didn't even whine.

Oh, man, I hope to hell I didn't kill him!

If I killed this damn dog they would search that house from stem to stern after they found him.

I started for the corner of the house. The garage was back here, a two-story thing with living quarters on the top floor. A paved driveway led around front.

Then I changed my mind and went back to the dog. He must have weighed fifty pounds. I picked him up and put him over my shoulder. He was still limp. If he came to while I was toting him, he was going to give me a serious hickey.

I went around the house, staying on the driveway, and then angled across the lawn for the spot in the perimeter fence where I came in. I knew I was leaving tracks in the soft sod, but it couldn't be helped. Maybe the guard, if that was who he was, would think they were his.

The dog didn't twitch. I could tell by the way his head flopped that I had broken his neck.

I changed my mind again, turned and hotfooted it for the main gate, which was a wrought-iron affair about ten feet high, and tried to stick the dog's head between two of the iron uprights, but they were too far apart.

I forced his head under the gate. It was a really tight fit, but the dog didn't protest. When I had him wedged in as tight as I could get him, I trotted for my tree.

The other dog was stirring.

I scrambled up that tree and out on the limb as fast as I could go, leaped toward the ground and twisted my ankle a little when I hit. I rolled over and was rubbing my ankle when the lights in the house came back on.

I keyed the mike button on my radio. "Where are you, Willie?"

"Where I'm supposed to be."

"Come get me. I'm beside the fence."

"Okay."

I was on my feet waiting when Willie pulled up. I opened the door and threw my backpack in. Then I collapsed in the passenger seat. He didn't even wait for me to get the door closed before he accelerated away.

"How'd it go?" he asked as I struggled to take off my goggles and radio headset. My hands were shaking and I was feeling the effects of an adrenaline overdose.

"There were two dogs."

"They get a piece of you?"

"No."

"You lucky fucker."

"Yeah. Shot with luck."

"I mean it. You're the luckiest fucker I know." That was Willie—he always could put things in the proper perspective.

"Let's go to Paris," I said. I reclined the seat and closed my eyes, which shut him up. I could hear my heart pounding in my ears. That dog—wheeyooo, that was close.

CHAPTER NINE

The next morning I listened as Conner washed and dressed and finally left her apartment. I was at the window when I saw her jog off down the street. I used the infrared goggles to check the buildings across the street, trying to find someone who might have me under surveillance—and saw no such person.

I went down to the street and walked around, looking in shop windows and paying particular attention to the vehicles. I didn't find anyone sitting in any vehicle within two blocks of my building. Surveillance teams often used vans or other closed vehicles for short-term setups; I located a couple that might fit the bill, but even as I watched, one, a flower delivery van, was driven away by a guy who had just carried an arrangement into a building.

The possibility that watchers were monitoring people coming and going, or bugs in her flat, could not be ruled out, I concluded. I hadn't found them, but that didn't mean they weren't there.

The women and their customers on the street? Now that I had time to think about it, I doubted if any of them were watchers. A new woman would draw the instant suspicion of the others, and men that hung out for hours on the street would be labeled as mashers, or worse.

What I really wanted to do was search Conner's flat. Not that I expected to find her DGSE building pass or a signed note from her boss. Still, whatever was there would offer some insight as to who she was, what she was interested in, or, perhaps, what she might do next. On the other hand, if she thought I might search her place, her apartment could be a trap. It was an interesting problem.

I suspected her next move was to give me the opportunity to know her better, sort of the same thing I did this past spring with the gal in Washington, Marisa Petrou. I wasn't quite ready for that.

I examined my collection of goodies that Jake Grafton had sent via Salazar. One of the items was an optical camera. It was a curious device. The lens was on the end of a long, flexible stalk, one about a half inch in diameter and ten feet long. The end of the stalk had some kind of wire material wrapped around it, so it would hold a shape. I bent it into a ninety-degree elbow and lowered it out my window. The end of the stalk had a quick-disconnect fitting on it, so I pushed that into the appropriate hole on the small television unit. The viewing screen was about three inches by three inches.

I turned the unit on, adjusted the gain and brightness, and eureka! The gadget worked. I could see most of the room. I played with the controls of the unit. When I finally got the picture as clear as I could, I studied the room below.

Her apartment seemed to be laid out identical to mine, with a large—I am being charitable here—room that functioned as living room, dining room and bedroom. In addition, there was a tiny kitchenette, a minuscule closet and a small bathroom with a tub that was only big enough to sit in. The whole thing was about the size of a standard hotel room. There was no telephone. Like me, Conner probably used her cell to communicate.

Terrific! I turned the unit off and disassembled it. Then I sat thinking about things.

I used the infrared goggles to inspect every inch of the apartment below, just in case. No people in sight. I put on my latex gloves, then went down one flight and examined her doorsill. No sensors, wires, nor any mark that hinted that the moldings had been removed in the last twenty years. I picked the lock and let myself in.

With the door closed behind me, I stood and looked. The time spent looking from the door was insurance; I was looking for markers that would show that someone had searched and memorizing the placement of every item I could see. One of the items in the goodie bag was a small ultraviolet flashlight, which I used now to see if perhaps Conner had dusted her room with a powder that can be seen in ultraviolet after it comes in contact with the oils on skin. I don't like the stuff because you can't get a surface scrupulously clean before you apply it, so it reveals itself in ultraviolet even before somebody smears it with a finger, and any pro worth a nickel wears gloves. She hadn't used the powder. I pocketed the light and began searching.

She had no cameras, no CD player or iPod, none of the usual electronic gadgets that trendy young adults can't get through the day without. A television was the only artifact of our time. I must say, I wondered how she did it. The answer, apparently, was that she was a reader. Lots of books, many still in boxes waiting to be unpacked. I glanced through the assortment that was on display; most of the titles were French, heavy books of philosophy and social commentary—Camus, Sartre, the struggle of labor, developing a fair trade policy, the economic challenge of the new world order and so on.

Still, the fact that she had no gadgets bothered me. She hadn't just arrived from planet Ork.

I worked as quickly as I could, checking everything. I found her packet of lock picks, which she probably used to visit my digs, and I learned the brands of her favorite toothpaste and soap and shampoo.

I didn't find her passport. No doubt she had that on her.

I was standing in the middle of her apartment when I saw the paperback on her nightstand. I had seen it when I first walked in, but the title didn't register. Now it did. *The Sum of All Fears,* by Tom Clancy. Were all the spies reading Clancy this year?

That was the only paperback in English that Conner owned, unless one of the unopened book boxes contained a few.

I made sure I knew how the book was positioned on the

stand, then examined it. It was certainly well thumbed. I found one word scrawled in pencil on the title page: *definite*. No other marks that I noticed. I replaced the book on the nightstand.

Finally I examined the ceiling, every square inch. I didn't stand on anything, just walked along using my eyes, which are excellent. I was looking for a bug, or a mark that showed a bug had been there—and found one, by golly: a circular mark about three inches in diameter that looked as if it had been made by a suction cup. It was over the desk, in a position she might reach if she stood on the chair. I looked at the seat of the chair—got my nose six inches from it and really looked. It was possible she had stood on it, I decided, but I saw nothing definite. Still, that round thing on the ceiling looked like a mark that a suction cup would make.

I went back to the television and turned it around so I could see the back of it. Well, how about that! The back was held on with four screws. A couple of the heads had marks on them, as if they had been in and out a time or two. I went looking for a screwdriver and found one under the sink in the bathroom.

Working quickly, I took the back off. There was the suction cup, a coil of wire, and a headset. I reinstalled the back and replaced the screwdriver under the sink.

A check of my watch. Seventeen minutes. I had been here too long.

I took one last look around to make sure everything was as I had found it, then left and locked the door behind me.

Henri Rodet was late again for his Monday meeting with Jean-Paul Arnaud.

Inside his office with the door closed, the director said by way of apology, "One of my Dobermans managed to break his neck last night on the automobile gate. Apparently he wedged his head under the gate and broke his neck trying to get free—a freak accident. And the power failed. The power fools are still working to replace the transformer."

The secretary had followed Rodet into the office, and now she served espresso to both men. Then she withdrew.

"I heard on the radio that the Israelis and Palestinians are at it again."

"A murdered policeman; more shelling in response."

Rodet opened the classified morning briefing sheet and scanned it as he sipped his coffee. Halfway through he laid it down. "That dog, Marcel—I don't understand how he did it. He was the brightest dog I have ever had." He paused, then added, "Without power, the household was in turmoil. There was no breakfast." He shook his head in frustration, then shrugged and picked up the report. "I will miss that dog," he remarked. "Nothing new on Bruguiere?"

"No, sir."

"An unsolved murder of a DGSE agent will cause us problems with all the foreign security people. I will speak to the minister. The police *must* do more. And *we* must do more. I want everything that man ever worked on reviewed. And check on the old gang from Algeria—they may know something."

Arnaud nodded.

They carefully went over current developments in European capitals and had moved on to the political situation in Iraq when the telephone rang. It was the secretary. "Monsieur Rodet, an unsecure call from the CIA Paris station chief, George Goldberg."

"George Goldberg," Rodet said to Arnaud, who lifted his eyebrows. Rodet punched the button. "*Bonjour,* Monsieur Goldberg."

After the usual pleasantries—exchanged in English, which Rodet spoke fluently—Goldberg got around to the reason he had called. "One of my colleagues is in town, and I wondered if I might bring him around to meet you."

Since this was an unsecure line, Rodet didn't ask who the colleague was or what he wanted to discuss. He glanced at his desk calendar, then said, "Of course. Perhaps Wednesday, about three in the afternoon."

"Perfect. I'll see you then."

"Good-bye."

Rodet said to Arnaud, "Goldberg wants to bring a colleague to meet me. Wednesday at three. Grafton, do you think?"

"It's very possible."

"Could you be here for that?"

"Of course."

They went back to their discussion of the situation in the Middle East and moved on to security preparations for the G-8 conference at Versailles.

That morning Jake and Callie Grafton were playing tourist. They were near the head of the queue when the Louvre opened and marched through the endless galleries with a purpose. Callie had the map, which she consulted regularly. Her husband kept his eyes peeled for signs. He pointed them out.

"That way."

They went up a wide flight of stairs and along a series of galleries, passing a seemingly infinite collection of old paintings that had little to commend them, Jake thought. Many were portraits commissioned centuries ago by the rich. Callie looked at yesteryear's aristocracy while Jake scanned the rooms of the old palace, trying to imagine the gentlemen in wigs and silk hose who had once walked these rooms on their way to see the king, and their ladies, with hair piled high, rouged cheeks, and wide skirts. The crowd today was more casual, in jeans and slacks, tennis shoes and cameras. It seemed as if everyone had a camera dangling from his neck.

They finally arrived at Callie's destination: the Mona Lisa. "It wasn't on display when I came with Amy," she whispered.

He left her to stare while he wandered on. He found dirty windows that looked out into courtyards that were either under renovation or abandoned, awaiting someone's attention, someday. The day was gloomy, with clouds rushing by overhead. Pigeons perched on every ledge and left their deposits to eat at the stone. No one paid any attention to the American standing with his hands in his jacket pockets, looking out.

He was still there when Callie found him a half hour later. She wrapped her hands around one of his arms. "You're wishing you were back in the States, aren't you?"

"I shouldn't have taken this job."

"Oh, Jake."

"I'm in over my head on this one, Callie. I have never in my life felt so damn overwhelmed."

"You've been in tough situations before," she pointed out. "I seem to remember you were up to your eyes when I met you, all those years ago. You've always found your way through the forest."

"Everyone strikes out, sooner or later."

She stood with him watching two workmen in the plaza below cleaning up construction debris.

"The world was simpler then," he said.

She squeezed his arm. "Let's go get some lunch."

"Okay."

Holding hands, they wandered along looking at tourists while the long-gone Europeans watched from the walls.

As they were eating lunch in the museum café, Jake said, "I have a little job for you, if you would like to help?"

Jake glanced around to ensure they couldn't be overheard, then told her about Henri Rodet's spy. He gave her the name he was given in Washington, Abu Qasim. "As it happens, Qasim is one of the names that a top Al Queda lieutenant, Abdullah al-Falih, uses occasionally. We know a little about him. He was originally from Algeria and spent time at the university here in Paris as a philosophy student. Al-Falih was one of the men the Egyptians swept up after the assassination of Anwar Sadat in 1981. They didn't think he was anything but a religious fanatic, or they couldn't find any evidence against him at all, whatever, so they didn't execute him. They kept him locked up for two years and then released him. Of course, he met many of the major figures in Al Queda while he was in prison."

"What is the source for the Qasim name?"

Jake smiled. His wife always asked the right questions. "Interrogation."

"Torture, you mean?"

"I don't know. But the name came up in an interesting way. The source claimed that Abu Qasim had a source inside French intelligence who passed him information."

"Do you believe that?"

"No, but it would be the perfect cover to pass information the other way. And we do know, or think we know, that the head of the DGSE got some critical intel from someone in Al Queda."

"So what do you want me to do?"

"Go over to the university this afternoon and ask questions. I would like to find at least one person who remembers Abu Qasim or al-Falih. I want a description, some fact or facts that will put flesh on this legend."

"Okay."

"If the DGSE has an agent, it's someone that Rodet recruited or someone he once knew well," Jake mused. He commented on how difficult it was to recruit agents, who were by definition traitors to the society in which they lived. The possibility of talking a religious fanatic on the inside into becoming a traitor struck Grafton as very remote, and to do it without endangering oneself or the prospective recruit, probably impossible. On the other hand, a man who had never believed and infiltrated . . . he might have a chance. A slim one, true, but a plausible chance. If he could live in the belly of the beast and keep his nerve.

"What if there is no record of him?" Callie asked.

"That would be a factor in the equation."

"You mean someone could have removed his name from the records?"

"Or he never existed. What we have is a tidbit spit out by the computer, a factoid someone once passed to an interrogator. It may be dross, pure fiction."

"Or a story woven around a germ of truth," Callie said thoughtfully.

Henri Rodet sat staring at a painting on the wall, an Algerian desert scene by a well-known young artist. "The old gang from Algeria . . ." He had used that phrase with Arnaud. The men he had known in Algeria all those years ago were either elderly or dead.

Except for Abu Qasim.

After he met Qasim, he checked on him the following week. Yes, he lived in a mud hut on the ragged edge of nowhere. There was the old man, Qasim's mother, two younger brothers, and a sister or two. The family had owned just one camel, and Rodet had killed it. The dressing on the wound in Qasim's arm had not been changed, and the wound was infected. If the boy didn't get medical treatment soon, he would lose the arm. Or die.

So there he sat, the Frenchman who caused it all.

"Inshallah," the old man muttered. As God wills it.

Using French and a smattering of Arabic, Rodet explained about the infection, how the wound must be cleaned and disinfected. He explained about germs. The old man was having none of it. No one was touching his son. It would be as Allah willed it. Finally it dawned on Rodet that the old man didn't know what germs were.

Why didn't he let the boy ride away on that mangy, half-starved camel? Why on earth had he shot the beast?

He went to see the company doctor, a fat man who had lived most of his adult life in Algeria, and explained the problem.

"Why did you return?" the doctor asked.

"Because I shot the camel and the boy broke his arm."

"You cannot save these people from themselves. They live in squalor and filth, ignorant, illiterate, besotted with God, and there is nothing you can do to save them. You understand, Rodet? Nothing!"

He had had it up to here with Algeria. He knew it was true. And yet . . . "I want bandages and disinfectant, sulfa powder, something to clean the wound."

The doctor threw up his hands. "They will not let you touch the boy. They will not thank you. They would rather watch him die. Whatever happens will be God's will, and man must submit. Don't you see, nothing can be done. It's useless to fight against your fate. The boy was doomed when he was conceived."

"We all were. Give me those things."

On the way back to the hut he bought a goat, paying twice as much as it was worth, and put it in the bed of the truck. The animal leaped out and he had to run to catch it while the seller laughed uproariously. He stuffed it into the passenger seat, where it promptly emptied its bowels and bladder. He rolled down the window and drove on.

The old man accepted the goat, which was a fine one. Food was food. After much talking about the animal, the old man led it away. While he butchered it, Rodet worked on Qasim's arm. The young man never whimpered, never made a sound as he scraped the wound, cleaned and disinfected it, and injected the boy with a massive dose of penicillin. After he dressed the wound, he rolled up his pant leg and showed the boy his scar, which he had collected in a motorcycle accident years before.

He left a stack of bandages and instructions to change the bandage daily. He stayed and ate goat and had to stop alongside the road when the vomiting and diarrhea got him.

Yet when he went back two weeks later the infection in Abu Qasim's arm was gone, the wound had a healthy scab, and the boy smiled at him.

Henri Rodet smiled back.

Callie Grafton started at the Sorbonne's main records office. It helped that she was herself a professor of languages at Georgetown University and that she spoke fluent French. The clerks were helpful, but after twenty minutes, they confessed defeat. They had no record of a student named Abu Qasim, nor one named Abdullah al-Falih.

The library was cool and quiet. Two hours later, Callie admitted defeat herself. She could find not a single scrap of paper in the building with either name written on it. Some of the records were incomplete, with the records of entire years missing. It was suggestive, she thought, but proved nothing.

She headed for the philosophy department, only to find the doors locked.

Tired and frustrated, Callie asked directions to the faculty club. Yes, the university had one. Armed with her passport and Georgetown University ID, she had no trouble talking her way in.

It was nearly six o'clock when Jake Grafton pulled the rental car over to the curb and watched his wife come out of the club. She was listening intently to the white-haired man beside her, who was talking a mile a minute. He held on to her arm to steady himself. As they approached the car, Jake realized the man was at least eighty.

Jake got out and came around to the passenger side. Callie introduced him to the man, Professor Heger, as cars swerved by the illegally parked vehicle. The French flew thick and fast. Jake nodded and smiled as passing cars beeped. Callie kissed the professor on the cheek and got into the car. Jake shook hands with Heger and got back behind the wheel.

When they were rolling along, he said, "You look as if you had a wonderful afternoon."

"Oh, I did. I met some delightful people. And Professor Heger is a gentleman, a ladies' man, and, believe me, he loves to talk."

When she fell silent, thinking about the conversations of the afternoon, Jake prompted, "Well, what did you find out?"

"Professor Heger taught philosophy until he retired, but he remembers no student named Abu Qasim."

"Huh," Jake grunted.

"He was lying," Callie said. "Chattered away about Paris and teaching and Americans he had known, tried to recall Abdullah al-Falih and couldn't. Then I mentioned Qasim's name, and he gave me an abrupt denial. He was lying—I'm sure of it. He did know Qasim, and now he refuses to admit it."

"We need more than a denial," her husband said gently.

Callie smote the dashboard with her fist. "I know that," she roared in frustration.

CHAPTER TEN

I could tell by the sound exactly what Elizabeth Conner was doing in her bathroom every morning, which was proof positive I was wasting my life . . . and probably should be locked up to protect the public. I listened on my floor bug while I performed my own ablutions. The thought occurred to me that audio voyeurism was like being married without sharing the toothpaste.

When I thought she was within a minute or two of completing her routine, I quickly stowed my stuff, shoved it under the bed, and let myself out. I slammed the door, rattled it to make sure it locked, then headed for the stairs.

She was coming out of her door as I trooped downward.

"Good morning," I muttered.

"Morning," she chirped, and fell in behind me. "Going running?"

"Getting cabin fever."

"I've been meaning to say hello," she said as we trotted down the stairs.

When we got to the street, I said, "Want to run together?" as I looked her over. She wore her hair in a modern, wind-blown style and was decked out this morning in blue Lycra pants, a sweatshirt, good running shoes and a headband. She wore a small fanny pack on her waist that probably contained her wallet, passport and door key.

"Okay," she said, and trotted right off. I fell in beside her.

"Do you run every morning?" I asked.

"Except when it's raining. I hate getting soaked and cold. Don't think the exercise does me any good when I'm in that condition, y' know?"

She ran at a good pace, so conversation became difficult. I concentrated on staying just behind her, out of traffic, and not running over pedestrians. The air was crisp and moist and there was a wind. It was very pleasant running through Paris, soaking up the sights and sounds and smells, running behind a woman who knew how to run.

Just when I was getting in rhythm, she picked up the pace. I lengthened my stride and managed to stay with her, but my days off were telling. She knew Paris better than I did, because I was thoroughly lost when we came pounding up to Sacré Coeur in Montmartre. Now she headed back to the Rue Paradis. When we began slowing a few blocks from the apartment building, I glanced at my watch. We had done about four miles, I thought.

"Whew," I told her. "You always run this far?"

"I'm addicted to it."

"So what are you studying?"

"European history. On a self-study program." She mentioned the university, one of the traditional women's colleges in the northeastern United States. "And you said you are a writer?"

"Travel writer."

"Have I read your stuff?"

"Do you read bumper stickers? 'Free the French: Whack Chirac,' and 'Make the world safe for war!' Those were mine. My biggest was 'Save Social Security: Free Cigarettes for Retirees.'"

She laughed. "You're kidding, right?"

"I freelance a lot. Working on a book on Paris just now, updating an existing guidebook."

"Sounds interesting." We were standing in front of our building.

"I like it. Enjoy the change of scenery and exploring. Long as I can pay the bills, I'll stay at it." I looked her straight in the eyes and grinned. That's a rule, you know—when you're lying, look 'em in the eyes and show 'em your teeth. Of course, whether she believed a single word of my spiel was another question.

She glanced at her watch. "I'd better get upstairs and get a shower."

"Thanks for the run," I said as she disappeared into the building. I smiled at the streetwalkers, nodded at a few prospecting johns, and after a minute or so, followed her up the stairs.

The limo slid to a stop near the curb; the driver got out and opened the door for his passenger, a well-dressed Middle Eastern businessman.

The man went into the building, which was old. He wandered along until he came to a sign that listed university faculty and the numbers of their offices. He went down the list, found the one he wanted, and walked to the stairs.

There were a few young people, men and women—students, no doubt—clad in jeans and sweaters and sweatshirts, talking to each other or striding purposefully along, on errands of great import. None of the young people paid any attention to him. Oh, a few glanced at him, then looked away. Wearing a suit and tie, he must have looked like a professor, one they didn't recognize. They refused to make eye contact.

He found the office he wanted and looked right and left along the hallway. It was empty. He rapped on the door with a knuckle.

"Come in."

He turned the knob and pushed the door open with the joint of a forefinger.

The professor was at his desk. He had white hair and wore a wool suit. He looked up and adjusted his glasses. "Come in, sir. Come in."

The visitor closed the door behind him.

The professor leaned forward, his right hand on his glasses. "*Mon Dieu!* Is it you? Qasim?"

"It's been a long time," the visitor said.

"Indeed it has. Come in, man, come in." The professor

rose and held out both hands. The visitor grasped the right one and shook. The professor held his hand with both of his.

"It must be twenty years or more since I've seen you, Qasim. Oh, my word, how the world has turned. Sit!" he commanded, releasing the hand and gesturing toward a chair. "Tell me of yourself, where you've been, what brings you to Paris. Tell me of your life."

The visitor seated himself on one of the two guest chairs. The room was very small, lined with books. He looked around, then focused on his host. "Professor Heger, I don't know where to begin."

"You should have stayed in touch," the old man said. "You were the best student I ever had. The very best. I got you that scholarship to Göttingen, but you didn't go."

"No. I didn't."

"I know, the Germans. What can one say? Still, it was a great opportunity, a great opportunity."

"Yes, it was. Life would have certainly been different if I had gone to Germany to study. For that opportunity, I owe you a great debt, one I can never repay."

"But you look healthy, prosperous," the professor said, adjusting his glasses again. "Life has treated you well. I trust you have made your mark, wherever you went." He paused, then said, "Oh, I had a visitor yesterday, a Madame Grafton, an American, asking about you." He lowered his voice. "Of course I denied knowing you, or knowing about you, as your good friend Rodet asked. Oh, it was so many years ago that he came to me. I am surprised that I remembered. But when she mentioned your name, I remembered that I was to say nothing."

His guest took something from a pocket and worked on it with both hands in his lap. The professor didn't seem to notice. He went on. "And then you appeared. What a coincidence! I confess, I hadn't thought about you in years, Qasim, until she mentioned your name. And I have thought of you fifty times since then. Wondered where you were, what you did with your life. It is so wonderful that you have dropped by for a visit. Tell me, please, about yourself."

The visitor looked up. "I wish I could, Professor. I wish life had worked out differently. I wish I could repay your kindness, your love of learning, your friendship and thoughtful humanity, but I cannot."

With that he raised a pistol; there was a silencer attached to the barrel. He pointed it at the old man's head and, as a startled look registered on the professor's face, pulled the trigger.

I stopped by the parked van on the Place des Vosges to check with the technician on duty. Rich Thurlow was there.

"Wow, nifty duds, Carmellini. I don't think I've ever seen you all duded up. What's the occasion?" I was wearing the best clothes I owned, all of which fitted perfectly. The sports coat I had had tailored so it didn't look as if it were hanging on a garden scarecrow.

"I'm working this morning," I told him. "What's happening, anyway?"

"One of the maids is in there, no one else."

"Marisa Petrou?"

"No."

"The guard who sits in the park?"

"Yeah." Rich pointed him out.

"Good. He's here for a reason." I checked my watch. Ten o'clock. Well, there was a chance. That's all you get in life, anyway—a chance.

"So did Al and Cliff Icahn get out to the château?"

"Yeah. All that stuff you planted there works the way it's supposed to."

That was a relief. I certainly didn't want to be told to do it again.

I patted my pockets, made sure I had everything, then asked Rich, "Do you have your cell phone?"

"Yes."

"Here's a number." I handed him a slip of paper. "If I get inside, wait exactly ten minutes, then call it."

"What do you want me to say?"

"Ask if they are the folks who ordered the furniture. You need to verify the address. Use French."

"Okay. Luck."

"Yeah."

I got out of the van, locked the door, and strolled across the square. The guard looked me over without interest—and, I hoped, without recognition. I took a seat on the bench nearest the entrance of Rodet's building. Thank heavens it was in the sun, because the air had a chill to it. I was wearing a sweater under the sports coat in case I had to sit here a while; if I got too chilled, I could always walk around. I pulled an Eve Adams paperback novel from my coat pocket, opened it and settled in.

Moms or nannies pushed strollers past; an old man with a small bag of grain fed the squirrels, which were greedy and fearless. Pigeons darted in to pick up the squirrels' leavings. An hour passed, then another.

I got up twice to stroll around, then resumed my seat. The second time I strolled the park I realized we had acquired another watcher, one who had just arrived in the square. He was an older man with a dark complexion and short gray hair, wearing a threadbare sweater, a pair of worn-out leather shoes and a nice pair of wraparound sunglasses. He was seated now, apparently watching the pigeons come and go and enjoying the sunshine, but I didn't think so. He was aware of who was in the square. Once I saw his head move a minute amount; he must have been scanning the people to his left, checking them out.

I thought he looked Middle Eastern. Perhaps North Africa? With the sunglasses it was difficult to say.

If the DGSE watcher noticed him, he gave no indication.

I went back to my novel.

The man in the sweater saw the American, Carmellini, sitting on the bench reading. He, too, was watching, but for what?

The Americans had a watch station in the plumbing van—he was sure of it. It sat there surrounded by cones, yet no plumbers came or went.

Americans were pouring into Paris. They were around the

George V Hotel, where the U.S. president would stay, and now were present in squads around the American embassy on the Place de la Concorde, men in sports coats and suits, carrying handheld radios. They visited with the French police, strapping, fit men wearing submachine guns and kepis. The French police operated in squads from small buses, which they parked on street corners and sidewalks near the American embassy and up and down the Champs-Elysées. No doubt by the time of the G-8 conference, Paris would be full of police and military units, brought in from all over the country.

Germans, Japanese, Russians, British . . . he had already seen security men from all those countries. Not a lot, but a few.

The rustle of branches in the autumn breeze caught his attention. Then a small whirlwind played with some fallen leaves.

Ah, Paris. It was so different from the desert. Who was it that said, "God loved the Arabs—He gave them the Koran—but He loved the French more: He gave them Paris"?

Callie Grafton was one of those people who enjoyed learning new things and being around schools and colleges. Her father and mother had been academics, so universities had been part of the warp and woof of her life ever since she could remember.

Today as she walked through the buildings of the Sorbonne, looking for Professor Heger's office, she remembered her parents. They would have enjoyed Paris, the Sorbonne, the faculty club. Ah, yes.

According to a student she questioned, the philosophy department was in an old building on a narrow street. She had no trouble finding it, or the sign just inside the door that listed the members of the faculty and the room numbers of their offices. A passing student confirmed the sign: Professor Heger's office was on the top floor.

The elevator had obviously been installed just a few years ago, probably much to the relief of the gray-headed professors who had spent their adult years climbing the building's narrow stairs. New or not, it creaked and groaned as it descended to the floor where she stood. She could hear it coming, protesting all the way. When the door opened she discovered that it was of modest dimensions—big enough for perhaps four average-sized Europeans or three porky Americans.

As she rode upward she went over her planned approach to Heger one more time. She needed confirmation of Qasim's name, and she needed it now.

Undoubtedly someone had asked him not to talk, and that was the promise he was honoring. Since he made that promise the world had turned, she would explain. Times had changed. For Qasim's sake she needed to know: All those years ago, had Qasim been a friend of Henri Rodet?

The elevator stopped with a bump, and the door protested as it opened. Somehow the French had accomplished the impossible—installed a brand-new old elevator in an old building.

She went along the hallway examining the numbers on the door. There it was. She knocked on the door.

No answer.

Well, he might not be here. He might be in class.

She rapped again. Heard a thump. Or was it her imagination? A noise from inside the room?

Callie tried the doorknob, and it opened.

"Professor Heger?"

She looked inside. The room was small, lined with books on shelves, two little windows, a desk, a computer . . . and behind the desk on the wooden floor, just visible, a shoe.

She stepped into the room. "Professor?"

He was lying behind the desk. "Professor Heger?"

She turned him over and saw the bullet wound in his head. It had bled some, and the blood had congealed on the floor and the side of his face. He also had a deep bruise where his face had hit the floor when he had fallen.

He was still alive, breathing erratically. His eyes were unfocused.

Callie reached into his mouth and cleared his airway. The man was obviously in a bad way, perhaps even dying. There was no time to lose.

"Professor Heger, I'm Callie Grafton. Yesterday you denied knowing Abu Qasim. It was twenty-five years ago, Professor."

The old man obviously heard her. He made a noise, swallowed, tried to focus his eyes.

"I know you promised not to tell who he was," Callie continued, "but the world has turned. Times have changed. It's a matter of life and death. I need to know. Did you have a student named Abu Qasim?"

He was trying to talk. Callie bent down. She heard the whisper.

It was incoherent noise.

Then Professor Heger lost consciousness. Callie talked to Heger in the hope that he might hear, but within a minute he breathed his last.

A t half past twelve the limo came slowly along the street and glided to a stop in front of Henri Rodet's building.

I stowed the paperback in my pocket and walked toward the long Mercedes as the driver got out and opened the right-side rear door.

A very shapely leg appeared, then another, and out stepped Marisa Petrou. She was wearing some kind of frock that ended just above her knees, a pair of high heels that consisted of a sole, a heel, and straps to hold it all together, and a little designer jacket. She reached back into the car for her purse, which was a large one.

Then she saw me. She didn't recognize me for a few seconds, then it hit her. She looked again at me and her mouth dropped open.

"Hello, Marisa." I walked over, closing the gap. "Travis Crockett."

"The man with the boots," she said. "You're a long way from Texas, cowboy."

The chauffeur was standing there respectfully, still holding the door. Being an American working man, I grinned at him and winked as she said, "Out for a stroll this morning?"

"Yep. Imagine my surprise at seeing you. I guess it's truly a small world, after all."

She moved away from the car and the chauffeur closed the door. She nodded at him; he got back behind the wheel and drove away.

As he did so, I looked around at the building we were standing in front of and said, "You live here? Cool neighborhood."

She was looking me over, apparently trying to figure out what I wanted.

"It's nice seeing you again," I said. "May I call you sometime? Perhaps take you out for a drink?"

"No." She bit her lip and glanced toward the park. "What are you doing in Paris, Tommy Carmellini?"

"My name is—"

"You left fingerprints. You're Tommy Carmellini, an officer in the CIA. What are you doing in Paris?"

"Standing on a Paris sidewalk in front of God and everybody chatting up a beautiful woman. And you?"

She grabbed my arm. "Come inside for a moment."

I went willingly.

What should I do?" Callie Grafton asked her husband. She was standing in Heger's office talking to Jake on her cell phone. She had told him everything, including the fact that Heger died without saying a word.

"Does he have a telephone on his desk?"

"Yes."

"Call the police. Wait for them. You've left fingerprints, so we don't want to send them off on a wild goose chase or get you in trouble. Don't tell them about Qasim. Tell them you met the professor yesterday and wanted to talk with him again."

"Okay."

"Are you all right?" Jake asked, although he knew the answer.

"Yes," she said.

"Call me later. I love you."

"I love you, too, Jake," she replied, and closed the telephone.

She and her husband made a point of saying "I love you" at the end of every telephone conversation. Life is short, random chance happens to us all—she glanced again at Professor Heger's body—and there is evil.

Evil exists. Filthy, obscene, virulent, evil is out there, ready to sear us all.

I love you, Jake, she whispered again, and picked up the telephone on Heger's desk.

Marisa Petrou unlocked the street door of her apartment building on the Place des Vosges. The door opened into a stairwell. There was no elevator, so we had to hike up two flights. She used a key on the only door on the third floor.

"Wow," I said when I was inside. The rooms were spacious, with ten-foot ceilings. The joint certainly didn't look like this in the Renaissance when the maids were emptying chamber pots out the windows. Someone, I assumed Henri Rodet, had spent serious euros remodeling and improving. Huge, original oil paintings hung on the walls, the ornate baseboards and moldings were gilded, thick drapes framed each window and antique chairs that looked as if they had welcomed Napoleon's bottom were scattered here and there. Modern sculptures sat in corners, illuminated by tiny spotlights. The place reminded me of a museum. It was something to see, if you like that sort of thing. I didn't particularly care for it, but I made polite noises.

Marisa marched through the place, checking every room, as I trailed along behind. She found the maid in the kitchen and asked her to run an errand, a trip to the market. She gave the maid money and sent her off.

Then we were alone.

She zeroed in on me. "What are you doing in Paris?" she asked again.

"Huh-uh. You first."

"I live here."

"In this place?" I looked around. "Nice work if you can get it."

Her mouth formed a straight line. Just then the telephone rang. She reached for it. I headed for the living room. From the window I could see the guard in the park. He was on his cell phone—probably checking with Marisa.

I could just hear the murmur of her voice. I was staring at a modern painting, trying to figure out what it was, when she came into the room.

She sat on the couch. "Sit, Tommy Carmellini." She patted the seat. I sat down beside her and left a few inches between us. "Let's start with the easy questions first. Why did you make a play for me in Washington?"

My eyes widened. "I seem to recall that you picked me up, not vice versa."

"So you knocked me out, had sex with me, then left me in a drugged stupor."

"If that's a question, I'm not going to dignify it with an answer."

She looked around the room, thinking.

"You could answer a question for me, you know."

"I'll be as honest with you as you were with me," she said.

"You had my fingerprints checked by someone, so you're not just the socialite daughter of a diplomat. Do you work for French intelligence?"

She kept her gaze on my eyes and didn't reply. The thought occurred to me that she was a knockout. Oh, well— that's the way my luck goes.

"If I show up for a visit with Henri Rodet and tell him my name is Terry Shannon, are you going to rat me out?"

"Rat . . . ?"

"Spill the beans. Tell him I'm not Terry Shannon."

"I don't know you."

"That's the spirit. I saw character in your face the first time I laid eyes on you."

Now it was her turn. "Are you going to tell Monsieur Rodet that we've met before?"

"A grand jury couldn't drag it out of me."

"Grand jury . . . ?"

"That's a political joke. I won't tell if you won't."

The phone rang again. Marisa made a face and went to answer it in the kitchen.

I was standing, closely inspecting a two-foot-high sculpture of a voluptuous, armless nude, when she returned.

"I am curious," I said. "There is a man sitting in the park that I would like to point out to you. I wonder if you know him."

She followed me reluctantly. "There's a DGSE man in the park. He saw you come in. I told him we had a mutual acquaintance."

"Who?"

"I didn't name her." .

"Okay."

The older man wearing sunglasses was still sitting in the same place. I pointed him out to Marisa. "Do you know him?"

She took a good look, perhaps fifteen seconds' worth. That pause convinced me she was a professional; if she ever saw him again, she would remember. "No," she said.

She led me to the door and opened it. "Good-bye, Tommy."

"Terry." I didn't want to leave. "So how is your father?" I asked.

A look of surprise crossed her face, then disappeared. "He died," she said.

"Oh. Sorry to hear it. He looked pretty healthy when I saw him."

"An automobile accident, in the Alps. Two months ago. A truck on the wrong side of the road."

"I'm sorry."

"Yes. Good-bye, Terry." She gently touched my elbow.

Hell, I can take a hint. I motored off and she closed the door behind me.

I had a lot to think about as I descended the stairs. I ignored the men in the park. Didn't look for or at them. I walked down the block and went through the arch under the buildings, which took me out of the square.

I called Rich on my cell as I walked. "Hey, it's me."

"Hey."

"Where is the watcher who was in the park?"

"He's still there."

"How many telephone calls did he make?"

"One."

"There's another one, an older guy in sunglasses, ratty pants and a sweater, Semitic features. Get a shot of him and ask Washington to come up with some ID, if they can."

"I see him," Rich said.

"I'm going home. Turn on the equipment, see what you can get out of those bugs. Make sure they work, then turn them off."

"What rooms did you put them in?"

"Living room, hallway and kitchen."

"Nice job," he said, and hung up.

I stretched my legs and marched.

I really didn't care if Marisa told her guy Henri that I was Tommy Carmellini—I just threw that in to see what she would say. Was she DGSE? If she already knew that the DGSE knew one CIA type named Carmellini was in town, she hid it well. She had seemed genuinely surprised to see me—and not pleasantly surprised.

If she wasn't a DGSE officer, then whom was she working for?

Jake Grafton leaned over Sarah Houston's shoulder so that he could see her computer screen and asked, "What do you have?"

"They used the computer at the château this morning after the power came back on."

"And . . ."

"I'm still sorting through what I have."

Grafton dropped into the folding chair beside Houston's small desk. "I want everything you can get off that hard drive, and the hard drive at his apartment in town."

Sarah Houston eyed him without warmth. "I know you don't believe in telling anyone anything, but until you tell me what I'm looking for, you can classify my efforts as recreational digging."

Grafton seemed to accept that with good grace. With him you never knew, Houston thought. The truth was he intimidated her a little, although she would never admit it.

"I've told you what I'm after. I want to know how Rodet and his spy communicate. And, obviously, what they say to each other."

Houston played with her keys a bit before she answered. "If you don't know how they communicate or what they say to one another, how do you know there really is a spy?"

"I don't," Grafton said with a smile. "All I have is a theory. Prove me wrong, if you can." He picked up Carmellini's file on Rodet's château and opened it.

"They may not use e-mail. Or if they do, they may use a public computer, such as one in a library or Starbucks, something like that."

"The agent might, but I can't see the director of the DGSE pounding a keyboard at a library."

"Why shouldn't the agent use a dead drop?"

"Too risky. This person is in a murderous conspiracy, surrounded by religious fanatics who are convinced that they are warriors of God, fighting God's battles. The least suspicion would cost him his life. So he doesn't go for walks alone, doesn't visit post offices, doesn't mail letters to foreign cities . . . none of that."

"A mailman?" This was a person who carried messages between the spy and his controller.

"Same objection."

"You have me searching for a needle in a haystack," Sarah Houston groused, "one that might not even be there."

"That kind is the hardest to find," Grafton admitted.

She frowned at her boss. He didn't seem to notice. He dug into the file, held up each satellite photo and examined it closely.

Jake Grafton looked amused as he listened to me tell of my success in getting bugs into Rodet's Paris flat. When I ran out of air he sat in silence looking around with unfocused eyes, lost in thought. There in the SCIF the only sounds were the hum of the air-conditioning and faintly, almost too faint to discern, the sound of background music. The speakers for the Muzak were inside the walls, floors and ceilings, to foil listening devices.

Finally he looked at me and blinked, almost as if seeing me for the first time. "That was a bold stroke," he said, "and regardless of what she does or whom she tells—in the French government—I can't see how we're compromised."

"In the French government?"

"She could be MI-6, BND, Russian, Polish, Italian, Israeli—even an agent of a terrorist cell."

"Okay, okay. Maybe I should have talked it over with you first."

Grafton sighed. "Perhaps. Perhaps not. You used your best judgment and acted on the information you had, which is the only way we're going to get through this." He smiled at me. "I spent my adult life in an outfit that operates that way and it's probably too late for me to change now. However it works out is how it works out."

"How do we know that she's anyone's agent? I thought that her father was the spy who—"

Grafton made a face. "Really, Tommy!"

I tried to explain. "Rodet thinks she's just a hot French tootsie. Maybe he's right."

Grafton rolled his eyes. "She's a beautiful, young, wealthy daughter of the establishment who is driven wild by the prospect of jumping in bed with a rich, powerful man old enough to be her father? Do you believe that?"

"No, but I know a few men who—"

"I doubt if Rodet believes it either," Grafton said. He picked up the photos we had taken of Rodet's apartment and began looking at them, one by one.

After a bit he put his feet up on the desk, leaned back and looked at each photo again. He must have looked at each of them three times when he handed the stack to me. "What kind of television does Rodet have?" he asked. He picked up the cell phone lying on the desk and fingered it.

"You mean what brand?"

"Brand, size?"

"I don't remember the brand. The one I saw at the apartment wasn't large. It was just a normal television. Floor thing, in a cabinet, kind of old-fashioned. Why?"

Grafton passed me a photo. "He has a satellite dish on the roof of the house. I would have thought he'd have a big Japanese flat screen, maybe a home movie studio, something like that."

I looked at the photo. Sure enough, there was the dish, sitting like a plate next to a chimney. "If he has a setup like that, I didn't see it," I said. "All I saw was an older television."

Grafton opened his phone and fingered it. Of course, it didn't work here in the SCIF, and he knew that. "Okay," he said, rising from the chair. "Now if you will excuse me, I've got to go upstairs to make a call."

I picked up the aerial photos and studied the dish antenna. They were sprouting all over Paris, it was true, yet Marisa hadn't struck me as a big fan of television, and I doubted that Rodet had the time.

Jake and Callie Grafton ate dinner at a hole-in-the-wall restaurant three blocks from their apartment. Night had fallen in Paris and the cool wind had picked up.

"The police accepted my explanation, had me go through it twice, and let me go. They said they would call me if they had more questions."

A few minutes later she said, "Poor Professor Heger. To die like that . . ."

"But he tried to answer your question?"

"He made a noise, Jake. I couldn't understand it."

"Could he have been trying to tell you the name of his killer?"

"I don't know. He was semiconscious, at best. I don't know how much he heard or understood of what I said. At the time I thought he was trying to answer my question. I asked about Abu Qasim. He made a noise. But do you think . . . Abu Qasim, here, in Paris?"

Jake Grafton shrugged and toyed with his wine glass. "It's a possibility to keep in mind."

"It's more than that. I ask him about Abu Qasim, and the next day he's murdered. It may be a coincidence, but—"

"Yesterday fifty people spoke to Professor Heger, about fifty different things. They couldn't all be cause and effect."

Callie wasn't going to take a brush-off that easily. "If Qasim is a killer, why would Rodet protect him?"

When her husband didn't reply, Callie said, "That was a stupid question. Twenty-five years is a long time."

"He'd have to be somewhere between forty-five and fifty," Jake said, musing aloud. "Maybe a year or two older."

Their food came and they ate in silence. When they finished and were sipping on tiny glasses of apple brandy, Callie murmured, "Professor Heger was a nice man."

"So it's possible that Heger recognized him," Jake mused. "Rodet might recognize him, too, if he saw him."

"Now *you* are assuming that Rodet's Al Queda spy is a killer. If he is, why did he tell Rodet about the Veghel conspiracy?"

Jake threw up his hands. "I wish I knew," he said.

CHAPTER ELEVEN

They were an unlikely pair, Henri Rodet and Abu Qasim. The Frenchman was eight years older than the Bedouin lad, they were from vastly different cultures and walks of life, and yet each found something in the other that made the friendship worthwhile.

Qasim was waiting one morning when Rodet drove by on a pipeline patrol. Rodet stopped, the boy climbed in the truck, and away they went. Qasim had nothing better to do, so they rode the pipeline twice a week. Rodet taught the boy French and Qasim taught him Arabic. They argued in both languages about God, religion, history, the world and man's place in it. Rodet enjoyed puns, and Qasim had a wicked sense of humor. They became like brothers who enjoyed each other's company.

The crisis came when the pipeline company laid off Rodet and hired a local man at half his salary. Two weeks after he went back to France, Rodet sent for Qasim. The boy didn't bother his father with the news—he merely walked away from home. A week later he showed up on Rodet's doorstep. Rodet's parents, both teachers, welcomed him.

Rodet went into the French intelligence service and Qasim went to school. After two years, he won a scholarship to the Sorbonne. He was just finishing his education when Anwar Sadat was murdered.

That was the day the earth moved, Rodet thought as he

stood looking out his window at Paris. That October day in 1981 was the dawn of the age of terror.

Islamic fundamentalists murdered Sadat, the president of Egypt, as he reviewed the army. The assassins were cut down by his security forces, but after all, they expected to die and were prepared for it. They were members of Egyptian Islamic Jihad, fighting to overthrow the old order and convert Egypt to an Islamic republic, a nation ruled by God. Why the God who created the universe and everything in it needed their help was never explained by the bearded holy men, but the warriors knew in their hearts that it was so. They wanted it to be so. And so they committed murder, paid immediately with their lives and were ushered into paradise.

Sadat's murder didn't just happen, of course. It was the culmination of months of civil strife between Muslims and Coptic Christians, which had resulted in bloody riots in some of Cairo's worst slums. With a stagnant economy, isolated from the Arab world for making peace with Israel, Egypt under Sadat was a powder keg. Sadat jailed the fundamentalists and Copts without trial, laying an iron hand upon them. They struck back and he died.

His successors crushed the Islamic movement in Egypt. They jailed its adherents, tortured prisoners for information and confessions, and executed without trial those they thought the most dangerous. The survivors of the purge fled Egypt and declared war on civilization.

Rodet had been working out of the French embassy in Cairo the year that Sadat died. He had witnessed the riots firsthand. Heat, dirt, squalor, blood, body parts . . . and the stench—he had only to close his eyes and he could recall that odor of wanton death.

"Your visitors are here, *mon directeur*."

The voice startled Rodet, bringing him back to the here and now.

I figured my trip with Jake Grafton to visit ol' Henri Rodet in the lion's den was my coming-out party. Every spook in town was now on notice that I was in the game, so I could expect an audience for everything I did and said. If I had been the kind of guy who liked to be the center of attention, a gig like this would have probably ruined me for polite society.

I met Grafton at his tiny cubbyhole office at the embassy. He was sitting there talking to Sarah Houston and George Goldberg when I arrived. I nodded at George and waited for Sarah to acknowledge my presence. She did. She was cool and professional, like a nurse ready to draw a pint or two of blood from one of your veins. Once she caught my eye when no one else was looking, so I winked at her. She quickly averted her eyes.

Grafton glanced at his watch, stood and motioned to me to follow him. I did.

"How's Callie?" I asked as we headed for the main entrance and the waiting car.

"She's talking about buying something in France, a little place that we can use summer or winter and commute from. I've got to get her home before she goes around the bend."

"How long do we have?"

"I don't know."

The driver was holding the door of the limo, so Grafton and I hopped into the back seat. The admiral didn't speak to the driver, who must have been told by someone else where we were going.

Grafton checked his reflection in the mirror and straightened his tie.

"Got any lines for me this afternoon?" I asked brightly.

"Just see and be seen. Don't say anything unless you are answering a direct question, and then give only unclassified information."

We didn't have far to go. Across the Place de la Concorde and the bridge, turn left on the boulevard along the quay, past the Musée d'Orsay and National School of Fine Arts, then left and across the Pont St. Michel onto the Ile de la Cité. On our left was the Palais de Justice, home of the criminal courts and judicial police. On the right was the Préfecture de Police, the site of a terrific street battle during the liberation of Paris.

I was gawking at the tourists when the driver turned the car into the courtyard of the Conciergerie. The driver told the guard who we were; we were waved past and directed to a parking place. From there, a man in civilian clothes led Grafton and me up a flight of stairs, past the metal detector and along a corridor with a twelve-foot ceiling. Our footsteps echoed on the stone floors and walls.

Video monitors were mounted high in every corner, as well as infrared and motion detectors. Every door we passed had a lock on it. It wasn't a people-friendly place, I can tell you. As I walked I could almost hear the wails of the damned as they were dragged from their cells to feed the guillotine. Yet today everyone looked normal—men in suits and sports coats, women in dresses or skirts. It could have been a scene from any large office building in any big Western city. Perhaps I was the only one hearing ghosts.

The receptionist showed us into Rodet's office, which was a big corner room high in the building. His view was west, down the river. He was of average height, maybe a bit over, with thinning hair, carrying no excess weight. It was obvious he exercised regularly. He also looked as if he had just returned from the beach—a nice tan.

He said hello in English and shook hands with the admiral. "My aide, Terry Shannon," Jake said, nodding at me. I shook, too. Rodet waved us to chairs, then dropped onto a nearby couch.

While Grafton and Rodet chatted, getting acquainted, I took a second or two to scope out his art. Looked old and expensive or trendily weird, which meant new and expensive. I was sort of glad I didn't have to look at any of it on a regular basis.

Jake Grafton explained that he was the new CIA ops man for Europe and made some remarks about being out of his depth, comments that didn't fool me for a second. I doubted if the Frenchman bought any of it either. Rodet looked like a very sharp man, with quick eyes that didn't seem to miss much.

Of course, I wondered about him and Marisa. She didn't

seem to want Rodet to know that she and I had met before, and I speculated about why that might be. Rodet didn't strike me as the insanely jealous type.

And who, precisely, was Marisa Petrou? Was she a French tootsie scaling the social register, or something else?

About that time Jean-Paul Arnaud came in, and Rodet introduced him. We shook hands. He was smaller than Rodet, intense, and reminded me of a mongoose. He sat down in a vacant chair in the back of the room.

Before long Grafton and Rodet were discussing security arrangements for the upcoming G-8 summit conference. "The Secret Service has sent a professional, of course, but I have been assigned to assist him. I wonder if we might go over a point or two?" Grafton produced an agenda from a coat pocket and went over it with Rodet.

At one point Rodet said, "We have beefed up our security at the border. We are stopping and checking every vehicle entering France, checking passports, and so on. As you know, normally travelers move freely back and forth across borders within Europe. Not now. Extra security at the airports, at train stations, every public place. The president has demanded that everything be done that can be done, and I assure you, it will be."

They discussed specifics for a bit, then Grafton moved on to various international matters, asking for Rodet's assessment of the current Middle East situation and inserting a pointed query on terrorist organizations in France, Spain and Germany. He listened carefully as Rodet talked, offering no opinions of his own.

It was interesting to watch Grafton work, in the same way that I suppose it is interesting to watch a snake charm a mouse. Not that Grafton was a snake or Rodet a mouse—far from it. Both men, I well knew, were competent, capable professionals. Still, I couldn't help wondering if Rodet understood just how competent and capable Grafton really was, or how ruthless he could be if he felt the situation demanded it.

Then, out of the blue, Grafton asked, "Who killed Claude

Bruguiere?" in the same tone he had used to ask about Romania's prospects in the EU.

"The police are investigating," Rodet said, showing not the least bit of surprise that Grafton knew about the death of a DGSE officer. "If they have a suspect, they have not shared his identity with us."

"Have they questioned you about the death?" Grafton asked.

"Of course not," Rodet said. "I have eight hundred employees in this agency. Why should they?"

"Bruguiere's name rang a bell when I heard it. If my sources are correct, he was the DGSE officer who went to Amman to complete a stock transaction on your behalf in the latter part of August."

"On my behalf?" The skepticism in Rodet's voice was barely discernible, but it was there.

"A quarter million shares in the Bank of Palestine were purchased in your name."

Rodet's face was a mask. When he said nothing, Grafton continued, "Two million euros. A nice chunk of change."

One would have thought that Grafton's knowledge of Rodet's Palestinian investments would at least raise an eyebrow, but it didn't. Rodet's and Arnaud's faces were impossible for me to read.

"You are misinformed, Admiral," Rodet said dryly, and stopped there without telling Grafton what he was misinformed about.

Grafton wouldn't let it rest. "In what way am I misinformed?"

Rodet weighed his words before he spoke. "I own no shares in the Bank of Palestine."

"I suppose a man should know what he owns," Grafton replied carelessly. "Obviously my informant was in error." I saw his shoulders rise and fall a quarter of an inch. He rose to his feet, so I popped out of my chair. I ventured a grin at Arnaud, who ignored me. His eyes were on Grafton.

"We'll not take up any more of your valuable time, Monsieur Rodet," the admiral said. "Thank you for the opportunity to touch base, so to speak, get acquainted and all that."

"Any time, Admiral, any time." Rodet rose to show us out. He looked as cool as he did when we came in. I instantly resolved to never play poker with him, not even for matchsticks.

"Oh," Grafton said as we left. "There's one more matter I would like to discuss, at a place and time of your choosing, but not in this building." He passed Rodet a slip of folded paper. "You can reach me at the embassy."

Rodet put the scrap of white paper in his pocket without looking at it. "I'll keep your request in mind," he said, and opened the office door. The escort who would accompany us to our car was waiting in one of the soft chairs.

The receptionist looked mighty nice. I managed to flash her a smile and collect one in return before I had to march off after the boss. She obviously didn't know I was a lackey.

The limo driver dropped us three blocks from the embassy due to traffic, and we walked. As we strolled along I asked the admiral, "What was in your note?"

He glanced at me, acknowledging the question, and didn't answer.

"So ol' Bruguiere was a bagman for Rodet?"

"He bought stock in the Bank of Palestine for Rodet."

"In Rodet's name?"

"Yes."

"Rodet doesn't strike me as the type that would be dumb enough to do that."

"That bothered me, too," Grafton murmured.

"Someone setting him up, you think?"

"More like taking him down," Grafton said sourly.

We were crossing the street when I glanced back and saw him. About thirty yards behind us was the man from the Place des Vosges. Not the DGSE agent, the other guy. Dark complexion, medium size, grizzled hair, wearing cleaner clothes than he had when I saw him last.

"We're being followed," I told the admiral.

"Anyone you recognize?"

"Yes."

After we gained the sidewalk on the other side of the street, I kept my eyes moving. That's when I saw the car, a dark four-door sedan, perhaps a Fiat. I couldn't tell how many people were in it. I saw it, or one just like it, in front of the Conciergerie when we came out. The walker behind us might have gotten out of that car when we abandoned the limo.

"Enjoying Paris?" Jake Grafton asked.

"No," I said, and meant it.

When the door closed behind Grafton and his aide, Jean-Paul Arnaud stayed for a moment. "The Bank of Palestine?"

"Check on that, please, and get back to me."

Arnaud left immediately and closed the door behind him. Henri Rodet returned to his chair behind his desk. The question about the stock in the Bank of Palestine from the American CIA officer had been unexpected.

As he thought about it, he fingered the objects on his desk, one by one, without seeing them, as he considered the matter. Anyone owning stock in the Bank of Palestine would appear to have a financial interest in the success of the Palestinian state and conversely, the demise of its blood enemy, Israel. Diplomatic protests would be lodged; his position would become untenable. So what could he do? Begin an investigation now? When the news broke in the newspapers, it could be made to look as if he were trying to cover up the facts.

Perhaps he should wait. When the news broke, someone's fingerprints would be all over it. That was perhaps the best course open to him, he decided.

In the interim, he should make sure that no one had gotten into his bank accounts and transferred money without his knowledge. He picked up his unsecure outside line and called his banker.

When they were finally connected and had exchanged pleasantries, Rodet said, "A situation has arisen, monsieur, that has caused me some concern. I wish you to verify the balances of my accounts and check to ensure that there have been no unauthorized transactions."

"Of course. It will take a few minutes. May I call you back?"

"At this number," Rodet said, and read it off.

The silence that followed after he replaced the instrument in its cradle was oppressive. Rodet rose from his chair and paced.

He could name two or three dozen people who would like to see him dismissed from the agency, including his wife and her father. And three former ministers and a half dozen sitting deputies. Not to mention his opposite numbers at some of the other European intelligence agencies. Running an intelligence agency wasn't a job for the squeamish. He had played rough and tough and made his enemies, which was inevitable.

A million and a half euros! A lot of money! All Rodet had to prove it was a few sentences from Grafton. *Does the American CIA officer really know, is he lying for reasons of his own, or did he hear a rumor and conclude that he might gain my trust by repeating it to me?*

What does he want, anyway?

Rodet remembered the paper in his jacket pocket. He fished it out and unfolded it. It was the corner of a sheet of plain white copy paper. On it were written two words in ink: *Abu Qasim.*

CHAPTER TWELVE

After the murder of Anwar Sadat, the Egyptians rounded up Islamic fundamentalists in massive dragnets. They interrogated and tortured everyone who looked interesting. Everyone who had anything to do with the assassination plot was shot, as were hundreds of zealots who appeared pleased that Sadat was dead. Yet the authorities knew that there was a real, if somewhat hazy, limit on how many zealots they could execute and not trigger a revolution, so they locked up everyone they didn't want to waste a bullet on.

Western observers of the Egyptian crisis watched with bated breath. The overthrow of the shah in Iran and the militancy of the Iranian clerics seemed somehow a part of the religious fervor sweeping the Islamic world, a brittle world atop a fossilized religion, one devoid of political freedom and chock-full of the desperately poor, a world threatened by encroaching Western civilization, with its prosperity, democratic values and freedom.

"The last iteration of bomb-throwing anarchists caused World War I," Henri Rodet's boss remarked. "This crop looks like they will be tossing them for the next half century. We need some agents inside the Islamic movement. Your job is to get us some."

Rodet couldn't believe his ears. "Recruit suicidal religious fanatics to spy on their friends? That would be the same as betraying God. No jihadist would take a chance on forfeiting his place in paradise by selling out his fellow holy warriors."

"I know it won't be easy," the boss acknowledged. "Getting good intelligence never is. Nevertheless, I want you to try. Get us some agents inside the movement. Jihadists they might be, but saints they aren't."

Rodet had spent two years in the French intelligence agency, and this assignment would undoubtedly be his last. There was no way under the sun that he could penetrate a cell of religious fanatics. It was a ridiculous assignment. Impossible. The boss didn't like him, he decided, and had picked this method of destroying his career. He would be back on the streets of Paris within weeks looking for a job.

Unless he had help. Someone who spoke Arabic like a native, who knew the people and the religion and the fanatic scene—in other words, a real Arab—could indeed recruit traitors. The boss was right: These people were just people. Regardless of their religious proclivities, they wanted money and sex and power like every other human on the planet. Some of them—well, a few, at least—could be bought or bribed or blackmailed. The real problem was finding those susceptible people.

He thought about writing to Abu Qasim, who was in his final year at the Sorbonne, taking a degree in philosophy, and explaining the problem to him. Qasim believed in civilization, and these people didn't. Still, his religion and ethnicity would allow him access to places and people that a European could not hope to match.

Rodet thought it over for a couple of days and decided to write. Qasim could always say no. He made that clear in the letter. "The job is identifying people inside the movement that we can target for recruitment. It's a job that needs doing."

A week later he got back a message, "Let's talk."

Rodet explained the situation to his boss, who was skeptical. Even so, he allowed Rodet to return to Paris. Rodet went by plane.

Even then Paris had a large population of Muslims, so he and Qasim had to be careful. He picked Qasim up one evening and they went for a ride.

They drove out of Paris and headed for a country inn that Rodet knew. At the bar three workingmen from the neighborhood drank calvados. The floor was uneven, the furniture old and scarred and the room chilly. Fresh from the heat and stench of Cairo, Rodet found it very pleasant. He and Qasim sat at a table in the corner.

Finally he asked the question. "Would you help us recruit some agents inside the Islamic movement?"

"Someone inside who will feed you intelligence?"

"Yes."

"It could be done," Qasim said simply. "But not if they know who is receiving the information. These people are committed to the depths of their souls, earning eternal life in paradise by fighting God's battles. They may be a lot of things, but they aren't hypocrites."

"How can we keep our identities a secret from them?"

"The agent will have to become part of their world. He will have to be in a cell, or perhaps a financier or an armorer. Only if he is a trusted part of the conspiracy will he be told things. He will be given pieces of the puzzle. That's about all one could hope for."

Qasim was right, of course.

"Our agent will have to actually help them," Rodet mused aloud.

"Indeed. He must become an actual part of the terror network and help them in a visible, material way. He must earn their trust every day. And if an operation is betrayed, he must remain above suspicion. It must be delicately handled."

Rodet laughed. "I thought you were studying philosophy?"

"I have been. And I have been reading history. This war between civilization and religious zealots has been going on for nine or ten centuries, at least. Heretics, torture, witches, people burned at the stake, God's kingdom on earth in the care of dedicated holy men . . . When holy men rule based on religious scripture, one gets hell on earth, not heaven."

"There's not a lot of flexibility in the 'Thou shalts' and the 'Thou shalt nots,'" Rodet agreed.

"The holy men are fighting for the right to rule Islamic society," Abu Qasim said. "History teaches that holy men always lose in the end. Even if they win the battles, they always lose their wars. It would be better for everyone if they lose this one quickly."

The inn served wine from barrels. Qasim savored a glass with Rodet.

"You need a man," Qasim said, "who knows these people and isn't afraid of them. Surrounded by fanatics who are absolutely convinced of the correctness of their cause, he must be even more so, believe in himself beyond any shadow of a doubt, believe in what he knows to be right with a faith that will withstand all adversity. And he must be willing to drive the knife in to the hilt."

"You are describing a superman, an idealist made of something other than flesh and blood," Rodet objected. "Jesus and Mohammed, perhaps. People like that do not exist in the real world."

"Oh, but they do," Qasim said lightly, and helped himself to more wine. "The world is full of them, which is, perhaps, part of the problem. The men who murdered Sadat were such men. A dozen popes, Henry VIII, Cardinal Richelieu, Robespierre, Marat, Napoléon, Lenin, Dzerzhinsky, Stalin, Hitler, Churchill, de Gaulle . . . the list goes on and on."

The proprietor brought their meals, but Rodet had no appetite. He stirred his food around with his fork and listened to Qasim talk.

"You need a man who can live by his wits, a man who is willing to play the game unto the last drop of blood. He must know the language, the religion and the culture. Any mistake will be fatal."

Finally his younger friend got around to it. "*I* am that man."

Rodet and Qasim finished their meal. Over the dirty dishes they discussed what the agent might expect to learn and methods of communication.

"If the agent plays it straight within his network, does his job and maintains his cover, he will do fine," Rodet said, "unless they discover how he sends or receives his mail. That will always be a risk."

"The biggest risk will be here in Paris," Qasim mused. "Everyone who knows about the agent in place is a potential danger. Everyone who knows of the mail system is a danger."

"In a perfect world only one man would know," Rodet remarked, "and that one man would be the handler."

"Then there is the problem of what use to make of the intelligence. Every terrorist arrested, every cell destroyed, every assassination plot thwarted will point, in some small way, back at the agent. He knew. Other people, too, but *he* knew. Eventually the noose will tighten."

"We must always appear to have another source."

"That will only work for so long. These people are paranoid. They don't need proof, just a suspicion. Sooner or later they'll get one, and from that moment on, the agent is a doomed man."

"This game will be brief," Rodet admitted. "Still, the intelligence could be valuable."

The workmen at the bar had long gone and they were nursing snifters of cognac when Rodet asked Abu Qasim, "Why do you want to do this?"

"I learned one thing at the Sorbonne," Qasim said, weighing his words. "Civilization is worth fighting for."

"That's not an explanation."

"Maybe I don't have one."

Henri Rodet thought about that for a while. The truth was that he didn't give a damn why Qasim was willing to risk his life. Qasim was a friend—well, more like a younger brother, really—and he didn't want him hurt.

"All right," he said after a while. "All right! We'll give it a try. But only if you promise to cut and run if they began closing in, or when you've had enough."

"I am not a martyr," Abu Qasim shot back. "Dead men win no battles."

That conversation occurred twenty-five years ago, and still Henri Rodet could remember every word as if it had happened yesterday evening. He was thinking about Qasim, about the life he must lead, when the telephone rang. The receptionist told him the man's name. His banker.

"I have your balance, Monsieur Rodet." He gave him the number. It sounded within a thousand or so euros of the sum Rodet estimated should be there. "Is there anything else I can do for you?"

"No, thank you," Rodet said. He murmured a pleasantry and said good-bye.

The watchers in the Fiat followed me when I left the American embassy late that afternoon. I walked, so they put one man on the sidewalk behind me, and the others—there were at least two more in the car—drove back and forth on cross streets or sat behind me in no-parking zones, always remaining within a block of me.

Grafton and I were pretty sure this bunch weren't French. Of course, everyone was into diversity these days, so they could be working for any agency on the planet. Yet if they weren't French, they were fair game. "See if you can find out who they are, Tommy," Grafton said just before I left the embassy. "Be careful. Don't let them hurt you and don't hurt them so badly that you get arrested."

"I understand," I said.

The weather was excellent, with the temperature in the sixties, mostly sunny skies, and a whiff of a breeze. I took off my suit coat and folded it over my arm.

Strolling the boulevards of Paris, I considered my options. I needed to get one of these guys alone for a few minutes. The watcher in the Place des Vosges had been alone, but would he be in the future? If he came back at all.

I walked through the gardens of the Tuileries, heading for the Seine. I walked briskly, purposely, looking neither right nor left, taking no precautions against the tail that I knew was back there. The car couldn't follow us and, with a little luck, would be struggling to get through late afternoon traffic on the Place de la Concorde.

My tail would have a cell phone with him, of course; he was probably on it right now. I didn't turn to see.

I crossed the Seine on the Passerelle Solférino, a walking bridge, and walked directly for the Musée d'Orsay, an old railroad station that had been converted to a museum. There was a line waiting to buy tickets, of course.

I joined the queue, ending up immediately behind a trio of young women from the States. From the comments they made, I learned that they were American students doing a semester abroad. One of them had met the love of her life a couple of weeks ago, so we heard all about him. As the girls chattered—they glanced at me when I got in line and then, due to my greatly advanced age and general decrepitude, ignored me—I glanced around.

My tail was in line, too, about fifteen persons back. He was from the Middle East, I thought, or perhaps a French Muslim. Clad in slacks and wearing a zippered jacket that hung open, he was studying a guide book. In my quick scan I noticed that he was holding his cell phone in his hand. That phone would be a little gold mine of telephone numbers, both called and received, that would provide a nice picture of the owner and the people in his organization, or cell.

I turned back toward the girls. My tail was in his mid-twenties, I suppose, of slightly above medium height, all muscle and sinew, weighing about 130 or 140. I hadn't seen any bulges under his armpits, so if he was packing, which I doubted, it was in the small of his back or an ankle holster. On the other hand, it would not surprise me to learn that he had a knife on him and could get to it quickly.

I shuffled forward, listening to the girls giggle and gush, paid for my ticket, took it to the guard at the turnstile and passed through.

I had spent an afternoon in this building six months or so ago, so I knew the general layout. The building is an architectural masterpiece, a great enclosed space with a vaulted ceiling.

From the entrance one walks through what was once the

waiting area into a huge open space where at one time trains sat on their tracks, chuffing smoke and cinders. On the wall above the old waiting area was a huge clock on an opaque glass wall. I glanced at my watch and found the clock was off by two minutes.

Most of the building had been converted to art galleries. Indeed, this museum was probably the best Impressionist museum in Paris. It was also full of really cool sculpture, some of it huge, by such folks as Rodin and Carpeaux. The biggest and heaviest pieces sat on the main floor. I went about halfway along the main gallery and arranged myself in front of a huge lion in such a way that I could see back toward the entrance.

Here he came, wandering along, looking at this and that. But where were his pals?

I didn't see them.

I proceeded to the far end of the building and joined the crowd waiting for the elevator. I watched for my tail's reflection in the marble wall . . . and saw him come around the corner looking for me.

I left the elevator crowd and took the stairs. I was the only person going up; everyone else was coming down.

I went up to the third floor, the top one, and perused the river-side galleries. There were some magnificent Impressionist paintings here, including several of the Rouen Cathedral by my favorite artist, Monet. Paying no attention to my tail, I wandered along with my hands in my pockets, absorbed in the art.

I passed the cafeteria—which was doing a land-office business—and turned the corner toward the men's room instead of going left into the gallery that led behind the huge clock.

For the first time since I entered the building, I was completely out of sight of every other person alive. I ducked into a janitor's closet and pulled the door almost shut. Looking through the crack, I could see anyone going into or coming out of the men's room.

This setup wasn't perfect, but it would have to do.

A man came out of the men's, then another. One man went in. None of the three noticed me inside the closet door, which was only open about an inch.

Three minutes passed, then four.

I was betting that my tail wasn't a pro. He had followed right along since I left the embassy without once trying to blend into the crowd. It was almost as if he wanted to be seen. Now, there was a scary thought. What if he *did* want to be seen?

What if—?

I ran out of time to contemplate the nuances. There he was! Standing at the door of the men's, trying to decide if he should go in or not.

His rabbit might not be in there. He was weighing that possibility, as I knew he must. I could have gone left instead of right.

He couldn't afford to wait to find out. Even now his rabbit might be walking out of the building. He opened the door a crack and peered in.

That was the moment I had been waiting for. His back was to me, he was concentrating on looking through the partially open door, and if he heard anyone behind him he would assume it was someone who wanted to use the restroom.

I stepped out, glanced back to ensure no one was watching, then hit him with a solid right in the side of the neck. He went down as if he had been shot.

I dragged him toward the closet and pulled him inside.

I patted him down for weapons. He had none. I snagged his cell phone and pocketed it. He had a French identity card in his shirt pocket that said he was Muhammed Nada, a resident of Marseille. I compared his face to the photo—it was him, all right.

Nada groaned. His eyes were unfocused, his muscles slack. He was going to have the sorest neck in town for a week or so, which was his tough luck. I stuck his ID card back in his shirt pocket and left him there. We had been in the closet about fifteen seconds.

As I came out of the closet there were two of them striding

toward me, young dark men, black eyes and unruly hair, no extra weight. They were sizing me up as they came—I could see it in their eyes. They made no attempt to avoid me or get out of my way. They separated just enough to get around me, and I heard one of them jerk open the closet door.

I bolted.

A couple topped the stairs and blocked the way, a portly man and white-haired woman. I spun around in time to set myself as the two Arabs raced toward me, digging hard. I went left and nailed the one on the left with a right to the jaw.

I ran back toward the cafeteria.

Now, I am a reasonably fast runner for a man of my size, and the guy who had come at me on my right side had had to reverse his momentum while his colleague went sliding face-first along the floor. Yet in two mighty bounds he was on my back, dragging me down.

I smacked my head against the floor, and that about did it for me right there. I saw stars from the impact and probably went about half out for a couple of seconds. I struggled to rise and actually got my feet under me.

Ahab the Arab was all over me. He slugged me in the face and gut, repeatedly. Through my haze I could hear a woman screaming.

I managed to latch on to one of Ahab's arms. Got him above the wrist and used his momentum to slam him into the wall. He went to the floor, temporarily stunned.

I tried to move and couldn't. With my head ringing like a bell, it was all I could do to stand there.

The woman sucked in a deep breath and screamed again.

I swayed, almost fell, and caught myself.

Ahab got it together and rose from the floor. Still sucking air and too stunned to run, I watched him produce a knife from a sheath in his pants and come at me holding it blade up. The fucker was going to gut me like a fish.

Maybe his bell was ringing, too, because he came charging as if he expected me to hold still while he ripped me from crotch to brisket. I didn't. I grabbed at the wrist that held the knife and threw him with a rolling hip lock. He went over the railing and through the opaque glass wall.

As the glass flew in every direction, he fell the long two stories to the main floor of the museum, screaming all the way. The scream ended abruptly with a serious thud.

I lost my balance and sat down hard.

The guy I had nailed with my fist, Ahab's pal, got up slowly. He took a long look at me, the hole in the glass wall, and the portly guy and out-of-air woman, then bolted down the stairs.

CHAPTER THIRTEEN

The police got my name, Terry G. Shannon, from my passport and took a statement. Fortunately for me, I had witnesses for most of it. The tourists were German, and they described the attack.

Five minutes after the police arrived, Muhammed Nada came staggering out of the janitor's closet. His neck was so stiff he couldn't turn his head. If he knew I had stolen his phone, he didn't mention it. The cops took him away for questioning.

I lied a little about ol' Muhammed. I told the detective that all three of them jumped me, and I slugged Nada first, and I didn't know where he went after that. Then I shifted to the truth: I was trying to flee but the other two persisted.

"At first I thought they intended to mug me," I said earnestly. "But now . . . I don't know. They may have been terrorists, looking for a tourist to beat up and rob for political reasons."

It was a lot of bullshit, of course, but my witnesses backed every word. They also latched on to the terror thing and ran with it.

The cops wanted to take me to a hospital; I refused. My head cleared and I was left with only a headache. I figured that with a night's sleep, I'd be good as new. An hour after the incident, they turned me loose.

They were still cleaning up the mess on the main floor when I left. Luckily the guy who did the swan dive through the clock didn't hit anybody when he arrived down below. The cop upstairs said he held on to his knife all the way down.

I hailed a taxi and rode over to the embassy. No one followed me, or if they did, they were so slick that I didn't spot them.

Jake Grafton was still in the SCIF, huddled with Sarah Houston. I told them about Muhammed Nada and presented his cell phone, and I told them about the other two.

"So one guy made a big mess on the main floor, the other dude ran, and Muhammed Nada went off to tell lies to the French police," I said in summation. "Mind if I sit down?"

Grafton took a look at my noodle while Sarah got the telephone numbers from Nada's cell phone. "Got a nice goose egg there," he said. "I thought I told you not to get hurt or hurt them badly."

"I tried."

"Lucky for you there were only three of them," Sarah said over her shoulder, without looking around.

"I'm slowing down as I get older. Happens to everybody."

My hands were still shaking from the adrenaline overdose and I was jittery. Sitting quietly watching Sarah work seemed to help. My headache gradually eased, too.

"Keep your eyes peeled for those guys," Grafton said. "They may try again."

I thought about that awhile. The problem, as usual, was that Grafton doesn't tell people what's going on. *He* knows, but he doesn't tell. Of course, a guy could always ask. I thought about that, about the pros and cons. It's not that Grafton is intimidating, either physically or morally. It's just that . . . well, he's the admiral, if you know what I mean.

I sat there thinking about things and worked myself up to it. "What's going on here, Admiral?" I asked.

He gave me a look, sort of measuring the height and width and breadth of my soul. "A lot of people want to know about Rodet's spy."

"What was in the note you gave him?"

"The name of the spy."

I guess I must have gaped. "Where did you get the name?"

A slow grin spread over Jake Grafton's face. "If I tell my secrets I won't have any."

That was a pretty snarky answer, if you ask me. Still, I could see that he wasn't going to say any more, so I dropped the subject.

Grafton managed to smile for Carmellini, but he wasn't feeling chipper. The fact of the matter was that he didn't know whether or not he knew the spy's name. Sure, the CIA database had coughed up a name from an interrogation—they hadn't told him the name of the informant or how the information was obtained or who the interrogator was, all information necessary to properly evaluate the intelligence. And yes, the name had been used by a known Al Queda lieutenant who someone else said had once attended the Sorbonne.

Even if Henri Rodet had known an Algerian named Abu Qasim once upon a time when they both were young, and Qasim had attended the Sorbonne, that didn't make Qasim a spy. Yet the Sorbonne had no record of Qasim under any of the names he was reputed to use. Henri Rodet certainly had the reach to make university records disappear, he reflected, and there was no reason to do that unless one wanted to eradicate evidence that Abu Qasim had ever existed.

Rodet could have had Professor Heger killed . . . could have done it himself, for that matter. Or Qasim could. But why? Because the professor knew Qasim's name?

It was possible, Jake concluded. So he had written Abu Qasim's name on a slip of paper and passed it to Rodet, who didn't bother to look at it in Jake's presence.

If Rodet called and wanted to talk, then Grafton would know.

And he would only be on first base. What Grafton really wanted—needed—was access to the intelligence Qasim was giving Rodet. If he was.

Why wasn't Rodet cooperating with Western intelligence?

One thing was for certain: With the arrest of the Veghel gang, the secret was out. Middle Eastern men had picked up him and Carmellini when they left the Conciergerie;

Carmellini had someone's agent living in the apartment under him—and then there were Claude Bruguiere and Professor Heger, shot in the head. Maybe the foreign powers didn't yet suspect Rodet of having a spy, but everyone knew Al Queda had sprung a leak somewhere.

Rodet must have known what would happen when he told George Goldberg about the Veghel bunch, and yet he did it anyway.

Jake Grafton looked at the calendar. The G-8 summit was next week. He took a deep breath and exhaled slowly. Maybe there was no intelligence to share. Perhaps that was the answer. He hoped it was.

It was a pleasure watching Sarah work on the computer. It only took her thirty-five minutes to hack into the main telephone records and come up with names and addresses for the telephone numbers from Nada's phone.

When she finished, Jake Grafton took the computer printout and studied it. Finally he lowered it and looked at Sarah. "Why don't you and Tommy go to dinner? A nice restaurant, very public, so everyone can see you. Look happy."

"Is this part of the assignment?" Sarah asked with a frown. I swear, that woman could squeeze the romance from a wedding cake.

"Yes," Grafton assured her.

"So Uncle Sugar is paying the bill?" I asked brightly, even though I knew the answer.

"You're on per diem," Grafton said flatly. Yep, that was the answer I knew.

"I had the dining room at the George V in mind, but I guess that's out," I remarked sadly. Sarah was looking at my reflection in the glass behind her computer. "How about a Big Mac and fries?" I said.

"I know a place," she replied, and turned off her cyberbox.

Amazingly, my headache had disappeared. The prospect of spending the evening with a beautiful woman always perks me up.

The place Sarah knew was a bateau that cruised the Seine.

We wound up on a dinner cruise, for which we had to pay extra. We went dutch, since we were both getting a per diem.

If there were any Middle Eastern types following us, I didn't see them. Didn't look very hard, either. We ended up at a table on the top deck. Fortunately we both wore jackets and there wasn't much wind or we would have frozen.

Sarah was attentive—not flirtatious, just attentive. She listened to every word I had to say, looked into my eyes, didn't even mention work or computers or the events of the day. I watched the wind play with her hair and told her she was lovely. She smiled.

After dinner we had a liqueur, then danced to a combo that played slow jazz as the boat made the return journey down the river toward its berth on the quay below the Eiffel Tower. Sarah felt good in my arms. Very good. We were young, this was Paris, and that night the future seemed to stretch away toward a glowing horizon.

As Grafton walked back to his apartment, he thought through the problem one more time. Rodet's agent must be someone he had known a long time. If it wasn't Qasim, it was someone else he had known from Algeria or his school days.

Qasim's name had never appeared in any of the DGSE's official traffic, encrypted or unencrypted. Of course, spies are routinely given code names, but none of the code names that the DGSE used seemed to match an agent with an ear in Al Queda councils. None of the employees of the agency, some of whom had been on the CIA payroll for years, had ever mentioned such an agent, nor even said they suspected that such a person might exist.

If Rodet had an agent, when did Rodet hold his hand? Spying is the most solitary of the human occupations, and one of the most dangerous. A spy alone was a case of a paranoia waiting to happen; controllers needed to hold their spies' hands occasionally, tell them that they were doing fine, that all was well, their work was valuable and the nation appreciated the sacrifice that the spy was making. When and where did Rodet hold hands with Qasim?

Grafton climbed the stairs to his flat and inserted the key in the door. As he was fumbling with it, he heard the telephone ringing, then Callie's voice.

He opened the door and closed it behind him.

The telephone was in the kitchen. He walked toward her voice. Callie saw him, then said, "Here he is now."

She listened for a few seconds, then held out the telephone to Jake. He raised his eyebrows.

"A man," she said silently, moving her lips.

He took the telephone and held it to his ear.

"Jake Grafton."

"We talked this morning at my office, Admiral. Perhaps it would be beneficial if you and I took time tomorrow for a personal chat."

Rodet!

D inner was the first meal Callie had fixed in her Paris apartment, so she tried to keep it simple—and elegant. The wine merchant in the next block selected a bottle of wine that he assured her was superb, at a reasonable price.

Jake was in a good mood, so dinner went well. He smiled and complimented her on her efforts and raved about the wine. It was all very pleasant, although she knew he didn't know a mediocre wine from a good one. Jake Grafton was a beer man.

After dinner he wanted real, American coffee, though, as he always did. Machines capable of making American-style coffee were unavailable in Europe, so Callie had mailed herself a new Mr. Coffee still in its box before she left the States.

Jake took an experimental sip of the hot, black brew and sighed contentedly.

An hour later they were walking on the boulevards, enjoying the sights and sounds of Paris, when Callie asked, "Why did you bring Tommy Carmellini to France, anyway?"

"Don't you like him?"

"Oh, he's all right, in a dangerous sort of way. But he's too flip, too cool."

Jake nodded. "Remember that time in Hong Kong when you were kidnapped?"

"Oh, yes."

"Carmellini volunteered to help rescue you. He didn't have to come with me."

"You never mentioned that before." She walked along in silence. "I knew he was there, but I guess I never thought about how or why he came with you."

"He's a good man to have around."

"Like Jake Grafton?"

Her husband laughed.

After the cruise boat tied up, Sarah and I had a devil of a time getting a taxi and ended up walking across the bridge and along the boulevards toward her hotel. No tail did I see. I was walking along with my hands in my pockets when she reached for my arm and held on to it. When I smiled at her, she smiled back.

I thought about kissing her in the lobby, thought I shouldn't, then did it anyway. She didn't slap me—just kissed me back, looked into my eyes and said good night.

Outside on the sidewalk I realized I was flat out of juice. Now the adventure at the museum came flooding back, and I looked around suspiciously for wild-eyed Semitic types. Didn't see any then, either.

I gave the bellman ten euros and asked him to find me a taxi.

CHAPTER FOURTEEN

When I awoke the next morning, I was so groggy it took me a long moment to get oriented. For some reason Sarah Houston was on my mind. Isn't it crazy how a woman who has shoved you out of her life can pop back into your psyche at any old time?

I tried to forget about Sarah and concentrate on the here and now. Grafton hadn't given me an assignment for today, other than checking on the guys monitoring the Rodet bugs, so I figured this might be a good time to tag along after my neighbor, Elizabeth Conner. It would be interesting, if nothing else, to learn what she did with her time when she wasn't listening on her ceiling bug to me snore or bathe. A quick squint through the infrared goggles revealed that she wasn't downstairs, so I figured she was out for her run.

I called Willie Varner. The phone at his room in the hotel rang and rang. He got it on the eleventh ring.

"Yeah." I had awakened him from a sound sleep.

"Hey, got a job for you. I need some help tailing a woman today."

"Oh, man, I ain't a mornin' person, and I got this jet lag disease, and I just got in bed an hour ago. Been tomcattin' around, y'know? How about this afternoon?"

"How about now, Willie? I need some help, man."

He consented with poor grace. I gave him the address and told him to step on it.

I scrubbed the molars and got dressed as quickly as I

could. I actually put on three shirts, each atop the other, and finished off with a hooded sweatshirt. The sweatshirt had a pocket in front, so I stuffed a baseball cap in there. I was putting on my shoes when I heard her door slam. She was back.

She was in the shower when I loaded my goodies in my backpack, stuffed my digital camera in my pocket, put on my windbreaker and shades, and locked the door behind me. The day was terrific—clean, clear and crisp, with a pleasant breeze in the street. The red, shiny Vespa looked wanton and wicked. Man, with a toy like this and a great city to ride it in, what was I doing wasting my time on other stuff? I left it locked up. If Conner went into a subway and I had no immediate place to park the scooter, I was screwed. Nope, it looked like a walking day.

I zipped over to the parking garage and ditched my backpack in the trunk of the rental. I thought it might be safer there than in the apartment.

My first problem was picking a spot to await Conner's pleasure. There were actually three Metro stations within easy walking distance—one to the left as you departed our building and two to the right, toward the Rue du Faubourg St. Denis. The most likely station that she might use, I thought, was the Gare de l'Est, a major station where three lines converged. Leaving our street, she would turn left on the Rue du Faubourg and walk two blocks to the Metro station, which was, of course, immediately in front of the railroad station. From the Gare de l'Est Metro station she could take the 4 train to the Left Bank, Sorbonne district. Or she could turn right on the Rue du Faubourg and go down a couple of blocks, then a block over to the Château d'Eau station on the Rue de Strasbourg, which was also on the 4 train line.

I was standing in a doorway, two doors down the street from my building in the opposite direction from those two stations, trying out my French on two hookers, when a taxi rolled up and stopped. Willie Varner got out. He paid the cabbie, then stood looking around. He saw me and came sauntering toward us. A big grin spread across his face when he got a good look at the girls.

"You didn't tell me you were livin' in a hot neighborhood, Carmellini."

"I'm a man of mystery."

"What you are is a guy who don't tell his friends shit."

He settled himself, sort of squaring his shoulders, grinning at the women. I got him by an elbow and led him gently away. "The subject is a cute American girl, about five five or so, athletic, brunette. You got a phone?"

He patted his pocket and gave me the number. Heck, it was a long distance call, clear to America. "That thing work over here?" I asked.

"Oh, yeah. Called my girlfriend on it."

I put his number into my cell phone and then put mine into his. "All you have to do," I explained, "is punch the 1 button just once and it'll ring my phone. Got it?"

"I dial any other numbers, anything like that?"

"Just push that 1 button once."

"Okay."

His eyes were slightly bloodshot, he had bags under his eyes, and he looked a little run-down. "You doing okay?" I asked.

"Oh, yeah. Just partyin' hard, y'know. Don't figure I'll ever get back this way again so I'm havin' my fling now courtesy of Uncle Sugar and the loyal taxpayers back to home. America's a great country."

"She should be coming out any minute," I said, anxious to get him briefed before the subject appeared. "If she turns this way, I want you to trot inside and stay out of sight, so she doesn't see you. Stay out of sight until I motion for you."

"Yeah."

"She knows me. You keep her in sight and I'll keep you in sight. If you have any problems, or lose her for even an instant, call me."

"Call you what, Terry or Tommy?"

"Just call me."

He was running his mouth about his adventures last night when I noticed two dark men talking to a hooker several doors down the street. I was looking at them in profile. Were they Arabs? Their clothes were nondescript; they were perhaps in their twenties, clean-shaven—

Just then Conner popped out of the door of our building, seventy-five feet down the street. I forgot about the Arabs. Sure enough, she turned right, toward the Rue du Faubourg. She was wearing a red jacket, slacks and sensible heels. She had her purse, which was actually more like a tote bag, slung carelessly over one shoulder. No hat. She walked like the fit, athletic woman she was.

"That's her," I told Willie.

"Okay." And away he went. I wished the gals a speedy au revoir, flipped the hood of my sweatshirt up to hide most of my face, and followed him.

I can't help it—I like following people. It's an art, really, tailing someone through a large city without letting them know you are behind them. An art, sport and secret trade. Not that I'm great at it, because I'm not. I'm probably about average as tailers in the spook business go, although I enjoy the work a little too much.

The problem was that ol' Lizzie Conner knew me on sight. One half-decent gander at me would ruin the game. She was way too smart to buy the coincidence thing, so we had to do it right or say good-bye. And I liked that, too.

She headed for the Gare de l'Est, which presented its own problems. I kept Willie in sight, hoping he didn't get too close. Of course, he didn't have a lot of experience at this, but he was the best I could get. The other guys were monitoring bugs for Grafton, which was probably a lot more important than finding out where Conner shopped or went to class.

She went down the steps into the subway and I saw Willie follow along. When I came down the stairs he was buying tickets at the booth. She wasn't in sight. He turned around, ticket in hand, saw the look on my face and shrugged.

He went through the turnstile and started down the stairs to the 5 train platform. "She go that way?" I called.

"I dunno," he answered. "I didn't have a goddamn ticket."

"Try the 4 train." I pointed. "Going downtown."

He trotted that way and disappeared down the stairs.

Jesus! Talk about a couple of incompetents! And I didn't know she was going downtown—I was just guessing. If she wasn't going to the Sorbonne, she could be on any of these six platforms. Oh, man! I wasn't going to tell Grafton about this one!

I followed Willie down the stairs. I stood on the stairway watching as he looked around, found her, then wandered over to the magazine rack. As he fooled around, pretending to look at magazines and actually keeping tabs on her, I decided I shouldn't have telephoned him this morning; he was having his problems following this woman onto a subway train. He was easy to miss in a crowd, sure, but if she didn't eventually spot the Wire, she wasn't the competent intelligence professional I thought she was.

Scanning the crowd, I looked for Arabs or North Africans who might be interested in me or Conner or Willie. Didn't see any. That isn't a politically correct remark, I know, but after my little adventure in the museum yesterday I was looking for swarthy faces. I saw some, too, although they didn't evince the slightest interest in Willie or me or Conner.

When I heard the train, I kept my eyes on Willie. He was glancing at Conner from time to time. The train stopped and the doors opened. He waited . . . I hoped he waited for Conner to board, but who knew? After a bit he wandered over to the train and got into a middle car. I waited five more seconds, then went for the last one. The door was closing on me as I stepped aboard.

The door slammed behind me, and the train got under way.

Now I had to find Willie, get him in sight, and hope he was cool enough to keep an eye on her and not get spotted.

The train slowed for a station, Château d'Eau, where she could have boarded this train. Willie stayed seated.

Another station, Strasbourg St. Denis, then two more, and in just another minute the train was pulling into the Les Halles station. This was a huge station, probably the biggest in Paris. If Willie lost sight of her in here . . .

He was getting up, leaving the car. I did, too, taking care not to turn toward Conner and Willie. I had the hood of the sweatshirt up, and with luck, she wouldn't recognize me if she didn't see my face.

A glance and I picked up Willie. He was going up a set of stairs. I followed.

She wound her way up and over and ended up on the platform for the 1 train to the west, toward La Défense. I risked a look around a column. There she was, reading a paperback as she waited. She was waiting to board the rear of the train. Willie stood in the middle. That left the front for me, as if I had a choice.

The train pulled in, and she got aboard. Willie climbed on, and so did I.

She wouldn't go far. She was changing trains to spot us, then she was going to ditch us and go on her way. I figured she would change again at the Concorde station, and sure enough, she did.

This time she stood in the middle of the platform waiting for the 8 train eastbound, toward Créteil-Préfecture. Willie wanted the aft end of the platform. I joined him so I wouldn't have to pass her.

"She's jivin' us," he muttered.

"Yeah."

She got on, and away we went. I got my pocket map of the subway system out and scanned it. My guess was that she would ride to the end of the line, watch me and Willie get off the train, then reboard for the trip back into the city. There wouldn't be many folks wanting to ride right back. We could either get back on the train with her or call it a bad day.

When she didn't get off the train at the last station where she could change lines, Daumesnil, I was pretty sure. "You stay aboard," I whispered to Willie. "She's going to the end of the line and catch this train back into town. Just stay with her. Call me when you start back to town. If she loses you, check in with me. Got it?"

"Okay."

I got off at the next stop, Michel Bizot, and walked up the stairs. The doors closed behind me and the train pulled out. I ran to the top of the stairs and waited. No Elizabeth Conner. She had stayed on the train.

I ditched the sweatshirt in a trash can and pulled on my baseball cap. Then I walked over to the eastbound platform and sat down to wait. Two French kids standing against the wall had a boom box and were serenading us with rap. It's everywhere these days.

A train pulled in and everyone on the platform except me got on. Blessed silence.

The minutes ticked slowly by. The longer I sat there, the angrier I got. Elizabeth Conner was playing me for a sucker. She broke into my apartment, listened to me on a wall mike, scribbled secret messages to God knows who, and now was riding the trains through Paris reading a novel and laughing her pretty little ass off. At me. Because I couldn't figure out what the hell was going down!

I climbed the stairs and went out on the sidewalk. France stretched away in every direction. I got out my cell phone and checked the battery charge.

The time had come to play a hunch. I punched up my list of numbers, found the one I wanted and pushed the button. Two rings, then a male voice answered.

"Hey."

"Hey your own self," I said. "Who else is there?"

"Just Al."

"That girlfriend of Rodet's. She still in the apartment?"

"Getting ready to leave, I think. She was talking to the maids about vacuuming while she was out."

"Is there a limo waiting?"

"Not down front."

"Tail her. You and Al. Don't lose her, and call me. I want to know where she goes."

"Okay."

I snapped the phone shut, then opened it again. I pushed the 1 button and listened to the ring.

"Yo."

"Where are you?"

"Damn if I know, man. Somewhere in France, I figure, out here ridin' through the suburbs. We're aboveground now."

"Get off at the next stop, get a cab, tell the driver to take you back to your hotel."

"You know how goddamn much that'll cost?"

I wasn't in the mood. "It isn't your money, Willie. But if you don't have the jack on you, walk back or take the subway."

He started to reply but I closed the phone and shut him off. There was a taxi sitting by the curb; I walked over and got in.

Talk to me," Jake Grafton said to Sarah Houston. She was sitting at a computer keyboard in the SCIF in the basement of the American embassy, so he pulled a chair around and sat where he could see her face.

"The key logger Tommy installed gave me the passwords to Rodet's computer and his files," she said, glancing at Grafton, "and the e-mail addresses to get in to two other computers he owns, one at the apartment on the Rue des Vosges, the other a laptop that either he or Marisa Petrou uses occasionally. I've managed to search the hard drives of all three computers."

"And?"

"None of the three is used to communicate with any secret agent anywhere."

Jake Grafton made a face. "I had hopes," he said.

"Don't we all?"

"How about encrypted e-mail?"

"Nothing long enough to contain a secret message—with, of course, the exception of unsolicited junk e-mail, but that stuff gets filtered out, and no one has ever done anything with those files, as far as I can tell. There is nothing on the hard drives to show that the junk has ever been processed."

"The Bank of Palestine investment?"

"The computer at the apartment is used to track three investment portfolios, all belonging to Rodet. If he owns a share of stock in the Bank of Palestine, there is not even a hint of it on that machine."

"So how does Rodet send and receive messages to his agent in Al Queda?"

Sarah didn't reply.

Grafton sighed. If he didn't use some kind of electronic communications, that left the regular mail. Who writes letters these days? Grafton thought that eventually long, chatty letters would arouse suspicions somewhere, especially in this day and age.

So what did that leave? Well, it left the entire world of third person com, couriers, dead drops, microdots, all of that. And yet, if that was indeed the method by which Rodet and his agent communicated, that meant there was a third person who knew the secret. That third person—if there was a third person, who was it? Someone who worked for the DGSE? Rodet's estranged wife? His girlfriend? Perhaps one of the agent's relatives who traveled back and forth fairly regularly.

If there was a third person, anyone really searching would find him or her. That fact alone suggested that the mysterious third person did not exist.

So what method did that leave?

The aerial photo of Rodet's château was pinned to the wall over Sarah's desk. Jake pulled the pins out, took the print down and studied the photo.

Henri Rodet told his secretary he was going to lunch and walked out of his office. In the courtyard he ignored the limo that was his to command and asked for an agency car. He got in and drove out the gate, turning right on the street.

He checked his rearview mirror at the first light, and the second. No one seemed to be following. Flowing with traffic, he drove to the large parking facilities that served the Pompidou Center and went in. There were four possible exits. He went straight though the building, ensuring that no cars were behind him, and exited.

He parked in a small lot near the Boulevard Richard Lenoir and walked. Ten minutes later he entered a modest restaurant. The staff were still cleaning and preparing for the luncheon crowd.

"Ah, Steuvels. *Bonjour*. Good to see you again."

"And you, Monsieur Rodet."

"Steuvels, I am expecting a friend, an American. He will be along in a little while, and I wondered if we might have one of your private rooms upstairs?"

"Pardon, monsieur, but they are not ready for lunch. You understand, we use them only in the evenings . . ."

"It doesn't matter. This is a private meeting."

"But of course. Come, follow me, and we will make a few preparations. What is your friend's name?"

"Grafton."

In the small room, which was just big enough for a table, eight chairs and a sideboard, Rodet had an excellent view out the window. He moved back in the room so that someone outside could not see him.

The day was bright; a square of light fell upon the table.

A waiter knocked, then bustled in with bottled water and two glasses.

"A beer, *s'il vous plait*," Rodet said.

When the waiter left Rodet loosened his tie and settled back to wait.

He and Qasim had had their last meal together in a brasserie in the Latin Quarter. The brasserie was gone now—the owner had a heart attack ten, no, fifteen or so years ago. These days the business on that corner sold ice cream to tourists.

Qasim had fallen in love with Paris. Rodet tried to talk him out of going to Egypt. "You don't need to do this," he said. "This isn't your fight."

Qasim didn't argue. He took tiny sips of wine and ate slowly, savoring every bite.

Rodet found that it was difficult to argue with a man who refuses to speak, so he gave up. He drank wine and watched people come and go and listened to conversations swirling around them.

When he had finished eating, Qasim ordered the best bottle of wine in the house. The proprietor brought it out reverently and opened it before them. Qasim took an experimental sip, then nodded his approval.

As the conversational hubbub engulfed and surrounded them, he spoke softly, so Rodet had to lean in to hear. "It will be a long time before I write to you. I'll write to your grandmother. In the letter a place will be mentioned. That will be where I am. Eventually, when it is safe, we will meet somewhere. I will tell you the place and time."

"It would be best if all our communications are in code."

"I understand. That will come later, when I have something to tell you. We must wait. The longer we wait, the more they trust me. The more they trust me, the more damage we can do them."

Rodet nodded.

"It is important that you understand, Henri. I may not survive. The Egyptian police may beat me to death or the fundamentalists may kill me. What happens will be God's will. But if God wants me to survive, it will be because He wants me to destroy these people."

Rodet drank more wine and said nothing.

"You see, I am a holy warrior at heart. Islam is the religion for warriors. A man must accept God in his heart and submit to His will. The rest is only details."

Rodet did see. He did not understand, but he saw the iron in the man before him.

They talked and talked until the wine was gone. Mostly Qasim talked and Rodet listened. In his new life as a spy, Qasim could only survive if he said very little, and then nothing that revealed the inner man. So now he talked freely, as if saying good-bye to himself.

He left the next day for Egypt. Rodet waited for several days, then followed along behind. When the Frenchman reached Cairo, Qasim was already in jail. Rodet didn't ask about him, but he saw the lists and found his new name.

Yes, he had to have a new name. Too many people knew Abu Qasim, philosophy student.

Months later Rodet failed to find the name on the newest

list. He didn't know if Qasim had died or been released. That was when the reaction to Qasim's choice hit him the hardest. Abu Qasim, he realized, was the greatest human being he had ever met. In an era when most people refused to get involved, Abu Qasim was willing to give his life for what he believed in.

The waiter knocked, breaking Rodet's chain of thought. Now the door opened and the waiter stuck his head in. "Monsieur Grafton."

"Show him in, *s'il vous plait.*"

S he's out and walking, Tommy."
    I was sitting in a taxi near the Gare de l'Est. The meter was running and my driver was leaning against the front fender, smoking and chatting with a colleague who had driven the taxi parked behind us.

The voice on the phone in my ear was tinny. "She crossed the square and is walking toward the Boulevard Beaumarchais."

"Both of you are on her, right?"

"Yeah. I'm on one side of the street, Al's on the other."

"What's she wearing?"

"Nice blue and white dress, a white fur wrap of some kind—looks like a short jacket—a designer purse hanging on a strap over one shoulder, and shoes with modest heels."

"Don't lose her and don't let her burn you."

"Comments like that are not productive, Tommy."

I tried to think of something snotty to say, couldn't and flipped the telephone shut. When I didn't move, the taxi driver lit another cigarette. He and the other driver were arguing politics, I think. I half turned so I didn't have to look at them, and checked the mirrors. There was a car parked about a hundred feet behind us containing three men. They were illegally parked too close to the corner. I couldn't make out their features, and I didn't want to turn around to look. It was a newer car, a dark sedan.

I tried to ignore them. On the seat beside me was a newspaper, probably left there by the cabbie's last passenger. The photo on the front cover caught my eye—a nice shot of the busted clock in the Musée d'Orsay. There was another shot of the guy who went through the clock, lying on the floor with a sheet over him. The reporter had used only two *n*s in Shannon. Since that wasn't my real name, I wasn't upset. Nor was I moved to save the article for my scrapbook.

There was also an article on the front page of the paper about the meeting next week of the G-8 leaders at the Château de Versailles, the Sun King's shack in the suburbs. Poverty in Africa and global warming were the issues of the day, not Islamic Nazis or terrorism. As you might expect, rock stars, tree huggers, anarchists, fundamental Christians and other socially committed, unhappy folks were planning huge demonstrations to protest almost everything. Already they were pouring into town; the hotels were filling up fast.

Last year French president Jacques Chirac caused a rumpus on the eve of the conference in Scotland by lambasting British cuisine. This year he was tut-tutting over hamburgers and hot dogs. I was deep into Chirac's explanation of the relationship between barbaric food and the Americans' bad attitude when the telephone rang again. As I opened it I glanced again in the mirrors. That car was still parked there.

"She's walking north on the Boulevard Beaumarchais, left side. There's a subway station a few blocks ahead, but she's dressed too nice. I think she'll catch a taxi or go into a joint right around here. Al's crossed the street."

"Un-huh," I said, trying to keep him talking.

"Oh, she's stopped to look into a window. She's checking for tails. She's hot. Let me call Al." The connection broke.

I leaned out the window and motioned to my driver. He took his time climbing in, the cigarette still dangling from his mouth, then started the engine and pulled his chariot into gear.

So she was checking for tails! That made me feel better. Running Al and Rich all over Paris was going to be difficult to explain if Marisa dropped into some boutique, bought a nightie, then went home.

As we rounded the corner I looked back. The sedan was pulling away from the curb.

My taxi sped toward the Place de la République. From there I thought we could go south toward the Boulevard Beaumarchais, and if Marisa Petrou didn't jump a cab and boogie, we'd eventually arrive in her vicinity. Like all plans, this one was subject to instant revision.

We had just about reached the Place de la République, the sedan following faithfully, when the phone rang again.

"She's walking west on Rue St. Gilles. I told Al to go up a block and parallel us. That way he's out of her visual universe."

"What the hell is this? NASA? Where'd you learn phrases like that, anyway?"

"I used to be somebody. 'Bye."

I looked at my map. "Boulevard du Temple," I told the driver. Like many European cities, the French renamed their avenues every few blocks. This one was soon to turn into the Boulevard des Filles du Calvare, then the Boulevard Beaumarchais. No doubt there was a logical reason for naming streets this way, once upon a time, but whatever it was, it has been lost to history. These days the system sells a lot of maps to tourists and foreign spies and fills up taxicabs with people trying to get from here to there.

Marisa was staying close to home base. She might even return home, although I was betting she wouldn't. She had a meet set up, and the person she was going to meet was Elizabeth Conner.

It's nice to be certain of something you have no proof for. I suppose that's a symptom of the human condition. Proof or not, I did have a suspicion. Conner used *The Sum of All Fears* as the basis for a code. Marisa's father had had a copy of the same book. Or did he? What if it was Marisa's book? What if Marisa was the spy and not her stuffy old man?

Well, it was a theory, anyway.

"Turn here," I told the cabdriver, and pointed. I might as well get ahead of Marisa so I'd be in the neighborhood if she went to ground or flagged a cab.

The phone vibrated again. I was holding it in my hand. "Yeah."

"She's crossed the Rue de Turenne. She dawdled twice to check for tails. Don't think she made me."

"If she does, drop off and let Al take her."

"I know how to do this, Tommy."

The connection went dead. I looked behind us. Yep, we still had a tail.

Who the hell were these guys?

The cabdriver was eyeing me in his rearview mirror. "It's alright," I said in English. "I'm working for Rumsfeld."

"Rums . . . ?"

"Forget it," I said in French. "Turn left."

But if Marisa and Elizabeth Conner were spies, who were they spying for?

The phone again. "She's marching up the Rue du Parc-Royal, headed straight for the Musée Picasso."

"Stay loose. There's bound to be cabs there."

"No joke." He hung up.

"Musée Picasso," I said to my chariot driver. He didn't seem flustered or excited, so I guess he knew where it was.

"She's inside," Rich Thurlow reported. "Went in the main entrance."

"Have Al go in and keep an eye on her. How many exits does that building have?"

"I dunno."

The taxi rolled sedately alongside the sidewalk outside the front entrance and drifted to a stop. Being a fiscally prudent government employee, I gave the driver a two-euro tip. I did, however, leave him the newspaper with the nifty photos.

I called Rich as I walked across the courtyard. "Where is she?"

"The Blue Period Gallery."

As I went in the door I saw the sedan stop and two guys get out. They might have been the same two I saw on the Rue Paradis, but I didn't take the time to make sure.

The museum is a mansion from days gone by. Built in 1656, it now houses the paintings and sculptures the French government screwed out of the Picasso heirs in lieu of death taxes; a monument, if you will, to the fact that Pablo didn't know any good lawyers.

I zipped across the courtyard and up the steps of the main entrance.

When I had gone through the short queue and passed the ticket lady, I took stock. It was nearly noon. The gift shop and café were on the ground floor. I headed in that direction.

I was in the gift shop hiding behind a rack of art books when I spotted Elizabeth Conner crossing the hall, heading for the café. I snapped a photo of her with the digital camera, then called Rich on the cell phone.

"We're doing his Cubist stuff now."

"Time to fade, fella. Leave her."

"I'm gone."

One of my tails came into the lobby and busied himself with a guidebook. I got four pictures of him. He didn't seem to notice.

Six minutes later Marisa Petrou crossed the hall and went into the café. I got a three-quarter photo of her face with the zoom out as far as it would go as she went by.

With both the women in the café, I strolled toward the exit. My tail turned his back to me as I walked past.

The sedan was still at the curb with the driver inside. I made a mental note of the license number. I walked to the Metro stop and went down the stairs.

Sure enough, two of them joined me on the platform, the guy from the lobby of the museum and another one. I ignored them. When the train pulled in, I got aboard. At the very last second, as the door was closing, I got off.

They didn't make it; the train pulled out with them aboard. They stood looking at me out the window, their faces expressionless, as the train went past, one of them with his cell phone to his ear. I wondered about the reception down here in this tunnel.

I climbed the stairs, crossed over to the other platform and caught the next train going the other way.

CHAPTER FIFTEEN

Henri Rodet had little to say to Jake Grafton as they waited for their wine, which Rodet had chosen. He watched the sommelier open the bottle, sipped experimentally and said, "*Bon.*"

The sounds of the street were strangely muffled, even though the window was open a trifle, admitting just a hint of cool autumn air.

Rodet savored his wine as he scrutinized the American's face. Grafton didn't seem to mind. He glanced at Rodet from time to time, looked about the room, studied the pictures, which were original oils by unknowns, and loosened his tie. His suit, Rodet noticed, was not well made, the fit only so-so. Still, Grafton looked, Rodet thought, like a man in perfect control of himself, supremely self-confident. Ah, yes, Rodet remembered: Grafton had been a combat aviator, one of those fools who bets his life on his flying skill, again and again and again.

So what, precisely, did the American know about Abu Qasim?

They were sitting in silence, each waiting for the other to begin the conversation, when there was a knocking on the door, then the waiter entered. Rodet raised his eyebrows at Jake, who made a gesture with his hand. Rodet ordered for both of them.

When the waiter departed, Rodet said, "You wished to talk, Admiral. This is your chance."

Grafton nodded. "You have an agent in Al Queda," he said. "I came to ask you to share the information he gives you."

Rodet took his time answering. He had been thinking all morning, trying to decide the best way to handle this, and he hadn't yet reached a decision. Finally he said, "Without admitting or denying that assertion, I wish to discuss with you the delicate position anyone would be in, if, indeed, he were privy to the information of such an agent. Needless to say, secret information begins to lose its exclusivity when the circle of people with access is expanded. In the world in which we live, inevitably, sooner or later, whispers that such information exists will begin to circulate."

Grafton said nothing, merely listened.

"Then there is the information itself. The greater the revelation, the greater the temptation to put newly acquired, valuable knowledge to use. Your use of knowledge reveals that you have it. If it was acquired by spying, those who have been spied upon will inevitably begin looking for the leak."

Now Grafton spoke. "All this is true, of course, and true of every piece of secret intelligence."

"Aah, not quite. The more possible sources there are for any given secret, the smaller the probability the owner will find the leak. In the hypothetical you describe, there could only be one source."

"One?"

"Just one."

"So you have arrived at a logical absurdity," Grafton said softly. "Your spy sends you information that you cannot use for fear of endangering him. His sacrifice is for naught, his information of no practical value."

Henri Rodet reached for the wine bottle and refilled his glass. When the bottle was again sitting on the table, he lifted his glass. Over its rim, he looked at Grafton and said, "I think you understand the problem."

"I am not so sure that you do," Grafton shot back. "When you revealed the Veghel conspiracy, you knew there were going to be arrests. And there were. So now the Al Queda leaders are looking for the leak they know must be there."

From a pocket Grafton produced the cell phone that Tommy Carmellini had taken from Muhammed Nadal and slid it across the table. "On that phone are nine telephone numbers. Here is a list of the people they belong to." From an inside pocket he produced a folded sheet of paper. This, too, he pushed across the table. "All these people are Muslims living in France. We think they are Al Queda soldiers."

"Where did you get the telephone?" Rodet asked.

"My aide, Terry Shannon, and I were followed yesterday when we left the Conciergerie. Shannon recognized the man. Then Shannon was followed yesterday afternoon when he left the embassy. He took the telephone off one of the thugs and threw another through the clock at the Musée d'Orsay."

"Oh, yes," Rodet said. He had seen the photo of the clock in the newspapers earlier and read of the incident in his morning brief. "And the list?"

"You can find anything on the Internet."

Rodet let that one go by. "A few obnoxious Muslim thugs do not prove your point. Nor do they prove your hypothesis, which was the assertion that I have an agent inside Al Queda."

"I am not a lawyer and this is not a court," Grafton said. "Contemplate the situation for a moment. Someone killed Claude Bruguiere, who, as it happens, had completed a transaction at the Bank of Palestine in your name a few months ago. One might theorize that he was killed because he knew too much about that transaction, that the man who sent him to Amman killed him to shut him up. That would be you or someone who wants to smear you. If the authorities suspect you of the murder or your connection to the Bank of Palestine becomes public knowledge, you will, at the very least, be forced out of the DGSE."

Rodet said nothing.

"And there is the murder of Professor Heger of the Sorbonne. I'm sure you have seen the police report. My wife discovered the body."

"Your wife. What business did she have with Professor Heger?"

"She wanted to ask him the name of the Algerian student

who was such good friends with you twenty-five years ago, one Abu Qasim, also known as Abdullah al-Falih. Our information is that he's a big wheel in Al Queda."

"That wasn't in the police report."

The fact that Rodet hadn't denied his friendship with Qasim did not escape Grafton's notice. "She didn't think the police needed to know that fact," he replied. "If you wish to pass it on to them, please do."

Grafton stood and walked to the window. With his back to Rodet, he said, "The man who could link you to Qasim has been murdered. The man who invested in Bank of Palestine stock on your behalf has been murdered. You are in an uncomfortable position, Monsieur Rodet."

He turned to face his host. "And on top of everything, you have become a target. You don't live in a bank vault. You have an estranged wife and a mistress. The Palestinians know of your bank stock investment, as do the Israelis. The fact is probably known to every terrorist and radical thug in that corner of the world. All these people have probably heard about the arrest of the members of the Veghel conspiracy. You are in the crosshairs, Monsieur Rodet."

"Is that a threat?"

Grafton opened a hand. "Not from us. But the folks in the Middle East don't hesitate to assassinate their enemies. Sooner or later they'll come at you. It is possible that they may come at you through your family."

"I have four men guarding my wife around the clock. Marisa and I can take care of ourselves."

Grafton came back to the table, where he stood looking down at Rodet. "You are the one who should be shouting at me. You have a sleeper buried deep and you've covered his trail so well that his identity has remained a secret for twenty-five years. Twenty-five years! Then he told you of a threat that forced your hand, and you passed it to the American CIA. And someone within the CIA is dirty. He told . . . someone, and the source of the information got out. Yet you have not complained to or berated any of us Americans. Not the American ambassador, not George Goldberg, not me, no one."

Grafton put his hands on the table and leaned forward. "Who is the CIA leak? Give me his name."

Henri Rodet opened his mouth, then closed it.

They were interrupted by the knocking of the waiter and the opening of the door. Behind the waiter came another man carrying a tray.

Grafton resumed his seat. When he and Rodet were served and the wineglasses recharged, the waiters disappeared. The two men ate in silence.

When they finished, Rodet pushed his chair back and sipped on the last of the wine.

"Your man has risked his life for many years," Grafton said. "If he is not under suspicion, he soon will be. His days are numbered. Yet he knows a great deal. If we can get him alive, we can destroy these people."

"If you cut off one head the monster will grow another," Rodet muttered.

Jake Grafton pushed his chair back from the table. "I am telling you the unvarnished truth," he said. "Your secret cannot be kept. If you leave your man in place, he will eventually be ferreted out and killed."

Rodet felt a huge weight pressing on him. The risks were great, yet no worse than they had always been. What a tragedy it would be for Abu Qasim's friend, Henri Rodet, to betray him. As for Heger, he was gone and nothing could bring him back.

"No," Rodet said, so softly that he thought Grafton might not have heard it. He repeated it louder and more clearly. "No. The time is not yet arrived. I ask you to trust my judgment on this matter."

"I would, except for the fact that you are wrong. The building is on fire, and we cannot wait."

Henri Rodet shook his head from side to side. "No," he repeated.

Grafton threw up his hands. "I will ask you one more question: Do you have any credible information, from any source, that Al Queda is planning an attack on the G-8 leaders at the summit?"

"We have heard rumors, yes, dozens of them. No doubt your agency has also heard them, or similar ones. But credible information, no."

"Thanks for lunch," Grafton said, and walked out. He closed the door behind him.

I took a cab back to my place and unlocked the Vespa. I needed to lower the frustration level. I had had it up to here with spies and ex-cons who couldn't follow a beer truck to a bar.

I went buzzing off, still stewing. The day was clouding up, so maybe it would rain. That would be the perfect ending to this day, let me tell you.

I was sitting at a stoplight, the little Vespa mumbling under my butt, when I realized that there were two really tan black-haired guys sitting in an old pale blue sedan in the next lane, and they were looking me over. This was not the late-model, dark sedan that had followed me to the museum. The paint on the car was chipped and sun-bleached. The tires were bald, the muffler sounded as if it were shot and a faint cloud of noxious smoke was spewing from the tailpipe. The third world had arrived in Paris.

The light changed and I goosed my ride. I putted off, riding between cars, right down the lane stripe, just the way we used to do it back in California. This maneuver left the grungy blue car behind.

Two lights later I was sure I'd lost them. I turned left and headed over to the embassy.

Grafton was down in the SCIF in the basement, staring at the photo of Rodet's country home, which he had taped to the side of a file cabinet. Beside it was a photo taken from a helicopter or airplane of Rodet's apartment building in town.

He gave me his full attention when I told him about my morning and produced my camera. "I would like to see if the CIA can match the photos of these women and the guy who followed me with anyone in the database."

Grafton palmed the camera and examined it. "Tell me about the men who followed you."

I did. I also told him about the old blue sedan I saw at the light and gave him the plate number of that car, too. "I think they're friends of that asshole I threw through the clock."

"But you don't know?"

"No."

"The guys who followed you to the museum—they knew you made them?"

"Sure."

Grafton sat down and idly examined the camera.

"I think Marisa and Conner are Israeli agents," I told him. "That code that NSA was interested in this spring might have been used by Marisa, not her father, Lamoureux. *The Sum of All Fears* could have been the key. And Conner has a copy."

"It's possible," Grafton admitted.

"Maybe you should share this possibility with your buddy Rodet."

"Not yet."

"He might be surprised."

"I doubt it."

I guess I gaped. "You think he knows?"

Grafton's eyebrows rose and fell, and he gave a minuscule shrug.

I lost it. "Jesus, Admiral, I'm trying to do you a good job and you don't tell me where you are!"

"I'm sorry, Tommy. The truth is I'm trying to figure out the puzzle myself."

That took the air out of my sails.

Grafton pointed at the photos on the wall. "Take a good look at those photos and tell me if there is anything unusual about them."

I did as he requested. That helped me get my blood pressure and heart rate back under control. My voice was absolutely normal when I said, "Look pretty innocuous to me."

"See the satellite television dishes. There's one on the château and one on the apartment building."

"Un-huh."

"I want you to go into Rodet's apartment and inspect that system."

"Okay."

"As soon as possible," he added.

"Want to tell me what I'm looking for?"

"I want to know how Rodet talks to his agent. The guys at NSA say it's technically possible to transmit encoded transmissions via the dish to the satellite, which will rebroadcast them. Anyone with another dish can pick the transmissions up. They will appear as a burst of static on the video or audio channels. With the right equipment, the static can be separated out into the coded message. The spooks like this method of broadcasting encoded traffic because it uses a low-powered ultrawide band signal. They say it's a good LPI signal—that's a low probability of intercept. Each party needs only a computer, one small transceiver, some plug-in cables, and a satellite dish." Grafton pointed at the photos. "Rodet's got the dishes, anyway. You see if you can find the other stuff."

"Yes, sir."

"Be careful, Tommy."

"I'll get Willie to back me up. If I find the stuff, what do you want me to do with it?"

"If you can lay hands on the computer, I want the hard drive. If you can't find it, I want to know if the transceiver is there. They tell me the transceiver can be pretty small, about the size of a cell phone. Just get me some kind of confirmation or tell me I'm barking up the wrong tree."

"Yes, sir."

"Thanks, Tommy," he said.

I got up to leave. "By the way, Sarah around?"

"Next door."

"I thought I'd just stop in for a minute and say hi," I explained.

"Oh, sure."

The uniformed policeman in his kepi strolled along checking every vehicle parked around the Place des Vosges. He took his time, checked the license plate, made a note and moved on to the next. It wasn't long before he arrived at the plumbing van parked against the inner square. He looked at the plate, then went around the front to inspect the parking authorization that was taped to the windshield. That's when Alberto Salazar saw him.

"Uh-oh. A cop," he said to Rich Thurlow. "Checking the front."

"Think he'll figure out that authorization is a forgery?"

"He might."

"What are we going to do if he pounds on the door?"

"We sit tight, he'll call a tow truck to haul this damn thing off."

As they debated the issue, the policeman came to the side door and rapped sharply upon it. It was locked.

"Okay, Rich," Al said. "You speak French. Get out there and schmooze him or jump in the driver's seat."

"I figure he'll jaw a while, and then we can leave," Rich said. "We'll want to park here later. We'll do another sticker. I'd better talk to him."

"A command decision," Al said sourly. "Go to it." The policeman rapped sharply on the van while he and Rich rigged blankets over the gear and computers so they couldn't be seen. The job took about thirty seconds, no more.

"Okay, open it," Al said.

Rich did so.

The policeman looked startled when the door slid back. He stepped right to the opening and looked past Rich to Al and the blankets.

Rich was trying to get out of the van, but the policeman stood in the way. As Rich launched into his monologue, the cop looked to his right and left, then pulled his pistol and shot Rich in the head.

There wasn't much noise. The pistol had a silencer attached to the barrel, so the report was just a pop. The impact of the bullet on Rich's head catapulted him backward into the van.

Before Al Salazar could react to what he was seeing, the cop had turned the pistol is his direction. A bullet hit him in the forehead before his brain recognized the muzzle flash for what it was. He died instantly.

The policeman shot each man in the head one more time, then holstered his weapon and pulled the van door shut. He walked on along the street, inspecting vehicles, until he got to the corner, then he walked out of the square.

When I left the embassy I had some of the stuff I would need for tonight, but I needed some of the gear that was in my backpack, which I had stashed in the trunk of the rental. I putted over to the Rue Paradis, parked the Vespa and walked three blocks, keeping my eyes open for watchers. Didn't see anyone.

The car was on the second floor of the parking garage. I looked around carefully as I walked up to it.

I was about to push the button on the key fob that would unlock the trunk when a little voice whispered in my ear. Something just walked on my grave.

I didn't push the button. I stood looking at the rental, wondering.

There was a greasy fingerprint on the driver's side window. I stood looking at it, trying to recall if I had had greasy or oily hands when I drove this thing.

Little cold chills ran up and down my spine, tiny fingers of fear.

I walked as far away as I could get and still see the car. This was about fifty feet.

Hunkered down behind another vehicle, I raised the key fob over the fender, pointed it at my ride, and pushed the button.

Nothing happened.

Okay, I'm getting paranoid. Losing my courage as I get older. Another year or two of this crap and I won't be worth a nickel to anyone.

I stood up, started toward the car.

Of course, the lights didn't flash when I pushed the button—maybe I was too far away.

What the hey. I hunkered down behind a car about fifteen feet away, raised the key fob and pushed the button again.

This time the lights flashed and the horn gave a tiny beep. *Bonjour, buddy. Let's go for a ride.*

I felt like a fool. I stood up, scratched my head and looked around to see if anyone had watched my shenanigans. No one had.

Well, you can't be too careful in this business. There are old spies and bold spies, but there ain't no old, bold spies.

I had taken two steps toward the car when it blew up.

The heat and concussion bowled me over backward. That probably saved my life. The air was filled with flying pieces, which were bouncing off the roof and other vehicles and ricocheting around. Not to mention the fire and heat. I didn't wait for things to settle down—I crawled away as fast as I could go.

Once the heat and fire seemed to dissipate, I scrambled to my feet and ran. When I got to the end of the bay, I looked back.

The smoke was so thick I had to wait to be able to see. After a few seconds the visibility improved somewhat. The bomb had been under the driver's compartment. The engine and front wheels were still there, blackened and twisted, but the rest of the car was rubble, and some of it was on fire. The roof of the parking garage was scorched black and the adjacent cars looked like they had been smashed by a runaway semi. The fuel in the tank had apparently helped feed the explosion, which had been a dilly.

An inventory of my own sensitive parts showed that all was still intact.

Talk about luck!

The next thought that occurred to me was that I didn't want to spend the evening visiting with the local police. I boogied.

CHAPTER SIXTEEN

I Vespaed back to the embassy and asked around for Grafton. He was in a meeting with the Secret Service top banana, but he motioned for me to join them. After the introductions, I told them about my car.

"You weren't hurt?" Grafton asked, scrutinizing me carefully.

"I'm all right. I think the local jihadists are out to get me."

He didn't comment on that, so I continued, "The police are going to snag me sooner or later. Seeing as how I'm running around town without diplomatic immunity, you had better be thinking about what you want me to tell them." I regretted that remark five minutes later, but it felt good when I said it.

Grafton just nodded. He was calm. Too calm. His manner offended me somewhat. It wasn't his fault that someone wanted me dead, but still, I was a little peeved, and, I guess, surly.

I stomped off to the cafeteria and had some dinner and real coffee while one of George Goldberg's flunkies hunted up equipment to replace the stuff that had been in the trunk of the deceased rental car. I wondered what the Paris police would say if they found enough of that equipment to figure out what it was.

P inckney Maillard didn't say a word until he and Grafton were alone, then he said, "I have heard that Carmellini is a thief. Do you really trust him?"

Jake Grafton smiled. "With my life. And I have done just that."

Maillard zigged away in another direction. "A car bomb, the murder of a DGSE agent in the streets, Muslim thugs attacking one of our people in a museum—I have to include all this in my report to Washington."

"So do I," Jake said without inflection.

"I also have to brief Ambassador Lancaster," Maillard said. "All these incidents will go into the assessment of whether or not it is safe for the president to attend the G-8 conference."

"Which will be presented to the president," Grafton said, "who will decide if he will attend."

"That's right. In the interim Lancaster will be discussing these incidents with the French government. He'll be making his own recommendation to the State Department. I expect he'll want to talk to you before he talks to the French."

"I expect you're right," Jake said, and sighed.

After dinner, feeling somewhat better and wearing my new backpack, I rode over to Willie's hotel and called him from the lobby. Woke him up. Resting up for a night on the town, I suppose.

"Hey, dude. We're going out among them tonight. Get up and get dressed. I'm down in the lobby."

"You don't really mean that, do you?"

"We have to work."

He said a dirty word and hung up on me. I picked up a newspaper and settled into a soft chair. My hands were still shaking from the adrenaline overdose, so the paper was hard to read. Still, I couldn't miss the big story about the guy who went through the museum clock. A reporter had been to see the family, who were Palestinians. They didn't speak French, although they said their late son was learning. They denied he was a terrorist or criminal: He was a victim, they said. The authorities were lying to protect someone. The paper had a photo of the family and a photo of the recently deceased from happier times.

I flipped over to the sports, which were soccer and tennis and what the bicycle racers were doing in the off-season. I was trying to get interested when I realized the bellboy was eyeing me from the door. Another dark, Middle Eastern type.

Maybe I *was* getting paranoid. Every Arab I met wasn't planning on doing the martyr trick or looking for a throat to slit. Still, I felt like a cowboy in Comanche country. Was it racial bias? Was I a bigot, in this day and age? I felt guilty. On the other hand, someone had put a bomb in the rental and I was the fish they hoped to fry.

Of all the wonderful folks I had met in Paris, who might the guilty party be? The French Muslims? Marisa Petrou? Elizabeth Conner? Henri Rodet? The person or persons unknown who killed Claude Bruguiere? I was trying to decide when the elevator door opened and Willie Varner stepped into the lobby.

He looked around, saw me, and headed for a chair. I hopped up and headed him off. He looked tired and worn out, and it seemed as if he had lost a little weight. Not that he had a lot to lose.

"Maybe you're hitting it too hard," I told him.

"I can rest up when I get home."

When he saw the Vespa and realized that it was our ride, he groaned. "Oh, Tommy, plee-ease!"

I laughed, and he started cussing me.

Okay, the Wire still had it. He wasn't over the hill yet.

Maybe I should have told him about the car, but I didn't. No use prematurely elevating his adrenaline level. The way things were going, he might need all the juice he had before this mess was over.

Jake Grafton ate dinner with Callie in their Paris apartment. Due to the possibility that the apartment was bugged, they never discussed anything of any import there. Sometimes that habit made for quiet dinners, like this evening. He had a lot to think about.

Had Tommy ticked off the local Muslim fanatics by tossing one of their flock through the museum clock? Were they out to even the score with Tommy, or had they decided to declare war on every CIA officer in France? Or were the locals following orders from Al Queda? How probable was it that events were building toward an attempt on the life of the American president? Or another of the G-8 leaders? Or all of them? Should the president come to France or stay in the United States?

"Come on," he told Callie as she finished the last of her dinner. "Let's you and I go for a stroll."

Callie asked no questions, merely began cleaning up.

Seven minutes later, they locked the door behind them.

There was still plenty of light in the evening sky when we rode away from the hotel on the Vespa, which was working hard to carry two men. Although Willie doesn't weigh 120 pounds dressed, I'm not small. Willie wore the backpack, and he had a devil of a time staying on the seat behind me. The problem was that he didn't want to hold on to me and there wasn't much else to grab on to. In Italy the girls sit sideways behind their guy and hold on to him lightly with one hand, if they hold on at all; they just sort of perch there.

Willie wasn't perching. He finally latched on to my belt with both hands in a death grip. If he went, I was going, too. Of course, we were only going about ten miles per hour at the time.

At the second stoplight two motorcycles turned and fell in behind me, one in the right rear and one in the left. The riders were wearing full-face visors on their helmets, so I couldn't see any facial features. They didn't look like big men, though. Medium size, maybe 140 or 150 pounds, lean and wiry, dressed in jeans, motorcycle jackets and leather gloves. They were mounted on Japanese bikes, apparently ones with decent engines. They could ride circles around our scooter with those things.

They stayed behind us, just following along as we rode through heavy traffic and stopped at each light.

When I putted away from the third light, dragging those

two along in formation, I said to Willie, "At the next light, bail off. I'll pick you up right here in an hour."

"What's wrong?"

"We have company," I replied, and for the first time I felt him turn to look back.

He didn't say anything, and the scooter was coming to a halt, he vaulted off the end. Willie Varner dishes out a lot of bullshit, yet when the chips are down, he's a guy you want in your corner. I watched him walk over to the sidewalk and turn, cross his arms, and look at the two dudes. The motorcyclists shot each other a look and stayed on their bikes. Willie's move had been unexpected, yet it was me they were after.

The light changed and I fed gas to the scooter. Without Willie's weight on the back, it fairly leaped ahead. Away we went, still in formation.

My mind was racing a mile a minute, even if my steed wasn't. If these clowns had guns, they could shoot me out of this saddle, race away and abandon the motorcycles somewhere, and they would be nearly impossible to find and convict. If they had guns. If the motorcycles weren't registered to them.

These thoughts were running through my mind as we rolled through traffic.

Darn, why didn't I get a motorcycle instead of this darn scooter? It had a puny engine and handled differently than a cycle. I spent a lot of my youth in California with a motorcycle between my legs and knew how to ride one of those. But a scooter?

Well, let's show 'em how we do traffic in L.A.

As we approached a light, I aimed the scooter between two rows of cars and kept going. In the mirrors I saw my riding buddies hesitate, then fall into trail.

I rode right up to the red light, dodged through the pedestrians without slowing, hung a hard right, and gave 'er the gun. Nearly got flattened by a delivery truck—managed to pass it on the right with two inches to spare and get in front of the thing.

I didn't wait to see how my friends were progressing but kept the hammer down, got in the crease and wound up that little engine.

We were flying down a boulevard—I don't know which one—toward the river. Traffic thinned and I caught a glimpse in my mirrors of the two bikes behind me, closing the gap.

A yellow light ahead! It turned red and the traffic on my left began to move. I beat the flow by a few feet.

Over the blatting of the engine I heard horns blaring and brakes squealing, then *whap!* A glance in the mirror . . . One of the motorcycles was down. With a little luck, the rider was on his way to frolic with the virgins. The other was right behind me, though.

I shot across the Seine with the remaining motorcycle inches from my fender.

We got a green light and the guy decided to see if he could dump me. He hit my rear fender with his front tire and I almost lost it. Fishtailed and goosed it while he backed off a trifle to stay up.

I shot right and tapped the brake and he was beside me. He looked my way, and for the first time, through his clear visor, I got a glimpse of his face, a mask of concentration. When you're out to kill a man you'd better work at it.

I aimed for the crease in traffic ahead—their brake lights were on—and goosed it just as the other rider glanced ahead.

He was too late! He was going to pile into the rear of that truck—but *no!* At the last split second the bastard saved it and fell in immediately behind me, three feet behind my taillight.

We shot down the boulevard between the cars, which were rolling right along. The quarters were too tight for him to use his speed and handling advantage, which was the only thing keeping me alive. I figured if I went down, I'd be dead before he rode away.

But maybe not. Maybe I should stop and break the bastard's neck with my bare hands. That would probably darken Jake Grafton's day and earn me a trip to a French penitentiary, but if it was that or the graveyard, I was willing.

Not yet. That was my hole card.

With my luck the dude would have a gun in his pocket and drill my silly self while I was trying to kung fu him.

These thoughts zipped through my mind while we shot down the traffic canyon between the rows of speeding cars and trucks. Once some Frenchie in a little van decided to change lanes and almost made a grease spot out of me. I saved it by the thickness of the skin on the knuckles of my right hand.

The guy behind me bumped my fender with his tire on three occasions, but he was trying to stay up and didn't put enough oomph on it.

As we came to an intersection where the traffic was stopped and cars were crossing, I knew I'd never make it. I darted to my right between two cars, slammed on the brake, then squeezed the scooter between two parked cars and got up on the sidewalk, hooked a U-ie and started back the way I'd come.

My maneuver had been unexpected enough that I put a serious amount of distance between us. The only problems were the human obstacles on the sidewalk . . . and the fact that my riding partner had a faster machine. I swerved violently a time or two to avoid pedestrians, yet they parted like the Red Sea for the guy roaring up behind me.

He looked like a runaway Freightliner in my rearview mirrors.

I was running out of sidewalk. I slammed on the brakes and swerved to avoid a light pole. Skidded out into the street and almost got flattened by a big Mercedes. Looked back just in time to see my pal hit the light pole dead center. He went over the handlebars and tried to drive his head through the thing.

At a glance, it appeared that the impact broke his fool neck.

My engine stalled. As I stood there pushing on the button and goosing the throttle, I could distinctly hear the *ooh-aah, ooh-aah* of a police siren.

Thankfully the tiny engine of my faithful steed fired before I flooded it. I putted off with traffic and took the first corner in order to quicken my disappearance. As my heartbeat began to slow, I noticed that I had broken the front brake hand lever—ripped it from the bracket that held it. It was dangling by its cable.

Willie was waiting for me where I left him. I pulled up to the curb, and he walked over to the Vespa.

"It took you long enough."

"Sorry," I said.

"They get tired of chasing you?"

"I think so. Hop on."

He climbed aboard. "What's going on, anyway, Tommy?"

"As if I knew," I told him. Man, I didn't have a clue. I just hoped Jake Grafton did.

As we rode through Paris I looked for holy warriors on Hondas but didn't see any. Now, however, I saw cops. Several of them glanced at the Vespa, but they didn't wave me over. I thought they might have heard about the Vespa that had run from the motorcyclists, yet if so, they were probably watching for a scooter with one man aboard.

We rode into the Place des Vosges and I parked the scooter in a motorcycle farm. I left it unlocked on the off chance that some idiot would steal it. Lost my enthusiasm for motor scooters, I guess. I wasn't having much luck with cars, either.

The van was parked in the usual place. "Wait here," I told Willie. I approached it from an angle that would shield me from any watchers sitting on benches in the park.

As I reached to rap on the side of the van, I saw that the door was slightly ajar. The fire alarm went off in my head.

Frozen, I stood with hand outstretched, listening. I leaned forward and put my ear up to the side of the thing.

Quiet as a tomb in there. Plenty of street noise, but nothing from inside.

Call it a premonition; I grabbed the door handle and jerked it open. The first thing I saw was a shod foot. Then another. I peered into the crowded interior. Al and Rich were there, and they were dead.

CHAPTER SEVENTEEN

Alberto Salazar had a small wet red hole in his forehead, a little off center, and a hole above his left ear. His face wore a surprised look. His arm was twisted up over his head. Apparently he had fallen off the stool, already dead, and his arm had caught on something and been pulled into the position where it was now.

Rich Thurlow sat facing the door with two holes in his forehead, about an inch apart. I could just make out the traces of powder around one of them. The gun had been nearly against his head for that one. Amazingly, he still had his glasses on.

I turned and found Jake Grafton standing there. He knew something was horribly wrong from the expression on my face. He took a step around me and looked inside the van.

Now he reached in and grasped Rich's hand. He kneaded it, then released it and pulled the door shut. "They haven't been dead long," he muttered. He turned to me. "How long have you been here?"

"Seconds. The door wasn't locked."

Jake Grafton walked away from the van about twenty feet to a place where he could see most of the park benches. I followed him. There were the usual tourists with cameras, and lots of couples—Parisians, apparently—out enjoying the evening. The nannies with prams one saw here in the afternoon were gone. Our DGSE man was also missing. The old man from the Levant was not here, either.

Grafton took his time looking at the cars, the people, the

facades of the buildings. He scanned the whole area, missing nothing.

"Do you have your cell phone?" he asked.

"Yes."

"I'll be your lookout. Go search Rodet's apartment."

"Okay."

I checked to see where Willie was and saw Callie Grafton standing near him. Both were watching us. I motioned to Willie; he came over and gave me my backpack.

I crossed the street, heading for the park and the building on the other side of the square.

Callie Grafton saw Tommy Carmellini walk away, and she saw her husband motion to her. She joined him and the black man by the van.

"Willie Varner, my wife, Callie," Jake said. He continued without a pause. "The men inside this thing have been murdered. I don't want the French seeing the equipment in there. Willie will drive the van back to the embassy. Callie, would you go with him and show him the way? Use your pass to get the van into the basement of the building."

She was staring at Jake, still trying to process what he had told her, when she felt herself nodding yes.

He gave a curt nod, glanced at Willie, and said, "The keys are in it. Go now." He touched his wife on the arm and turned away. She stood rooted watching his back as he looked right and left, then crossed the street, walking toward the park. She saw him remove his cell phone from his pocket and dial it as he walked.

Trying to keep her composure, she walked around the van and tugged at the handle on the passenger door. It was locked. She waited. The black man got behind the wheel and glanced once over his shoulder; then she heard the door click. She opened it and climbed in.

It took two tries to get the door firmly closed. Callie looked behind her. She found herself staring at the open, dead eyes that were focused on infinity.

She turned around and sat looking forward.

◆ ◆ ◆

At this point in my Paris vacation I was beginning to get nervous. I figured the holy warriors who followed me into the museum were out for my scalp. The artist who installed a bomb under my rental car certainly had something on his mind. Perhaps the bellboy at Willie's hotel called his pals from the mosque when he saw me sitting in his lobby, obviously still alive, and they came zipping over on motorcycles to get their pound of flesh. On the other hand, vengeance didn't seem to be the motive of the shooter who iced Rich Thurlow and Alberto Salazar. He *knew* that U.S. agents were sitting in that van, and he didn't want them listening to the doings across the street at Henri Rodet's apartment.

Rich and Al had each been shot in the head, and their heads didn't explode: That meant the weapon was small caliber or a low-powered 9 mm, something that could be silenced. No one on the sidewalk had called the police; it was probable that no one heard the shots.

What didn't the bad guys want Rich and Al to hear?

These questions ran through my mind as I walked through the park toward Rodet's apartment building. I didn't have a gun. CIA illegals running around France aren't armed. It's France, for Christ's sake!

And where was the DGSE watcher? Was this his day off? Or was he sleeping somewhere with a hole in his head?

I was waist deep in the Okefenokee Swamp. There were alligators in here, and they were obviously hungry.

The streetlights were on now; the sidewalks contained the usual number of tourists and locals—no one in sight that I knew. I crossed the street and walked into the entrance to Rodet's building. The security door that was normally locked was ajar.

Uh-oh! It looked as if Rodet had been burgled.

The flesh on my arms formed goose bumps.

I paused and took three or four deep breaths to get myself under control while I considered. Even if the burglars were gone, it was going to be rough if the cops caught me in there. Rougher if the burglars were still there—with that silenced pistol. The shooter had just iced two guys with it; a third would be no big deal.

I used a knuckle to open the door and stepped inside. The door swung shut and didn't latch. Aha—the old burglar's trick, one I had used a dozen times myself: A small stone carefully placed prevented the door from swinging completely shut. Once in, a burglar didn't need to worry about getting out; all locked doors in dwellings open without a key from the inside so occupants can escape from fire. No, this trick was used so the guys who were coming along behind the burglar could get in without the burglar opening the door for them, or so the thieves could carry out stuff by the armfuls and zip back in for additional loads. When they left, burglars left the rock jamming the door in the hope that some curious kid would come in for a look around. He would mess up the evidence, leave fingerprints all over and, with a little bit of luck, manage to be caught inside, increasing the burglar's chances of escaping scot-free.

Leaving the rock in place, I looked at the elevator, rejected it, and began climbing the stairs.

What if Marisa Petrou was up here, stretched out on the floor with a hole in her head?

I climbed on the side of the narrow staircase, where it was least likely a board would creak. I went up as silently and quickly as I could.

The doors on the apartments on the first two floors were closed. I climbed the last flight, pausing at the landings to listen. Street sounds, muffled traffic, a faint low rumble that might be a jet running high, but nothing else.

Okay, I'll admit, this was foolhardy. If Jake Grafton hadn't told me to come, I would be down on the street watching to see if anyone came out. *So, what is it with you, Tommy? You do anything Grafton tells you? You keep this up, boy, you'll collect about as much of your pissy pension as Al and Rich are going to get of theirs.*

I eased the top of my head up and looked at Rodet's door. It was standing open about a foot.

I climbed the rest of the stairs and stood in the doorway listening. Not a sound.

Taking a deep breath, I pushed the door open with a knuckle and looked into the room. Things were strewn everywhere. They had even used knives on the stuffed chairs and couches. The place had been ransacked.

I slipped in. Trying to avoid stepping on things, I moved to the interior doors and looked. No people, living or dead.

When I had checked every room, even the bathrooms, I paused to engage the brain. Every single room had been searched, thoroughly. The contents of the refrigerator and cabinets were strewn over the kitchen floor. There were footprints in the flour, floury white footprints throughout the apartment. The beds had been ripped apart, the mattresses slit open, the closets emptied onto the floors, the drawers pulled out of highboys and dumped on the floor, Rodet's filing cabinets emptied and overturned. They had even peeled back the edges of the carpet.

They hadn't found what they were looking for.

That conclusion popped into my criminal mind. I had done enough burglaries to know, when you found the thing you came to find, you left. They hadn't found it.

Maybe it wasn't here.

As I surveyed the damage, another thought occurred to me. Maybe they didn't know what they were looking for.

Or . . . maybe they found it and didn't know they were looking at it.

I was disassembling the satellite television control box, which was behind the TV in the sitting room, when I heard a noise behind me. I almost lost it right there. I spun around with the screwdriver in my fist, ready to stab.

Jake Grafton was standing there. "Sorry," he said.

I got back after it. "These screws have been taken out of here a bunch of times," I told him. "Look at the wear in the slots." I passed him one to examine.

He looked it over and passed it back to me.

When I got the innards out of the casing, he leaned over my shoulder to look. The stuff was mounted on a board, jammed in there tight so as to keep the unit as small as possible. I turned it over in my hand, to the extent I could with the electrical cord still attached. Then I saw two jacks into which leads would be plugged.

I glanced at the aluminum casing. There were no holes for the plugs.

I pointed out the jacks to Grafton. Together we examined the thing as well as we could without disassembling it. He saw it first, of course. He pointed.

The device was about the size of a large cell phone. Two wires ran to it from the jacks, and one from it to a unit I thought was probably the main lead to the outside dish.

"That's it. Put it all back together and let's get out of here."

I was finished in three minutes.

We didn't say anything until we were outside, walking across the park. The sky was dark and the air crisp; lovers were strolling; all in all, it was a great night to be alive. Yet it was all over for Rich and Al. It would be all over for me, too, one of these days.

"That thing was just a transmitter, right?" I asked Grafton.

"Transmitter and receiver. There's a computer someplace. If the people who went through that apartment had found it, they'd have quit and left. He writes the messages on a computer, encrypts them, plugs in the leads and transmits. It's an ultrawide band signal, a UWB, superimposed on the regular television signal. He receives the same way."

"Why haven't the wizards at NSA picked it up?"

"Oh, now that we know what to look for, they'll intercept the signal. The question is, Can they decrypt it? If he and his agent use some multiple of really large prime numbers as the basis for the code, it could take years to factor the number, even with huge computers."

"So you really want Rodet's computer?"

"Yes."

Grafton picked a park bench with a view of Rodet's building and plopped down on it. "Let's wait a while," he said, "and see what happens."

I didn't know what he had up his sleeve, and I didn't really care. It had been a long, long day for me. So we sat there in the middle of that old square with its symmetrical buildings and ghosts, as Grafton made telephone calls. His cell phone was a peach, a bit larger than the usual. "It's encrypted," he said, when I remarked on it.

His first call was to someone at NSA, I surmised, as I listened to his side of the conversation. He told the person on the other end about the transmitter/receiver on the satellite television system, listened a while, then grunted good-bye.

"The French might have broken that code," I suggested, indicating his telephone.

"It's possible," he admitted, "but improbable. Still, everything in life is a risk."

"I suppose."

The night wore on. My butt got tired and I shifted around to maintain circulation. I decided I wasn't going to do this for a pastime if and when I got out of the agency. At least I had my scooter jacket, which kept me reasonably warm. Grafton had only a sports coat, yet he didn't complain. He received two telephone calls on his encrypted cell and made another. I didn't try to figure out what the conversations were about. His side of the discussions consisted mostly of grunts and yeses and noes.

After the last call, he told me, "The guys were set up to record the sounds from the apartment when they were shot. Sarah and Willie listened to the burglars search and trash the place. There were muttered comments in a language they can't understand. They even got Callie in to listen, and she doesn't understand it."

His wife was, I knew, a linguist who spoke seven or eight languages.

"Sarah will send the stuff to Fort Meade and see if they make sense of the comments. I suspect it was just something like, 'Look over there.'"

"Be nice to know which language it was," I suggested.

He didn't reply to that.

While we sat on our bench, three people went into the building. One was a single man in his sixties, well dressed with what appeared to be a nice warm coat. The other two were a couple, in their forties, I would say. From where we sat, about a hundred feet away, it was hard to tell.

It was a little past 10:30 in the evening and downright chilly when a limo rolled up in front of Rodet's building. The chauffeur hopped out, zipped around the car and opened the right rear door. In a few seconds I saw Marisa Petrou's dark brown hair. Seconds after that Rodet appeared, standing a head taller. As he spoke to the doorman, Jake Grafton rose and strolled in that direction.

Being a loyal trooper, I cranked myself erect and fell in behind him.

CHAPTER EIGHTEEN

After Rodet and Marisa went into the building, Jake Grafton waited about two minutes, then followed. He didn't tell me not to come, so I clumped up the stairs right behind him, more out of curiosity than anything else. It was going to be interesting to see Marisa's face when she saw mine.

The door was standing open and Grafton walked right in. Marisa was surveying the mess when she saw us. She managed to keep a grip on her face, which impressed me. Coming home to find your place trashed, and then seeing the last guy in town you expected, had to be difficult.

"*Bonjour,*" she said automatically, without inflection.

"We were in the neighborhood and thought we'd drop by," Jake Grafton said in English.

Rodet came out of the sitting room. He looked tired, stressed. His gaze went to Grafton. If he even saw me, he gave no sign.

"You've had some messy visitors."

"Burglars," Henri Rodet said curtly.

"One would think they were searching for something," the admiral said as he surveyed the wreckage.

"You know anything about this?" Rodet asked, scrutinizing Grafton's face.

"Not a thing. Is the whole place like this?" Grafton walked past him and looked into the sitting room, then the kitchen. He whistled when he saw the mess on the floor. He turned back to Rodet, looked him in the eye and leaned slightly toward him. "Did they find it?" he asked.

No one ever accused Jake Grafton of messing around. Rodet wasn't used to the direct approach, and I could see that he wasn't sure how to handle it.

"Perhaps you and I should have a talk," Rodet said to Grafton. "Marisa, will you entertain this gentleman for a moment while I visit with the admiral?"

As Rodet led Grafton into the wreckage of the sitting room, I gave Marisa my best honest smile. When the two superspooks were out of earshot, I said earnestly, "We're just here to sell you a good used car."

My pathetic attempt at humor went right over her head. She, too, had a lot on her mind. "What do you know about this?" she asked, searching my face.

I looked around a bit before I answered. "Looks to me like they spent at least an hour at it. Two or three guys, I'd say. Where were you and Rodet this evening?"

"At a party."

"The maids?"

"This is their evening off."

"Convenient, you must admit. Did you tell your Mossad pals that the coast was clear?"

She looked daggers at me.

"Maybe you should make an executive decision," I continued earnestly. "Decide that we're on the same side and tell me what you know."

She half turned away from me.

"Well," I said, surveying the stuff on display like a suburbanite at a yard sale, "they didn't find it. You've been living here and you haven't found it, so I wonder why they would think they could in just an hour?"

That stung her. "You talk too much," she snarled.

"Probably." I decided a shot in the dark wouldn't hurt. "Maybe Elizabeth Conner isn't who she seems. Maybe she brought some friends over for an Easter egg hunt."

She acted as if she didn't hear that comment.

I went to the nearest chair, an antique by the looks of it, cleaned off the seat by dumping the contents on the floor, examined the slashed padding, then parked my fanny.

Marisa seemed lost in thought.

I prattled on anyway. "Remember that evening in Washington that you and I danced the night away? Who would have suspected that we were going to have a long-term relationship? I should probably write to Jack Zarb to thank him for starting something grand."

She ignored me. That didn't bother me much; women have been ignoring me all my life.

The forensic scientists were busy swabbing explosive residue off the floor and ceiling of the parking garage when Jean-Paul Arnaud arrived. Inspector Papin was conferring with another police official. Arnaud saw Papin glance at him, so he merely stood and watched until Papin finished his conversation and came over.

"Ah, Arnaud. They have decided to call me on every police matter that might have any intelligence implications, so you and I are going to become closely acquainted." The inspector gestured with his hand. "A car bomb."

"Victims?"

"Apparently none. The car was a rental. It was rented to an American, a Terry Shannon." He held out a slip of paper with the passport number and local address. "One of our clerks did a routine check and it came back a hit. So we called you."

Arnaud glanced at the paper. "Shannon . . . Wasn't he the American attacked by thugs at the Musée d'Orsay?"

"Yes."

Arnaud folded the paper once and pocketed it as Papin briefed him on the investigation so far of this bombing. "Initial indications are that the explosive was a military type. We'll have more when the chemists finish their work. We have yet to determine how the bomb was triggered. We'll be examining the wreckage, but that will take a while."

"Suspects?"

"Not yet. Nor have we questioned Shannon. Do you have any objections?"

"Treat it as a routine police matter."

"Very good. We'll try to find him this evening."

"Keep me advised, will you?"

"Of course."

"And the Bruguiere killing? Anything new?"

"Nothing yet." The inspector hesitated, as if trying to make up his mind.

Arnaud waited, perfectly willing to give the man his moment.

"This afternoon two French Muslims on motorcycles chased a motor scooter through Paris. They crashed. One is dead, the other is in the hospital. We will question the survivor as soon as he is fully awake, although, as you know, these people usually refuse to say anything. And, of course, none of the people we talked to noted or remembered the license number of the scooter. I did have the motor vehicle registration people run a check, and, as it happens, several days ago Terry Shannon bought a scooter."

Arnaud frowned.

"Shannon is having a memorable visit to Paris, by any measure. Islamic thugs attacked him yesterday in the Musée d'Orsay, this afternoon his car exploded, and this evening he may or may not have fled from two thugs on motorcycles."

"Perhaps he should go home," Arnaud muttered.

"One wishes he would," the policeman said. "He has been extraordinarily lucky so far, but with luck there is always a limit. The examining magistrate may forward a request to the ministry that he be expelled from France."

Arnaud scrutinized Papin's face, then nodded curtly. "Keep me informed," he said.

As the deputy director of the DGSE walked away, he thought about Papin's comment: "With luck there is always a limit."

The people who searched your apartment are trying to discover the method that you use to talk to Qasim," Jake

Grafton said conversationally to Henri Rodet as they stood in the center of the disaster area.

Rodet could think only of his friend Qasim. Even looking at the trash strewn about the floor, the personal danger this mess implied seemed but an annoyance. Qasim laid his life on the line every single minute of every single day, and he had been doing it for twenty-five years. And yet . . .

Those bastards! Breaking in here!

From his pocket he pulled a pistol. He aimed it at a painting on the wall of the Algerian desert, one he acquired as a youth, and pulled the trigger over and over again.

The booming roars filled the room.

The action was so unexpected that Jake Grafton stood stock still, watching.

Only after Rodet had jerked savagely at the trigger several times and gotten no reports because the pistol was completely empty did the American breathe again.

Rodet pocketed his weapon and stalked into his bedroom. He rooted through the pillow feathers and underwear and clothes strewn over the floor until he found a box of cartridges. Then he returned to the sitting room.

When the pistol was reloaded and back in Rodet's pocket, only then did Jake Grafton say, "You've been passing Qasim's intelligence to the Israelis for years, and they haven't used it in a manner that would betray him. Why don't you trust the Americans?"

"I could write a book."

Grafton took a deep breath, sighed, then stirred the trash with a toe. "They are getting very close," he said softly. "Qasim's life is hanging by a thread. So is yours." He gestured angrily and roared, "These people mean business, and they don't give a damn who knows it. If you don't use some sense and get him out of there, they'll kill you. If that doesn't shut him up, they'll purge their organization, kill everyone who might be the leak. Think Joe Stalin. Now, that outcome wouldn't be a disaster, *if* your man was already out of there." He paused and scrutinized Henri Rodet's face. "Think about it," he said softly.

"I have been thinking," Rodet said, "and probably not too clearly. The truth is I'm in over my head, and so is my source." He rubbed his face with both hands. "I love Abu Qasim like a younger brother . . . or the son I never had." He took a few seconds to compose himself, then spoke again. "Did you ever have a son?"

"Thousands," Jake Grafton shot back.

Rodet looked surprised.

"Have you ever been to the American cemetery at Normandy?" Grafton asked. He didn't wait for a reply. "Young Americans have been fighting for freedom, for liberty, since the American Revolution. They've fought kings, rebels, dictators, Communist oligarchies, and now religious fanatics. They've been maimed and killed on battlefields all over this planet. Black, white, yellow, brown, they come from the four corners of the earth and obey the orders of elected officials. Those officials have made many mistakes, sometimes grievous ones, but still young people step forward to wear an American uniform, to fight for the flag. They're my sons and daughters; all of them—soldiers, sailors, Marines, airmen— every last one of 'em."

"But a son you have known and loved?" Rodet said, unwilling to drop the point.

Grafton gathered himself. "When the planes crashed into the World Trade Center and the buildings were on fire, Port Authority police and New York City police and firefighters rushed to the site and charged into those buildings to save as many people as they could. They died by the dozens when the buildings collapsed." His voice was husky now. He leaned toward Rodet; their faces were only a few inches apart. "On that day three thousand innocent people were murdered by madmen. *Those people* were my flesh and blood—I claim them all."

Rodet found a place to sit. He closed his eyes so he wouldn't have to look at his ransacked apartment.

Finally he spoke. "So far we've been lucky—the Islamic fundamentalists have used true believers as soldiers. But they're sitting beside the biggest river of money the world has ever known. It was inevitable that sooner or later they would use some of that money to pay infidels to go places they can't, to supply expertise they don't have, to fight the holy war as hired mercenaries. They're doing all three now."

Jake swept the trash from a chair and sat down as Henri Rodet continued to talk.

When I heard the shots, my heart about stopped. If that frog bastard shot Grafton—

I scrambled for the door to the sitting room and jerked it open. Saw Rodet put another one into a painting. He killed it dead as hell. When his gun was empty I closed the door and went back to Marisa. Her face was a study as she scrutinized mine.

When I didn't say anything she moved toward the sitting room door. She stood about six inches from it and looked rapt. She might as well have glued her ear to the door. I thought she got most of it.

When she looked my way, I waggled my finger. She ignored me. It was amazing how good she was at that.

Time dragged. I got tired of looking at Marisa and sat thinking about Al and Rich out there in that van.

Finally, after an age and a half, Rodet appeared in the door. He motioned for Marisa, who by then was over by the sink noisily storing things in cabinets. She picked up her purse and went into the sitting room.

I sort of followed along to see what was happening. I was standing in the doorway when I saw her hand something to Grafton, who glanced at it and put it in his pocket. Then she turned and came out, sweeping by me as if I weren't even there.

Grafton shooed me away with a head nod.

It would sure be nice if for once I were a party to whatever was going down!

I snarled at Marisa, who was standing at the sink looking about distractedly. She paid no attention. Ah, me!

Five minutes later Grafton came out of the sitting room.

Marisa met his eyes but didn't say a word. He jerked his head at me and marched for the door. They probably don't do a lot of marching in the Navy, but Grafton learned to cover ground somewhere. I was halfway to the sidewalk, following Grafton, when I realized I hadn't even grunted au revoir to the Israeli agent.

Grafton got to the sidewalk and set off at a good clip. I fell in beside him. "What'd you get?" I asked hopefully.

When he didn't answer, I thought maybe he didn't hear me, so I tried again. "What'd you learn?"

He ignored me. It was that kind of day.

As we walked the streets, he made a few telephone calls on his encrypted phone. After the second one he said, "The police are looking for you. They know about your car."

I groaned. I wasn't up for a night at a police station answering questions. Truthfully, I was whipped.

Grafton walked along the Paris sidewalks with his hands in his pockets, his head down. If he knew where he was going, he wasn't sharing that, either. The wind was downright chilly, and I was so tired I shivered. Grafton didn't seem to notice. Finally he said, "I suggest you crash at the embassy. I think they have a cot or two over there for the staff when they pull all-nighters. Tomorrow I want you and Sarah Houston to betray your country."

"Okay by me," I said with a sigh. "You American bastards deserve it."

In the basement of the American embassy, Secret Service personnel and young Marines placed the bodies of Alberto Salazar and Richard Thurlow in coffins and packed dry ice around them. The technician, Cliff Icahn, sat in the van playing with the equipment while Jake Grafton and Pink Maillard watched from the open door.

"They had the interior tape running, which is standard procedure," Cliff said. "It's a four-hour continuous loop. Here is the sixty seconds before the shots." He played it. Jake stood with closed eyes concentrating as he listened to the words, the sound of the door opening, the fast two pops, a pause, then two more, then the door closing.

"That's basically it," Cliff said. "Want to listen again?"

Jake and Pink looked at each other and both shook their heads. "No," the admiral said.

"A cop," Pink mused.

"More precisely, someone dressed as a policeman," Jake said.

They walked away from the van. Pinckney Maillard had his hands in his pockets. "The ambassador isn't going to like this," he muttered, more to himself than Jake. "How are we going to get the bodies back to the States? We don't have death certificates for the immigration people."

"We can take them to Germany and put them aboard an Air Force transport," Jake said. "No one checks vehicles crossing the French-German border."

"That's illegal, a violation of God only knows how many international treaties and laws," Maillard protested. Sneaking bodies around . . . Jesus! Stunts like that weren't the way to get ahead in the Secret Service.

"Someone around here could gin up some fake death certificates," Jake suggested, "if that will make you feel better."

"That isn't very damn funny."

"Maybe the best course is to pass the buck to Washington, let someone there figure it out."

"Yeah," Maillard agreed. That was the only safe approach. Then he added, "Of course, Lancaster is gonna blow a gasket." An outraged U.S. ambassador shouting his name wouldn't do him any good at the Treasury Department, either.

Grafton paused for one more look at the coffins, then headed for the elevator. Maillard followed along.

The Graftons' apartment overlooked a tree-lined boulevard. Callie referred to it in her letter to her daughter, Amy, as "the perfect apartment," and that was how she thought of it. It was a third-floor walk-up in an older building, the plumbing was antique, the pipes groaned, the kitchen was tiny and the refrigerator was barely large enough to hold a six-pack. There was a small balcony, just large enough for two chairs and two flowerpots, where she and her husband, when he was home, could sit and watch the endless traffic and, in the evening, Parisians stroll by on the sidewalks. It was Paris the way she had always dreamed it would be.

Of course, the place had a few drawbacks. The major one was that Jake said it was probably infested with electronic bugs, so no discussion could take place about anything remotely connected with what Jake was doing. When they had moved in Callie thought the possible presence of bugs no big deal, and she had forgotten about them. After the murders of the CIA technicians, she felt strangled. She wanted to discuss the situation with her husband, but she couldn't do it here.

Tonight she stood on the balcony watching the sidewalk, waiting for Jake. The tops of the trees on the sidewalk were just below the balcony. Birds liked to light on the now bare branches, there to ride the swaying limbs as the fall winds blew through the canyon of the boulevard, quite unconcerned about her presence or the precariousness of their resting place.

Then she saw him, still almost a block away, walking this way, looking at the people, glancing into store windows occasionally. Jake Grafton. He was still the warrior she married, but he was no longer the young stud with the aroma of jet exhaust embedded in his clothing and hair. Yet at times she fancied that she could still smell it on him.

She went into the apartment and closed the doors to the balcony. She turned off the lights and locked the apartment behind her. The stairwell was dark, lit only by twenty-five-watt bulbs that dangled from sockets on each landing.

Callie stepped out onto the sidewalk just as Jake arrived. He reached for her hand but she hugged him instead. He wrapped his arms around her, pulling her tight against him. With her head on his chest she could hear his heart beating.

"Let's go for a walk," she whispered.

"Sure." They set off down the sidewalk hip to hip, with his arm draped over her shoulder.

• • •

"Could we be under audio surveillance even here, walking along the sidewalk?" Callie asked.

"It's possible," he said. "Not too probable unless someone wants to spend a lot of time and money."

"Can we talk?"

"I'm sorry about sending you off with Willie Varner and two dead men. I wanted you out of there and knew Willie didn't have a clue where the embassy was."

"I understood. And I've seen dead men before. Still, it's hard to take. They didn't deserve that."

"No," he agreed. "They didn't."

They went into a patisserie and got ice cream cones. When they came out, Callie asked, "What happened after I left?"

Jake was not in the habit of sharing classified information with his wife, even though she was the personification of tact and discretion. Still, in this instance, a woman's perspective might be helpful. So he told it, about going into Rodet's apartment with Tommy Carmellini only to find it had been searched and trashed. "You might speculate that the people who searched the apartment knew Al and Rich were listening and killed them before they went in. Of course, even with our guys dead, the audio from the bugs was recorded. After you and Willie returned the van, the folks at the embassy listened to the recording. All they heard was sounds of people searching and garbled voices."

"So the searchers were pros?"

"Perhaps. Or very careful."

"Did they find what they were looking for?"

"No." He continued with the narrative between licks on the ice cream cone, telling her about waiting for Henri Rodet and Marisa Petrou to come home, then following them into the apartment. "Of course, Rodet suspected me of searching the place, then waiting until he came back to let him show me what I had failed to find." He shrugged. "I'm sneaky enough for a trick like that, but in this case I happened to be innocent."

A trace of a smile crossed Callie's lips. She finished her

ice cream and tossed the paper the cone came in into the first trash can she passed. Then she licked her sticky fingers. She walked along holding on to his arm as she listened to the rest of the story.

"He gave me the high-end telephone computer, a Palm, that he used to compose and encrypt the messages he sent to Qasim, and to decrypt the messages he got from him. I put the thing in a safe at the embassy."

"The searchers didn't find it? Where did he keep it?"

"His girlfriend, Marisa, had it in her purse."

"And she's Mossad?"

"Perhaps."

"Why didn't she jet off to Israel with the computer?"

Jake merely glanced at his wife, who answered her own question. "Oh. She's in love with him."

"That's my take on it."

"Or she thinks there is nothing on the computer's memory to get," Callie said.

"I liked the love angle better."

"Men always do," his wife said. "They're hopelessly romantic."

He went on, telling her about his conversation with Rodet. "He gave me some names of people that Qasim says have been hired by Al Queda, and he gave me that computer, which may or may not have anything on it. And . . . he didn't tell me anything about Qasim."

"Nothing?"

"Said he loved him like a son. But he didn't tell me where he is or what he's doing—none of that."

"So if he gave you the computer he uses to communicate with Qasim, how is he going to do it now?"

Jake Grafton stopped, turned and stared at Callie. "I didn't think to ask him that," he admitted, and started walking again.

They walked along in silence for a few minutes. Finally Callie said, "It sounds as if Rodet is trying to protect him."

"The best thing he can do for that man is get him out of wherever he is."

"Maybe he's trying to protect Qasim from himself." When her husband eyed her, Callie added, "Perhaps Qasim doesn't want to leave. Perhaps there is nothing more Rodet can say to him. Or . . . Qasim has nothing more to say to Henri Rodet."

Jake Grafton stared at Callie for several seconds. Then a big grin split his face and he kissed her. "You're a genius," he said, laughing. "Man, am I glad you married me!"

"What did I say?"

"I've been racking my brains, and you just explained everything—*everything*!" He snapped his fingers. "Just like that!"

He walked along in silence, holding her hand. Finally he said, "Man, I would really like to know what's on that little computer."

"Can't Sarah Houston or the NSA cryptographers give you a plain English text?"

"Oh, given enough time, I'm sure they can, but we're running out. The G-8 meeting is next week."

"So you don't have many options. Your only choice is to assume you know the contents and go on from there," she said. "You'll have to fake it."

He grinned. "Why not?"

CHAPTER NINETEEN

The next morning Jake Grafton found Sarah Houston in the SCIF. She had the photo that Tommy Carmellini took of Elizabeth Conner on the screen of her computer.

"Her real name is Ruth Cohen," Sarah said. "Her parents immigrated to Israel when she was five years old." She hit a key, and a photo of Cohen in a school uniform appeared. "This was taken five years ago in Tel Aviv when she graduated from high school." Another picture. "This one was taken last year in Iraq. She was with a group of Israeli scientists looking for evidence of weapons of mass destruction."

Another keystroke, and Carmellini's photo of the man who followed him appeared. Sarah pronounced his name. "The computer matches this photo with one the French took for his internal ID card. He is an emigrant from Morocco."

Now the picture of Marisa Petrou appeared on the screen. Keystrokes followed, and photos appeared one after another. In each one she got younger. "School pictures, passport photos," Sarah murmured. In the last one, Marisa looked to be about twelve years old. "This is the oldest one I can find. She was a student at a private school in Switzerland. Name was Marisa Lamoureux."

"How about a birth certificate?" Grafton asked.

"Nothing yet."

"Keep looking when you have the time. Today is the day you and Tommy turn traitor."

• • •

Sarah and I walked from the embassy to the Metro, rode it for a few stops, then walked toward the river and the Conciergerie. It was a raw, windy day, with clouds of autumn leaves swirling around. Just keeping your hat on in the gusts took some doing. I kept my eyes peeled for Arabs on motorcycles or in junker cars and didn't see any. Sarah was quiet, walking with her hands in her pockets.

"I don't think this is a good idea," she told Jake Grafton before we left the embassy.

"Objection noted," Grafton said. He looked tired, as if he weren't getting much sleep. I had no sympathy—I spent a miserable night on a basement bunk and was wearing the same clothes I wore all day yesterday. Someone produced a spare toothbrush and disposable razor, so I felt as if I were still a member of the human race. On the other hand, perhaps I should have had my visit with the Paris police, then retired to my cozy garret on the Rue Paradis, complete with hot water and bathtub, clean clothes and comfy bed. Say what you will, but the truth is, war is hell.

"I don't know if I can do this," Sarah said to Jake Grafton when he sat us down to brief us.

"It's only for a few days," Grafton replied. "Pretend that you're in love. Hold hands, look soulfully into Tommy's eyes, hang on his every word, even when they aren't watching, because they might be."

"That's the part I don't like," she said acidly. "I volunteered to serve my country and all that, but this is very close to prostitution."

"Perilously close," I chirped. "What would your mother say?"

"Objection duly noted," Grafton said with finality. He went on to discuss codes and protocol and other technical stuff that Sarah understood and I didn't. Finally he got around to it. "I want you to tell your tale to Jean-Paul Arnaud, the deputy director. Ask for him and refuse to talk to anyone else."

I got a sick feeling in the pit of my stomach. This whole thing was going south, and quickly. "Why not Rodet?" I asked. "The way we planned it?"

"There's been a change of plans."

"Why do I have this feeling that you're not telling us all of it?"

"I don't want to burden you with all of it. Unless I am seriously mistaken, you're going to be strapped to a polygraph before the day is out."

"Oh, joy," Sarah said bitterly.

"The less you know the better."

"Oh, for the love of—," I began, but Grafton cut me off with one of his looks. The admiral's stare, with those cold gray eyes, could stopper Niagara. Needless to say, it always did a job on me. Those were the moments when I was glad I had never been in the Navy.

Sarah cleared her throat and said, "And just how do you propose that we pass polygraph exams?"

Grafton grinned. "I thought you'd never ask. Here's how you're going to do it." And he told her. Me, I didn't ask. When you've told as many lies as I have, you get pretty good at it.

As we walked along, the cold wind gave Sarah's cheeks a nice rosy hue. Except for the fact that she had a seriously warped psyche, she was a nice person. I reminded myself that no one is perfect.

"How can you be so calm?" she asked.

I was tempted to tell her that I was a pro, but decided maybe the truth was best. "It's an act."

We hiked over the bridge to the island and presented ourselves to the guard at the gate. He waved us into the reception room. "We'd like to see Jean-Paul Arnaud," I said to the uniformed gendarme. "We don't have an appointment. My name is Terry Shannon."

"Passport, please." The man was portly, with a mustache that needed trimming. He had sad eyes. His younger colleague, who hadn't been eating as well, looked bored.

I surrendered the document, and the portly man held out his hand for Sarah's. I was watching his eyes, and they showed no surprise when she produced a diplomatic passport from her small purse. Traitors must call here on a daily basis.

"Have a seat," he said, and glanced at a row of molded plastic chairs. We perched there.

"Maybe we oughta hold hands," I suggested, and reached for one of hers. She slipped it into mine. It was cool and firm, very pleasant. Ah, yes. I remembered.

There is a theory about the power of the human touch, something about it being the most subtle form of sex. Certainly it is the most sensual. Not that I was getting some sort of perverted thrill out of holding Sarah Houston's hand there in the public reception area of the Conciergerie as the man with the sad eyes ignored us, the bored fellow read a newspaper and a cleaning lady worked around us, but I was enjoying it. I even gave her hand a tiny squeeze and got one in return. When I met her eyes she glanced away; her hand stayed where it was.

The woman was one hell of an actress. If I didn't know better, I would have thought she still liked me. Believe me, if the guards were paying attention, they would have been fooled. It is a pleasure working with a pro. And her hand felt really good.

Life is short—enjoy it.

Ten pleasant minutes after we arrived, a man in a suit and tie appeared and escorted us along a hallway. I had been here before with Jake Grafton, but this was different. If we screwed this up, we weren't going to be strolling out of here—we were going to the basement to see the toys. For some reason I felt warm and my palms were sweating.

Arnaud's office was on the floor below Rodet's in the same corner of the building. His workspace was not as nicely furnished—I saw no original art—and the carpet didn't cover as much of the floor, all in keeping with his status as Number Two. Apparently French bureaucrats worry about these things as much as American ones do.

Arnaud could have moonlighted at Madame Tussauds wax museum—his face was that expressive. The man who brought us here pointed toward two chairs. We sat as Arnaud examined our passports. He spent two or three minutes with each of them, apparently satisfying himself that they were genuine.

Believe me, I wasn't calm now. Arnaud's office seemed warm. I swabbed at my forehead and found it was wet. Sarah looked a little nervous, too, I thought, and her hand was warm and slippery. She kept a firm grip on mine.

I had been thinking about how I was going to handle this moment. Sarah and I practiced once this morning with Jake Grafton playing Arnaud. I was up for doing the scene several more times, but Grafton nixed that. He wanted us to wing it.

That's precisely what I did: looked into Arnaud's cold, waxy face and told him what was in my heart. "We want to make some serious money." That was the bald truth that defined my life. Maybe it will be my epitaph. Everything that followed that remark was almost true but not quite. I told him that Sarah and I were in love and wanted to run away together. We were tired of the workaday world and ready for a little piece of paradise, somewhere. He listened to my whole spiel, glancing from Sarah's face to mine. I waited for him to brighten when I discussed the CIA's intelligence Internet links, but he didn't.

"He's not going to be interested in a peek at our stuff if a traitor has already given or sold him access," I pointed out to Grafton earlier that morning.

"Oh, but he will," Grafton shot back. "There is always the possibility that you were sent to determine if indeed he already has such access. If he does and appears disinterested, he knows we would suspect the truth, endangering his source. Even if he has access, he has to buy what you have to sell." Heaven help us, that kind of circular logic is the way spies think. Life is a giant forget-me-not. He loves me, he loves me not, he loves me . . . etc.

Arnaud fingered my passport. "Is Terry Shannon your real name?"

"No."

"Ms. Houston? Is that your real name?"

"Yes," Sarah lied.

"Why did you come to France, Monsieur Shannon?"

"My agency sent me."

"What is your assignment?"

"I'm Admiral Jake Grafton's assistant. I do what he tells me to do."

"And your specialty is?"

"Breaking and entering, planting listening devices, burglary, safecracking, that kind of thing."

"The Paris police are looking for you."

"I thought they might be."

"They wish to question you about several unfortunate incidents that occurred yesterday."

"I spent some of the day sightseeing."

"How did you travel?"

"A motor scooter."

"Were you involved in a chase?"

"Several men on motorcycles tried to make me crash. A traffic incident. You know Paris traffic."

"Indeed. It can be harrowing. And where is your rental car?"

I tried to look suspicious. "How'd you know I had a rental car?"

He ignored my question. "Where is it?"

"I assume it's still parked in the garage where I left it." I gave him the address.

"How do you propose that we structure this deal?" He glanced at Sarah, and then his eyes came back to me. When I hesitated, he added, "One assumes that you have given the matter a great deal of thought."

He was trying to make me nervous, so I let it show. I wiped my hands on my trousers, glanced at Sarah, and launched into my spiel. The codes to Intelink-C were changed weekly, and we would provide them for a fee. If he liked what he saw, Sarah would arrange permanent access when she returned to the States. He would then pay us a onetime sum of two million dollars, and we would change our names and disappear.

"Two million dollars is not a lot of money these days," he

remarked with another glance at Sarah. I had no worries there; she could wear a poker face with the best of them.

"We're not greedy," I told him. "And enough is enough. Pay us out of the Christmas party fund."

"It is enough, however, if you sell the same thing to a variety of people and collect two million American dollars from each of them."

I glanced down at my lap and swallowed hard, then looked at him and smiled. "We wouldn't do anything like that. If too many people see what's on the Intelink, the fact that it's been compromised will get out."

"One suspects so," Arnaud said dryly. "Fortunately you are honest."

I could see that I was going to have to say something. "We have to charge enough to make the risk worthwhile, yet not so much that you say no and hang us out to dry. Sarah and I decided on two million. That's our number."

"How do you know that I won't call Admiral Grafton and report your attempted treason?"

I didn't reply to that comment.

As the silence deepened he sat watching Sarah's and my faces. Finally I said, "It's ten grand American for a peek."

When he didn't reply, I stood. "Why don't you think about it? You know where to find me." I turned to Sarah, who was already up.

"We aren't finished yet," Arnaud said flatly. The words were barely out of his mouth when the door opened and three of the biggest, toughest Frenchmen I ever laid eyes on came into the room. They weren't smiling.

"Do you guys practice these entrances?" I asked the one in front.

I had speculated on what the DGSE had in the dungeons of the Conciergerie; now, unfortunately, I found out. They had renovated the basement at some time in the last century or so, and they had little interrogation rooms down there. They put me in one and led Sarah off to another. I caught a glimpse of two women, matrons. I didn't know if that was good or bad.

I ended up with the friendly trio from Arnaud's office. They didn't do any rough stuff, just made me empty my pockets on a table and strip naked. As one of them began going through my stuff, the other two led me along a corridor to the cells, which looked like they dated from the Franco-Prussian War. They stuffed me in one, clanged the door shut and left me there. Still wearing my birthday suit, I discovered that the place was damp and chilly.

Is there anything worse than a cold, slimy stone floor on your bare feet? I was going to get athlete's foot, sure as hell.

Grafton had told us to expect interrogation and isolation and reminded us that anywhere we were put would probably be equipped with listening devices. Sitting on the edge of my wooden bunk in my eight-by-eight Paris cell, I silently congratulated him on his foresight. I also wished he were here instead of me.

The light wasn't great in that hole. After inspecting the floor and the cotton mat on the wooden bed for mouse droppings, I amused myself by looking for bugs. Didn't find any. I figured Sarah would be along shortly, and she was. She was wearing a new shiner on her right eye and that was about it. The matrons put her in the cell across the corridor. They didn't even glance at me, to my relief.

"Had an accident?" I asked Sarah when we were alone.

"The bitches did a body cavity search. I think they enjoyed it."

"Hard to get decent help."

"I think I broke one of those women's nose."

"I certainly hope so."

"Stop staring at me, you pervert."

I turned my face to the wall. I glanced at my wrist from force of habit, and was mildly surprised to find my watch was missing.

It's hard to believe that I am so damn stupid that I do this for a living. That thought shot through my head, and I almost said it aloud—but stopped myself just in time.

• • •

L et me see if I have this right," Ambassador Owen Lancaster said. He had Jake Grafton, Pinckney Maillard, and George Goldberg in his office, but he was talking directly to Grafton. "One of your men killed a French citizen in a museum, led another to his death after a merry chase through Paris traffic and had his car bombed in a parking garage."

Lancaster paused, but the admiral said nothing.

"Then last night two of your men were murdered in a surveillance van. You didn't notify the French police. Their bodies are in coffins in the basement. Have I got that correct?"

"Yes, sir."

"Why didn't you notify the French police?"

"The murdered men were conducting an illegal clandestine surveillance of the residence of the director of the DGSE, Henri Rodet. I thought that fact would cause us more diplomatic problems than a police investigation would solve. If you think I was in error, we could notify the police now and let them take the bodies to the morgue and confiscate the van."

"Don't be insubordinate, Admiral," Lancaster snarled.

"Pehaps, sir," Agatha Hempstead interjected from her seat on the sidelines, "it might be productive if Admiral Grafton explains precisely why his business with Mr. Rodet— whatever it is—cannot wait until after the G-8 conference."

"Thank you, Agatha," Lancaster said evenly, without taking his eyes off Grafton. One of Hempstead's many functions, apparently, was to help the ambassador keep his temper under control. "I seem to recall that you mentioned cooperating with the French officials providing security for the summit, not harassing the official in charge. Really, surveillance of the director of French intelligence—in France—is more than a little too much."

"Unfortunately I am not at liberty to discuss ongoing intelligence operations with people who lack the proper clearances, sir, as you are well aware."

"Why didn't you just say you were here on a classified matter?"

"Everything I do is classified, sir."

Lancaster turned his head a millimeter and focused on Pinckney Maillard. "So, Mr. Maillard, you see how it is. My staff operates under the old adage, 'Ask me no questions and I'll tell you no lies.' It's a miracle that America has *any* friends. But I must ask you: Is France safe for the president of the United States?"

"My job is to make reports to my superiors at the Treasury Department, sir. They make those judgments, not me."

Lancaster lowered his head and shook it. "Now let me tell you people the facts of life: The president will attend the G-8 conference, even if it takes the entire Secret Service and the armed forces of the United States to guarantee his safety. Our relationship with France is more important than anything the CIA could possibly be doing in Paris. Admiral Grafton?"

"Yes, sir."

"I want no more incidents, no more bodies, no more interest at the French cabinet level in our conduct as guests of the French nation. And I am giving you a direct order: Stop spying upon and harassing the director of French intelligence. Have I made myself clear?"

"You have."

"It would be embarrassing for everyone if I have to call your superiors and demand that you gentlemen be recalled. It would be even more embarrassing if the French government throws your silly asses out of the country."

"Definitely not career-enhancing," Maillard agreed. Suspecting insubordination, Lancaster glared. Grafton managed to keep a straight face.

"President Chirac will not tolerate being humiliated by American diplomatic personnel," the ambassador continued. "The secretary of state understands that, the president understands it and you had better. People, we are public servants and we must act in the public interest. The public interest just now is to ensure the G-8 summit happens as scheduled."

He dismissed them. Out in the corridor Maillard squared his shoulders and said, "The American public might be less than pleased if their president gets murdered in Paris."

"Probably would," Goldberg agreed, nodding.

"I suspect so," Grafton murmured.

As they walked, Maillard asked Grafton, "Sounds as if your man Shannon is having a rough time. Does he need a weapon?"

"Not right now. He might, though."

"You and your wife? Any concerns for your safety?"

"We're possible targets, yes, but the French would freak if they caught any of us with guns."

"Maybe I can help. The CIA has loaned us some experimental weapons, wireless Tasers if you will, made by an outfit in Arizona called Ionatron. The ones they gave us are about the size of a small automatic. They fire a laser, which ionizes a path through the air, then an electrical charge zips across the path."

Jake Grafton chuckled. "It's a ray gun," he said.

"The agency!" George Goldberg grumped. "First I've heard about this."

"They're developing these things to zap cars carrying bombs," Maillard said. "Ruins the driver's day, let me tell you. I've got a couple I can loan you."

Sarah Houston and I spent the noon hour in our windowless cells. We got more miserable with every passing minute. Sarah began to shiver, and after a while, so did I. We wrapped the mats from the beds around ourselves for warmth. There was a hole in the floor that I put to its intended use. I think Sarah used hers, too, but gentleman that I am, I didn't look to make sure.

She didn't say anything to me and I said nothing to her. I figured if the place was bugged, after a while they'd get tired of waiting for us to talk to each other. The less we said, the sooner we'd be out. Sarah must have thought so, too. Once I almost said that we'd laugh about this experience someday, but thought better of it.

My guess is that about three hours had passed when they came for Sarah—the same two matrons, and they brought one of the burly fellows along for a backup. No handcuffs. Sarah went right along.

After they left I was really alone. A fellow could disappear into one of these holes and never come out, and who would know?

In my case, who would care?

I amused myself by counting the stones in the walls, and by counting my pulse. At least my heart was still beating.

One thing for sure, institutional life was not my thing.

I was dozing, sitting on the bed with my head against one wall, when they came for me. The same three dudes.

I was really ready and trotted along in the middle.

Two flights up, they led me into a room similar to the one where they made me strip. There was a chair, which I was told to sit in, and a desk. A little guy wearing glasses and a white shirt sat behind it. In front of him was a polygraph machine. The big guys got me strapped up, then left the room.

The exam took about an hour. The operator talked and marked his tape, and I answered in monosyllables.

When it was over one of the studs brought me my clothes. I dressed; then he led me back to the cell in the dungeon. Sarah was back in hers, dressed.

She looked at me. I looked at her, shrugged, and lay down on the bed.

The polygraph operator took his tapes with him when he had his interview with Jean-Paul Arnaud.

"The woman, Houston, refused to cooperate. I didn't get any readings on her."

Arnaud looked puzzled. "Did she answer the questions?"

"Randomly. Said yes to three questions, then no to three, yes to four, no to four, and so on. After a while she began sobbing and refused to say anything. It was hopeless."

"I understand."

"I am sorry, Monsieur Arnaud, but there was nothing I could do."

Arnaud waved it away. "And Carmellini?"

"Results inconclusive."

Arnaud waited.

"The polygraph detects the body's involuntary responses,

respiration, heart rate, blood pressure and perspiration. The theory is—"

"I know the theory. You are the most experienced operator at the agency. Give me your professional opinion."

"His answers didn't vary from the baseline, which I established by asking him his name, employment, and various questions about Paris."

"His body responses indicated that he was telling the truth?"

"His body responses seem to indicate that Carmellini has himself under perfect control. I got the impression that if he wanted me to think he was lying, the needles twitched. If he wanted me to think he was telling the truth, they didn't."

"Yet he may have been telling the truth?" Arnaud insisted.

"That's one possibility. Another is that he is a sociopathic personality, one of those individuals who lacks any sense of remorse or anxiety when he lies. Or it may be that he is a very skillful liar."

"That's a useful asset in any era," Arnaud said thoughtfully.

The polygraph expert thought it wise not to reply to that observation.

When we finally got back to Arnaud's office, I was hungry, tired, thirsty and dirty, and I knew Sarah felt the same way—we were channeling each other by then.

"I am sorry for the inconvenience this afternoon," Arnaud said smoothly. "We must take precautions against liars and provocateurs."

"In which category did you put us?" I asked politely, trying to show interest.

"We have decided to accept your offer. We will give you ten thousand American dollars for a look at Intelink-C."

"Tomorrow," Sarah said loudly, which was the first word she had spoken in my presence since she called me a pervert, down in the nether regions. "I am hungry and filthy and I need a hot bath."

"Tomorrow, then. Shall we say two o'clock?" He rose and came around the desk.

"Two o'clock is fine," Sarah agreed. As he reached for her hand she slapped him hard, a real stinger that sent his glasses skittering across the carpet. Then she headed for the door.

"She's a tough broad," I told Arnaud. "She'll get over it."

I followed her into the reception area, where our escort was waiting.

CHAPTER TWENTY

It was a gloomy afternoon, misting rain, when Sarah and I reached the sidewalk. "That bastard," she said darkly. "I have never been so humiliated in my life."

I reached for her hand, and she let me take it. I pulled her up short and she looked me in the face. "Bugs," I mouthed silently, and pointed to her earrings, her purse and my belt buckle. I certainly didn't know if the French spooks had planted bugs, but they could have. It was a trick I wouldn't have missed if I had been running their show, and they were probably smarter and sneakier than I was.

Sarah was quick on the uptake. She nodded. Hand in hand, we set off for the Metro stop with the fine mist cooling our faces. After a few paces she latched on to my upper arm and walked with her hip against mine.

"Do you think he'll do the deal?" she asked.

"I hope so, babe. I hope so."

We rode the Metro to the stop nearest her hotel and walked from there. Up in her room she stripped and got into the shower.

As the water ran I examined her watch, a small self-winding Swiss one. The case didn't look as if it would have any room for extra machinery, so I laid it aside. Her earrings, dangly, shiny things, were another matter. Sure enough, a close inspection revealed that one had been cut in half, then put back together, with superglue, probably. It seemed heavier than the other one, but perhaps that was only my imagination. One of the buttons on her coat had a similar minute slice along its length, as did one of the buttons on her jacket.

The hotel provided laundry bags, so I put all her stuff in one, including the shoes she had worn.

I was inspecting my belt buckle when Sarah came out of the bathroom. She had a towel wrapped around her hair and one around her middle.

She paused; I held out my arms. She settled into my lap.

She smelled of soap and shampoo and her lips tasted delicious.

After a while she whispered, "You should take a shower, too."

When I came out she was in bed waiting for me.

We ate dinner in the hotel coffee shop, then headed for the Metro. I was carrying the bag. We got off the Metro at the Concorde Metro stop, the one nearest the embassy. As we came up the steps out of the ground, a squad of uniformed police was waiting.

"Terry Shannon?"

"Yes."

"Passport, please."

I produced it; one policeman examined it as two other cops looked me over. There was usually a squad or two of police in this area, the huge square in front of the American embassy, but this evening there must have been fifty. Many of them were carrying submachine guns on straps over their shoulders.

"Come with us, please." The cop kept my passport. I handed Sarah her bag of clothes, but one of the policemen took it from her hands.

"This is mine," she protested.

"Passport, please."

She whipped out the diplomatic passport for examination as one of the cops pawed through the clothes and shoes and ladies' underwear.

One of them talked into a lapel radio, but apparently they

had no pickup order on Sarah. They returned her passport, gave her the laundry bag and said, "You may go."

I shrugged at Sarah and was escorted over to the police van. When I glanced back I saw that she was walking on toward the embassy.

Everything was sweetness and politeness at police headquarters until I demanded to speak to an American diplomatic official. "You are not under arrest, Monsieur Shannon. We wish only to ask you a few questions about your car, a Hertz."

"I want to see an American diplomat."

They shouted; they said regrettable things about me and Americans and people who refused to answer questions. One of them even reminded me that I was a guest in their country. When I remained obstinate I was shown to a cell, my second of the day. This one was much nicer than the lockup in the dungeon of the Conciergerie. One might think Martha Stewart had been a guest here. I flopped on the bed and tried to sleep. It was going to be difficult with the drunks singing two cells away. They sounded like Americans—yep. They were from the States, all right. And they liked country.

What the hey—it wasn't rap.

George Goldberg was going over each item from Sarah Houston's purse with a magnifying glass when Jake Grafton touched her on the arm and led her away. In the SCIF in the basement, he motioned to a chair.

"Tell me all about your day. Everything you can remember."

When she told him about the polygraph examination, he asked her to tell him each question they asked. She could remember most of them, much to her amazement, because she had tried to ignore them when they were asked and answer yes or no according to the progression.

"What did the polygraph operator think of your tactic?"

"I don't know. I was ignoring him, too. Really, stripping a

woman naked and strapping on those leads and firing questions at her is not a method I would adopt to get at the truth."

"You were angry?"

"Infuriated and humiliated."

"Perhaps Arnaud expected to get more from the bugs than the polygraph. The polygraph was merely to set the mood, so to speak."

"When we were out of there I would have said the wrong thing instantly," she admitted, "but Tommy stopped me. As soon as they took our clothes away, he knew they would insert bugs."

"Tommy has a devious mind," Jake Grafton said blandly, and Sarah Houston laughed. The thought of Tommy Carmellini brought a glow to her cheeks. A smile lingered on her lips.

Jake Grafton saw that glow and smile and decided to move on. He produced the handheld computer that Henri Rodet had given him. "Ever seen one of these before?"

She inspected the device. "No, but I've read about them. Telephone, camera and computer all in one."

"Hidden in plain sight. This is the computer that Rodet used to communicate with his agent in Al Queda. The messages were transmitted over a satellite television system."

"Clever. How did you get this?" She held it up.

"He gave it to me."

"Where did he keep it?"

"His girlfriend carried it in her purse."

"Well, well, well," Sarah murmured.

"Indeed!" Grafton sighed. "These computer phones have been available for a couple of years, and I suspect that's about how long Rodet and his man used the system. In any event, I want you to get the messages off the memory of this thing."

"Oh, I'm sure he's tried to erase them."

"No doubt he has. I want the messages."

"I may have to take it apart," Sarah said.

"Whatever. And I have another little errand for you. Remember Gator Zantz, from London? He's going to be along in a few minutes. He'll have to leave his cell phone outside like everyone else. When you see him, go out, get the phone and get all the numbers off it. Find out who the numbers belong to. I want to know who he's been calling."

"Okay."

He left her there with the cell phone in hand. She was working on it when she saw Gator Zantz go by the door. She waited until Zantz had disappeared, then got up and left the SCIF.

Upstairs George Goldberg held up a tiny transmitter for Jake's inspection. "This was in the heel of her shoe. It's a homer."

"So they know that she's at the embassy and Carmellini's visiting the police?"

"So it would seem."

"The folks at the desk received a call from the police. Carmellini is demanding to speak to an American diplomat."

"Send somebody over," Jake Grafton said. "I hope they don't keep him all night. That boy needs some sleep."

Kirby Jones was the name of the man from the embassy. He was a slightly built fellow in his late twenties, I suppose, who wore horn-rim glasses and a bow tie. You don't see many bow ties these days, so I stared.

He stayed a safe distance away from the cell bars and pronounced his name. "I understand you wanted to see a diplomat?"

"Yeah," I said, tearing my eyes away from that bow tie. "Got any credentials?"

"My heavens, man," he said in the purest Boston accent, "you think the American embassy would send over a Russian?"

"I'm sure if they wanted to these Frenchies could dig up a frog who sounds like the Ding Dong Daddy from Dumas. Got any credentials?"

As he produced them from his jacket pocket I asked, "Where'd you get that tie, anyway?"

"There's a store on Harvard Square that sells them."

I looked through his stuff. Well, it looked official as hell to me. Jones was even wearing a bow tie in the photo on his diplomatic passport. I handed the packet back through the bars. "Get me outta here."

"An automobile that you rented at the airport last week blew up in a parking garage yesterday. A bomb, apparently. The police want to ask you some very reasonable questions about it."

"I didn't blow it up, if that's what you're getting around to."

"I don't think they suspect that you did, but they have some questions. It would be in the best interests of Franco-American relations if you answered them politely and truthfully so they can do their duty."

"I see."

"With the G-8 meeting in Versailles next week, the police have some very real concerns. You see that, don't you?"

"I'm not answering any questions."

Kirby Jones frowned. "If you persist in that stance, I'm afraid they may eject you from the country."

"You mean, like, send me home?"

"Yes."

"It's tempting." The drunks were caterwauling again. It wasn't my fault that I didn't have a diplomatic passport. If I had one I wouldn't be wasting an evening in this damn cell listening to that chorus.

"They also have some questions about a motorcycle chase that took place on the streets of Paris yesterday."

"You been in France long?"

"Three months."

"Know George Goldberg?"

He gave me a hard look. "I know who he is, yes."

"Why don't you call him? Then get back to me."

Being in jail is a humbling experience. It's too bad it is an experience reserved for the dregs of society and occasional drunks, like my fellow Americans a few doors away. More people should do it. More people should lie on a cot in a cell with nothing to do but stare at the ceiling and think about . . .

I thought about Al and Rich for a while, how they looked dead. They looked so surprised, as if they were shocked that life could end so suddenly, and for so little reason. I thought about the guy I threw through the clock; I got a glimpse of his face as I threw him, and he was surprised, too. Maybe the motorcyclists were surprised when they realized they were going to crash. And I thought about Marisa Petrou and Elizabeth Conner, the Israeli agents. It was a hell of a game, and it was being played for blood. Did they know? Would they be surprised?

Would I?

Finally I got to thinking about Sarah Houston. I liked the way she looked, the way her skin felt, the way she smiled . . . She was a smart cookie, and I liked that, too. Smart women are hard to come by these days. It seems that some of the smart ones don't really want to be smart.

I was asleep when I heard a key in the door. A uniformed policeman opened the cell door and motioned to me. The bow-tie man, Kirby Jones, was standing behind him. The drunks, who had sobered up somewhat, were shouting, "Hey, we want out, too," and Kirby, to his credit, was ignoring them.

When I got out in the corridor he said, "The director of the DGSE called the police. He said to let you out. You're free to go."

"It's Kirby with a *K*, right?"

"That's right."

"I'll name my first daughter after you."

I had to sign my name twice to reclaim my belt, my shoelaces and the contents of my pockets. I almost scribbled my real name before I remembered that I was Terry Shannon. When we were out on the street, Jones said, "Who are you, anyway?"

"Nobody you want to know," I told him as I shook his hand. I walked away in the direction of the nearest subway stop.

He called after me, "I've read about you. You're the clock guy, aren't you?"

My flat above the Rue Paradis looked terrific. The water in my little bathtub was hot and wet. I sat in it awhile staring at my knees. After I toweled off, I said good night to anyone listening, then crawled between the sheets. Aaaah!

CHAPTER TWENTY-ONE

When I awoke the next morning a fine cold rain spattered on my little window and gurgled in the gutter and downspout, which were right outside. I had the window open a couple of inches, so I went over and sat on the floor where I could feel the cool breeze coming through the gap.

This little room was a very pleasant place, and Paris was a great city. I wished I were really Terry G. Shannon, travel hack, with nothing on my agenda but visiting tourist sites and updating guidebook descriptions of hotels and restaurants. "Sorry, but the cassoulet isn't up to your rating. Au revoir and better luck next time."

I took the belt out of the trousers I wore yesterday and casually inspected it as I listened to the rain running off the roof and let the cool autumn wind play across my arms and face.

Grafton had said I could leave the agency after this assignment, and maybe I should. I was thoroughly sick of spooks and spies and vans with bodies.

I guess I was really sick of myself.

Sarah Houston was a nice woman; she had made her mistakes and paid for them, and so had I. Maybe—

There was a listening device in my belt. The French technicians had cut a small hole in the leather for it and woven the transmitter antenna wire into the stitching. The wire was tiny, about the diameter of a human hair, difficult to see unless one looked closely.

Should I wear this belt, or my other one?

This one, I decided. The game was up in the air, still to be decided.

Part of the problem was that the admiral wasn't in the habit of sharing his ratiocinations with me, which was to be expected, I guess, since I had a part to play in his drama. I was sure he thought there was nothing to be gained by burdening me with superfluous information.

Such as, why did he change the plan? When we came to France, we were going to dangle the Intelink in front of Henri Rodet. After all, he was the dude with the Al Queda source. But now we were conning Jean-Paul Arnaud, the Number Two spook. Did Arnaud and Rodet talk? Was Arnaud the villain? Did Rodet really have a spy buried in Al Queda, or was that a fiction for foreign consumption? Why was the Mossad stooging around? Was Marisa Petrou a double agent? Who shot Claude Bruguiere? More to the point, who the heck shot Alberto Salazar and Rich Thurlow?

It could have been me in that van instead of Al and Rich. Me! Mrs. Carmellini's son, Tommy.

I could have been sitting there thinking a twisted little thought when the door opened and pop, pop, life ended for me, just like that.

I was examining that reality when my cell phone rang, making me jump. I snatched it up and looked at the number. Willie Varner.

I reminded myself that the DGSE techs were listening to my side of the conversation, and perhaps Willie's too.

"Hello."

"I'm in a Seven Four Seven flyin' over England, Carmellini. Adios, asshole." The reception was perfect, his voice right in my ear. I figured he was lying. He continued. "I told you I was gettin' outta frog-land when the shit hit the fan, and by God, I meant it." Yeah, he was lying. "I'm still alive, no thanks to you."

"You could have borrowed my Superman suit, you know, so those bullets would bounce right off."

He sighed. "You don't believe me, do you?"

"No."

"The sailor has me doing important secret shit. I can't tell you anythin' about it. Don't call me wantin' somethin'. And stay outta trouble, dude."

"Okay."

He hung up.

I knew Willie Varner wouldn't boogie, no matter what he said. Willie would stick like glue. If he wasn't that kind of guy, he wouldn't be worth knowing.

The sailor was, of course, Grafton. If they were monitoring the cell phone conversation, the French spooks would never figure that out. Right. But what did Grafton have Willie the Wire doing? I spent a couple of minutes speculating, then gave up.

I hoped Jake Grafton knew who the players were and who had the ball. I certainly didn't.

I levered myself up and headed for the bathroom.

"There are the contents of Rodet's hard drive," Sarah Houston said to Jake Grafton. She pointed toward the computer screen. Grafton stood looking over her shoulder at a sea of computer symbols. They were in the SCIF in the basement of the embassy, in a tiny little room. On the walls were a calendar and a photo of the World Trade Center collapsing.

"The contents are encrypted," Sarah explained. "The code breakers at NSA are going to have to sort this out."

"Okay. Send it to them. Encrypted, of course."

Sarah attacked the keyboard. A minute later she said, "It's gone. Sorry I couldn't crack it."

"Well, it was a long shot." Jake dropped into the only other chair.

She handed him a single sheet of paper. "You asked for the telephone numbers from Gator Zantz's cell phone. Here they are."

Grafton looked them over. "You're sure about all of these."

"Yep."

Grafton folded the paper once, very neatly, then doubled it up, making all the edges touch. He inspected it to make sure it was perfectly square. Then he put it in his pocket. "Let's talk about your visit with Arnaud," he said. "Are you comfortable with the technology?"

She nodded. "It'll let him into your fake files."

"This won't work unless you sell him. He has to believe that you're madly in love with Tommy and want to run away with him."

"Why Arnaud?"

"If Rodet is telling the truth, it can't be anybody else."

"You couldn't convict a man of a parking violation with that kind of logic."

Grafton frowned. "That's true, but this isn't a trial."

"Is Rodet telling the truth?"

Grafton leaned back in his chair and took a deep breath while he considered. "That's a fair question and it deserves an honest answer. Let me put it this way—he's telling me part of the truth." He paused, considering. "Perhaps a better way to say that would be, he's telling me what he thinks is part of the truth."

"What kind of truth are you looking for?"

"The kind that leads to a living man, one who knows things that can help us catch the masterminds of Al Queda."

"They're leaders in the terrorist movement," Sarah admitted, "but if they are arrested or eliminated, others will take their place."

"What is the alternative?"

"I don't know."

"We're in a war against religious fanatics, madmen, who are trying to crack the foundations of Western civilization by murdering the innocent," Jake Grafton said. "The conflict between the demands of secular government and religion has shaped civilization, but Islam has been fossilized, frozen in time. The good news is that history is on our side—in the long run, religious zealots always lose. The Europeans fought true believers of every stripe for centuries and finally won. Look around you at this city, this nation. France is secular civilization in full flower, and it's worth fighting for."

"Win or lose, the fanatics will murder a lot of people," Sarah Houston said thoughtfully.

"Our job is to see that they don't," Jake Grafton said grimly. "Let's get on with it."

Elizabeth Conner's door slammed in the room under mine, so I was at the window watching when she went jogging away along the sidewalk, past two bored old hookers smoking cigarettes. At least the rain had stopped, although the sky was low and slate gray.

Conner was another puzzle I hadn't figured out. Was she really an American? Or an Israeli pretending to be an American? Did it matter?

I wondered if another search of her flat would turn up anything useful. Was there another way to learn her story?

Of course, anything she told me would be just that, a story. Still, it would be a place to start. We could check every fact she let loose of, to learn . . . what?

DGSE officer Claude Bruguiere could have been hit by the Mossad. In fact, Lizzie Conner might have done the shooting. For that matter, dear, sweet, innocent Marisa might have pulled the trigger.

Around noon I met Sarah Houston in the dining room of her hotel. I stood as she approached the table, and she kissed me. Her tongue grazed my lower lip in a contact lasting several heartbeats. It was a darn nice kiss, the kind that speeds up your heart ten or fifteen whacks a minute. She broke it off as my blood pressure soared, then backed away a few inches and gave me a tiny smile.

I helped her with her chair and almost tripped getting back into mine. That's when I handed her a note that said my belt had a bug in it. She read the note, nodded and handed it back. I wadded it up and stuck it in my pocket, to be discarded into a toilet.

"I'm not looking forward to seeing that man," she muttered as she glanced at the menu.

"We'll get through this," I assured her warmly, laying my

hand atop one of hers. "Ibiza will be worth it. You'll see. Just the two of us, lazy mornings, walks in the afternoon, life slow and easy."

"You make it sound so tempting." She turned her hand so her fingers touched my wrist.

We chatted on, about how great it would be to be modestly rich and have each other. I hoped to hell the frogs who were listening were getting all this. Actually, it was an easy conversation to do. Sarah was lovely, smart and the kind of gal a guy like me could spend his life with.

Where did that thought come from?

Come on, Tommy! This is just an act. Remember?

We didn't have any trouble getting into the Conciergerie this time. The guard took one look at my Terry Shannon passport and motioned us on through. One of the security men accompanied us to the elevator, watched our faces as we rose two flights, then ushered us along to Arnaud's corner suite. The receptionist took one look, then buzzed the great one, and we were shown in. The security man stood beside the closed office door.

"Hello," Arnaud grunted unenthusiastically.

I have played my share of poker through the years and learned a thing or two about reading faces. Right then I would have bet my stack that Arnaud was on the fence: He wasn't sure we were genuine and he wasn't sure we weren't. The truth be told, this was a better position than Grafton and I thought we might be in. We figured he would be pretty close to dead certain that we were conning him, so we were ahead of the game.

I attacked. "I didn't appreciate you siccing the police on me last night," I said aggressively. "I had to get a diplomat involved and do a lot of explaining to my boss."

Arnaud regarded me icily from under bushy eyebrows. Now his face was expressionless, which I thought was probably his usual professional demeanor. "Two men on motorcycles tried to run you down. Why?"

"My guess would be that they were trying to get even with me for throwing their pal through the clock at the museum, but I certainly don't know. They very nearly made me a traffic statistic. If the police in this town were any damn good they'd be trying to find out if the motorcycle dudes knew the clock diver."

"Who blew up your car?"

"Maybe those guys, or some friends of theirs. You obviously have a lot of assholes running around this town."

"Why didn't you call the police?"

We weren't getting anywhere with this, and we both knew it. I was in no hurry, however. If Arnaud wanted to spend the afternoon beating around the bush, that was fine with me. Cons only work when the mark sells himself. While he was barking questions, his natural greed was percolating. I also knew a thing or two about greed.

After two or three more questions, his eyes strayed to Sarah. That's when I knew we had him hooked.

"Don't look at me like that, creep," Sarah snapped.

For a hundredth of a second, he looked startled. Then the mask dropped.

This was too easy. Maybe he was conning us.

"C'mon, Sarah," I said, rising from my chair. "Let's get the hell outta here."

"Sit!" Arnaud ordered coldly.

I obeyed.

"I want to see it," he said.

"First the money."

"First I see it."

"No," Sarah said firmly.

I leaned across and got hold of a hand. "Hey, babe. This is our chance. Let's do the deal."

"Don't 'babe' me, Terry. I don't trust this slimy bastard. I want the money first. Ten grand."

I got in front of her, lifted her from the chair and led her to the corner of the room farthest from Arnaud. I held her in my arms and we whispered. I told her I loved her and a bunch of other stuff, strictly part of the con. She let tears leak and swabbed at them with a fist.

Man, she was *good!* Looking at her red eyes, watching that lip tremble, I'd have given her my life savings to help a Nigerian prince get money into the States.

She capitulated.

Arnaud gave her his chair. She turned to his computer, which was on. She began talking, telling him about the walls around the Intelink to keep out riffraff. Talking slowly, showing him every keystroke, she led him to her rathole. At one point he got too close to her, and she recoiled like a scared cat. He backed off.

She looked up at him. "You're recording all this, right?"

He didn't say anything.

"Because I'm not doing it again unless you pay me a lot of money."

"I will try to remember your words, Miss Houston."

She got back to it. Five minutes later the opening page of Intelink C came onto the screen.

Sarah rose. "You owe us ten thousand dollars."

Arnaud sat playing with the scroll buttons as he read. After a moment he turned, nodded at the security man, who was still standing over by the door, and said to us, "Tomorrow morning. Ten o'clock."

He was still staring at the screen when I went through the door and glanced back.

Sarah Houston stayed in character when we were out on the street. "Do you think the bastard will buy the whole package?" she asked.

I grinned at her. It's a pleasure to work with a pro, and she certainly was one. "Hard to say," I replied. To give the unseen watchers material for their report, I put my arm around her shoulder as we walked. She felt mighty good as we strolled across the bridge over the Seine and the wind whipped at us.

At the embassy I went into the men's room. Sitting in a stall, I used a penknife to pry the transmitter out of my belt. I twisted it loose from the antenna and dropped it into the trash when I left.

Pink Maillard and Grafton were huddled in the admiral's office. I looked in, gave Grafton the Hi sign, and stepped back outside. Pink looked worried. I didn't blame him; I'd be on tranquilizers if I were responsible for keeping the president alive in this day and age.

Gator Zantz was there, too. He looked properly humble, having been summoned from his London sinecure to help fill the hole created by Al and Rich's sudden departure.

"Hey, Tommy," he said when he saw me sitting beside Sarah, holding her hand. He merely nodded at her; I wondered if he remembered her name. "What in hell have you guys got going around here?"

"G-8 meeting, spies all over, assassins . . . another day in the CIA. That's going to be the title of my memoirs."

"Always the clown."

"How's every little thing in merry ol' England?"

"Still there. Wanna make a little bet on the Monday night game?"

"Man, I don't know who's playing, and I don't want to take your money. Don't you have a car payment or rent or something like that?"

"Very funny," he said, and went away. Which was fine. Personally, I never liked the guy, but then, there are a lot of guys I don't like. Dozens, scattered all over the world.

Grafton wanted to see me before I left, someone said. I winked at Sarah and went to see if he was alone. He was.

The admiral wanted to know every word and detail of our performance at the Conciergerie. After fifty questions, he asked my opinion. I rubbed my chin while I considered. "I think he bought it, but maybe not."

Grafton grunted. His parting comment didn't give me much comfort. "Be careful, Tommy. Watch yourself out there."

"Yeah." That's what I told him. Yeah. Sure. Always. I'm going to live forever.

Sarah and I had dinner, just to keep up appearances, at an

intimate little place George Goldberg recommended. He certainly knew his restaurants.

Sarah was—but I don't need to bore you with that.

I dropped her at her hotel and took a cab to the Rue Paradis. Riding through the streets I remembered Rich and Al, and how I felt when my car blew up. Now wasn't the time to start coasting. I sensed that matters were coming to a head; this thing was going to be over pretty soon, one way or the other, and I was going to be a free man. What was I going to do without the CIA—and the green paycheck?

I thought about that as I checked the traffic and scanned the pedestrians. Where were the local sons of Islam? I'd thrown one through a clock, and two had crashed. Maybe they bombed the car, maybe they didn't, but I was blaming them for it until a better candidate showed up. Then there was Al and Rich—somebody iced them.

I had the cabbie drop me two blocks from my place. I stood there on the sidewalk watching the cab drive away, breathing deeply and soaking up some Paris. No other cars whipped up and let people out. It was nearly eleven o'clock. At that hour on the sidewalk in that neighborhood, it was just me and a few stray johns dying to meet some of the neighborhood cuties.

I paused at the top of my street and looked over the scene. I couldn't find anything out of the ordinary.

Man, I've been doing this too long.

So where am I going to go and what am I going to do when I get back to the States?

The stairwell was narrow and dark, as usual. I paused by Elizabeth Conner's door and listened—could faintly hear television audio. I kept going, unlocked the door to my palace, stepped inside and took off my shoes.

After I got out of my clothes and brushed the fangs, I pulled out my infrared goggles and put them on. I looked downward and fiddled with the gain and contrast controls.

It took me several seconds to realize what I was looking at. Elizabeth Conner was lying motionless on the floor, and she was difficult to see. I changed positions while I adjusted the gain control. No help there. Contrast didn't seem to make any difference. The battery?

I looked at the hot-water pipes. About as usual. Back at Conner, her legs akimbo . . .

I tore off the goggles. Grabbed my lock picks. Left my door standing open, charged down the stairs three at a time. Pounded on her door. No answer, of course.

The television ran a series of ads for something or other as I worked with the pick and torsion wrench. I was all thumbs. God damn it all to hell!

The lock gave and I threw open the door.

She hadn't moved. Her eyes were open and she was staring at nothing at all.

CHAPTER TWENTY-TWO

Elizabeth Conner was very dead and had been for hours. How many I don't know, but her body was cool to the touch. Of course. That was why her body was just a ghostly shadow on the infrared.

Ah, me. She was wearing her bra and panties, nothing else. A towel lay under her.

She had been strangled. Her neck was a mass of bruises. I tried not to look at her face.

The contents of the room had not been touched, as far as I could tell. Whoever murdered her had apparently come for that purpose. Someone knocked, she wrapped a towel around herself, then opened the door. Whoever was standing there advanced, seized her by the neck and began to squeeze violently. Maybe she took a couple of steps backward. When his victim was dead, the strangler left, pulling the door closed behind him.

You've probably read the mysteries and seen the *CSI* shows where the victim has big gobs of the killer's DNA under her fingernails. I have, too, so I looked. Well, I didn't see any obvious wads of skin and hair, although she did have two broken fingernails. The broken nails looked jagged, as if they were fresh breaks.

I forced myself to look at her face. Whoever did that . . .

Suddenly I felt embarrassed, as if I were shaming the dead. I was in the presence of sudden, unexpected violent death, and I was wearing only shorts and a T-shirt.

I pulled the door shut and smeared my palms around over the back of the knob. The killer wouldn't have left any prints, and I certainly didn't want to decorate the knob with mine. Nor did I want it wiped clean, just covered with useless smeared prints.

Back upstairs I sat down for a think.

After a few minutes, I called Jake Grafton on his cell phone. "Elizabeth Conner's dead. Strangled in her flat. I just found the body."

He groaned. "Damnation."

After a moment of silence, he said, "Go get her cell phone. Bring it with you tomorrow."

I was losing my patience with Jake Grafton and this whole spy gig. "You know whose number is on it, don't you?" I said roughly.

"I think I know who killed her, if that's what you mean. Please, go get the cell phone before the police find the body." He hung up on me.

Jake Grafton stared at the computer screen, trying to concentrate. He had two pages of text in front of him. He scrolled through it, reading it again, word for word. Then he hit the print button. When he had the pages he folded them carefully, put them in a shirt pocket, and turned off the computer.

I stopped to put my pants on before I went back downstairs. I picked the lock again and went into Conner's room, leaving the door open so I could hear anyone coming up the stairs.

I tried not to look at her. Even in her underwear, she looked obscenely naked.

I began frantically looking for her cell phone. Alone in a bedroom with a strangled woman, listening for the heavy tread of policemen, I could feel the tension ratchet up with every passing second. Of course, as the tension tightened, I developed an urge to pee, which got steadily worse. I tried to put all the extraneous stuff out of my mind and concentrate on thinking logically about my task. It was difficult.

Three minutes of searching did it for me. I convinced myself that her cell phone wasn't in the room. It was possible, I suppose, that it was under her, but not very probable. In any event, I wasn't going to move the corpse to look.

I locked the door behind me, smeared the knob one more time, and went upstairs. Safely back in my hole, I made a beeline for the bathroom. When I had relieved the pressure, I called Grafton and gave him the bad news.

Jake Grafton was walking toward the embassy's main entrance when the phone rang. He signed out at the security desk as he listened to Tommy.

"Do you know what's going on?" Tommy demanded.

"Well, I have made some guesses. Based on evidence, I suppose, or lack thereof. But it's thin. We're not there yet."

When I heard that comment, I couldn't restrain myself. "Maybe you should tell somebody what you're thinking. Don't think I'm being pushy, but if on the way home tonight you get crushed by a falling piano, it would be nice if some other human on planet Earth had an inkling of what the hell you think is going on in Paris."

Grafton sure took his time answering. "I suppose you're right," he said finally.

I waited expectantly.

He began with random comments, then finally got into the groove. He told me about Abu Qasim and Henri Rodet, and he told me what he could prove, what he surmised, and what he thought might happen as events played out. The recitation took about twenty minutes.

As I listened I sat at my window and watched the first snowflakes fall into the streetlights.

Finally Grafton ran out of words. I thanked him for taking the time to talk to me and hung up.

A few minutes later I climbed into bed. I lay there listening to the wind sing as it passed my window, which was open about half an inch.

I tried to think about something besides Elizabeth Conner. I thought about Sarah, and about a woman I used to know and had sort of decided to wait for, Anna Modin. But it didn't work. Their faces faded and I was left with the image of Elizabeth Conner lying dead on her floor, strangled, her eyes bulging, every muscle in her face taut, frozen in death. The image was ugly, and I began thinking evil thoughts.

It was a few minutes past midnight when Jake Grafton put his cell phone into his pocket. As he talked he had taken shelter behind a pillar on the portico of the embassy. Now he stood looking at the Place de la Concorde, and at the two police vans parked in a side street to his right. On the sidewalk beside one of them, a small knot of policemen stood smoking and drinking something hot. Grafton could just see the steam rising from their cups.

There wasn't much traffic in the huge square. No taxis in front of the Hotel de Crillon, which was next door, and none zooming along the Rue de Rivoli, ready to career through the plaza and across the Seine on the Pont de la Concorde. He fastened the neck buttons on his coat, jammed his hands in his pockets, and set off for the Metro stop. A few snowflakes were falling, melting when they hit the pavement. The wind had a nasty bite, so he hurried the last few paces toward the stairs leading underground.

There were four or five people on the platform; he didn't pay much attention. He walked out to within four feet or so of the edge and unfastened the top buttons on his coat, looking idly at the billboards advertising haute couture jeans and expensive tennis shoes.

Grafton was thinking about Elizabeth Conner when he realized that the man on his left was walking toward him. He looked. The man was young, Midde Eastern, of medium height and build.

Jake glanced right. Another man, also Middle Eastern, advancing toward him.

He heard a noise. Two behind him—he had walked right by them when he came out onto the platform.

They had been waiting for him!

He was outnumbered four to one. There were no other

people on the platform at this time of night. No, there was one other person on the platform, sitting on the bench, a man in a long coat.

Grafton turned to face the young thugs.

They kept coming. One of them pulled a knife from his pocket.

This might be an excellent time to try out the wireless Taser, Grafton thought. He pulled it from his coat pocket and flipped the switch on the side to turn it on. What was it Maillard had said? The thing took ten or fifteen seconds to charge the capacitor?

"You guys stop right there."

They did stop, momentarily, their eyes on the weapon. Then one of them realized there was no hole in the barrel. He laughed, pointed at it, and made a comment to his friends, who grinned.

The man on Jake's left pretended to piss, and laughed. *They thought the thing was a squirt gun.*

The admiral raised the weapon and pointed it right at the man with the knife, who was about eight feet away, still immobile. "I wouldn't, if I were you."

The man lunged—and Jake pulled the trigger through the first detent to the last stop, as far as it would go.

Even he was surprised at what happened next. There was a flash as a finger of visible light shot out and illuminated the man's chest. A second later a streak of lightning reached out with a loud, high-pitched cracking sound, the finger of God, and hit him right where the light had rested. The lightning strobed once, twice, and disappeared.

Half-blinded by the intensity of the glare, Grafton watched as the man he had zapped dropped his knife and toppled to the concrete. Then he groaned.

Jake looked at the weapon. He had the intensity set on the middle setting. "Best to keep it there," Maillard had said, "halfway between kill and tickle."

Grafton swung the weapon, pointing it at the others, who had already retreated a few steps. "Anyone else want some?"

The thugs turned their heads toward the figure sitting on a

bench against the wall. For the first time, Grafton really looked at him. He was an older man, wearing a ratty coat and brimmed hat—and he had a pistol in his hand, an automatic of some type with a silencer on the end of the barrel. There was no mistake about the silencer, which was as big as a sausage.

He raised the pistol, pointed it at Grafton.

Jake didn't wait. He leaped from the platform onto the track as the pistol popped and he heard a bullet zing past.

As he ran he could hear bullets pinging off the concrete. Hitting a running man at fifty feet with a pistol without sights would be a challenge for an expert, which the shooter plainly wasn't. He had a lot of bullets, though. They spanged around Grafton and stimulated his adrenaline mightily. He ran toward the dark tunnel ahead as hard as he could go, still carrying the thunderbolt weapon in his right hand.

He had reached the dubious sanctuary of the darkness when he heard the oncoming train—heard the rumble, heard it decelerate, then heard the squeal of brakes. The train was entering the station from the other direction. In a few moments it would be coming this way.

He glanced back and saw two men running toward him, both looking back.

Grafton felt for the weapon's intensity knob, cranking it as far as it would go. He aimed at one of the oncoming men and pulled the trigger.

The light reached out and—*crack!* The strobing lightning . . . and the man he had aimed at fell to the tracks.

The other one didn't pause in his charge. Grafton pointed the weapon and pulled the trigger again. Nothing.

Damn thing needs to recharge the capacitor.

Grafton braced himself to receive the charge—then he saw the gleam of the knife blade!

He turned and ran into the darkness. He stumbled on the ties, recovered, and ran hard.

Slap, slap, slap. His feet pounded on the gravel. Behind him he could hear the panting of his pursuer.

He was running into total darkness. Not a glimmer of light

ahead . . . no, a faint glow. The track turned up there, and now he could see the reflected glow from the next station.

He would never make it. The man behind was getting closer.

Grafton risked a look and saw only a blur, a few feet behind. He could hear the man's rasping breath—he wasn't in shape, but he was thirty or more years younger than the admiral.

Grafton felt a touch on his shoulder. He spun with the weapon leveled in his hand and pulled the trigger as he turned.

The knife went by his face. Then came the flash, the report—and a scream as the man fell onto Grafton, who was falling himself, going down on his back.

The man went on screaming in agony as the lightning pulsed between them.

When the darkness came again, the sound stopped. All sound.

Jake's attacker was lying across him. And he wasn't breathing. The admiral felt for the pulse in the man's neck. There wasn't one.

Jake Grafton pushed the corpse aside and rose shakily to his feet.

He heard the train get under way, felt the rush of air. He scrambled over the hot rail, carefully avoiding it, and hunkered down against the tunnel wall.

The headlight illuminated the bodies on the track, but the train continued to accelerate. The noise rose to a painful level. The wind became a gale; Jake braced himself against it. Then the train thundered by, its steel wheels singing on the rails. The sides of the cars passed inches from Jake's shoulder.

CHAPTER TWENTY-THREE

On Saturday morning Agatha Hempstead led Grafton and Goldberg toward the ambassador's office. She marched in front and both men found that they had to lengthen their stride to keep up. The receptionist had anticipated their arrival and was manning the door. He opened it for Hempstead and her entourage, then closed it behind them.

The ambassador was on the scrambled telephone. When he saw them, he punched the button to put the audio on the telephone speaker.

"Mr. President, they are here now."

"Very well," the president said in his distinctive voice. "Well, Owen, please repeat your request for their benefit."

"I would like Grafton and Goldberg recalled," Lancaster said. "Last night Grafton killed two men in the subway with some kind of electric weapon. The police released him after verifying his diplomatic immunity. I have talked to the foreign minister, who is of the opinion that the government will declare Admiral Grafton persona non grata unless we act first and recall him. They are very unhappy that he had a weapon."

"I assume they would be less agitated if he were dead?"

If Lancaster understood the irony in that remark, he ignored it. "Then it would just be a tragedy, you see. The minister would issue an official apology, routine condolences, etc. Now the press is screaming about a weapons violation, accusing the government of bias toward the United States."

"Can't we make some noise about Middle Eastern thugs attacking diplomats in subway stations?"

"Not unless you're willing to be called a racist on the eve of the summit."

"Uh-huh," the president said. "What's their gripe about Goldberg?"

"He is the CIA station chief, a fact of which the French are well aware. I think he's worn out his welcome, too."

"I see. Grafton, are you there?"

"Yes, sir," Jake said.

"I read your report of last night's incident. How are you coming on that matter we discussed before you left?"

"Still working it, sir."

"Any way you can get someone to put in a good word for you with the French government?"

"Are you referring to Rodet?"

"Yes."

"I can call him."

"I suggest you do that. And I want a complete brief from you when I get over there."

"We should have most of the answers by then, sir."

"Terrific. Goldberg?"

"Yes, sir."

"Better behave yourself if you expect to complete your tour."

"Yes, sir."

"Owen, I hate to put you on the spot like this, but you're going to have to kiss some more frog ass. Tell the minister you've been chatting with that I ripped Grafton and Goldberg a new one and respectfully request that they be allowed to remain in France, at least until after the G-8 conference is over."

Owen Lancaster didn't turn a hair. He'd been doing this for more years than the president had been in government. "Yes, sir," he said evenly. "See you Tuesday."

" 'Preciate it, Owen. Knew I could count on you."

The connection broke, and the speaker began buzzing. Lancaster pushed buttons to silence the noise. "*I* don't appreciate being put on the spot like this," he said.

Grafton and Goldberg were still standing in front of his desk. He hadn't asked them to sit.

"This weapon the French said you have—do you have it with you?"

Grafton nodded affirmatively.

"May I see it, please." It wasn't a question. Lancaster held out his hand.

Jake Grafton removed the weapon from his pocket and flipped on the power switch. He held it so Lancaster could see it but didn't offer it to him.

"I'll take that, Admiral," the ambassador said curtly.

"I think not," Jake responded. "I may need it again."

Lancaster's eyes narrowed. "I understand you killed two men with that thing. That makes it a deadly weapon. There is a centuries-old tradition that diplomatic personnel will be unarmed—it's really a point of international law—and it's a tradition that I personally support."

"I'm not going to become a victim of street thugs just to make your life more comfortable," Grafton said. He pointed the weapon at the television set in the corner and pulled the trigger.

The laser beam shot out; a long second later, the electrical charge vomited forth in a clap of thunder that was painfully loud in that enclosed room. As the lightning strobed, the television picture tube exploded, showering glass fragments in all directions. Fortunately everyone slammed his eyes shut or managed to cover them.

The silence that followed was broken only by the patter of tiny bits of glass raining down until Grafton said, "Come on, George," and headed for the door.

I was in a foul mood when I got to the embassy. I'd only had a few hours' sleep, and each time I dropped off I awoke with nightmares. The corpse on the floor of the apartment below weighed heavily on my mind. It wasn't right that her body should be left to rot.

Gator Zantz was manning the guard desk outside the SCIF. Apparently security guard was the one job in the agency he was completely qualified for. I snarled at him, "Admiral Grafton in?"

"He's up in the ambassador's office getting chewed out."

"About what?"

"Couple of guys he killed in the subway last night."

That took the juice out of me. "Oh," I managed, and dug in my wallet for my pass. After Gator prayed over it, I tossed my cell phone into the basket and went in to find Sarah.

She was working on a computer in the bowels of the SCIF. Of course, the screen was arranged so that anyone coming into her cubicle couldn't see it—security, you know. I dropped into the chair.

"The admiral told me about Elizabeth Conner," she said, glancing at me.

I didn't know what to say. "It must have happened while we were eating dinner, or maybe a little before," I muttered.

"You look as if it hit you hard."

That comment surprised me. In my profession you can't let your emotions show. Man, I was slipping. Getting old, I guess. And real tired of this . . . this . . .

Sarah picked up a sheet of paper from the desk and handed it to me to read.

After two sentences my heart almost stopped.

Henri Rodet has passed to the CIA information from his undercover agent in Al Queda, which has been planning a major attempt on the lives of the G-8 leaders in Paris. The agent reports that Osama Bin Laden feels that even if the attempt is only partially successful, the mere fact the organization is strong enough to launch such an attack will have major political implications in the G-8 nations and the Islamic world.

I tried to whistle and nothing came out. "Wow," I said. "I guess the admiral's got it in spades, huh!"

"Ah, there you are!" Grafton's voice, behind me in the doorway. I still had the page in my hand, so he said, "What do you think of my effort?"

"So the wizards at the NSA decrypted the stuff on Rodet's

telephone, eh? Jeez, when you were talking to me last night you didn't say—"

"Oh, that's all bullshit. I wrote it yesterday evening, and Washington posted it on your private Intelink for Jean-Paul Arnaud to find." Grafton waved a hand distractedly. "The NSA code breakers are still working on Rodet's telephone, but we've run out of time. That's what I think Arnaud thinks might be on that hard drive."

"So you're trying a finesse?"

"Call it whatever you like."

I'd seen Grafton in action before. He wasn't sweating or breathing hard yet. "What do *you* think is on that hard drive?" I asked.

He stepped into the cubicle. "If I were a betting man, I'd bet Qasim hasn't sent Rodet anything of significance since he gave him the Veghel stuff."

"But that's crazy," I protested. "Why was Rodet trying to protect the device if there's nothing on it?"

"He's trying to protect Qasim, not the hard drive of that pocket computer. There's a large difference."

"You're implying Qasim gave Rodet the Veghel stuff to win his trust—"

"—Or win it back."

"Sacrificing the Veghel conspirators? To checkmate the king?"

"To kill the kings, perhaps," Grafton said, nodding. "It's possible." He looked at his watch. "My wife and your pal Willie are due to relieve Cliff Icahn in the listening van at Rodet's country estate in about an hour. Why don't you go pick them up and drive them out there? Stay with them. I'll have my cell phone in my pocket—I want to know what you hear and if anyone comes by there."

A little ride in the country! I stood up and shook down my trousers as I glanced again at Grafton's composition. "If you got this figured right, after Arnaud reads this, he and his pals will zip right on over to have a piece of Rodet."

"I'm sorta hoping they will," Grafton said, and grinned. He pulled something that looked like a plastic water pistol from his pocket and handed it to me. "Better take this along."

As I examined the device, Grafton explained how it worked.

"How noisy is this thing?"

"About as loud as a pistol shot."

"Got any knives in the building?"

Grafton nodded. "Keep that," he said, and disappeared through the door.

I dropped back into the chair. "When we get out of this, if we do," I said to Sarah, "Grafton's going to let me resign from the agency. Why don't you talk to him about getting out of your job?"

She eyed me with interest. "That a proposal?"

"Aah, actually . . . no. Just a suggestion."

"I'll keep it in mind."

We sat in silence, not looking at each other. I played with the ray gun, looking it over. "This thing really work?" I asked Sarah.

"Last night in the subway he injured one man and killed two others with it, or one like it," she said dryly.

"Sounds like a recommendation," I agreed.

Grafton returned several minutes later. "Goldberg said you can use this. It's from his personal collection." He produced a Fairbairn-Sykes fighting knife, complete with wrist scabbard, an artifact if ever there was one. I only knew what it was because I'd seen one in the Imperial War Museum. "Guy in MI-6 gave it to him," Grafton added. "His grandfather used it in World War II."

"I would have guessed World War I," I said, and rolled up my left sleeve. As I was strapping it on my forearm I asked, "What about the ten grand Arnaud owes us? Sarah and I were going by this morning to collect."

"He'll probably be too busy today to pay off. Let's hope so, anyway."

"Darn," Sarah said with a sigh. "I had plans for some of that money."

I wasn't quite finished. "If you've got this hairball all figured out," I said to Grafton, "who shot Rich Thurlow and Al Salazar and strangled Elizabeth Conner? I'd like to know who the players are."

Sarah opened her mouth to say something, but Grafton silenced her with a glance. "Not yet," he said.

"By chance, do you have any Snickers bars in that desk?" I asked Sarah. She shook her head. I looked at Grafton. "So what do we do if Arnaud shows up?"

"Call me. Pink Maillard and I will be close by with a couple of his men. We can be there in five minutes."

"The cavalry! So we're the bait for the lion, huh? Callie know that?"

Grafton snorted. "Know it? Hell, this was her idea. I didn't have the guts to say no." He pinned me with those gray eyes and said softly, "Be careful, okay?"

"Sure, Admiral."

That's what you always say to Jake Grafton. Sure. He's that kind of guy.

After Carmellini left, Grafton dropped into the chair beside Sarah's desk. "This older man I've been seeing—I think Tommy took his picture. Did the agency match it up with anything in the database?"

"No," Sarah said, and stroked the keys. The photo appeared.

Grafton got out of the chair and moved so he could see the screen. "That's him, all right. He was in the subway last night with four young toughs." The admiral examined the photo, then backed away and squinted at it. "What would he look like if he were younger?"

"I can manipulate that image and pass it back to Langley," Sarah said. She attacked the keyboard. "Oh, by the way," she said as she typed, "I can't find any record of Marisa Petrou in Europe before she was ten years old." She looked at Grafton. "Suggestive, don't you think?"

"It raises questions," he admitted.

• • •

I picked up Willie Varner at his hotel. I called ahead and got him on his cell, so he was waiting in front of the joint when I pulled up.

"Hey, man," he said as he pulled the door shut.

"Hey."

"Nice car. I thought yours blew up."

"Yeah. Must've had a short in it or something. This is an embassy heap."

"Well, I want to tell you, it's been fun working with Mrs. Grafton. She's quite a lady. Got better personal habits than you do and doesn't cuss as much."

"What you been up to?"

"Sittin' in that van out at Rodet's, lookin' and listenin'. The sailor thought that ol' Rodet and his girlfriend might get snatched by somebody. We were supposed to call him if anybody did that." He kept talking, nattering on about Mrs. Grafton and how nice she was and all that.

I wasn't paying much attention to Willie, I'm afraid. I was looking for my Muslim friends as I drove and wondering why Grafton thought that Qasim was a false agent or, even worse, a double agent.

Mrs. Grafton was also waiting on the sidewalk when I pulled up. Seeing her there, a target for anyone who wanted to get even with Grafton, brought me back to full alert. I was going to need all my brain cells to just keep myself, Mrs. Grafton and Willie alive. Grafton was going to have to do the thinking.

"Hello, Willie. Tommy." She climbed in and shut the door. I muttered a good morning as I watched for a hole in traffic. I got one and rolled as Callie and Willie chattered away like lifelong friends.

When he was with me, Willie Varner didn't show the slightest interest in Paris, France, Europe, the people, how they lived, any of that. As we rode out of the city he plied Callie with questions. By the time we had left the suburbs behind, they were talking art.

As they visited I began worrying about Cliff Icahn, who

was alone in the surveillance van near the Rodet estate. Oh, man, it would be a really bad scene if he were dead when we got there. I dug my cell phone out of my pocket, and as Willie discussed the Impressionists' use of light and color—please, I am not making this up—I dialed Cliff. He answered on the third ring.

"This is Cliff."

I relaxed a little. "Tommy. What's happening?"

"Slow morning. When are you going to get here?"

"Twenty minutes or so."

"Gardener arrived a half hour or so ago, and a grocery delivery van came by. That's it. For all I know the folks are still sound asleep."

"I doubt that. We'll see you soon." I slapped the phone shut.

Willie knew more about art than I thought he did, but still, he couldn't talk it for more than ten minutes. Mrs. Grafton deftly changed the subject, talked about Washington, the city where Willie Varner had spent his life, except when he was in prison. Between the two of them, they knew every nook and cranny of that town, let me tell you.

The van was parked about a mile from the entrance to Rodet's estate in a little public pull-off about fifty yards up from the three-way intersection on Rodet's side of the Marne bridge. We could see anyone crossing the bridge and turning east toward Rodet's. Of course, we couldn't see traffic coming in from the other direction to Rodet's entrance, but there was nothing out that way but some camps and old farms. Everyone going to or coming from Paris came this way.

Cliff was sitting behind the wheel of the van wearing a headset when I drove up. He had the window down and was resting his elbow on it. He wriggled a finger at me. There were no other vehicles or people in sight. I parked the government sedan behind him, got my backpack from the back seat and walked over with my hand in my pocket holding the zapper. I had the battery switch on, so the capacitor was charging, just in case.

I faced the door. "Hey."

Cliff yawned. I didn't think he'd do that if there were

someone behind him with a pistol in his neck, so I relaxed. Still . . . I leaned in just enough to look. Yep, the van was empty. I motioned to Willie and Callie Grafton, and they got out of the car.

"What's going on in the house?"

"Not a damn thing," he said, and opened the door to get out. "They're listening to music. Classical. I dozed off a couple of times." He yawned again, then said hi to Willie and nodded at Mrs. Grafton. I introduced him and they chatted a little bit. After I gave Cliff the key to the sedan, he flipped a hand and climbed into the thing, turned it around, crossed the bridge and turned left for Paris.

Willie and Callie got into the back of the van and played with the equipment. I tossed my backpack onto the passenger seat, yet I didn't want to get in. That thing last night with Elizabeth Conner . . . nothing else that had happened in Paris had hit me like that. The guy I threw through the clock, the assholes on the motorcycles—they sallied forth to commit mayhem or murder and they got smacked instead. Al and Rich—I felt sorry for them, sure, but . . .

Conner, strangled . . . I couldn't get her face out of my mind.

I walked around the van taking deep breaths and looking at everything. A car came along the road from the northwest and crossed the bridge, then hung a left for Paris.

Now isn't the time to stress out, Tommy-boy. A few more days, then you can have your breakdown.

It turned out I wasn't going to make it a few more days. I started retching. I went over in the weeds and put my hands on my knees and heaved my breakfast and kept heaving until there was nothing in there to come up.

When I got myself more or less under control, I went back to the van. I heard Willie and Callie in there talking, their voices just murmurs.

Okay, Tommy, get it ratcheted up, guy.

Okay. I'm okay!

I took some more deep breaths and climbed behind the wheel. The headset that Cliff had been wearing was lying on the console, so I put it on. A symphony . . . I didn't recognize the composer. Not that I know much about music. Truth is, there is a lot I don't know about.

The stuff I do know about isn't the kind of stuff that any sane man really wants to know.

Apparently the radio was automatically channel surfing, listening for five seconds or so on each set of bugs. Now it switched again; the symphony was faint. No voices.

At the count of five, it switched again. Nothing on this set. Nor the next. The next was music, faintly, still the symphony.

Then back to the symphony at full cry.

There was a bottle of water in the cup holder on the dash that Cliff had apparently been drinking out of. Hoping he didn't have anything contagious, I finished it off and felt a little better.

Let's see, I put those bugs in the office, the library, the two sitting rooms, and the dining room. If the music was in the library or one of the sitting rooms, where were the people?

I turned around. "Can you get the video from the office?" I asked Willie.

"Oh, yeah," he said, and played with the controls. He reached up and turned the small monitor above his head so I could see it. The little camera was looking at the desk and computer. No one was in the picture.

"Got any more water back there?" I asked.

Callie passed me another bottle. It was warm. I drained it anyway.

Whew!

The leaves were blowing, the branches swaying. The overcast was up high, but it obscured the sun.

Two cars came across the bridge, but they went straight instead of turning toward Rodet's. They passed the van and the people in the car ignored me; maybe they knew I was an American.

"Something's not right," I said as Callie flipped through the audio channels another time. "We should hear some voices unless everyone's asleep."

She looked at me, and I saw the guts and intelligence in

that face as she asked, "Do you want to call Jake?" Not "Are you sure?" or any of that.

I wasn't sure, though. Maybe I should have been, but I wasn't. I listened through another round of the channels and wondered if I was going to heave again. Apparently not.

"Not yet," I told Callie.

But something was wrong. I had that feeling. Or I was breaking out in paranoia again. Is there a pill for that?

Darn, I'll bet those bastards swept for bugs and found them.

"I'm going in there," I announced. "Going to see what's what." I reached for my backpack, got out of the van and put it on. Willie handed me a radio headset. I turned on the batteries and put the thing on. "Testing, one, two, three."

"Works fine," Willie said in my ear.

"I have any trouble, I'll scream," I said.

"You want one of those electromagnetic bangers to cut the power?" Willie asked.

"We do that in the daytime, they'll know I'm coming."

"Watch yourself, Tommy," Callie Grafton said as I closed the door and latched it.

Walking along the road felt good. I was wearing a light jacket, which was enough coat if I didn't do any serious sitting. The truth was, I didn't have any more sitting in me. I wanted to be up, moving, doing something. I was being nervous and silly, I knew, but there was nothing I could do about it. I was out of patience. Didn't have a drop left.

I suppose I wasn't thinking logically. For some reason Marisa Petrou was on my mind, and Henri Rodet. Jake Grafton didn't want them dead, and I sure as hell didn't want to find them in that condition.

I took some deep breaths as I walked along, trying to think.

There were three of them; they had Jean-Paul Arnaud tied to a chair in the room over the garage. They said nothing to him, merely tied him up with a rope they had with them and waited. They were armed. One of them was always at the window, looking out.

He heard steps on the stairs. A head appeared, that of a grizzled old man. Yet he came up the stairs lightly, without much effort. The old man wore a threadbare coat and baggy trousers with visible stains. He spoke to the three in Arabic.

While they were talking Arnaud heard someone else ascending the stairs. Henri Rodet!

"You bastard," Jean-Paul hissed. "You're in with this scum."

The old man removed the pistol from one coat pocket and the silencer from another. In no hurry, he screwed the silencer into the barrel while Arnaud struggled against the ropes.

When the silencer was tight against the barrel, the old man pulled the slide of the Beretta back until he saw the gleam of brass, then let it go forward. Rodet watched impassively.

"This used to belong to a Mossad Kidon man. He used it to kill my son. Then I killed him. Now I use it to kill infidels."

"Killing infidels—will that bring my brother back from the dead?"

The old man turned. Marisa was standing at the head of the stairs looking at him. He hadn't heard her footsteps.

"Bah, woman, what do you know?" the old man hissed. He drew himself erect.

"You ask me to sell my soul—and I have obeyed because you are my father. I have a soul also, and you have never once thought of me. You think only of yourself, and vengeance. God sees! He knows."

"You think it was easy in that Egyptian prison?" the old man asked. "They tortured us, made us scream for mercy, and they showed no mercy. Still, I believed in civilization. With all my heart I knew that the world of the French—the world of ideas, grace, beauty—all of that was superior to the mud and dirt and squalor of the Arabs. God didn't love the Arabs more—he loved the French. I, Abu Qasim, knew the truth. So I betrayed them. Betrayed their jihad. Gave their secrets to their deadly enemies, who used them to thwart and murder the men of the faith.

"Yes, woman, I did that. I, your father. Covered my hands with the blood of the faithful, covered myself with sin that will never wash off. And God sent me a sign. He sent a Mossad killer who murdered your brother . . . my son. My only son, whom your mother died giving birth to. God spoke to me, and the message was blood. Evil for evil, wickedness for wickedness, betrayal for betrayal, drop by drop and dram by dram I was to suffer until the whole foul debt was paid in full!

"At long last, I listened to God. Listened and thought again, for the thousandth time, of the men I had betrayed. And I saw God's will. I, Abu Qasim, was to take up the sword and slay the infidels. And I have. *I will.* I swear it on the beard of the Prophet."

With that, he extended the pistol to arm's length and pointed it at Jean-Paul Arnaud's forehead.

"*Allah akbar,*" he said, and pulled the trigger.

CHAPTER TWENTY-FOUR

Going over the fence in broad daylight was a little different than doing it after midnight. For one thing, the night vision goggles weren't going to do me a lot of good. On the other hand, my unassisted eyes might. The yin and the yang . . .

I made sure the ray gun was on, with the capacitor charging, but left it in my pocket. If it went off accidentally I would never need a vasectomy.

As I walked I kick-started the brain. They had surveillance cameras on trees, but was anyone watching the monitor? The bugs seemed to indicate that no one was in the main house. Maybe and maybe not. If they had discovered the bugs, they might have moved them to the basement and put a radio nearby. Or the people might be camped out in the attic. Or using another building on the property—as I recalled, there was an apartment over the garage, a barn or two, and a couple of outbuildings. Or they might be sleeping off a wild night of sex and alcohol, which wasn't very likely.

I got tired of weighing the ifs. When I came to the corner of Rodet's property, I looked around for possible passersby or gawkers—and didn't see any.

"I'm going over," I said to Willie.

"Okay," he replied. With Mrs. Grafton sitting beside him, he had apparently cleaned up his act.

I climbed the fence and worked my way over the barbed wire on top, managing to rip my trousers on a barb and put a nasty groove in the back of my thigh. I silently cussed a little, but I didn't really mean it; I figured things would probably get worse.

I dropped onto the ground on the other side and hunkered down behind the nearest tree. "I'm over the fence."

"Okay."

I scanned the trees for cameras and the grounds for dogs while I probed my wound with my fingers. The dang thing stung. Fortunately I had a tetanus shot just last year. There was a camera in the tree, all right, but not a dog in sight. I twisted around for a look at the tear in my trousers and the hole in my hide, which was bleeding. Well, it wasn't going to kill me and there was nothing I could do about it now.

I got out my ray gun and checked it. A little green light glowed on the top. No use sneaking. Trying to ignore my smarting leg wound, I trotted for the main house.

One thing was certain: If anyone was watching the video from the surveillance monitors, life was going to get interesting very quickly. I didn't think Rodet or his hired hands would just shoot me, but they would undoubtedly loose the dogs and come looking.

I got to the wall of the house. I froze against it, listening. "I'm against the house," I reported to Willie, who merely clicked his mike twice in reply. He was learning.

My head was on a swivel. I was in the field of view of the monitor on the corner of the house. If there was anyone watching he had to see me.

Nothing moved except the bare limbs of the trees. The leaves on the ground hadn't been raked; they were too wet to blow around.

Where were the people?

More to the point, where were the dogs?

From where I stood I could see the main gate and portions of the long driveway that wound up through the trees and curved in behind the house. The barns, garage and dog pens were back there. I moved along the wall toward the rear of the house, detouring for shrubbery, listening . . .

Not even the sound of a dog barking. The wind was carrying my scent away from the dog pens, thank heavens.

In better days I would have enjoyed this. As a kid I always liked sneaking around, going places I wasn't supposed to go, seeing things I wasn't supposed to see, learning things that other people thought no one knew. No doubt shrinks would say I had a problem, and one did, by the way—a doc who worked for the agency. He had a serious ethical dilemma: He had to explain to the brass why I liked my work, then offer help to get my head on straight, yet not cure me so much I would be useless to his employer.

I came to the rear of the house and eased over between the shrubs and the wall. Getting as low as I could and still see over the greenery, I eased my head around.

The shrink's solution, which I thought was sorta neat, was to declare me neurotic but not psychotic. Apparently there's a very thin, crooked line in the dirt that separates the serious sickos from the rest of us twisted freaks, people like you and me, and mental health pros are the only people who know where that line is. In any event, they pretend to know. We amateurs—

I saw something descending toward my head just in time and jerked it back. A machete! The man wielding it had tried to take my head off!

The force of the downward blow carried the big blade to the ground. The man had swung it so hard he couldn't stop it. I dropped the ray gun and grabbed at the wrist that held the weapon with my left hand while I drove my right at his neck.

He rolled away and my knuckles smashed into his cheek.

Before I could close, he rolled and came up with the machete ready for another swipe. He looked like an Arab, young, wiry, medium height. I outweighed him by at least thirty pounds and was four or five inches taller. Didn't matter—with that machete he looked big as King Kong.

He waggled it and stepped to his left to clear the house and shrubs.

If I turned around to retrieve my ray gun, I was going to

lose a few body parts. I reached up my sleeve and pulled out the fighting knife.

When he saw it, he charged, swinging the big blade.

That was the wrong move. I went over backward, under the arc of the singing machete, and let his momentum carry him onto the knife. It went up to the hilt in his solar plexus.

Impaled, he tried to draw a breath as his eyes widened. He drew back the machete . . . and dropped it.

I gave the knife a savage twist, then shoved him off it. He fell over backward, tried to rise, gasping, then fell back.

I hunted around for my ray gun, wasting valuable seconds. Where was it?

Under this juniper. Must have kicked it. I dropped to my knees and retrieved it.

I didn't know anything about knife wounds, didn't know what my assailant's prognosis might be. Was he going to get up, go for help, follow me for another try, or die quietly dreaming of the virgins that awaited him in paradise?

Since I didn't know, I helped him on his way. I stabbed him in the throat with the knife and jerked it upward, slashing, as I pulled it out. Blood shot all over the place—the sight and smell of it hit me like a hammer. Maybe I shouldn't have done that. Probably have to answer for it at the Pearly Gates, if I ever get that far.

I keyed the mike on my headset. "Better call the cavalry. I just got attacked by a raghead."

"You okay?" Willie asked, worried.

"Yeah. Get Grafton and tell him to step on it."

I stood over the rapidly dying man, looking around. The grocery van was parked beside Rodet's Mercedes. Another car was there, an older small Fiat; figured that belonged to the maid or security man. Beside it was a small pickup. The gardener? Hell, for all I know, French upstairs maids drive pickups.

I headed for the dog pens.

When I was fifty feet away, I saw a body lying beside the fence. I slowed. Walked. Before long I saw the corpses of the dogs inside. I couldn't tell if they had been shot or poisoned, and it didn't really matter. The man, though, had been hacked with the machete.

I stopped. Looked around at the buildings and the empty windows looking back at me. Could hear the wind sighing in the big pines that shaded the pen.

Where were the people?

"Dead man here by the dog pens," I said to Willie. "Dogs look dead, too. Grocery van still here."

"Grafton's on his way."

"Don't know where the people are," I said to Willie. "Gotta be here someplace."

One of them is coming," Muhammed Nada told the old man. "The infidel warrior, Shannon."

"The others will be here soon," Abu Qasim said, and carefully knotted the rope around Marisa. He stepped around the chair that held the sagging corpse of Jean-Paul Arnaud and checked the rope that held Henri Rodet to his chair.

"You have been a brother and father to me," he said softly to Rodet. "Someday I will welcome you to paradise."

"It will be soon, I think," Rodet said.

"Oh, no. You have much to do before that day. Allah will help us both."

With that, he removed a cloth from his pocket and used it to gag the Frenchman.

"Your precious faith," Marisa said acidly as her father was tying the knot. "What if you are wrong? What if hell awaits murderers?"

"Don't blaspheme, woman."

"Can't you admit that there is no way to be absolutely certain you are right?"

"With Allah there is no doubt."

"Only a fool is absolutely certain of anything in this life," she shot back.

"She may betray us," Muhammed Nada suggested to Qasim. "One word from her, and all our preparation and suffering will be for nothing."

Qasim finished the knot behind Rodet's head and looked at his daughter.

"One word," Nada repeated.

"He's right," Marisa Petrou said, and bowed her head. "Why take the risk? I am tired of living and I loathe you all. Kill me. And explain that crime to God, if you can."

Rodet made a noise, and Qasim glanced at him. He was shaking his head from side to side.

Abu Qasim walked over to Rodet with the silenced pistol in his hand. The Frenchman closed his eyes. At a distance of three feet, Qasim aimed carefully and squeezed the trigger.

The barn was nearest, so I went to the door, eased it open and looked into the gloom . . . and saw nothing. Not even a horse. The building was empty. I put on the goggles, flipped them on, turned them to infrared and studied the ceiling. No humans up there, I concluded.

Raising the goggles onto my forehead, I checked the courtyard, then stepped outside. One other barn, the garage, or the house. They had to be in one of them.

I pulled down the goggles and looked. The daylight shining on the walls had warmed them so much the goggles were nearly useless. I played with the contrast control, trying to see something, anything.

Wait! In the garage . . . on the second floor. The apartment above. A moving shape. At least one.

I pulled up the goggles, checked everything I could see one more time, then trotted for the personnel door of the garage.

I was halfway across when the door opened and a man with a submachine gun stepped out. He didn't hesitate. God, he was quick! He braced the weapon against his hip and started shooting.

He should have aimed. As the bullets went over my head, I dropped down and squeezed the trigger on the ray gun. The laser shot out.

I kept the trigger down for what seemed like an eternity. When nothing happened, I thought *I* had had the stroke. This guy might not be a marksman, but he had lots of bullets and it would only take one to do me. Despair and panic welled up in me, and then the lightning flashed and strobed from the weapon in my hand.

The report was almost lost in the thunder of his gun, but the effect on him wasn't. His back arched and the gun muzzle went up and he fell with the weapon still hammering. I held the trigger down and the lightning pulsed across the thirty feet that separated us.

The lightning stopped about the same time his gun went silent. The pulse lasted maybe half a second, though it sure as hell seemed longer. I could see smoke wisping from the corpse.

"God almighty!" I whispered, stunned.

Mesmerized by the smoke rising from his flesh, I walked over to him. The electrical charge had hit him in the chest, burned a hole in his shirt and cooked his flesh. The smell turned my stomach.

Still standing there like a blithering fool, I glimpsed a motion in the doorway. Another man with a gun.

Before I could get the ray gun up, his gun flashed—that was the last thing I saw. A tremendous blow hit me on the head and everything went dark.

Jake Grafton was in the car that roared up alongside the van. Another car was right behind. Callie was already standing outside; Willie was in the van, monitoring the radio, waiting for Carmellini's call.

"Tell him Jake's here," Callie said through the window before the cars braked to a stop.

Willie complied. "No answer," he said, and hopped out of the van.

Willie and Callie piled into the rear seat of the lead car with a man neither of them knew. Jake turned around in the passenger seat and said names. "Pink Maillard," indicating the man at the wheel, "and Inspector Papin, of the French police."

"*Bonjour,*" Callie said to the Frenchman. She was all business. She said to Jake, "Tommy called on the radio and said he had been attacked by an Arab. Now he doesn't answer when we call."

"Sounds as if they arrived a bit quicker than I thought they would," Jake muttered as the car sped along the road adjacent to Rodet's estate. "Did he say where the people were?"

"I don't think he ever got inside."

"Yeah, he would have said," Willie added. Then he pointed. "Up there on the right. That's the entrance."

"What if the gate's closed?" Pink Maillard wanted to know.

"Go right on through anyway," Jake Grafton said matter-of-factly. He glanced through the rear window. The other car was immediately behind them. The admiral grabbed the hand strap and held on firmly.

"This the first time I ever been in a car with the *po*-lice without wearin' handcuffs," Willie declared as Maillard braked for the turn ahead.

Fortunately the gate was still open. Maillard feathered the brake and slewed the car, then accelerated up the driveway.

Two guys were dragging me up a flight of stairs when I came to. It took me a few seconds to figure it out, and that was the answer I came up with. Each had an arm, and they were yanking and lifting and tugging as my feet dragged over each step. Something was wrapped around my face; I thought it was the headset or straps for the night vision goggles. Whatever it was obscured my vision—or maybe the blow I took had affected my eyesight.

I tried to move and couldn't. My head was splitting; my face was numb; my legs felt as if they were being hammered on by lumberjacks. I must have moaned or something, because one of them paused and slugged me in the face. Then they resumed their ascent.

Somehow I knew we were going up the stairs to the apartment over the garage. I don't know how or why I knew that— I just did.

I was in damn big trouble—that I also knew. Two of these holy warriors had already tried to kill me. These two and however many more were waiting upstairs were going to finish the job if I didn't get to kicking and scratching pretty damn quick. My muscles didn't seem to work. Panic set in, probably stimulated by a quart or so of adrenaline.

As these two dragged me up the stairs they were jabbering loudly in some language I didn't recognize—calling to someone in the room above, a man who answered them.

As Pink Maillard braked to a stop near the rear corner of the house, he stuck his arm out the window and motioned for the car behind to pass him. It did. It roared between the garage and the house and stopped near the dog pens, where the four men inside came tumbling out. Someone in a window of the apartment over the garage opened fire with a pistol.

One of the men below was hit in the arm, and he dived back behind the car. As one, two of his colleagues opened fire with submachine guns at that window. The glass shattered; the framing around the window splintered. Pieces rained down.

The third man ran for the door of the garage.

I was going to die. Unable to move, I was going to be slaughtered like a steer by these Arab lunatics.

Not like this—no!

I tried to move, to resist, oh, my God, how I tried, but I couldn't make my muscles respond!

Then I heard the pop of a pistol, followed by the roar of submachine guns.

One of the men released an arm. They were going to kill me right here!

I grabbed a handful of balls and tried to rip them out. The man they belonged to screamed and went nuts. In that enclosed stairwell, the sensation was like being in a barrel with a tiger. His high-pitched wail of agony was like a tonic to me.

The other man tried to release me to get to his weapon but found that I had him, rather than the other way around. I didn't have a good hold, though, and there wasn't much I could do about it with this other guy kicking and pounding on me, trying to get me to release his scrotum.

Somehow I got my feet under me and regained my balance. I was screaming, too, I guess, because the noise in there was unbelievable.

Muhammed Nada ran into the bedroom in response to a call from the lookout as the two cars roared in. He got there just as the lookout fired his pistol out the window, then died under a hail of submachine-gun bullets.

Nada was tempted to rush to the window and return the infidels' fire, but he changed his mind: They couldn't get in through the window. He scrambled for the stairs.

Jake Grafton and Pink Maillard also charged for the stairs. Grafton was carrying a borrowed pistol and Pink had a submachine gun. They arrived behind the Secret Service officer from the lead car. The three of them started up the narrow staircase just as Muhammed Nada opened the door at the top.

He looked over the men struggling at the top of the staircase, ignored the screaming of tortured souls, and fired his pistol at the men at the bottom of the stairwell.

I didn't really have a grip on the man on my left; I was banging him off the walls as I tried to rip the balls off the man on my right, who was down, kicking wildly, threatening to break my ribs. I was about all in, at the absolute limit of strength and endurance, when the gun went off right over my head.

I let go of the man on my left and fell on the man who was down.

A burst of submachine-gun fire followed, and the man beside me collapsed over me. I tried to shrug him off and couldn't.

I couldn't breathe under his weight. With all this wrestling around, I lost my radio headset and night vision goggles. Relieved of the obstruction, I found that my eyes still worked, even if I wasn't getting much air.

I let go of the scrotum I had been tearing at and transferred my attention to the guy's throat. That stopped his screams. As another burst of submachine-gun fire assaulted my ears, the guy under me struggled feebly, tugging at my wrists; I stopped squeezing when I felt his larynx go and he went limp.

I fought to free myself of the dead weight on me and get my feet under me, fought to fill my lungs. As I did, my hand hit something that I recognized. My ray gun. One of these guys had pocketed it. I pulled it loose and felt the switch to ensure it was charging.

Somehow I managed to fight loose of the corpses and crawl up the stairs. Nearing the top, I saw a body on the floor. I recognized him at a glance: ol' Muhammed Nada, holy warrior, a little worse for wear now that he sported at least five bullet holes that I could see.

There were three other people in the room, all tied to chairs. I looked at Rodet, who was slumped in the chair with blood covering his left side. I raised Arnaud's head and saw the hole in his forehead.

I heard voices, turned, and saw the good guys coming into the room.

There was another figure slumped in a chair. No clothes. Covered with streaks of blood. Long hair.

Oh, my God!

I walked toward her. Lifted her head. They had sliced her terribly. I couldn't even tell for sure who she was. Then I saw her eyes flicker.

"She's still alive! Somebody—quick!"

Two people rushed by. One was a woman—Callie Grafton—and Willie Varner. They began tearing at the ropes that held the woman to the chair.

"Rodet's alive, too," Jake Grafton said. He and a man I didn't recognize were examining him.

The room was spinning by that time. Later they said I had a concussion from the bullet that ricocheted off the night vision goggles. Whatever, everything faded to black; that was the last I remember.

CHAPTER TWENTY-FIVE

The first ambulance departed with Marisa Petrou aboard. Jake Grafton and Inspector Papin had a moment with Henri Rodet after the crew of the second got him into their vehicle. He had taken a bullet in his side at some point in the gun battle.

"It was the old man who led this rabble," Rodet hissed. "He wanted to know about Qasim. Wouldn't believe me when I said I didn't know who he was now. So he butchered Marisa."

And got away. The police quickly established that the old man wasn't on the grounds. The vehicles were all there, but Rodet's boat was missing from its dock on the river.

"Marisa has a chance," the American admiral told Rodet. "The ambulance attendants were giving her plasma. My wife went with her to the hospital."

"I've mishandled this whole mess," Rodet moaned. "I should have told everyone what I knew, as soon as I knew it." By everyone, he meant the Western intelligence services.

Jake understood. "Wouldn't have made any difference," he said. "The fanatics in Al Queda would not have believed, even if they heard it from your lips. That old man didn't believe."

"If there is a God, that old man will rot in hell." Rodet struggled to breathe, then began coughing.

Jake whispered, "Why Arnaud?"

When the coughing subsided, Rodet said, "He brought them here this morning, to the château, shortly after dawn.

They paid Arnaud for information about Qasim. I think Arnaud wanted to ruin me." The pain drew a groan from him. "He always hated me."

"I'll come visit in the hospital," Grafton said. He and Papin got out of the ambulance and watched the crew close the door and roar off down the driveway.

Carmellini went next. Inspector Papin and Pink Maillard stood watching as the police loaded him in an ambulance while their radios squawked and tinny French echoed between the main house and the garage. Carmellini was still unconscious.

"So," Jake said to the French policeman, "who killed the DGSE officer, Claude Bruguiere?"

"I have no evidence to give to the magistrate."

"Probably won't get any, either. Arnaud hated Rodet, thought he might be named director of the DGSE if only Rodet would leave. So he invested some Oil-for-Food money in the Bank of Palestine, knowing Rodet would be ruined if and when the press found out. Bruguiere completed the transaction for Arnaud after the original man had a heart attack on the plane. Since he knew who had really supplied the money, he, too, had to die. Had things sort of run their course, I am sure Jean-Paul would have tipped a friendly reporter about Rodet's big investment. That's one theory anyway."

Papin pounded his pipe on his hand, then slowly refilled it from a leather pouch. "As I say, I have no evidence. Not that I need any, with Monsieur Arnaud dead, the victim of Arab terrorists."

"Of course, another theory is that the old man up there killed Bruguiere," Grafton suggested. "The magistrate might like that theory better."

"Indeed," Papin said thoughtfully. "I think the old man will also be an easier sell on the killings of your men, Thurlow and Salazar, than Jean-Paul Arnaud. Avoids messy diplomatic problems."

"Yes," Jake agreed, and eyed Inspector Papin askance. The policeman had the wireless Taser that Tommy had used in his hands. He inspected it carefully, one more time, then handed it to Grafton.

"What about Elizabeth Conner?" Inspector Papin asked. "The concierge of her building discovered her body this morning. She had been strangled. I immediately thought of your friend Shannon, or Carmellini, as the case might be."

"He didn't kill her. He found the body last night, after he got home from dinner. If you blame her murder on the old man upstairs, I will see that her killer gets justice."

"You know the real killer's name?"

"Yes."

Inspector Papin lit his pipe as he watched the police carry a body on a stretcher out of the garage apartment entrance. When he was puffing like a chimney, he said, "Perhaps you should share it with me, just in case, as they say in America."

Jake pronounced the name as Papin smoked. The two men stood silently watching as the morgue crew loaded Rodet's gardener and maid into the meat wagon.

"Why did he kill her?"

"He has a severe gambling habit and was selling her information. She passed it to her agency, the Mossad, because that was her job, and to Marisa Petrou because she was her friend. Of course, Marisa passed it to Henri Rodet. Apparently the killer panicked when he learned that her apartment was immediately below Shannon's. He thought we were getting too close. Frightened men do illogical things."

"You will try him in America? For treason?"

"The prosecutors there would probably say that we don't have enough evidence."

Papin smoked in silence. Finally he looked at Pinckney Maillard. "Do you wish to say anything?"

"No," Pink said. He nodded at Jake. "He's the man."

"Conner worked for the Mossad," Jake said to the French policeman. "We'll tell them who killed her and why."

Papin puffed furiously, then nodded. "*Bon*," he said finally. "*Bon.* They will see that justice is done. They have that reputation."

"Yes," Jake Grafton said. He felt the ray gun in his pocket. "Indeed they do."

"Of course," Inspector Papin added hastily, "you might tell them that it would be better if justice were done somewhere else. Not in France."

"I'll pass that along, too."

Papin and Maillard left together, leaving only a few forensic men, who were busying themselves with cameras and measurements when a car rolled up and Sarah Houston got out. Gator Zantz was with her. Jake was sitting on the steps of the back entrance of the château.

They listened in silence as Jake related the events of the morning. Amazingly, the time was only a little past noon.

"Is Tommy going to be all right?" Sarah asked, the concern evident in her voice.

"He has a concussion." He told her the name of the hospital the French were taking him to. "You may go check on him, if you wish. Zantz can ride back with me in the van."

She didn't say good-bye, just climbed back in the car.

"Wear your seat belt," Jake called. She started the engine, turned the car, and drove off.

Grafton turned his attention to Gator, who was standing on the walkway watching two plainclothes forensic men taking photographs of the dogs, which had been shot. "Want to tell me about it?"

"About what?" Gator asked, apparently baffled.

"About Elizabeth Conner."

"What is there to tell?"

"Why you killed her."

Gator looked Grafton over. Then he looked at the policemen, busy with other things. "I don't know what you're talking about."

"You were selling her information that you had access to in the London office. Being a Mossad agent, she passed it to Tel Aviv. Since she was a friend of Marisa Petrou, she also gave it to her. Marisa passed it along to Henri Rodet."

"Got any proof of that?"

"You had Elizabeth's telephone number on your cell phone. We found it on your phone when you tossed it into the basket before you went into the SCIF."

"So I called her. That doesn't prove I killed her," he blustered.

"Marisa isn't dead. Neither is Henri Rodet. Do you seriously think Elizabeth didn't tell Marisa the name of her source in the CIA? My God, man, she was paying you. I'll bet you a thousand against a doughnut she told her control whom she was paying, what your job was . . . name, rank and serial number. Do you honestly think the Mossad doesn't know?"

Gator Zantz looked hastily around, right, left. He had his hands free and he was shifting his weight from foot to foot. When he looked back at Grafton the admiral was still sitting comfortably, but he had the wireless Taser in his hand—wasn't pointing it anywhere, just holding it. Zantz stared at it, mesmerized.

"So the question remains, Why did you kill her?"

Zantz swallowed. Cleared his throat. Finally he said, "You don't have enough evidence to convince a jury of anything. Speculation won't cut it in court."

"I feel responsible, in a way," the admiral mused. "I knew you had her telephone number and that was enough to initiate an internal investigation. I should have done that. If I had, Elizabeth Conner might still be alive. I thought we could investigate when things settled down. And, truthfully, I didn't think you were so damned stupid that you'd kill somebody."

"My God," Zantz declared, "she was an Israeli spy!"

"And you're an American traitor. If I just kill you where you stand, it'll be no big deal, right?"

"You wouldn't kill me."

"You like to gamble. How much you want to bet?"

Zantz just stood there looking at the admiral, breathing in and out, not saying anything.

"Give me your diplomatic passport and embassy pass."

"Does this mean I'm fired?"

"Take it any way you like."

Zantz thought about it for a moment, then removed both documents from his pocket. He tossed them on the ground. "How am I going to get out of France without a passport?"

"Your problem."

"Now, listen here, goddamn it! I'm an American citizen, an agency employee. I'm innocent until proven guilty. You can't treat me like dog shit."

Grafton shrugged. "If you like, we'll waive your immunity. The French will probably be willing to arrest you and see if they can put together a case. You don't have the right to remain silent in a French court—you talk or go to prison. Or we can take you back to the States and prosecute you for espionage. Who knows, maybe the Mossad will cooperate, Rodet and Marisa Petrou might be persuaded to talk, you might get a cell beside Jonathan Pollard. Or you might beat the rap."

"Fuck you."

"You really are stupid. I've wasted enough air on you. Scram."

"What?"

"I'm giving you a running start, Zantz. Make the most of it. The Mossad will be looking for you."

"Are you nuts? I might defect, sell secrets to the highest bidder. Then you'll look like a fool!"

"What country is going to want you? Israel? France? You don't know anything the Russians want to know and you'd be an embarrassment. You're a problem no one needs. On the other hand, perhaps Iran—"

"You bastard! I'll see you in hell."

"No more badmouth. Beat it." Jake pointed the weapon and squeezed the trigger. The laser beam shot out and touched Zantz on the chest. Jake released the trigger before the capacitor discharged. "Now!" he said.

Gator Zantz turned and walked along the driveway until he disappeared around the house.

Callie Grafton insisted on staying with Marisa Petrou in the emergency room as the nurses prepped her for surgery. One of the nurses was washing her, cleaning her up the best she could.

One of the doctors tried to explain in poor English, and Callie asked him to switch to French.

"Cleaning and suturing her wounds should be done in the operating room. I don't think she is in immediate danger unless she goes into shock. She has lost a lot of blood. Still, she is young, with a strong heart."

"What about her face?" Being a woman, Callie had to ask.

"I have sent for the plastic surgeon. We will see what he says."

"I must see Monsieur Rodet before he goes into surgery. It is urgent."

The doctor nodded at one of the nurses, who led Callie through the hallways to the X-ray department. Rodet was on a gurney. The bullet had ripped a gash in his side and apparently broken a rib. The staff was going to X-ray him to ensure no fragment of the bullet was in his chest. He was conscious.

She leaned over so he could see her. The nurses were installing IVs on both arms. His face was pasty, covered with sweat. "I am Callie Grafton, Admiral Grafton's wife. Marisa is going into surgery. The doctor was hopeful. He says she has a strong heart."

"Her heart . . . ," he whispered.

"They are going to sedate you momentarily and operate. Before they do, you must tell me what you know of Abu Qasim."

"I know nothing. Those fools . . ."

"When you saw him twenty-five years ago, what did he look like?"

"Medium height, strong features, an expressive mouth, the Arab nose."

That was almost useless. Callie tried to maintain her composure. "How did you pass him the telephone computer?"

"A dead drop in Riyadh. Two years ago when the telephone first came out."

"And the code?"

"Onetime pads."

"*S'il vous plait, madame,*" a nurse said. "We must X-ray him now."

"A moment more," she pleaded. She touched Henri Rodet on the hand. "Where is your pad?"

It took him a second to process it. "It's a memo pad on my desk," he whispered. "You must apply heat." She had to lean over and place her ear near his mouth to hear the rest of it. "Place des Vosges . . ." That was all he managed, then the sedative put him under.

Callie watched the nurses move him from the gurney to the X-ray table, then left.

As she passed the waiting room, she glanced in and saw Sarah Houston there in earnest conversation with the attendant. She had never met her, but she knew who she was. She went in.

"I'm Callie Grafton," she said. "May I help?"

"I can't make this man understand," Sarah explained. "He doesn't speak English. I want to see Tommy."

She stood there watching as Callie and the attendant shot French back and forth at each other. The attendant made a telephone call, then shook his head.

"Monsieur Shannon is conscious," Callie related. "They're moving him to a room. It'll be a few minutes."

The women moved to a window. "Thanks," Sarah said. "*Bonjour* is about all I can manage."

The two women talked desultorily, unwilling to say anything that might be overheard about the events at Rodet's château, or even why they were in Paris.

Soon they were on their way to see Carmellini, who was in a private room.

I had been awake awhile and talking to the one nurse who spoke a little English when Sarah Houston and Callie Grafton walked into the room. They both looked pretty damn good, let me tell you, although they were a little fuzzy. I was having some trouble focusing my eyes. "Hey."

"Hey there yourself, cowboy," Sarah said. "What have you been into this time?"

"Got a hole in my leg. They stitched it up in the emergency room, they said. Took eight stitches. Barbed wire. They gave me another tetanus shot. I get one every year, seems like."

"You should get into another line of work," Callie said, reaching for my left hand. Sarah had already latched on to my right, and her hand felt terrific.

"No joke."

"Nothing else wrong?"

"Little concussion and some bruises. I'll be out of here in a little while."

"They said we couldn't stay long. I'll let you and Sarah chat. I'll be in the waiting room, Sarah."

"Okay."

Callie bent over, gave me a peck on the cheek, and left.

"Cool lady," I told Sarah.

"Are you really leaving the company when you get home?"

"Yeah. I've had enough."

"Me, too, I think."

"You talked to Grafton?"

"Not yet."

"Better do that."

The doctor came in and said something in French, and the nurse told Sarah she had to leave. She kissed me on the lips, then she was gone.

Life was looking up.

Jake Grafton was strolling aimlessly with his hands in his pockets when Pink Maillard drove up Rodet's driveway in a government car with one of his men. "You going to stay here all day?" he called to the admiral.

"Just thinking."

"Want to do it over some food?"

"Sure."

Maillard told his man to take the van back to the embassy, and Jake got into the passenger seat of the car. They stopped at the inn on the Marne, across the river from Rodet's estate. The police were working on a boat at the pier; Rodet's, no doubt. The old man had crossed the river on the boat and someone had picked him up. It was that easy.

"I screwed up the timing," Jake said when they were seated, sipping on beer. "Arnaud must have found that item I wrote on the Intelink last night, a few minutes after we posted it. He didn't waste any time. Got the old man and his thugs and charged right over there."

"Why didn't your listener, Icahn, hear anything on the bugs?"

"He was probably asleep." Jake sighed.

"You can't blame yourself. These were desperate people."

"Shit!" Jake muttered.

"When I first saw him," Pink mused, "I thought that old man might be Qasim, artificially aged a little."

"That is a possibility," Jake replied, "but in any event, Abu Qasim is still out there. Have you asked yourself why all these people were suddenly so interested in Rodet's spy?"

"The Veghel conspiracy was busted six months ago."

"Indeed. Six months pass, and suddenly all hell breaks loose."

"Breaks loose just before the heads of government of the eight largest industrial powers on the planet have a summit meeting in Paris."

Jake watched a couple come into the small room and seat themselves at a table beside the window so they could watch the ducks on the river. The man nodded at Grafton.

"I think he's here, in Paris," Jake said to the Secret Service man. "Callie went to Professor Heger, trying to learn if there was any truth to the Abu Qasim legend. When she went back the next morning, the professor had a bullet in his head. He died while she watched."

"Rodet didn't kill the professor," Pink said. "Arnaud didn't. The old man and his thugs had no reason to do so."

"What if Qasim wasn't just the answer to her question but also the name of the killer?"

After lunch, they went out onto the riverbank. The police

had finished with the boat and taken it back across the river to Rodet's boathouse. There was one die-hard fisherman casting into the river. It was late in the season, but he wasn't ready to quit. Squadrons of ducks paddled furiously about, looking for food.

"When we get back to the embassy," Pink suggested, "perhaps you and I should go see Lancaster. He's going to get an earful from the French politicians."

"Fine," Jake said.

"I'm tempted to call Washington and tell my boss that I recommend against the president's participation in the G-8 summit. We can't guarantee his safety—and the French can't—and it's time to admit it."

"The French will dispute that. Even if the president backs out, they'll have the summit anyway with whoever comes. And, boy, will they heap the stuff on the Americans for chickening out. You *know* the president will come, regardless of what you tell Washington."

"Well, they pay me for my opinion, so I'm going to tell them. They can do as they please with it."

"And they will. So we're stuck with an insoluble puzzle: What is Al Queda planning?"

"And where does Abu Qasim fit in?"

Callie drove. She explained to Sarah. "He said the code was onetime pads. What are those?"

"They are pads for encrypting messages. Each sheet in the pad is intended to be used just once, then discarded. If the pad is used that way, the messages are nearly impossible to decode since the code is based on random numbers. Even if you break one, you can't break any of the others since the code changed from message to message."

"He said the pad was on his desk. 'You need to apply heat,' he said. Is that possible?"

"Oh, yes. The pages of the pad could be printed with invisible ink, which heat makes legible."

They rode the rest of the way in silence. Each woman had a lot on her mind.

The door to the apartment in the Place des Vosges was locked. Callie pounded on the door. Finally the maid opened it a few inches.

"There has been an automobile accident," Callie said in French. "Monsieur Rodet and Mademoiselle Petrou are in the hospital. He asked us to bring them some clothes."

The maid looked at Callie, looked at Sarah, then held the door open. "Are they going to be all right?"

"I hope so. You know the doctors—they will tell us nothing."

"*Mon Dieu!* Where was the accident?"

"Uh, on the highway near the château."

"Oh, the traffic! People drive like maniacs. No one is safe." She shifted gears. "Someone broke into the apartment several days ago. We are still making amends."

"Think nothing of it! We will find what they need. Do you have a suitcase?"

The maid scurried off to look. Callie and Sarah went looking for Rodet's office.

The maids had been working on it, but only half the room was cleaned down to the floor. Callie and Sarah glanced at the desk, opened the drawers . . . and Sarah pulled out a curling iron, its cord wrapped around it.

"Look at this."

They rooted through the stuff strewn about on the floor and came up with three memo pads, in three different colors.

Sarah was ready to plug in the iron to test them when they heard the maid coming along the hallway. Callie pocketed all three pads.

"Keep looking," she murmured to Sarah. "Look for more pads."

But they could do no more looking. The maid entered the room with a small valise, then led them to the bedroom. While the maid was bent over opening the valise, Sarah passed Callie the curling iron. She took it and the pads and went into the bathroom.

With the door locked, it took but a moment to warm the iron and pass a sheet of memo paper through it. Nothing happened with a sheet from the first pad. Nor the second. Callie was sure none of the pads was the right one when letters and numbers began to appear on the top sheet of the third.

With the valise full of toiletries and nightclothes for Rodet and Marisa, the women thanked the maid profusely and departed.

Back in the car, Callie showed the pad to Sarah.

"Hidden in plain sight," Sarah muttered.

"Can the messages on the telephone-computer hard drive be decoded with these?" Callie asked.

"No. These were for future messages. See the gummed backing sticking out? Rodet tore off each sheet as he used it, then destroyed it. He could have burned it, flushed it down a commode, or wadded it up and eaten it. The pages are water soluble."

Callie said a cuss word. She looked at the pad dubiously.

"Won't hurt to have them," Sarah continued. "If there is another message, we can read it."

"There won't be any more messages," Callie said bitterly. She smacked the steering wheel with her hand. "And I thought we were getting somewhere!"

"If we had an identical pad, the entire pad, with copies of the missing sheets," Sarah told her, "then we could read them."

Callie found Jake in his cubbyhole office in the embassy, with the lights off, his feet on the desk and a cold washcloth on his forehead. He had finished a session with Ambassador Owen Lancaster a half hour ago and it had not been pleasant.

Callie snapped on the lights and tossed the pad onto the desk. Jake put his feet on the floor and set the washcloth aside. He picked up the pad and looked at it, then put on his glasses and looked again carefully.

"Where'd you get this?"

She told him, and pulled up one of the two chairs.

"Rodet told you where it was?"

"Yes."

"And it was on his desk in his apartment?"

"It was on the floor beside the desk. Along with two other pads, both of which appear to be simple memo pads."

"Huh."

"That wasn't the best part. In a drawer of the desk we found this." She passed him the curling iron.

"In a drawer?"

"Yes. It was there. Sarah and I found it."

He snorted, raised his glasses to his forehead and sat looking around. Then he got up and went to the only window, which looked into the courtyard at the back of the building. He stood there for a moment, lost in thought. Finally he turned to Callie and smiled. "You sure know how to cure a headache, woman. Come on, let's go get some dinner."

"What are you thinking?"

"That I've been a fool! And you've showed me the path out of the wilderness. I need to think some more on this, but in the meantime, let's *celebrate!* I want some good food and music and your smile."

Callie was baffled. "Why don't you tell me what you're thinking?"

He grinned at her, took her lightly by the elbow and raised her from the chair. He kissed her cheek. "All in good time, beautiful lady. All in good time. Come! Let's find Pink Maillard and George Goldberg and take them to dinner."

CHAPTER TWENTY-SIX

On Sunday morning Callie took Jake to the hospital where the casualties from the shootout at Rodet's estates had been taken. After much talking, they were admitted to post-op. The policeman outside the ward refused to let them in, so Jake demanded that he call Inspector Papin, which he finally did. After a few sentences in French, he handed his cell phone to Jake.

"*Bonjour,* Inspector. This is Admiral Grafton."

"Good morning, Admiral. I spent a few minutes with Mademoiselle Petrou earlier this morning, immediately after she awoke. Her statement was exactly as you and I discussed yesterday. Such a tragedy!"

"Yes, isn't it? I understand she is very ill, but I need to ask her a few questions myself. I, too, have superiors I must please."

"Of course. Let me talk to the policeman again."

Jake passed the telephone back. He and Callie were admitted to the ward and shown to the bed where Marisa Petrou lay. She was covered in bandages, but she was conscious.

Callie did the talking, in French. "I'm Callie Grafton, and this is my husband, Admiral Jake Grafton. Do you know who he is?"

"Yes."

"Can you tell us what happened yesterday? Everything you can remember?"

"We were having breakfast, and Jean-Paul Arnaud came.

He went into the study and talked to Henri. I heard them arguing, but I could not hear what they were saying. They were in there a few minutes—"

"Did Henri make any telephone calls?"

"He might have. I don't know."

"Did Arnaud leave the study?"

"No. I heard a vehicle drive up and glanced out the window. I saw these men getting out, an old man and some others. Four or five, I think. They had weapons. I ran into the study and told Henri and Jean-Paul, but before they could do anything the men rushed into the house—the outside door must have been unlocked. Henri had a pistol, and they took it from him. They gagged me and Jean-Paul and took us to the apartment over the garage. They tied us up, began beating Henri and Jean-Paul, demanding to know what Henri had told . . . your husband. 'Tell us what you told Grafton. Where is Abu Qasim? Who is he now? We want that traitor!' "

"What did Henri say?"

"He told them the truth, that he knew nothing. He knew Qasim years ago, but not now. He couldn't tell them what he doesn't know, and they refused to believe. One of them began cutting on me, trying to force Henri to talk."

She paused here, swallowing, perspiring as it all came flooding back.

"I could feel the knife. Amazingly, it didn't hurt so much, but I knew what he was doing, butchering me. I tried to scream—couldn't breathe, fought the gag—" She paused again, swallowed, collected herself. "The old one, the one that did the talking, said Jean-Paul had been paid. He had betrayed them. Failed. Then the old man shot him. I heard the shot, a pop. I knew then that they intended to kill us, Henri and me, so it didn't matter . . . didn't matter . . . what they did—did to me."

She lay there immobile, rigid, staring at the ceiling, as her IVs dripped and the squiggly lines danced across the screen of the heart monitor beside the bed.

"I passed out. I don't remember any more."

Callie translated all this for Jake, whispering so her voice wouldn't carry. He listened, looking at Marisa or watching the heart monitor. Once he reached out and touched an IV bottle.

Callie asked Jake, "Why didn't the bugs pick up Rodet and Arnaud in the study?"

"Rodet found the bugs and moved them, I suspect." He made a gesture of dismissal. "That's enough. She's told us all she can." He reached down and found Marisa's hand and squeezed it gently. "I'm sorry," he said. "Truly sorry." Then he led the way from the room.

Callie lingered a moment, then bent over the bed, whispered that she would be back in a day or two, and followed her husband.

When the doctors came around that Sunday morning, I talked to them about leaving the hospital, and of course they hemmed and hawed. French is a good language to do that in, I discovered. I whispered a few old Anglo-Saxon words I happened to know and resigned myself to my fate.

About midmorning, Willie Varner came sailing in.

"Carmellini, you idiot, I told you to be careful."

"It's Shannon. Terry Shannon."

"You know I can't remember stuff like that. How smart do you think I am, anyway?"

We discussed that at some length, then he said, "Lucky for you that bullet hit that damn night vision thing. If it had hit your hard little head, it would have cracked it like an egg. Maybe even punched a hole in it. I tell you, Tommy, you're wearin' out your luck."

"Don't I know it."

"You gonna eat that crossaint-thing there on your tray? Well, I guess not or you'da already done it, huh? You ain't got nothin' contagious, I don't reckon, 'cept stupidity, and that's been goin' around forever. Fought it off a few times my own self. Mind if I scarf that thing down?"

"Be my guest."

"I hope Grafton's got this mess all figured out," Willie said with his mouth full. "Man, I don't know what the game is!

Truth is, I don't even know who's playin'. Of course, nobody tells me nothin'."

"You don't have a need to know, Willie," I said. "Got that problem myself."

He was running his mouth, talking trash, when Jake Grafton came by. The admiral shook hands with both of us and asked me how I was doing.

"Okay. Ready to go, but the doctors said I have to stay another day."

"Are you dizzy?"

"No."

"Double vision?"

"No. Honestly, I'm fine. Just had a whack on the noodle. Got some bruises and I'm mighty sore. They took eight stitches in my leg, bandaged it up and gave me some shots." I tried to flip back the sheet to show him my bandage.

"I don't want to see it," Willie declared. "You keep that thing under the covers." He said to the admiral, "He'll be okay. His head's pretty hard."

I asked Grafton about ol' Henri. He had a few dozen stitches and a broken rib, Grafton said. He and Callie had checked on Rodet and Marisa before he stopped by to see me. Marisa was conscious and talking, and the doctors said her prognosis was good.

"None of this has hit the papers yet," Grafton said. "The French government is keeping the lid on. They want the G-8 summit to go as planned."

"I figured," I admitted. "The first priority is to look good. But I want to know which of these bastards iced Elizabeth Conner."

"What would you do if you knew?" Grafton asked.

There must have been an edge in my voice, because as I was mulling an answer, Willie put his two cents in. "Don't tell 'im! Don't tell 'im. He don't need no more shit to tote through life."

"I just want to know, that's all," I insisted.

What Grafton might have said I don't know, because just then Callie came in. Turns out she had been talking to the doctors in French. She shook her head from side to side at Jake, who obviously had something on his mind.

"Well, you've laid around here long enough," he said to me. "Get dressed. Doctors or no doctors, we have work to do. You can check yourself out."

Uh-oh. Saddle and ride. "Where are we going?"

"I need some help. You can come, too, Willie."

"Sure. I got nothing to do until tonight," Willie replied, a comment Grafton ignored. With Willie the Wire, you have to ignore things.

I wasn't as enthused as Willie. Sarah was going to stop by later. I was sorta looking forward to holding her hand and soaking up some sympathy. There isn't much sympathy in the world these days—you've got to get it where you can, when you can.

Willie and Grafton wandered off to the lobby. I got out of bed and put on my ripped pants and dirty shirt and stinky socks while Callie stood in the hallway having an earnest discussion with the staff. I was so damned stiff and sore that getting dressed took several minutes.

There was some difficulty about the bill; Grafton whipped out a credit card. After a while, I scribbled my name a few times and they gave me some pills to take four times a day. Then we were escorted to the street.

"If you've got anything important in mind, I'd like to take a bath and change clothes," I told the admiral. He was downwind of me, so he knew how it was.

He didn't care.

"Later," he said, and led the way to his car.

So what's the gig?" Willie asked when we were rolling along with Grafton at the wheel.

"We're going back out to Rodet's estate on the Marne," Grafton told us. "Yesterday afternoon Callie and Sarah Houston searched the apartment on the Place des Vosges and found a onetime pad written with invisible ink that had been sitting in plain sight on Rodet's desk."

"It was lying in the trash beside the desk," Callie said. "And we found a curling iron in one of the desk drawers."

"What's a onetime pad?" Willie asked.

Callie told him, even passed him the one she had found. He looked it over and passed it back.

"So why are we searching today?" Willie asked.

Grafton tilted the rearview mirror so he could see my face, then asked, looking at me, "Doesn't it strike you as strange that someone searched Rodet's apartment from top to bottom—ransacked it—and didn't find that pad? With the curling iron right there in the desk drawer?"

"Well . . ."

"If you had found that iron in an office drawer, what would you have thought, Tommy?"

"Heat. Ink. But maybe they just missed it."

"Maybe," Grafton agreed.

"Why not go back there and see what else we can find?"

"I'd thought we'd do the country place first. You may have to get us in."

"Oh, man!" Willie said dramatically. "Breakin' and enterin'. The last time I got out of the joint I promised my ol' mama that I'd never do that again."

He was lying, of course. His mother died when he was a teenager. I laid my head back against the headrest and tried to sleep as Willie entertained the Graftons.

Rancho Rodet looked properly somnolent that warm, sunny Monday morning. It should, since the old man and his thugs had killed a maid and the gardener, who doubled as the outside security guy and fed the dogs. They didn't have any dogs left, either, which almost brought a tear to my eye, but not quite. And no cops in sight.

Grafton handed me my backpack; he had rescued it yesterday from the police after I passed out. I went to work on the back-door lock while he and Callie and Willie stood by the car looking around like tourists. Innocent tourists.

Opening it took a while. My headache had subsided to a

buzz, yet I was a little shaky and, truthfully, a bit dizzy. I kept trying one pick after another. Finally I paused, wiped my head and took a deep breath, then started all over again with the pick I had first started with. Got it that time.

After Callie and Willie went in, Grafton told me to sit down for a minute. I plopped down right on the step. He sat down beside me.

"How you doing?" he asked.

"Okay. Want to tell me what you hope to find?"

"I've got a theory," he said. "I want to prove it or disprove it."

"Uh-huh."

But he didn't explain, merely got up and went inside. I wiped my face and levered myself erect.

Each of us took a room. We took that house apart. Looked everywhere, in everything, examined everything. One of the first things I found was an electromagnetic sweep set in an aluminum case; no doubt Rodet used it to check the house for bugs. Terrific.

We found a lot of dry pens, receipts from years ago, old photos, dust balls in places the maids obviously hadn't visited in years. It was hard, dismal work and got us exactly nowhere. We took pictures off the wall and cut the backing off. We rolled up carpets, examined the baseboards, disassembled radios and televisions, flipped through every book on the shelves—and ol' Henri had a lot of books. I wondered if he had read them all.

In midafternoon Callie fixed us something to eat. We only had three rooms left to do at that point, two bedrooms and a kitchen.

"Tommy, why don't you tackle the barns?" Jake said.

He didn't have to say it twice. I gobbled the rest of my sandwich and went outside.

The big barn smelled of horses, yet it was empty. A few flies buzzed on that warm, late autumn day, and a couple of cats slunk around.

There weren't a lot of places to hide anything in that barn.

I looked under the walkway. Cobwebs and dirt, a pathway for the cats. No human had ever crawled under there.

I went over the ground floor inch by inch. I probed the cans that held the horse feed with a shovel handle. Obviously it would have helped if Grafton had told us what he was looking for, but I sort of figured he didn't know. My impression was that he was feeling his way along, which bothered me. I confess, I didn't understand what Arnaud or Rodet had been up to, nor why Rodet didn't share what he knew about Qasim. I had a few theories of my own. I thought Arnaud killed Al and Rich so the old man and his Islamic gang could sack Rodet's apartment in peace. But if that was true, why did the old man kill Arnaud? Did he think he double-crossed him and the cause?

A ladder led up to the loft. I climbed it and inspected the loft as carefully as I could in the poor light. There were no electric lights up here, merely daylight coming through air vents overhead. Bird droppings were splattered everywhere.

There was hay in square bales, a lot of it. Moving all those bales didn't appeal to me. Not by myself, anyway. Some old saddles and tack, really old. Horse-drawn equipment that ought to be worth some money at an antique store. A couple of wood-burning stoves that I looked in. One of them was filled with rusty wire. I pulled it all out.

This barn reminded me of the one my uncle owned back when I was growing up. It was a cool barn; I liked it because my uncle had a stash of girlie mags in an old trunk in the loft, which he liked to study for inspiration. I know because I liked to follow and spy on him. He never found out that I was watching.

Finally I had searched everything in the loft. I stood looking up at the joists, which were also filthy with bird droppings. There was a platform way up there on one end of the barn, right under the roof, but there was no way up.

I looked around on the floor—and saw two scrapped places where the feet of a ladder might have stood.

The ladder! It was lying against one wall, wedged in behind the hay bales.

I moved four bales and worked the ladder free.

It was an extension ladder. I managed to extend it and put it up against the platform. The feet fit the scraped places perfectly.

I wasn't feeling myself, so I went up very carefully.

There was a suitcase up there. Nothing else. It had something in it—I could tell by the weight.

I almost dropped it getting it down to the floor of the loft—had to hold it in one hand and get myself down with the other without falling.

I put it on the floor and opened it.

There was a pistol, a silencer, a box of ammo, a police uniform complete with badge, and the pièce de résistance, a small computer and a onetime pad with about a dozen sheets left on it.

I was inspecting this treasure when I heard someone call, "Hey, Tommy."

"Up here."

In a moment Grafton's head appeared at the top of the ladder. "Got something?"

"Yeah. Come on up."

He looked at everything. "Where was it?"

I pointed.

He glanced up, then sat down beside me and examined the computer carefully.

"Is this what you were looking for?"

"Looks like the jackpot. Did you touch that pistol?"

"Huh-uh."

"Remember Al and Rich? Talking about the cop outside the van, just before they were shot?"

"I remember. Who wore this outfit, Arnaud or Rodet? Who was trying to frame who?"

"You can make a case either way, but it was Rodet. Qasim and his local soldiers were going to trash Rodet's apartment, pretending to look for a computer. He didn't want us listening."

"So the old man was Qasim?"

"Yes. Wearing makeup."

I couldn't believe it. The old man was Qasim? "Rodet must have recognized him!"

"Oh, yes."

"But . . . Qasim shot Rodet! Cut up Marisa!"

"Uh-huh."

"That means Marisa's in this up to her eyes. She *let* them cut her up."

"Yep."

"So Rodet and Qasim are both terrorists?"

"I don't know what they are. Let's forget labels for a moment. Marisa was the link between Qasim and Rodet. The proof is right here, in my hand." He meant the computer. "Rodet told me that fancy telephone was the way he wrote and encrypted his messages to Qasim, and he gave us four sheets of a onetime pad that had been lying on his desk in his Paris apartment. He said NSA will eventually sort out the zeros and ones, make these two devices give up their secrets. I suspect this is the computer that was used to program the telephone computer Rodet gave us. Qasim never had one."

"How'd you figure it out?"

"Rodet telling Callie about the pad on the desk. And in the desk the women found a curling iron to apply heat to the pages of the pad. There it was, right in the drawer. You saw that place after it had been trashed. They broke the lamps, ripped pillows apart, tore up the carpets, even broke the light-bulbs. Don't you remember? I thought at the time that it looked as if everything in the place had been put through a blender. Rodet's mistake was to go back and put the pad beside the desk for Callie and Sarah to find. To clue them that it was there, he left a curling iron in the desk drawer, a place where the iron wouldn't normally ever be used for its designed purpose. He was worried that I wasn't buying the story he wanted to tell—or the French police wouldn't—so he tried to tidy up with one too many touches."

"But what about that scene yesterday?"

"The whole thing was an act. Let's go through it: Arnaud sees my short story on the Intelink and rushes right over to tell his boss, the man in charge of the security for the G-8 summit. Rodet goes to the bathroom, or a bedroom, and makes a call to Qasim, who jumps in the van, picks up his soldiers and motors right over. Marisa said the bad guys arrived immediately, but she was lying. They arrived later, much later, maybe two hours or so later. Remember, Cliff Icahn saw the van arrive, but he didn't notice Arnaud in his car, which had passed hours earlier.

"They rolled in, shot the gardener and maid, and took Arnaud and Rodet and Marisa out to the apartment over the garage. They tied them to chairs and set the scene for us. They knew we would be along in a little while. They hoped to be gone by then. We would have found Arnaud dead, Rodet wounded, and Marisa sliced up. Rodet would have probably worked his way out of his bonds and called the police. That timetable went out the window when you showed up. They knew we would be right behind you. A quick shift in plan. The holy warriors would fight, perhaps escape, but even if they didn't, they were going to kill some of us and go down fighting. Didn't matter either way, because they would earn a spot in paradise."

Grafton took a deep breath, then continued. "Arnaud had to die. He was always the fall guy, the man they were going to blame for everything to keep Rodet in the clear. Arnaud was supposed to have framed Rodet on the Bank of Palestine stock purchase. He was supposed to have shot Claude Bruguiere to permanently close his mouth. He was supposed to have shot the two Americans in the surveillance van in the Place des Vosges."

"But why did they need a scapegoat?" I asked.

"*Rodet* was the man in charge of renovations to Versailles in advance of the G-8 summit. *Rodet* was the man in charge of security. So after the assassination of the leaders, *Rodet* will need a villain, someone to blame for betraying the security arrangements. Arnaud is that man. It would look as if he sold out to the terrorists and attempted to implicate his boss."

Grafton paused. "That scene yesterday wasn't as impromptu as one might think. Rodet and Qasim probably planned to kidnap Arnaud sometime before the summit, act out this scene and kill him. His rushing over merely speeded things up."

He laid the computer back in the valise on top of the folded police uniform.

"Shit!" I muttered.

"Marisa is in it as deep as Rodet. Maybe they injected her with a local anesthetic. Qasim could have taken the needle and drug with him when he left."

Grafton stood. He reverently closed the suitcase and smiled at me. "Thanks," he said.

"Jesus Christ, Admiral! I am *so* confused. I thought Rodet had a spy in Al Queda. He gave us the Veghel conspiracy!"

"Oh, no, Tommy. You're looking at cause and effect the wrong way round. You're looking at a mirror image of the truth. The truth is precisely the opposite. Abu Qasim is *not* spying on Al Queda. *Henri Rodet is Al Queda's spy in the West.* The Veghel conspiracy was sacrificed to ensure that no one suspected that Rodet was passing information to Al Queda. He's a double agent." He patted the suitcase. "This computer will tell the tale."

All this was a bit too much for my criminal mind to process quickly. "But no one suspected that," I objected.

"Oh, they will," Grafton said heavily. "They will! When Al Queda assassinates the G-8 leaders—the president of the United States, the prime ministers of Great Britain and Japan, the president of France, the chancellor of Germany, and the others—the investigators are going to turn over every single stone. The fallout from that event will make the Warren Commission look bush league. *Then* Henri Rodet will have the alibi he needs. He selected Arnaud to take the fall months ago. When I arrived in Paris and began nosing around, Rodet began to worry that they didn't have Arnaud wrapped tightly enough. So he improvised."

"And nearly killed his girlfriend."

"If she had died after she told her story, he wouldn't have cared."

"What about those thugs who tried to kill me? You think Rodet ordered them to do that?"

"No. Personal vendettas and vengeance isn't his style. After you threw that guy through the museum clock, the jihadists declared war."

"They tried to kill you, too."

"I think Rodet and Qasim were afraid of me by then. They wanted you dead, too. That car bomb should have done it."

"Elizabeth Conner?"

"You really want to know?"

"Yeah."

"I need your word that you are not going to get personally involved."

Uh-oh. He knew I wasn't going to like this. So it wasn't Rodet or Arnaud or the soldiers of Islam. "Okay."

"Your word?"

"My word."

"Gator Zantz."

"That son of a bitch!"

Grafton hefted the suitcase, lifting it experimentally as if he were weighing it. "We found two more electromagnetic sweep sets after you came out here. So Rodet actually had three sets in the house. He found the bugs and put them in two bedrooms upstairs, then turned on a radio. That's what Icahn was listening to."

"I figured it was something like that."

Grafton nodded. "In this business we must have good people. Icahn listened to the bugs all night and heard nothing but music. He didn't think a thing about it. You listened for, what—ten or fifteen minutes?—and knew we were being had."

"Lucky, I guess."

"Lucky? Maybe lucky for Marisa Petrou. Those people weren't doctors. That fool with the knife might have killed her. She might have bled to death."

"Maybe she wishes she had."

Grafton didn't say anything to that.

I went down the ladder to the ground floor first and he handed the suitcase down to me. He climbed down carefully.

"Marisa is in love with Rodet," I said when he was beside me. "I thought the bastard loved her."

"Maybe he does, in his own twisted way," Jake Grafton mused. "Yet there's someone he loves more." A moment later he muttered, "Qasim may have started out as Rodet's spy. Somehow that relationship got seriously twisted."

CHAPTER TWENTY-SEVEN

The Rue Paradis didn't look the same. Oh, it still had its hookers and johns, but it felt as if the air had gone out of it. The narrow stairwell of my building echoed with my footsteps. I paused at Conner's door. The police had sealed it. I kept climbing.

My little room looked . . . well, little. Grubby. Old. Paris had lost its charm.

The bandage on my leg would get soaked if I sat in the tub, so I did the best I could with a washrag at the sink. Got water all over the floor.

I opened the window a couple of inches and fell into bed. Must have laid awake for two whole minutes thinking about things. The next thing I knew my cell phone was ringing. I opened an eye. It was morning and light was streaming through the window. The room was chilly; I was really snuggled in.

"Yeah."

"Grafton. Rise and shine. Come see me when you get here."

"Okay."

Another day at the war. I rolled out.

I wore my best suit—well, my only suit—and best dark red power tie. Over that I put on a windbreaker. I set forth on the Vespa.

The town was full of paramilitary police with submachine

guns hanging on straps across their chests. Pairs of them were on every corner, standing around watching people and traffic and looking bored. How they stand it I'll never know.

The motorcycle rack was nearly full, but I lucked out and found a spot and locked up my ride. I stuffed the windbreaker in the little plastic saddlebag and locked it up, too, and locked the helmet to the thing. Then I strolled over to the embassy and went right in the front door like a real person.

The place was hopping. Jake Grafton had had a stormy session with the ambassador early that morning, someone said, and was now in conference in the embassy theater, where all the big briefings were held. He wanted me there, according to one of the security guys.

Who should I find outside the door but Willie Varner, also sporting a suit, with a blue tie over a blue shirt with a white collar. I whistled. "Didn't know you owned a suit."

"Own one and this is it," he said. "Bought it to be buried in."

"You're looking kinda poorly, too."

"Grafton said to send you in when you got here."

"This been going on long?"

"Just got started. Ever' high muckety in the French gover'ment is in there listenin' to Grafton tell them about Rodet. There was a lot of tight jaws when they went in. I hear the prez and PMs all show up tomorrow, so he's upsettin' their applecarts."

The guard let me in and I found an empty seat in the back of the little auditorium. Grafton was on the stage—also decked out in a suit. I'll bet that he had never had a more attentive audience in his life. The place was quiet as a morgue, and Grafton was Mr. Cool, as if he were making a presentation at his neighborhood homeowners' association. Sitting in a folding chair on his left was Inspector Papin of the French police. On the right was a white-haired man of distinction. I asked the guy beside me who he was.

"Ambassador Lancaster."

When Grafton finished his indictment of Henri Rodet, he opened the suitcase that we took from the barn at Rodet's place and displayed the items one by one. His audience stared in silence at the pistol, at the silencer, at the police-man's uniform, at the cop's hat and shoes, at the remaining sheets on the onetime pad, but they were mesmerized by the computer. Every eye in the place was on it as Grafton ex-plained what it was and how Rodet had used it.

Someone stood up. "I helped develop the security plan. There are no holes in it."

Grafton responded, "I have no doubt that it's as good as can be devised. The point is that Rodet probably passed it to Al Queda. We can assume that the bad guys have the summit agenda, the flow plan, the photo op plan, and the security plan."

There were a few more questions; then the high mucketys huddled in front of the podium. I made my escape. Willie wasn't in the lobby.

I went down to the SCIF to find Sarah Houston.

"Hey."

"Hey yourself. You're looking better this morning than you did yesterday."

"What a difference a day makes, huh?" I dropped into a chair. "Did you talk to Grafton?"

She played dumb. "What about?"

"About your future?"

"Not yet. No use leaving the agency until I get a better offer."

"I see." Believe me, I did see. Life is for the living, and here she was—but I couldn't pull the trigger. Maybe I should have zigged, but I zagged. "Seen Gator around?"

"Nope."

"He owes me money. Know where he is?"

"You may have trouble collecting. I heard he quit."

"Quit what?"

"The company."

I scratched my chin as I considered. I figured that Grafton turned him over to the French police, who probably had him locked up someplace, and the admiral wasn't broadcasting the fact. I wouldn't, either, if I were him. Too much going down. *Le Monde* would have a field day with Gator Zantz. Ah, me.

Good-bye, Lizzie.

The phone on the desk rang and Sarah picked it up. She grunted a few times, hung up and said, "The Secret Service honcho, Pink Maillard, wants to see you and Willie." She concentrated on her computer screen and went back to tapping keys.

"Keep it warm, babe," I said, and levered myself up. I was still stiff and sore—felt like I had gone a few rounds with a gorilla.

"Don't 'babe' me," she said without enthusiasm, not bothering to look up. I closed the door behind me.

Pink had already corralled Willie when I found him in Grafton's closet office. "I don't have much time. The security team is reconvening in a French government building in half an hour. The admiral says I can use you guys as additional spotters at the summit tomorrow and Thursday."

"I ain't with the gover'ment," Willie said. "I'm just here in Paris on a consultin' basis, checkin' things out, lendin' my professional expertise to the spooks. For money, of course."

Maillard didn't quite know what to make of Willie. "You won't be carrying weapons. I want two more sets of eyes out there. You see anything suspicious, and I mean anything, tell one of my agents or a French officer. Okay?"

"Sure," Willie said. "But I ain't doin' nothin' dangerous, you understand? Ain't bein' paid enough."

"Put us on the duty list," I said cheerfully.

"I want you to go out to Versailles and look around. Stay out of the way—just look."

"We get to wear those cool little radios with the lapel mikes and earpieces?" Willie asked.

"No." Maillard started to say something cutting, then thought better of it. What he did say was, "I need eyes. The guys downstairs will give you a pass with your photo on it. Go take care of it."

"You bet." I took Willie by the elbow and got him out of there before he managed to convince Maillard we were a couple of ding-dongs.

◆ ◆ ◆

We rode out to Versailles on the subway and strolled the street of the tourist trap that the area around the château had become. Neither of us had eaten, so we had brunch in a café on a corner. We were given a seat against the window where we could watch the passersby. Willie looked at the menu and launched into a monologue about the prices. I tuned him out; been doing that for years.

Two tourists—obviously Americans, wearing casual clothes and armed with digital cameras with big lenses—were seated at the next table. In answer to their questions, the waitress told them that the château was closed to the public. They were disappointed.

After we ordered, I watched the people on the street. The day was blustery, with small puffy clouds racing overhead and casting shadows that came and went quickly.

The only people in the Sun King's palace today and during the summit were going to be officials, security people, and the press. Al Queda knew that. If Rodet passed along the security plan, they knew precisely how the whole staged event would go. I didn't, but if I could corner Grafton or Maillard, they would give me the outline. Might even let me read the whole plan, which wouldn't help me much.

So if I were a terrorist, how would I assassinate eight heads of state? Or seven, or six, or as many as I could get?

The problem was that I wasn't an assassin. Nor was I suicidal. I didn't have the mind-set for the job.

"You haven't heard a word I said," Willie remarked.

"Sorry."

"Practicing up for gettin' married, huh?"

I snorted.

"Talked to ol' Sarah this morning. She's got her sights on you, Tommy."

"Terry."

"Yeah."

The entrance to the palace grounds lay at the end of a broad, tree-lined avenue. A small crowd of camera clickers stood outside shooting pictures through the fence. Willie and

I threaded our way through, presented our passes to the para-military police at the gates, and were admitted.

Without tourists, the place looked deserted. Actually, it probably looked much as it did when Louis the Whatever came riding up in his carriage with Marie Antoinette at his side. The huddled masses yearning to be free were kept outside the gates in those days, too. Versailles was, and still is, an extraordinary monument to the vast chasm that existed between the filthy rich at the top of the pecking order and the 99 percent of the populace at the bottom. No wonder the French had a revolution.

We hiked along looking the place over. The château, or palace, was an extraordinary, sprawling building, the second largest palace in Europe. The first? The Louvre, the king's house in town. Today Versailles is a Paris suburb, but back then Paris was a much smaller town centered on the two islands in the Seine.

Even though they chopped off Louis' head, the revolutionary French were proud of the palace, and today's French still are. They love to hold state functions here to show it off. The glory and grandeur of France, and all that.

Bomb squad trucks were parked at some of the entrances. The explosives experts were searching every square inch. No doubt Abu Qasim and Henri Rodet knew they would, so I doubted if a basement full of dynamite was on their list of possibilities. I ran through every explosive possibility I could think of and rejected them one by one.

Airplanes? Mobile antiaircraft missile batteries were already in position and being checked over by troops. I saw two and knew there were more. If the bad guys planned on crashing a plane into the building, or driving a truck through the gate to blow it up alongside the building, they would make a big splash in the news media and probably not kill a single politician. If that was the plan, there was little Willie or I could do about it except get out of the way. The truth was, if they did that, they would prove how impotent they were.

They didn't think of themselves that way. They needed a success.

Snipers? The French had snipers on the rooftops. I saw uniformed men with rifles moving around up there.

No, I decided, if an attempt was going to be made, it would be one man, or a small group, that came through the gate with passes. Politicians, cameramen, reporters, the château staff . . . or the military or police.

Rather than go inside, I led Willie away to look at soldiers. Over the next two hours we saw a bunch. We were footsore and ready for a restroom when Willie finally complained. We headed inside.

There was a stack of tourist brochures just inside the door; I picked one up. The usual tour-group guides had the week off, so we were on our own. A paramilitary cop with a sub-machine gun stood in every doorway. We met two groups of police with bomb-sniffing dogs working the rooms systemat-ically, looking for anything out of the ordinary.

The G-8 finance ministers were meeting in the library, and we were turned away. The working press was herded into an-other room a few doors down. We looked in there. The room had been set up for press conferences, which were going to be held later this afternoon when the ministers had some agreement to spin for the folks back home.

We wandered along, looking at this, looking at that. The ceilings were way up there, like twenty-five feet above the floor, and everything was gilded in real gold, or painted to look like it. The gold was accented by white pillars and walls, although occasionally a brilliant color had been used for con-trast. All in all, it was a hell of a palace, but I wouldn't have wanted to live there back in the good old days, B.T.P.— before toilet paper. Those were chamber-pot days, long be-fore running water. Makes me shiver just thinking about it. Maybe that's why camping has never had much appeal to me.

"Maybe you ought to get married," Willie said, right out of the blue, while we were contemplating a huge painting of a queen with the royal children.

The American philosopher Jerry Lee Lewis once said that too much sex drives a man insane. No joke. Willie had lost it.

"Sarah's pretty serious, you know," he added, quite unnecessarily.

"What would you know about marriage? I seem to recall that you are a lifelong bachelor."

"Thought about gettin' married. Once. Years ago."

We strolled on, looking at paintings. I was kinda glad I didn't have this kind of art in my apartment.

"Was datin' a redheaded nymphomaniac who owned a liquor store," Willie said a moment or two later. "She was easy to get serious about."

"You're lying."

"Well, to tell the truth, she wasn't really a redhead. Dyed her hair and straightened it and made it stand up. Looked pretty good, actually."

"You never took her to the altar."

"Never got seriously into liquor, man. Beer's my drink. But Sarah, she's a nice woman. Gonna make some guy a wife for life."

"Let's talk about something else, like global warming, the tax code, or who's going to get to the Super Bowl."

When we got to the Hall of Mirrors, the big hall on the back of the building, we found another crowd. Workmen were setting up a huge conference table, a microphone system, enough lights to stage a rock concert, and a bank of television cameras. This was where the presidents and prime ministers were going to meet to talk about important political stuff. Under the constant scrutiny of a squad of paramilitary police, we walked slowly along looking at everything.

"This is where it's gonna happen, if it happens," Willie declared. "While they're all together. On television, even. This may be the only time they're all together. Maximum impact."

I looked at the cops, at the television cameras, at the statues lining the walls, at the mirrors, at the vaulted gilded ceiling way up there. This room obviously inspired several generations of railroad station architects. But if Al Queda intended to strike here, how were they going to do it?

If I knew the answer to that one, I'd be running the Secret Service, not wandering around with a daffy ex-con with marriage on his mind.

We strolled on to the other end of the room and past the squad of paras. A couple nodded at us after they inspected our passes, which were hanging on little chains around our necks.

Behind them, covering the wall, hung a curtain that reached all the way to the floor. I had seen other curtains here and there throughout the building, but now the implications sank in. I felt the curtain and found the part. Easing it back a little, I saw a door. It wore a common European lock.

"Look at that," I said to Willie.

He wasn't impressed. "Hell, I could open that with a bobby pin," he scoffed.

"Got one on you?"

He scrutinized my face. "Are you nuts? They'll throw our asses outta here."

"We got passes and we know people. Do you have a pin?"

"Yeah." Willie removed one from his shirt pocket and straightened it out somewhat. I reflected that old habits die hard.

He slipped behind the curtain while I stood there looking at the backs of the troops. Ten seconds passed, fifteen, then half a minute.

"Got it," he said in a barely audible voice. "Come on."

No one was watching me. I went through the curtain and the door, which Willie was holding open. He came in behind me and pulled the door shut until it latched. Then he grinned. "Still got it, dude. Still got it."

We were in a narrow hallway, perhaps four feet wide, lit by naked bulbs in fixtures on the wall just above head-high. The wire that ran from fixture to fixture was stapled to the wall.

"Slave hallway," Willie said softly.

"The frogs didn't have slaves."

"The hell they didn't! They were all slaves—that's why they had a revolution. Lead off. Let's see where she goes."

We walked along and came to a ladder leading upward. We were inside the interior wall of the Hall of Mirrors. I consulted my tourist literature, which had a rudimentary map of the château's rooms. We were between the Hall of Mirrors and the king's bedroom. Sure enough, a few paces farther on, we came to a doorway that must lead to the king's chamber. I said as much to Willie.

"Want to look in there?" he asked.

"No." We walked on. The passage was endless. Doors opened into every room. Narrow stairs led up and down. We took one leading down, went down and down, and came to another passageway that led away in two directions. These servants' passageways apparently led all over the building.

"The kings and queens didn't want the help parading through the big rooms," Willie said.

At the bottom of another staircase we found only a door, so we opened it. We were in a kitchen. Seated at a table were Jake Grafton and the French police inspector, Papin.

"Ah, Terry. Willie. You've been exploring, I see. Come sit down, have a drink of wine."

Willie marched right over and parked his bottom. "Howdy," he said to the Frenchman as Grafton poured him a small glass of white wine. I accepted one, too.

"How did you get into the passageways?" the Frenchman asked in good English.

I jerked a thumb at Willie. He tossed his bobby pin onto the table.

"I see."

This cop had obviously been around. I turned my attention to Grafton. "You think this Abu Qasim is going to try for paradise tomorrow?"

"Perhaps, but I doubt it," the admiral said. "However, someone might. Inspector Papin has been briefing me on Muslim fanatics here in France, which seems to have its share plus a few."

"Suiciders," Willie said sourly, and slurped more wine. He drank it as if it were beer. The Frenchman didn't seem offended.

"Inspector Papin was telling me about the renovation of this building that was completed this past spring," Grafton said. "All the rooms on the main floor were extensively refurbished."

He looked at me and I looked at him.

"Tomorrow I want you and Willie in those servant hallways," Grafton said.

"Okay."

He slid a ray gun across the table. It looked like the one I used at the Rancho Rodet.

"The batteries all charged up?" I murmured.

"Yep."

I checked that the power was off, then pocketed it. Papin had his head turned and didn't seem to notice.

"What are you guys going to do about ol' Henri?" I asked the police inspector.

Papin shrugged. "I am just a policeman," he said.

"Next week, after the summit, Henri Rodet will be asked to retire for medical reasons," Grafton said.

"*Next week?*" That just slipped out.

"The government doesn't want a breath of scandal now, during the summit."

"I see."

"If he refuses to retire, he will be fired," Grafton added. "He'll retire, I think. The authorities don't have enough evidence to prosecute him."

"Prints on the gun? The magazine? Ammo? Suitcase? Computer?"

"None, they tell me. Wiped clean."

"You're joking." I could see that he wasn't, so I added, "Hairs on the uniform? DNA?"

Grafton shrugged. "If there is an attempt made on the lives of the G-8 leaders and somehow it can be tied to him, that decision could change, of course."

"Gotta have evidence," Willie declared, and slurped more wine.

I was thinking of Marisa. "Very civilized," I said, and nodded at the inspector.

CHAPTER TWENTY-EIGHT

As Willie attacked his second glass of wine, Inspector Papin glanced at his watch and excused himself. Watching Willie slurp it kinda bothered me, too.

Grafton waited until the policeman was out of the room. Then he said, "If you were going to kill eight world leaders, how would you do it?"

"Wait until they were all in one place," Willie said, "then blow it up. While the television cameras watched."

"The only place all eight will be together on television is upstairs in the Hall of Mirrors. Oh, Wednesday evening they'll all go to a state dinner hosted by the French president at his residence in Paris, but that won't be televised live."

"It'll be here," Willie Varner insisted. "While the world is watching."

I agreed with Willie. Still . . . "The bomb squads have had dogs in the building all day."

"Indeed they have, but dogs are trained to smell certain types of explosives. No dog can be trained to find everything in the chemical cornucopia that can be made to go bang."

We discussed it and decided to start in the basement and work up. We found a door to the dungeon, all right, a damp, dark place of massive stone walls and iron beams. The beams were at least a century old, installed to replace the original oak beams, yet the iron looked serviceable. It had been painted recently with some kind of red rust inhibitor.

Grafton had a pocket flashlight, and we used that to supplement the poor light from the overhead light fixtures. The fixtures and wires looked as if they dated from the nineteenth century. We found the remnants of ancient cells that probably once held political prisoners, back when the musketeers were dashing and slashing.

"The dungeon," Willie whispered.

After my recent jail experience, the place gave me the shivers—and an uncomfortable, closed-in feeling.

It seemed to get to Willie, too. "Man could get that clause-tro-phoby in a place like this," he remarked at one point. "People musta been smaller back in them days."

"How much explosive would it take to knock out the supports and bring down the building?" I asked Grafton. He was a naval officer; he must know more about explosives than I did.

"A few hundred pounds if it were placed right. A whale of a lot more if it were just packed in here."

"They don't have to bring down the building," Willie pointed out.

"That's right," Grafton admitted with a sigh. "But I don't think there's anything here. Let's go upstairs."

When we got back to the kitchen, the door to the stairwell was locked. As Willie worked on it with the bobby pin, I said, "A man could go far with a thing like that."

Willie opened the door with a flourish.

"All the way to the penitentiary," Jake Grafton said as he walked by.

We walked the passageways looking at everything, not that there was a lot to see. The floors were wooden, the walls and ceiling plasterboard, and there were lights and wires and doors. That was it. So we walked along looking for discontinuities, something out of the ordinary, such as a floorboard that had been removed and replaced, a section of the wall that had been repaired, anything. It was time-consuming and tedious, and, of course, we found nothing.

We had been at it an hour and were in the south wing of the building when two paras came along with a bomb-sniffing dog. They looked at our badges, then looked us over while I eyed the dog—it wasn't interested in us—edged by, and went on.

"We'll never manage to walk through all these passages," Grafton remarked. "Let's go back to the main building where the summit meeting will be held."

"In the main building on the main floor, in the passageway between the king's bedroom and the Hall of Mirrors, there are ladders—actually just boards nailed to the wall," I told him. "A dog couldn't climb them."

"We'll try that," Grafton said.

The first ladder we came to went up into the ceiling, yet the trapdoor was screwed shut. We walked along, looking. There were three ladders, and all three had secured trapdoors.

"I saw some hand tools in the kitchen, Tommy." Grafton told me where they were, and away I went. I found them and paused for a drink of water, then headed back.

I took off my coat, got up on the middle ladder, and started screwing. Ten screws, with paint covering the heads. It took a while.

I got the honor of going up first. When I opened the trapdoor in the ceiling, it was dark as a tomb above me. I stuck my head up and felt around, found a switch, and flipped it. Way up high, a naked bulb illuminated among the rafters and braces. The space between the massive uprights of the walls of the Hall of Mirrors and the king's bedroom was criss-crossed with wooden braces that stabilized everything and tied the whole building together. It was dusty and gloomy up there. There was only that one bulb, and in that huge dark space, it looked like a firefly in the night.

"We're going to need a flashlight," I said.

Grafton, who was below me on the ladder, passed up a small pocket flash. "Callie always packs these when we go anyplace, just in case the power goes out."

I took the flash, put it in my shirt pocket, and climbed into the loft. Grafton, then Willie, followed.

There were spiders and webs. Didn't look as if anyone had been up here in a while.

Willie cussed as he climbed. "This is my good suit, I'll

have you know. Paid near two hundred dollars for it. It gets ripped, I'm gonna bill the gover'ment. Grafton, just want you to know."

"He got it at the Salvation Army," I said.

"That's a damn lie."

Near the top of the ladder was a catwalk. I climbed up on it. The lightbulb was in a ceramic fixture screwed to a rafter. Scanning the flash around, I could see that the rounded ceiling of the Hall of Mirrors was suspended from the rafters and joists and braces. The joint work looked superb to me. I could see by the different shades of the wood, and the texture, that the beams were of various ages. Across the space was the outside wall of the château; the beams and boards there butted into the masonry.

"Bet some of these boards are as old as the building," Grafton muttered as he joined me on the catwalk.

I looked down the ladder. Willie was going back down to the passageway below.

"Hey," I called.

"You don't need me up there. I'm too old for this shit, anyway."

Grafton took the flash and went down the catwalk, looking at everything. I followed along. We went all the way to the end of the catwalk and worked back to the other end. It was a nice distance, at least a hundred feet, but the room below was huge.

All we saw was beams and dust and spiderwebs and sawdust from the construction last winter and spring. Finally Grafton sat down on the catwalk. I did, too. We could hear chairs being set up in the hall below, plus some other banging and clanging.

"Maybe we figured this wrong," Grafton said disgustedly. "Maybe it won't be a bomb. Maybe a submachine gun, a pistol, something for the evening news."

"Who's going to pull the trigger?"

"A cop? A paramilitary guy? A fake cameraman? I don't know." Grafton smacked his fist on his thigh.

"If that was the plan, Rodet wouldn't have needed a scapegoat," I told him. "Maybe we should go over to the hospital and sweat the guy, make him an offer he can't refuse."

"I know you didn't really mean that, but don't say those things. By three o'clock in the morning I'll be ready to do it." Grafton idly played the beam of his flashlight back and forth over the timbers.

"Maybe Abu Qasim himself. Whaddaya think?"

Grafton turned off the flash and sat silently in the gloom. "Maybe, but I doubt it. Anyone could push a button." He flipped on the light, then flipped it off. "If it was going to be Qasim, Rodet could have told us a tale, who Qasim was, where he was, knowing that would send us off on a wild goose chase and clear the way for Qasim here. But he didn't."

"He didn't because you would have figured he was lying, and since he said it wasn't so, it was."

Grafton wasn't going to waste time chasing his tail. "Only place we haven't looked is over there," he said. The beam shot out across the hump of the ceiling in the hall below, pointed at the far wall. "On the other side of the apex there's an area that can't be seen from the catwalk."

I hoisted myself erect and flexed the leg with the stitches in it. "I can get over there."

"You fall, you'll go through that ceiling and land down below. Make a splash, maybe even the evening news."

"Get famous, sign a book contract for my autobiography, get rich and retire." I put Grafton's flashlight in my trouser pocket, stripped to my undershirt, climbed up on the railing, then began working my way across the beams. I got some splinters in my hand and did a little quiet cussing. It was just so dark out there.

I stopped just ten feet from the other side, eased the flashlight out without dropping it, turned it on and began looking. The beam wouldn't reach either end of the hall, so I started right below me, in the trough where the roof met the exterior masonry.

And by God, there it was. A small black cylinder, perhaps three feet long. It was strapped to a timber, I could see that. There was a valve on one end, and a hose leading to the ceiling of the room below. A wire led from the valve . . . to a black box of some type. A radio receiver!

I tried to keep the excitement out of my voice. "I think I've found something. Crawl over here and look."

"Gimme some light here," Grafton said as he inched himself in my direction.

When he arrived, I ran the light over the cylinder and the box. "What do you think is in that cylinder?"

Grafton didn't answer immediately. He took his time, looking everything over with the flashlight. Finally he said, "High-pressure gas, highly flammable. Explosive. A push of a button and the radio control unit opens the valve, venting gas into the top of the room below. Somewhere around here there's an igniter. After the cylinder empties—and it would only take five or six seconds, I imagine—a push of another button ignites the mixture."

"A radio-controlled bomb."

"Yep. The concussion will probably kill everyone in the room. If it doesn't, the resulting fire will." He scanned the flashlight right and left. Finally the light stopped moving. "There's another one."

There were five cylinders and four igniters, which were also attached to radio-control units.

When we finally got back to the catwalk, I could see the sheen of perspiration that covered Grafton's face. He pulled a shirttail out, unbuttoned the shirt, and used the tail to wipe his face and hands.

"What kind of gas, you think?"

"Good Lord, I'm not a chemist. Hydrogen with an enhancer would be my guess."

"This stuff wasn't installed last week."

"It was installed during the renovation, probably just before they closed up this area."

"The location for the G-8 summit wasn't announced until a few weeks ago," I mused.

Grafton shook his head vigorously. "Just before we came to Europe. But Rodet knew long before that. He may even have recommended this site. Probably promised ironclad security."

"Think the batteries in the radio control units are still good?"

"I expect they are, but just in case, look here." He bent down and used the flash to illuminate the underside of the beam that he had just crawled out on.

I looked and didn't see anything. Then I did. There was a black cord there, taped under the beam. The end was within easy reach.

"That cord is looped around the cylinder valve. If the radio won't open the valve, it can be opened manually." He went along searching under beams. Sure enough, each cylinder had a cord, and each igniter. The two different kinds were even color-coded.

"Moving the summit to another location at this late date is out of the question," Grafton said as he inspected the cords with his flash. "Questions will be asked that the French government won't want to answer. The powers that be wouldn't consider it."

I didn't argue.

"We'll take the actuating wires off the gas valves on these cylinders," he continued. "The easiest thing is probably to just cut the wire. Our bomber can push his button until his thumb wears out and there won't be any gas to ignite. And, of course, we can cut the cords."

I thought that would work. "We need to get sweep gear up here, ensure we've found all the radio control units."

"You stay here. Don't let anyone touch this stuff. I'll be back after a while."

He left me the flashlight and disappeared down the ladder. I turned the light off to save the battery and found a place to sit.

That turned out to be the longest night of my life. Grafton came back after a couple of hours with Inspector Papin and a few other Frenchies. One of them was a bomb squad guy, and he disconnected the radio-controlled actuators from the cylinder valves. All I did was hold a flashlight and keep it pointed at his work. He didn't need it since he was wearing a miner's light strapped to his forehead.

While he worked the other technician crawled back and forth over the beams working with the sweep wand, which had an extender that lengthened it to over twelve feet. He had a heck of a time maneuvering it around the framing in there, but he verified that there were only four igniters. The bomb squad man disabled them and removed one to take back to the lab.

Finally the frogs left, and it was just me and Grafton. We sat on the catwalk with our legs dangling, listening to the workmen in the Hall of Mirrors below us. You could hear the sound of voices, although words were indistinguishable, and bangs and thumps from people dropping this or that or scooting things around.

"If you're willing, I'd like for you to spend the night here," Grafton said as he watched my eyes. "Don't want to take a chance that anyone might come up here and reconnect this stuff. Or crawl out on those beams and open the valves manually."

"Sure."

"We'll get you a bucket to pee in and food and water. You can sleep in the hallway."

"I need to visit the facilities awhile before you leave."

He nodded. "Better go now," he said.

So I went down the ladder and on down to the kitchen in the basement and used the small restroom there. After slurping some water, I headed back to where Grafton waited. He was standing in the hallway at the bottom of the ladder.

"You can sleep right here, if you want. We'll bring a pillow and blanket."

"See you later," I said.

He stuck out his hand to shake and smiled at me.

When he was gone, I was still glowing. It wore off quickly, though. I strolled the hallway, sat a while, and strolled some more. I sang silently to myself, whistled, thought about After, when this was over. I was bored silly.

About seven that evening Willie showed up with a bucket, a box of really good grub, water, wine, a flashlight, a blanket, and a pillow. "So you guys found a bomb, huh?"

"Yeah."

He wanted to know all about it. When I finished talking, he whistled.

"Did you bring a book or magazine or newspaper?"

From the depths of his bag he whipped out a paperback. A romance. "This was all I could find in English."

At that point I had no shame. I took it.

"You don't look like yourself, Tommy," he said, scrutinizing my face. "You get some sleep."

"Okay."

"Take care of yourself, man."

"I got the zapper."

He nodded, looked at me again, then was gone.

After I ate I dove into the book. The heroine was a sweet young thing, innocent, who fell in love with a jerk who was trying to find himself. A rich jerk, which is the very best kind. Finally I gave up and tried to sleep.

Several times during that long night, someone—I don't know who—rattled the doors to the hallway, checking the locks. Each time I came wide awake and lay there with the ray gun pointed at the door. But the doors didn't open.

I was never so glad to see anyone in my life as I was Jake Grafton on Wednesday morning. I heard someone fussing with the lock on the door, so I popped around the corner into the hallway that led to the right wing of the building while I turned on the battery of my ray gun. When I heard footsteps, I eased an eye around.

"Tommy?"

"Here." I stepped out and hit the ray gun's power switch.

"Breakfast."

"I need a potty break."

"Okay."

I took the bucket with me down to the kitchen and dumped

it in the commode. When I got back upstairs, Grafton was pacing the hallway.

"Long night?" he asked as he handed me several newspapers. One was in English, even.

"You have no idea."

"We spent the night sweeping this building. My pension against a doughnut there aren't any more radio-controlled devices."

"We're going to be in big trouble if you're wrong."

"Oh, no," Jake Grafton said. "If I'm wrong, our troubles are over. We're going to be dead."

It was a long, noisy morning in the hallway. I felt like a monk in his cell, cut off from the world, yet it was just beyond the walls, thumping and bumping. I read all three newspapers, flipped listlessly through the pages of the romance. Nibbled some on the breakfast items that I hadn't eaten. Peed in the bucket. Walked the hallway, back and forth, back and forth. My headache was back—the concussion, I figured—and I was stiff and sore from being pounded on by gorillas and sleeping on the floor.

I knew Abu Qasim was the guy coming to press the button and send the G-8 leaders and their entourages to wherever it is that good suicidal terrorists don't go, someplace without virgins. Then I convinced myself that it wasn't him, that it would be someone else, anybody. A team maybe, anxious to share in the glory.

There was no guarantee that we had found all the bombs. For all I knew, I had slept on one. Underestimating the terrorists was an error that would prove fatal for a lot of people, me included.

Hijack a plane and crash it into the château? It was certainly within the realm of possibility. As I walked, the scenes of the World Trade Center collapsing ran through my mind, over and over.

Well, we had Jake Grafton on our side. Maybe that leveled the playing field.

Fire and blood.

Damn, boy, you gotta get away from this.

I felt clammy and sweaty and started swallowing repeatedly. I should have known! Seconds later I ran for the bucket and heaved my breakfast. I felt a little better afterward, but not much.

I was about ready for the straitjacket and funny farm when Jake Grafton came up from the kitchen at 10:03 A.M. I knew because I'd been checking my watch twice a minute since he left my breakfast.

"Here's a key to the door Willie picked yesterday," he said, holding it out. "Want a break?"

I snatched the key, grabbed the bucket and started hiking for the stairs.

"Come back in an hour or so."

"You bet." I took the stairs down two at a time, dropped a *bonjour* on the five or six plainclothes security folks sitting around the kitchen table, and hopped into the restroom. When I was done there I went through the kitchen to the great outdoors.

I found myself on the back side of the château. I needed a walk, so I circled the building. That takes a while, but that's how long I had. I was stunned when I rounded the north wing and saw the courtyard, which looked like the parking lot at the Super Bowl. There must have been two dozen media trucks there with satellite dishes on the tops; miles of cable ran everywhere in a hopeless tangle; here and there stood a generator truck with its diesel engine snoring loudly; and there were even a couple of private buses.

Three reporters gripping microphones stood with their backs to the château in front of cameramen. A couple appeared to be on the air, chattering into their mikes.

As I watched, a helicopter descended onto the paved area behind the main gate and a small knot of people got out. They walked past the statue of Louis XIV toward the château and the waiting television cameras. It looked like a Hollywood premiere—all they needed was a red carpet and a hot dolly or two draped for action.

Trailing along at a respectful distance, I had to run a gauntlet of security types, some in uniform wearing submachine guns, some in plainclothes with bulging armpits. Every one of them scrutinized my face and the pass dangling from the chain around my neck.

Inside the building was bedlam: television lights, cables strung willy-nilly to trip the unwary, cameras, and the technicians and on-air people to make the magic; needless to say, all these people were talking loudly to each other. Several interviews were in progress in front of large blue drapes, which allowed the producers at home to put in any background they wished any time they wished. I recognized none of the interviewers or interviewees, which is natural since I've led a sheltered life of quiet contemplation.

In one of the rooms, press secretaries were briefing the working press on agreements and statements that the ministers had issued after yesterday's meetings. More uniformed paras, police and plainclothes security guys.

Pink Maillard was huddled with a couple of women carrying Secret Service purses. The women were hardbodies who looked as if they would enjoy shooting me or breaking my neck just for practice. I gave Pink the Hi sign and he jerked his head at me in acknowledgment.

Of course I looked around for Arabs and North Africans and didn't see a one.

Then I did, a delegation in white robes and beards. They appeared to be Saudis, but who knows?

The newspeople were a polyglot lot: their stories and broadcasts were going all over the globe. I leaned against a wall for a while and watched them interview government stooges and ministers and each other. They never tired of it.

As I watched, another knot of people came in, Japanese security types surrounding their leader. Just as I was glancing at my watch, noting that my hour was almost over, the president of Russia arrived. These heads of state were shuffled off to await their summit in the north wing, where they could visit with their own ministers or each other free from press scrutiny.

I stared at the people, scrutinizing them one by one. Which one was the guy with the radio transmitter? Which one had a gun?

That camera—that could be a gun! I walked over, looking at the camera. The guy had a ponytail and wore jeans.

I must have had a strange look on my face, because he said, "Who the hell are you?" in a Texas accent.

I realized I was making a fool of myself and turned away.

Qasim. It would be him. But which one was he?

The key that Grafton had given me opened the door behind the curtain that we had gone through yesterday. No siren went off and no one started shooting. I pulled it shut behind me until it latched, then rattled it.

Jake Grafton was sitting on the catwalk at the top of the ladder. I climbed up to join him. My head was thumping like a toothache and I was perspiring freely, so I held on to the rungs for dear life as I climbed.

"We've done everything that can be done," Grafton said when I was seated beside him, clinging to the rail with a death grip. "The French have searched this building from end to end, including both north and south wings. They've swept it for electronic devices of any sort and swept it with magnetic detectors looking for suspicious metal in the walls, and they've got people stationed everywhere. Antiaircraft missile launchers are on the grounds around the building, concrete barriers have been erected at every entrance to force vehicles to slow to a creep to get through, and tanks are stationed where they can take any vehicle out at can't-miss range. Oh, and troops are out in town patrolling to minimize the chance that someone could shoot a shoulder-launched missile at the château."

"Food and drink have been inspected," I suggested.

"Yep. And no one is in the building except authorized staff, newspeople, security folks, and the political delegations from all over. Absolutely no tourists."

"Sounds like you have it covered."

"I'm just praying there was only the one bomb."

He departed for the security command center, which was a

trailer outfitted with three different global communications systems that sat by the door in the courtyard, right outside the main entrance. It had been obscured by the news trucks, so I hadn't noticed it. Grafton assured me it was there, and I believed him.

It did figure that there was only the one banger. Two doubled the chances that one would be found; then the building would be searched like a Colombian nanny. But since I saw it that way, maybe there were indeed two. Or three.

The problem was that I was a little dizzy. I climbed down from the catwalk gingerly, making sure my feet were properly placed on the rungs. The irony of the moment made me want to cry. I'm a rock climber, for Christ's sake, a cat burglar. I can free-climb a brick wall, and here I was, holding on to a ladder like a kid climbing an apple tree for the very first time.

Safely on the floor, I propped my head on the pillow and lay down on the blanket I had slept under the previous night. Closed my eyes and tried to ignore the pounding in my head. Tried to shut out the noise that seeped through the walls from all sides. Tried to sleep, but it didn't happen. The person on my mind was Abu Qasim.

Grafton found Willie Varner in the basement kitchen watching the ceremonies on television. He was alone. "Carmellini still upstairs in the hallway?"

"He hasn't come down."

"The door is locked, right?"

"Yep. I checked a little while ago."

"Don't let anyone through that door to the servants' hall. Anyone."

"Got one of those radios for me?" Grafton was wearing a radio earpiece in his left ear and a lapel mike. The wires ran to a radio transceiver hooked to his belt.

"No. I got the last one they had." He pulled out a cell phone, made sure it had a signal, and passed it to Willie. "This is Callie's. Call me if anyone wants to go up. Just open the phone, push the green button, then the number 1."

"Okay, boss." Willie put the cell phone on the table.

"I don't have a weapon for you, either. Think you can do this?"

Willie opened several drawers, searching. Finally he pulled out a large knife. "Yeah," he said.

"Good man," Jake said. He patted Willie on the shoulder, and went up the staircase that would take him to the main hall.

Willie Varner pushed the knife up his left sleeve. He opened the refrigerator, which held nothing of interest, then filled a glass of water from the tap. He eyed the television as he sipped it.

The helicopter settled onto the pavement in the vast square in front of the château, but no one got out. The rotors slowed and eventually stopped.

Jake Grafton was standing near the command center, adjusting his radio earpiece, when Pink Maillard's voice sounded in his ear. "He wants to see us, in the bird."

Jake clicked the transmitter button on his belt transceiver twice and began walking toward the helicopter. Maillard caught up with him and matched him stride for stride.

They walked past the media trucks, the paras and the waiting diplomats. A crewman wearing a helmet was standing beside the open door as they approached the helicopter. They climbed aboard and found the president of the United States and the U.S. ambassador to France, Owen Lancaster, seated side by side. The president pointed to the facing seats; Grafton and Maillard sat down.

"You found a bomb."

"Yes, sir." Jake described the cylinders and igniters and explained how they would work.

"So who has the radio control unit that would have set these things off?"

"Someone who is already here," Pink Maillard said tightly. "The French have sealed this place off. No one gets in without a pass."

"But our bomber probably already has a pass," the president said.

"That's right."

"And it could be anyone," the president mused. "Any politician, staffer, cook, policeman, soldier, reporter, cameraman . . ."

"Anybody," Jake agreed.

"Have the terrorists got a Plan B?"

No one answered that question.

When the silence had gone on too long, Owen Lancaster said, "The French have given me assurances. They know the risks as well as we do."

"Right."

"Anybody," Grafton repeated.

"Sweet Jesus," the president muttered. He rose from his seat and climbed out the door of the helicopter.

Pink motioned to one of the Secret Service men who was getting off to follow the president. "Give me your pistol."

The man produced it and passed it to Pink, who handed it to Jake Grafton.

Outside, the president walked toward the row of television cameras and waiting dignitaries.

T he British prime minister was the last to arrive. He made his way into a foyer where he was greeted by the president of France. The two of them walked shoulder to shoulder toward the Hall of Mirrors as the other G-8 leaders came in from the north wing of the building.

Grafton was already in the hall with his shoulders pressed against the back wall. He was amazed at the crush of newspeople, cameramen and bodyguards. The room filled quickly as the heads of government shook hands and seated themselves around the large conference table in the middle of the room.

Grafton watched the crowd and listened to the radio chatter among the security men. He didn't have a good vantage point—he had three men with large videocams on their shoulders directly in front of him—and there was no way he could easily and unobtrusively move to a better one. That's when he glimpsed a face he thought he knew on the other side of the room. Then it disappeared.

• • •

Henri Rodet pushed the button on the transmitter in his jacket pocket repeatedly. He glanced up, waiting . . . and saw nothing out of the ordinary. Well, the gas might be colorless.

He counted silently to ten, took a deep breath, and pushed the button on the other transmitter.

Nothing.

Mon Dieu! Perhaps he had accidentally switched transmitters. If so, the gas was coming out now. He kept counting . . . seven, eight, nine, ten! And pushed the button on the first unit again.

Nothing.

Had they found the bomb and disabled it? Or were the batteries dead?

Jake, this is Pink. The French just got several hits on their radio receiver. Someone is transmitting on the bomb activation frequency. They didn't get a location."

"Pink, Grafton. I thought I just saw Rodet."

"He's in the hospital."

"Maybe he's out. It could have been someone else, but it looked like Rodet."

"What's he doing here?" This rhetorical question went unanswered. "I'll check with the French."

Grafton moved left, elbowing his way around the room as the president of France spoke into a microphone. He scanned the crowd. Rodet had disappeared.

"Papin says Rodet came through the gate twenty minutes ago," Maillard told Jake over the Secret Service net. "He had a pass. No one told the gate people that it was invalid."

Jake clicked his mike twice and kept moving, trying to find Rodet among the hundreds of onlookers.

The batteries, Rodet thought. *They were always the technological weak link. Ten months they had been in place, through the heat of the summer.*

At the top of the staircase to the basement he passed two

paras, who nodded at him. He went down the stairs as quickly as he could. He was favoring his left side, but with the tight wrapping, it didn't hurt too badly.

I'll climb to the bomb. That is the best way.

As he entered the kitchen he glanced around. A slender black man sat at the table. He had been watching the television. He rose.

"What are you doing here?"

Rodet went to the door that would admit him to the stairs to the servants' hall. He removed a key from his pocket and inserted it in the lock.

"You can't go up there! Get away from that door!" The black man came at him. He had a knife in his right hand.

Rodet reached into his coat pocket and grabbed the pistol. But it had no silencer. If he fired a shot here, it would bring an army of paramilitary police and security men. He palmed the pistol, and as the black man stabbed with the knife, he hit him in the side of the head. The man went down and stayed down.

Rodet looked at his side. The knife had gone through his coat, ripping it, but it hadn't penetrated the vest.

He unlocked the door, went through, and pulled it closed behind him.

Stunned, Willie Varner levered himself from the floor and fought to clear his head. He had recognized Henri Rodet, stabbed him—and the knife hit something hard.

He struggled to his feet and grabbed the door handle. Locked. He had the key Grafton had given him. Swaying on his feet, he fished for it.

Should call Grafton, but no time.

He inserted the key in the lock, opened the door, and started up the stairs.

The commotion in the Hall of Mirrors got my attention. I could hear the sonorous French over the PA system, hear every word.

I was standing there in the hallway nursing my headache when I saw the man come up the stairs from the kitchen.

I turned toward him. *Holy . . . ! Henri Rodet!*

I walked toward him.

He saw me, pointed his pistol at me and kept coming, closing the distance.

"You fucking bastard!" I screamed. I had the ray gun out, so I raised it and aimed. Rodet's arm came up, the pistol in his hand.

I squeezed the trigger; the laser leaped across the space and hit Rodet in the chest.

He fired the pistol and something whacked me in the left arm. I released the trigger of the ray gun, steadied myself and pulled it again as I launched myself toward him.

I got the laser on his chest just as his pistol cracked a second time and Willie Varner shouted, "*No, Tommy! He's wearing a bomb!*"

We were only twenty feet apart when the finger of God shot from my fist in a brilliant flash, strobed once . . .

Henri Rodet disappeared in a blinding explosion.

The expanding fireball raced toward me and smacked me like a giant hammer; I flew backward through the air . . . That was the last thing I remember. Everything went black.

Jake Grafton heard the muffled shots, barely audible over the PA system, then the dull whump of an explosion. Pieces of plaster flew off the wall behind the French president and several mirrors shattered.

The president paused just long enough to shoot a glance at the falling glass, then continued his speech without missing a word.

The crowd shuffled their feet, restless, but nothing else happened, so they settled down almost immediately.

Jake Grafton forced his way through the onlookers behind the cameras and made for the stairs to the kitchen as Pink Maillard's voice sounded in his ears, giving orders to his men to enter the servants' hall and report to him.

CHAPTER TWENTY-NINE

When I awoke I was in a hospital bed. I moved my eyes—an IV bottle hung on a hook, sun streamed in a window. I tried to move, but the effort required was too great.

"He's awake." The voice was French, in heavily accented English.

Two women's faces came into view. One I recognized: Sarah Houston.

"Hey, babe." My voice came out a whisper.

"Hey babe yourself, Tommy Carmellini. Welcome back to the land of the living."

I swallowed a time or two and worked my eyes around. My head . . . I couldn't turn my head. I tried to lift my right hand; the effort required was huge. Then I got it going and lifted it to my head, which was swathed in bandages.

"You have a fractured skull. Bullet hole in your left arm, some burns, a ton of bruises—that's about it." Her face was maybe a foot from mine. God, she looked good!

"How long have I been here?"

"Four days."

I thought awhile, trying to remember. I recalled Willie shouting, and the explosion. "How's Willie?"

"Oh, he's okay. Got singed some, but only his head was sticking up above the stairwell. They kept him for a couple of days, then sent him home. He's back in Washington."

"Good. Another week in the whorehouses would have finished him off."

She sat on a chair beside the bed and grasped my right hand. "The summit is over. The French never told the press about the bomb. They explained that there had been a minor accident in the next room, and that was that."

"Minor accident . . ."

"I'm supposed to call Grafton when you wake up."

"Don't hurry. I want to look at you awhile."

She had a good smile. In fact, her smile reminded me of my mother's, back when I was young. And I really liked her eyes, which were big and brown. Say what you will, brown eyes are the best.

"Hey, babe," I said. "When we get back to the States, what say you and I move in together?"

The smile widened. "Yes," she said, and kissed me.

Jake Grafton brought his wife, Callie, when he came. After the three of us visited awhile, Callie excused herself and the admiral pulled the chair over to the bed. They had me cranked up and told me I was going to sit up the next day, but I wasn't there yet.

"Do you know you're in the same hospital that Henri Rodet checked himself out of?"

That thought hadn't occurred to me. I told him so.

"He shouldn't have gotten onto the château grounds, and wouldn't have if the French had told their security folks that he had been fired. But this being France, they were afraid someone would leak it to the press and questions would be asked that would embarrass the government. So they *still* haven't told anyone that he was fired. Only that he died in an accident."

"Don't you love it?" I said.

"It turns out that the morning the summit began, Rodet had a visitor here in the hospital. The ministry had pulled the guards since Rodet was no longer on the team, but, as I said, they didn't tell anyone, including the guards." Grafton gave the French Shrug. "The visitor stayed about fifteen minutes. No one could discover how he arrived or how he departed, except for the fact that Rodet apparently drove a stolen car to the Conciergerie, went up to his office for a few minutes, came down and drove off. The stolen car was found parked at a subway station a couple of stops from Versailles."

"This visitor. Abu Qasim, you think?"

"Perhaps. It's a possibility, anyway. The French investigators couldn't get a description. They fingerprinted the room, but two days later, after the room had been cleaned twice. It was hopeless. No one who saw the visitor had any reason to remember what he looked like."

"Nondescript," I muttered.

Jake Grafton leaned back in his chair and exhaled a bushel of air. "Boy, would I like to have been a fly on the wall when those two talked. Maybe the visitor was going on to the château with the radio transmitters to set off the bomb. Maybe he was wearing the vest containing a bomb. Maybe Rodet insisted that he go in the other man's place. We'll never know."

"So this Qasim, if he exists, is still out there."

"Yep." From an inside pocket Grafton produced a picture. It was actually a computer-drawn picture of a face. "Recognize him?"

The face was of a man in his forties, perhaps fifty, clean shaven, intelligent, with regular features. "Well . . ."

"Sarah made this from the photo you took of the old man in the park."

"Abu Qasim," I said.

"Perhaps," Grafton said, and pocketed the picture.

I thought about it awhile; about terrorists and traitors and bombs. This really wasn't a world I wanted to live in. Who the hell would? "I want out of the agency," I said a bit later. "I've had enough."

"That was our deal. We'll keep you on the payroll until the docs say you're well, then . . . What are your plans?"

"Don't have any."

"I'll be back to see you in a couple of days to see how you're doing." The admiral held out his hand, and we shook. "Thanks, Tommy," he said.

◆ ◆ ◆

A couple of weeks passed before the French doctors were willing to let me leave the hospital. They took my bandages off and I got my first look at my new, pink hide. My arm healed up and so did the gash in my leg. I felt like a new man. Looked like one, too.

Since the Graftons were in Europe for another six months, the admiral said Sarah and I could use his beach house in Delaware until we got a place of our own. He even gave me a key, which I thought was a nice gesture. Shape I was in, it would have taken me an hour to pick the lock on his door.

So we flew home and landed at Dulles. Someone from the agency met us and drove us to Delaware. Grafton had called ahead, and the guys had my old red Benz coupe parked in his driveway.

The first few days were great; then Sarah got bored and started talking about going back to work. She had to have something to do, she said, and someone was going to have to support us. She lasted through the weekend, but Sunday afternoon I drove her to Maryland and dropped her off at her place. She kissed me and told me she'd see me on Friday night. I drove back to Delaware alone. I'd been alone most of my life, but this time it felt different.

I managed, though. I got out on the beach every morning, watched storms come in, walked for miles and thought about things. It was winter, so the winds were raw and it rained almost every day. Rain or shine, I walked the beach. I worked my jog up to a run and began increasing the distance every day. I worked out at a gym in town. The football wars were entertaining; I didn't read the newspapers or watch the news on television. Life was very pleasant, especially on the weekends, when Sarah came over to the beach.

Still, the sword was hanging over my neck and I could feel it: I was going to have to figure out what to do with my life. Sarah told me that a time or two, just a reminder. Even so, I was in no hurry. The world kept turning, just as before.

The lease on my apartment in Maryland expired, so I spent three days moving out. Some of my stuff I put in storage, but most of it went to the Salvation Army. I was ready to move on. What the heck—maybe we could live at Sarah's place.

Willie Varner drove over from Washington one Saturday evening for dinner. I grilled some steaks and Sarah made a huge tossed salad.

"What you gonna do for a living, Tommy?"

"I'm listening for your answer," Sarah murmured. See, that's how women work—they apply pressure until you buckle like an empty beer can.

"Watch you work our lock shop and take half the profits," I told Willie, after a glance at my roommate, who was up to her wrists in lettuce.

He reached into his pocket and pulled out some coins. He put four quarters on the kitchen counter. "There's your half of what was left this month after we paid my salary."

I laughed and left the quarters there. He didn't pick them up, though.

He wanted to talk about Paris and Henri Rodet. "Thought we were goners when you zapped ol' Henri. I knew something was bad wrong, him being there in the kitchen, after what you and Grafton said, so I went after him with a big carvin' knife. It was like stabbin' a wall. He whacked me in the head with a pistol, slowin' me down somewhat. But I knew he was wearin' somethin' under his coat, probably a bomb like those damn suiciders. That's why I shouted at you when you were gettin' ready to zap 'im. Thought we were goin' to get blown to kingdom come, and sure 'nuf, damn if we didn't. That thing popped and about cremated us."

A little later he said, "Wasn't much left of ol' Henri, Grafton said, and what there was was fried. We was real lucky, Tommy. Real lucky that Henri didn't get his ass up that ladder and pop that thing in the attic where those cylinders were. Might have set them off. Then you and me would be singin' in the angel choir, and we'd have a lot of company."

I nodded and turned the steaks. Luck is a fickle lady; she's here one minute and gone the next.

After Willie left and Sarah and I were alone, I asked her, "I know it's classified and all that, but what did the code breakers get out of those telephone computers we got from Rodet?"

"Nothing."

"That's what Grafton said they'd find."

"I worked with the wizards. They used random number decryption theory and everything else they had on the stuff and got zilch. There was no code to crack, because there was no message. It was just random letters and numbers."

I was beginning to see a glimmer. "So they didn't communicate with the computers," I said slowly as I thought it through. "They were red herrings. Marisa was the mailman, the go-between."

"The computers and the codes were there to deflect attention from her," Sarah explained. "Rodet was trying to protect her."

"You think he loved her?"

"I think she is Qasim's daughter, and he loved Qasim."

Sarah said that like she believed it, but I wasn't buying it. "Are the French sweating her?"

"She's disappeared."

"You're kidding."

"Nope. Grafton told me Abdullah al-Falih, who might be Qasim, had a daughter and a son. The Mossad assassinated the son a couple of years ago."

"And the daughter?"

Sarah shrugged. "Marisa is about the right age."

I still didn't believe it. Seeing the look on my face, she added, "It's a possibility, nothing more. Someday you'll have to ask Abu Qasim."

"Naw. I'm out of it," I said, "and I intend to stay out. Someone else can hunt 'em."

Having definitely and absolutely eliminated one of the ten thousand possible ways to spend the rest of my life, I felt better. I was making progress. Only 9,999 more to consider.

Sometimes I thought about Al Salazar and Rich Thurlow and Elizabeth Conner. Sometimes I wondered how Marisa

Petrou was doing, how she was getting on with her life. Was she Abu Qasim's daughter?

The more I thought about it, the more likely it seemed. Yeah, I know, true believers sign up for paradise and they do whatever it takes to get there. Still, letting those clowns cut on her face . . . The women I knew would need more than faith to undergo that ordeal, even with an anesthetic.

Abu Qasim—willing to sacrifice his daughter and his friend for his vision of God's war. Whew!

That reality was so alien to my world that I didn't want to think about it. I wanted to watch football and walk on the beach and enjoy my moments with Sarah. Aren't we all like that? Don't we all wish to retreat occasionally from foul reality?

Finally I broke down and started reading the newspapers again. Mainly for the sports, you understand. More earthquakes, bankruptcies, volcanic eruptions, political shenanigans, terrorism; the French put a tax on international airline tickets sold in France to fund the war on African poverty. The Denver Broncos looked like the team to beat in the postseason.

However, one morning I found an interesting three-paragraph item on an inside page of *The Washington Post*: Richard Lewellan Zantz, an American expatriate, age twenty-eight, was shot to death the previous day at a sidewalk café in Rome. Someone walked up, pulled out a sawed-off shotgun, and blasted him four times with buckshot. Then the shooter walked away into the crowd. Eyewitness identifications were nebulous—no one got a good look at the killer. Too busy taking cover, I guess. Italian authorities promised to bring the villain to justice.

Ol' Gator. Five ounces of lead administered in four doses. Adios, asshole.

Two months after Sarah and I arrived in Delaware we still hadn't rented an apartment in Maryland, and I hadn't figured out what I was going to do for a living. Sarah was getting very testy.

One Friday morning the telephone rang: Jake Grafton was calling from France.

"Hey, Tommy," he said.

"Although my wishes are a little late, happy new year, Admiral. Your house weathered the holidays and is none the worse for it."

"Had enough loafing yet?"

"Well . . ."

"Ready to go back to work?"

"What do you have?"

"UPS will bring you some airline tickets tomorrow. It's snowing here. Pack accordingly."

I took a deep breath. "Okay," I said. We talked for a bit about Sarah and Callie, but it was a transatlantic call.

After we hung up, I called Sarah. "Hey, babe, you'll never guess who called."

"Let's see . . . Your mother is in Hawaii, the president is in China, you said no to that movie producer and the ballet company . . . Was it Jake Grafton?"

"How'd you know?"

"He called me first. Wanted to know if I thought it would be okay to call you."

"And you said yes."

"I love you, Tommy, more than you will ever know. But you have to keep being you—I know that. I'll be here when you come home."

"Thanks, Sarah. See you tonight."

After I hung up, I remembered her comment a few weeks earlier about Marisa. So when did she and Grafton have that little conversation?

The more I thought about it, the more amusing it was. She knew all along that Grafton would eventually call me. Women!

ACKNOWLEDGMENTS

A novel such as this would be impossible to write without help. The author is blessed with the world's finest editor, Charles Spicer, whose wise counsel and patience have proven essential to the creative process for the past ten years. The author's wife, Deborah Coonts, delights in plot twists and contributed several to this tale. Gilbert "Gil" Pascal brought the Ionatron, Inc. wireless Taser, a real product being developed for the CIA, to the attention of the author, who altered and "improved" the device for his own nefarious ends.